SUPERMAN ADVENTURES

the NEVER-ENDING BATTLE

Written by:
Mark Millar

Colored by:
Marie Severin

Illustrated by:
Aluir Amancio
Terry Austin
Mike Manley

Lettered by:
Lois Buhalis

Superman created by **Jerry Siegel** and **Joe Shuster**

Dan DiDio
VP-Editorial

Mike McAvennie
Editor-original series

Frank Berrios
Assistant Editor-original series

Scott Nybakken
Editor-collected edition

Robbin Brosterman
Senior Art Director

Paul Levitz
President & Publisher

Georg Brewer
VP-Design & Retail Product
Development

Richard Bruning
Senior VP-Creative Director

Patrick Caldon
Senior VP-Finance & Operations

Chris Caramalis
VP-Finance

Terri Cunningham
VP-Managing Editor

Alison Gill
VP-Manufacturing

Rich Johnson
VP-Book Trade Sales

Hank Kanalz
VP-General Manager, WildStorm

Lillian Laserson
Senior VP & General Counsel

Jim Lee
Editorial Director-WildStorm

David McKillips
VP-Advertising & Custom Publishing

John Nee
VP-Business Development

Gregory Noveck
Senior VP-Creative Affairs

Cheryl Rubin
VP-Brand Management

Bob Wayne
VP-Sales & Marketing

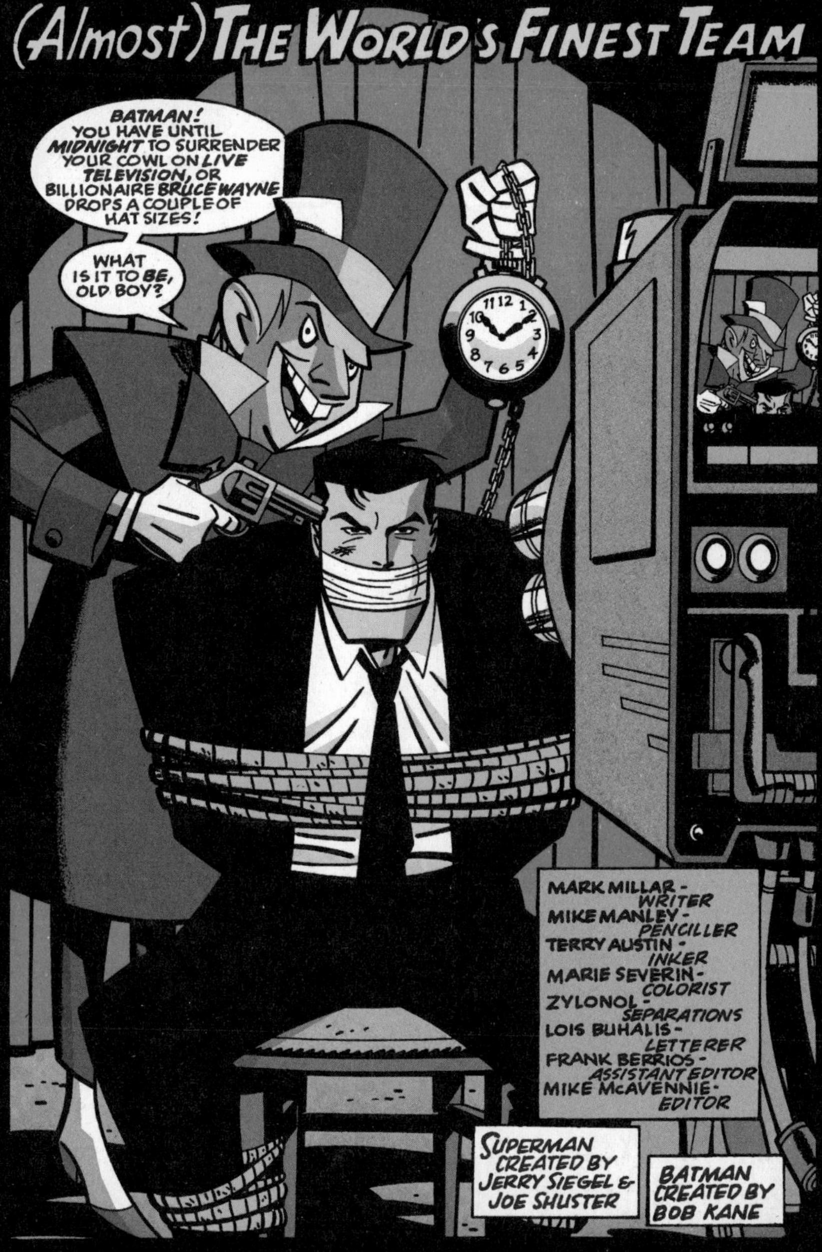
(Almost) The World's Finest Team
BATMAN! YOU HAVE UNTIL MIDNIGHT TO SURRENDER YOUR COWL ON LIVE TELEVISION, OR BILLIONAIRE BRUCE WAYNE DROPS A COUPLE OF HAT SIZES!
WHAT IS IT TO BE, OLD BOY?
MARK MILLAR - WRITER
MIKE MANLEY - PENCILLER
TERRY AUSTIN - INKER
MARIE SEVERIN - COLORIST
ZYLONOL - SEPARATIONS
LOIS BUHALIS - LETTERER
FRANK BERRIOS - ASSISTANT EDITOR
MIKE McAVENNIE - EDITOR
SUPERMAN CREATED BY JERRY SIEGEL & JOE SHUSTER
BATMAN CREATED BY BOB KANE

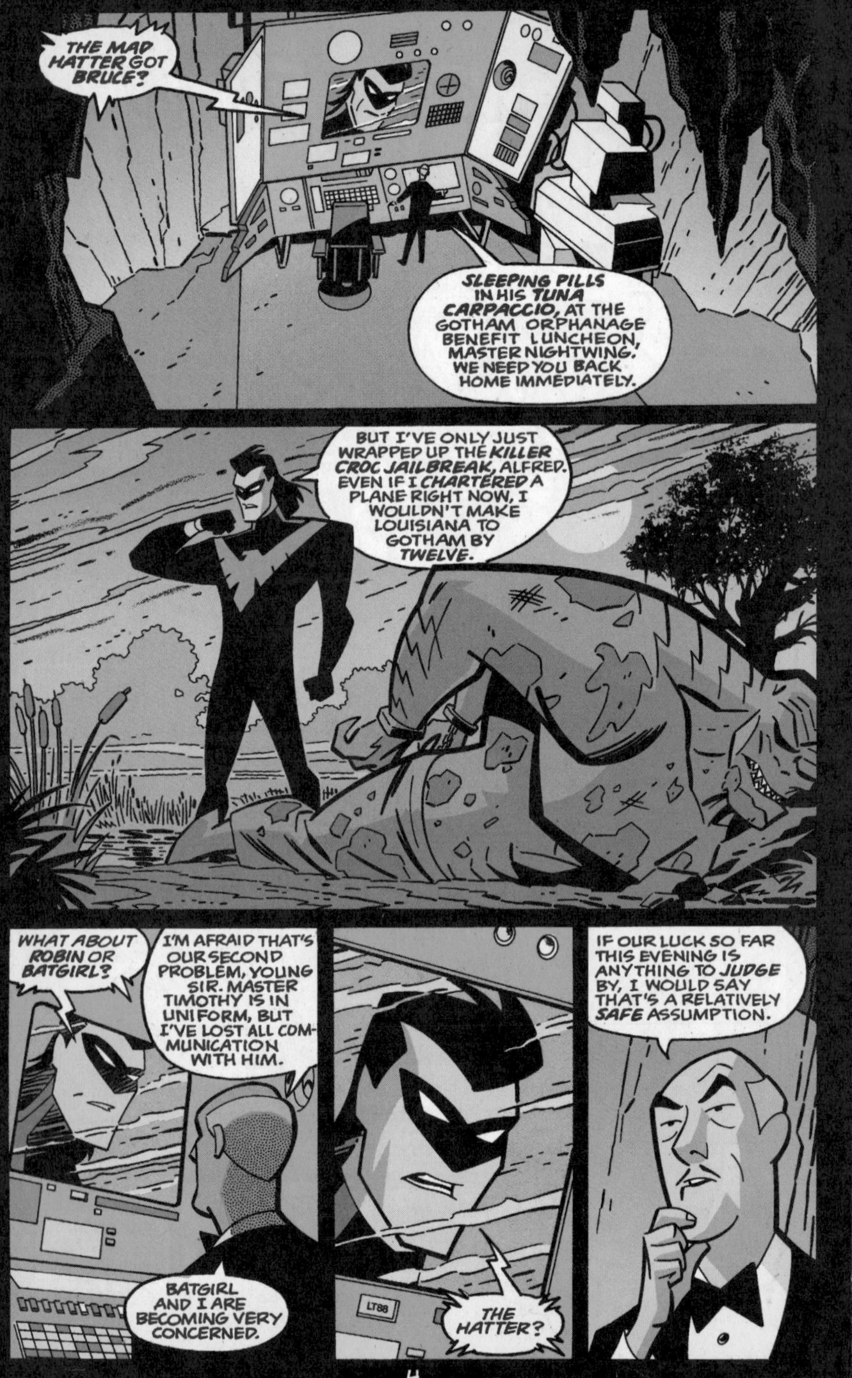
THE MAD HATTER GOT BRUCE?
SLEEPING PILLS IN HIS TUNA CARPACCIO, AT THE GOTHAM ORPHANAGE BENEFIT LUNCHEON, MASTER NIGHTWING. WE NEED YOU BACK HOME IMMEDIATELY.
BUT I'VE ONLY JUST WRAPPED UP THE KILLER CROC JAILBREAK, ALFRED. EVEN IF I CHARTERED A PLANE RIGHT NOW, I WOULDN'T MAKE LOUISIANA TO GOTHAM BY TWELVE.
WHAT ABOUT ROBIN OR BATGIRL?
I'M AFRAID THAT'S OUR SECOND PROBLEM, YOUNG SIR. MASTER TIMOTHY IS IN UNIFORM, BUT I'VE LOST ALL COMMUNICATION WITH HIM.
BATGIRL AND I ARE BECOMING VERY CONCERNED.
LT88
THE HATTER?
IF OUR LUCK SO FAR THIS EVENING IS ANYTHING TO JUDGE BY, I WOULD SAY THAT'S A RELATIVELY SAFE ASSUMPTION.

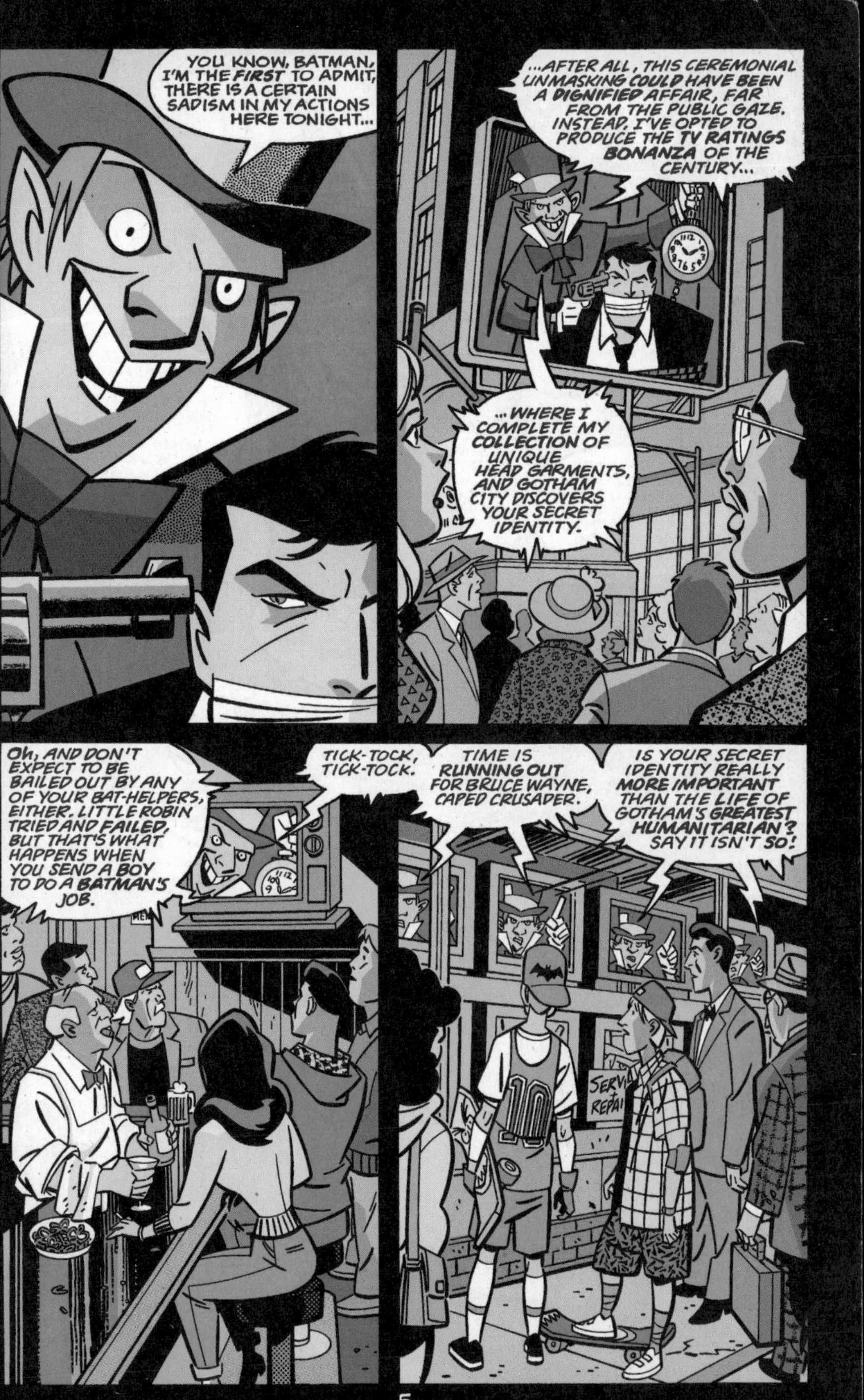
YOU KNOW, BATMAN, I'M THE FIRST TO ADMIT, THERE IS A CERTAIN SADISM IN MY ACTIONS HERE TONIGHT...
...AFTER ALL, THIS CEREMONIAL UNMASKING COULD HAVE BEEN A DIGNIFIED AFFAIR, FAR FROM THE PUBLIC GAZE. INSTEAD, I'VE OPTED TO PRODUCE THE TV RATINGS BONANZA OF THE CENTURY...
...WHERE I COMPLETE MY COLLECTION OF UNIQUE HEAD GARMENTS, AND GOTHAM CITY DISCOVERS YOUR SECRET IDENTITY.
Oh, AND DON'T EXPECT TO BE BAILED OUT BY ANY OF YOUR BAT-HELPERS, EITHER. LITTLE ROBIN TRIED AND FAILED, BUT THAT'S WHAT HAPPENS WHEN YOU SEND A BOY TO DO A BATMAN'S JOB.
TICK-TOCK, TICK-TOCK.
TIME IS RUNNING OUT FOR BRUCE WAYNE, CAPED CRUSADER.
IS YOUR SECRET IDENTITY REALLY MORE IMPORTANT THAN THE LIFE OF GOTHAM'S GREATEST HUMANITARIAN? SAY IT ISN'T SO!

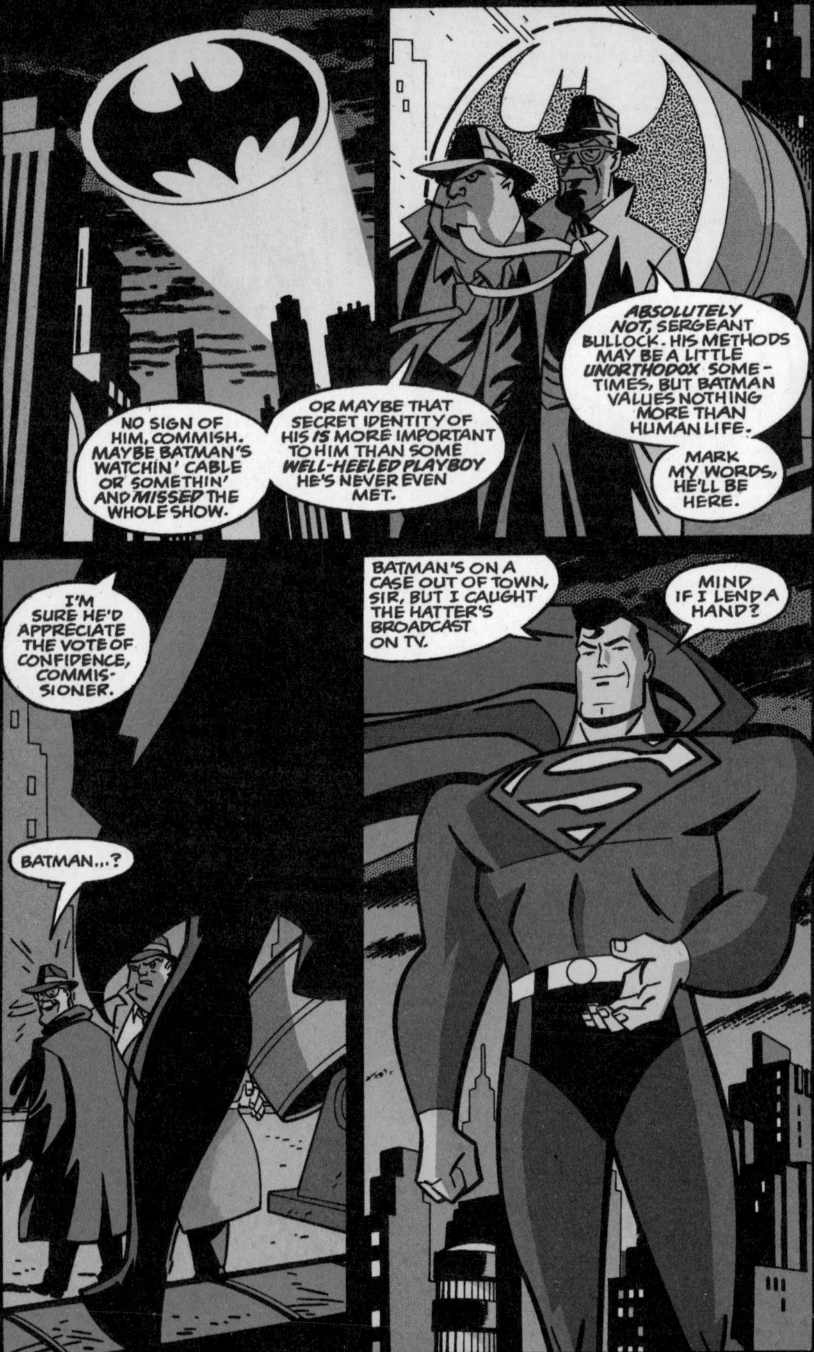
NO SIGN OF HIM, COMMISH. MAYBE BATMAN'S WATCHIN' CABLE OR SOMETHIN' AND MISSED THE WHOLE SHOW.
OR MAYBE THAT SECRET IDENTITY OF HIS IS MORE IMPORTANT TO HIM THAN SOME WELL-HEELED PLAYBOY HE'S NEVER EVEN MET.
ABSOLUTELY NOT, SERGEANT BULLOCK. HIS METHODS MAY BE A LITTLE UNORTHODOX SOME-TIMES, BUT BATMAN VALUES NOTHING MORE THAN HUMAN LIFE.
MARK MY WORDS, HE'LL BE HERE.
I'M SURE HE'D APPRECIATE THE VOTE OF CONFIDENCE, COMMIS-SIONER.
BATMAN...?
BATMAN'S ON A CASE OUT OF TOWN, SIR, BUT I CAUGHT THE HATTER'S BROADCAST ON TV.
MIND IF I LEND A HAND?

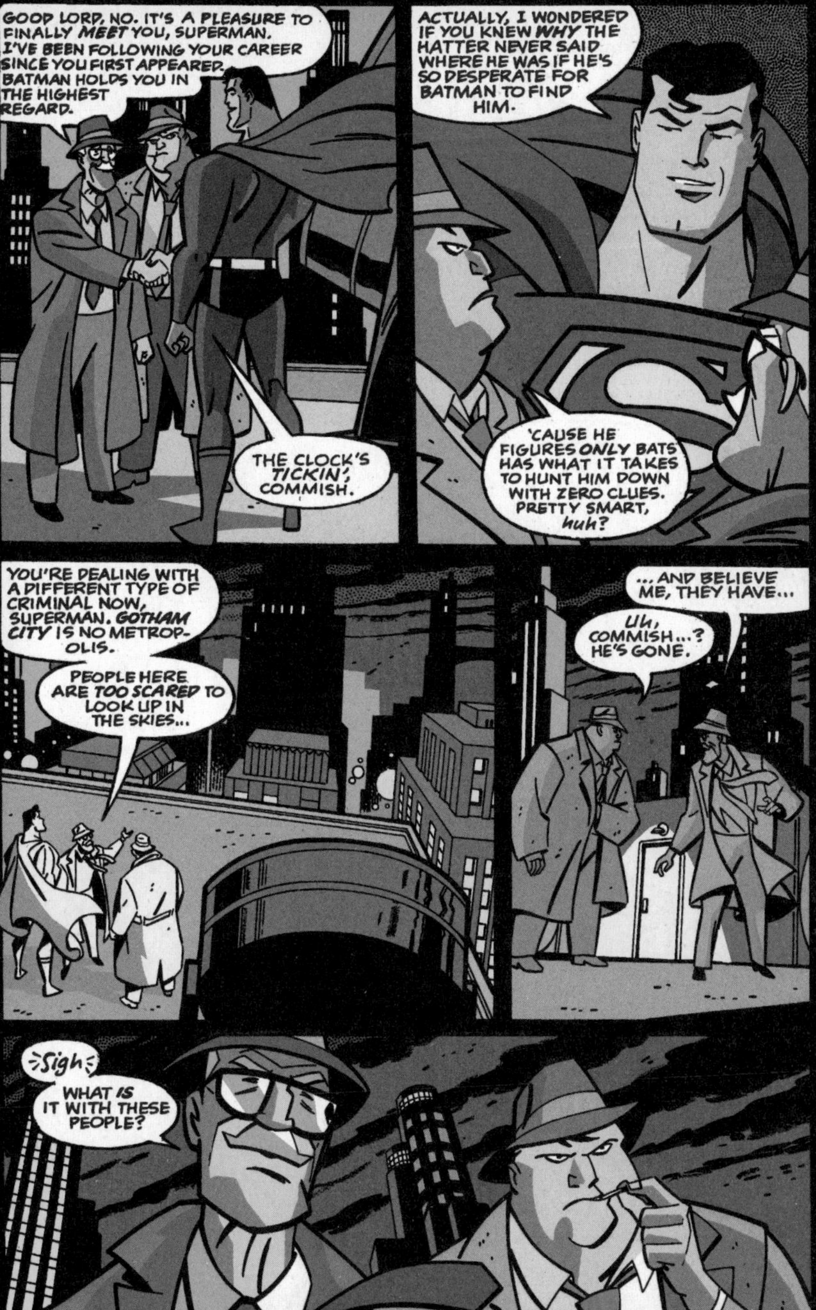
GOOD LORD, NO. IT'S A PLEASURE TO FINALLY MEET YOU, SUPERMAN. I'VE BEEN FOLLOWING YOUR CAREER SINCE YOU FIRST APPEARED. BATMAN HOLDS YOU IN THE HIGHEST REGARD.
THE CLOCK'S TICKIN', COMMISH.
ACTUALLY, I WONDERED IF YOU KNEW WHY THE HATTER NEVER SAID WHERE HE WAS IF HE'S SO DESPERATE FOR BATMAN TO FIND HIM.
'CAUSE HE FIGURES ONLY BATS HAS WHAT IT TAKES TO HUNT HIM DOWN WITH ZERO CLUES. PRETTY SMART, huh?
YOU'RE DEALING WITH A DIFFERENT TYPE OF CRIMINAL NOW, SUPERMAN. GOTHAM CITY IS NO METROP-OLIS.
PEOPLE HERE ARE TOO SCARED TO LOOK UP IN THE SKIES...
...AND BELIEVE ME, THEY HAVE...
Uh, COMMISH...? HE'S GONE.
Sigh
WHAT IS IT WITH THESE PEOPLE?

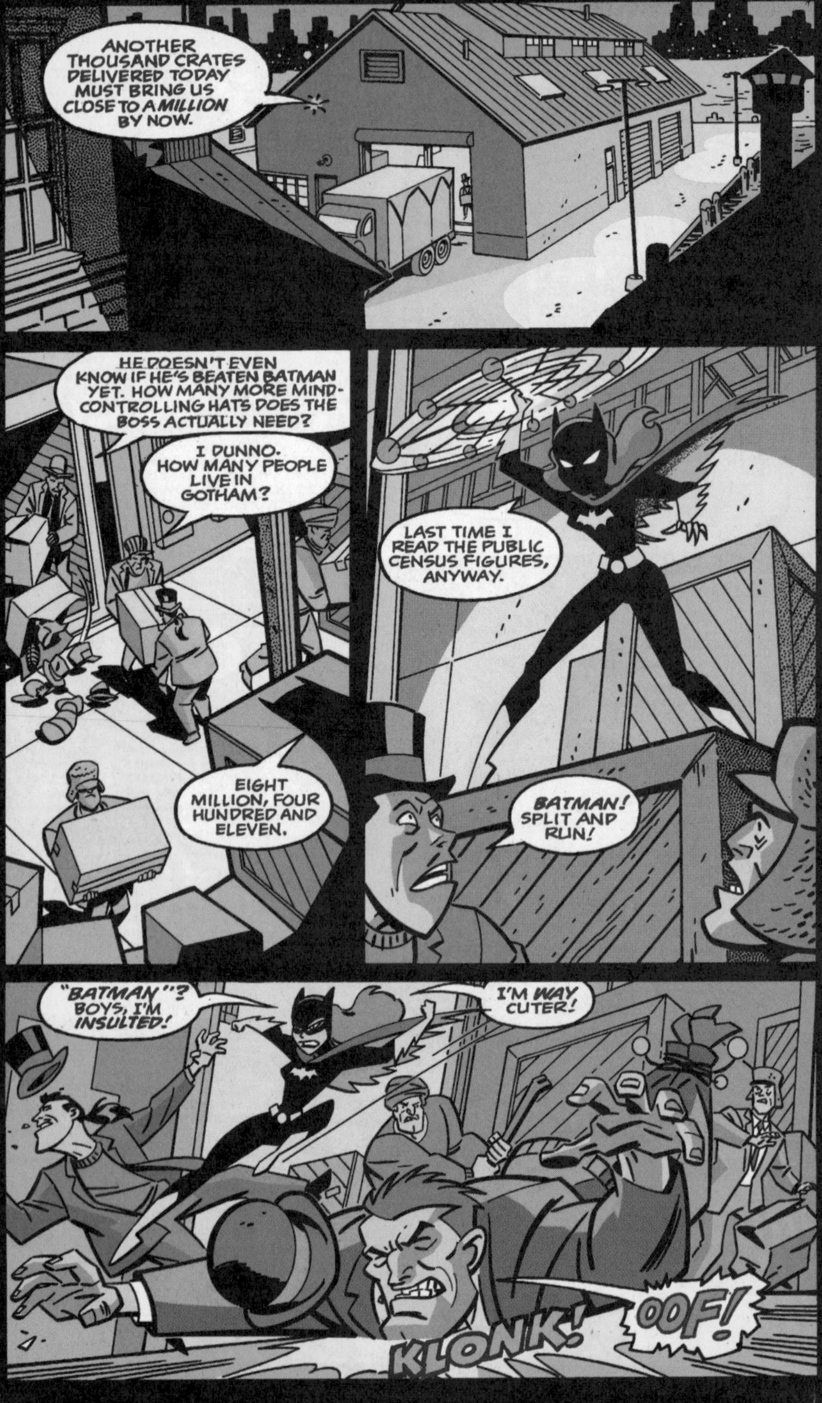
ANOTHER THOUSAND CRATES DELIVERED TODAY MUST BRING US CLOSE TO A *MILLION* BY NOW.
HE DOESN'T EVEN KNOW IF HE'S BEATEN BATMAN YET. HOW MANY MORE MIND-CONTROLLING HATS DOES THE BOSS ACTUALLY NEED?
I DUNNO. HOW MANY PEOPLE LIVE IN GOTHAM?
EIGHT MILLION, FOUR HUNDRED AND ELEVEN.
LAST TIME I READ THE PUBLIC CENSUS FIGURES, ANYWAY.
BATMAN! SPLIT AND RUN!
"*BATMAN*"? BOYS, I'M *INSULTED!*
I'M *WAY* CUTER!
KLONK!
OOF!

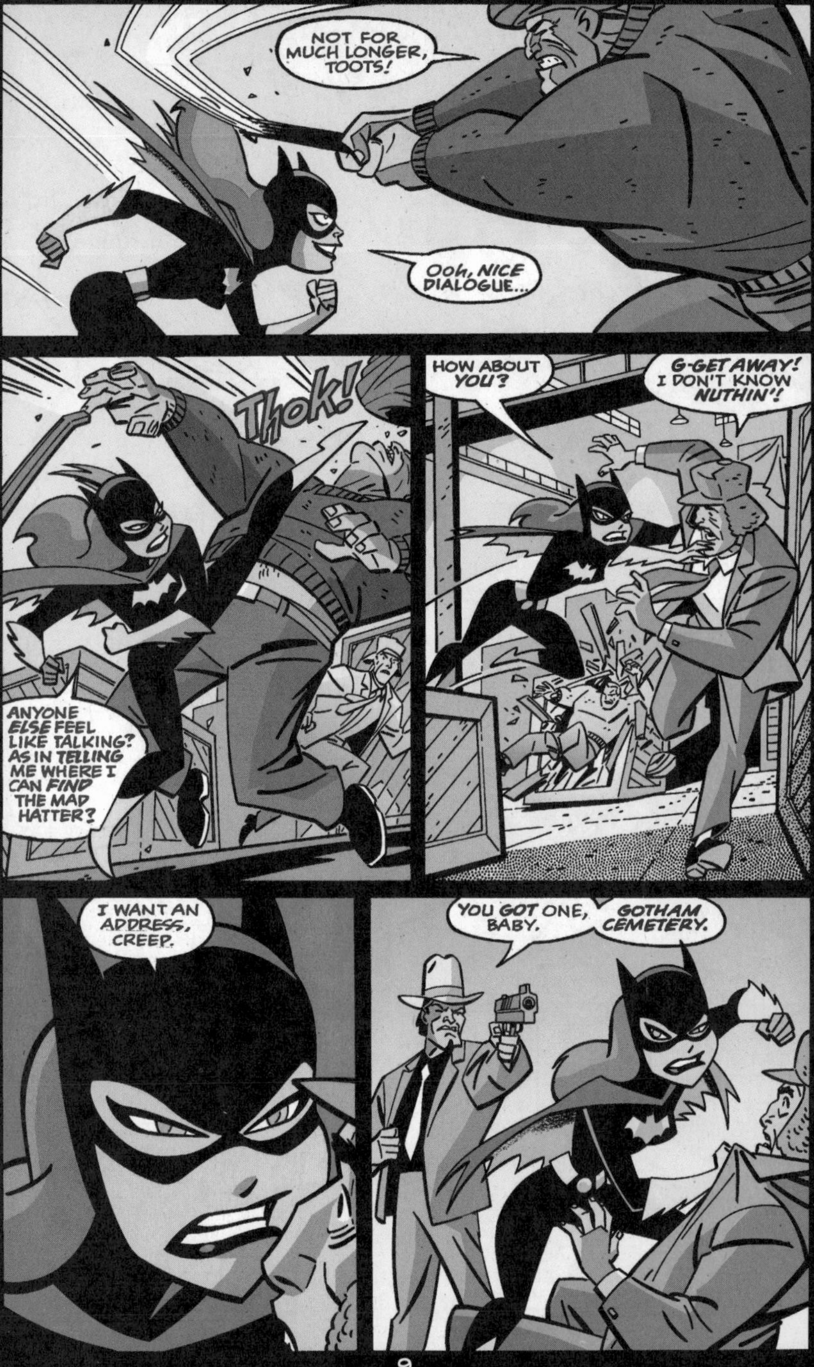
NOT FOR MUCH LONGER, TOOTS!
Ooh, NICE DIALOGUE...
THOK!
ANYONE ELSE FEEL LIKE TALKING? AS IN TELLING ME WHERE I CAN FIND THE MAD HATTER?
HOW ABOUT YOU?
G-GET AWAY! I DON'T KNOW NUTHIN'!
I WANT AN ADDRESS, CREEP.
YOU GOT ONE, BABY.
GOTHAM CEMETERY.

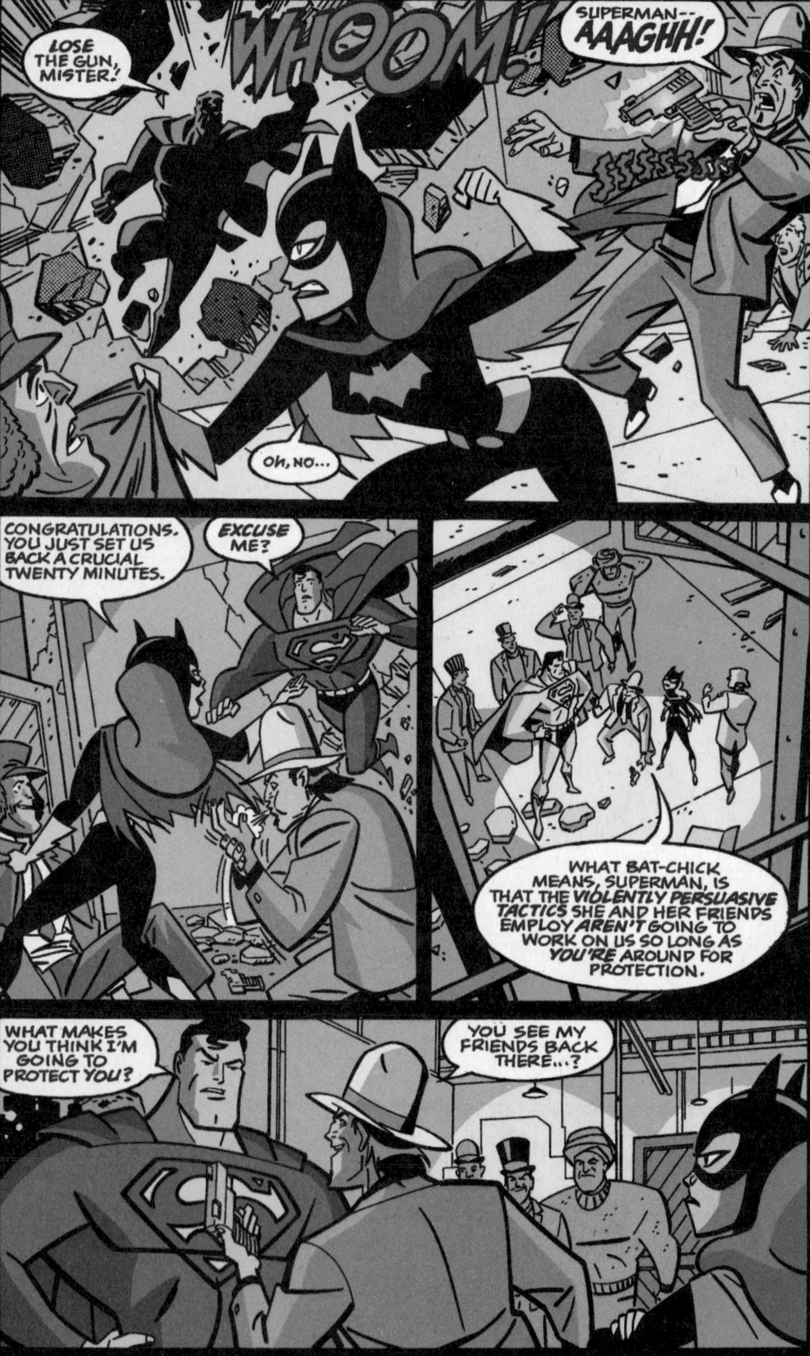

LOSE THE GUN, MISTER!
WHOOOM!!
SUPERMAN-- AAAGHH!
Oh, NO...
CONGRATULATIONS. YOU JUST SET US BACK A CRUCIAL TWENTY MINUTES.
EXCUSE ME?
WHAT BAT-CHICK MEANS, SUPERMAN, IS THAT THE VIOLENTLY PERSUASIVE TACTICS SHE AND HER FRIENDS EMPLOY AREN'T GOING TO WORK ON US SO LONG AS YOU'RE AROUND FOR PROTECTION.
WHAT MAKES YOU THINK I'M GOING TO PROTECT YOU?
YOU SEE MY FRIENDS BACK THERE...?

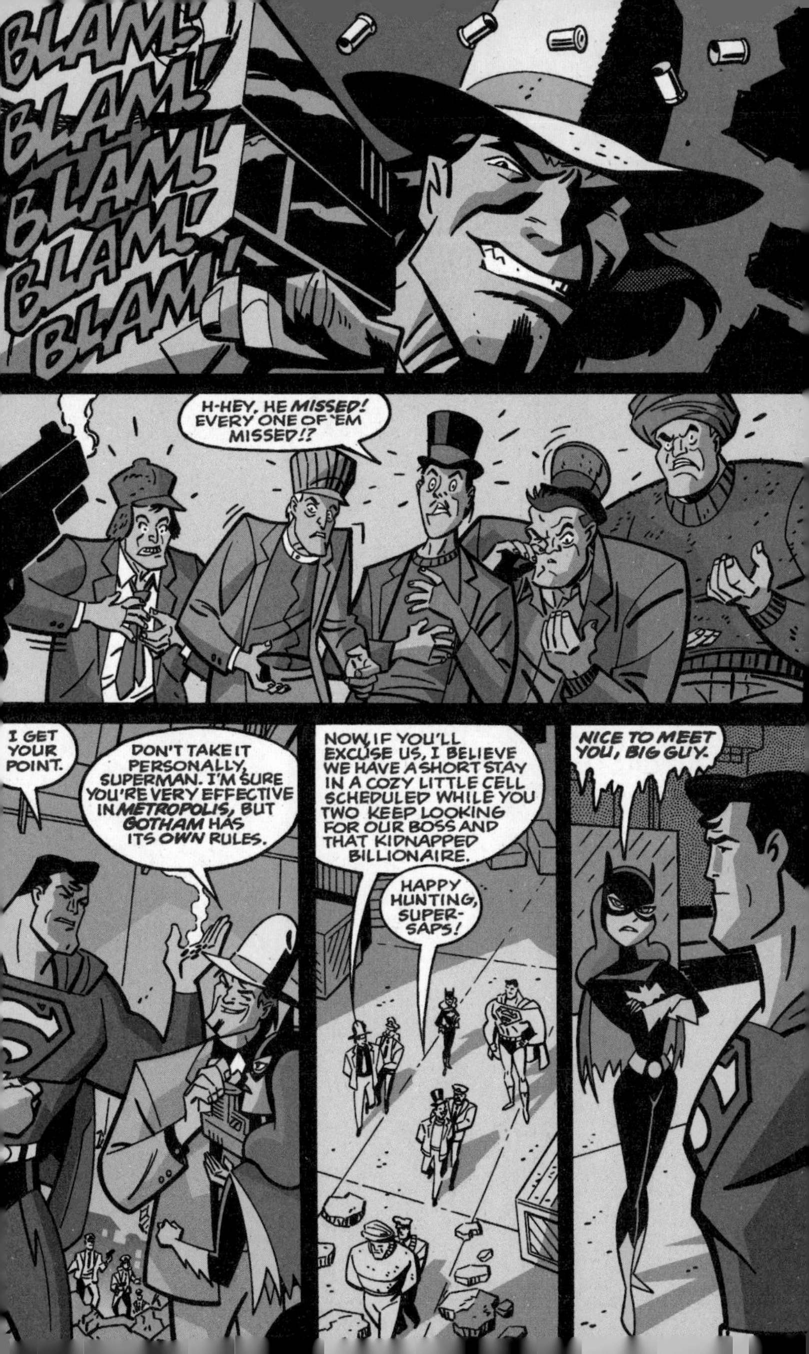

BLAM! BLAM! BLAM! BLAM! BLAM! BLAM!
H-HEY. HE MISSED! EVERY ONE OF 'EM MISSED!?
I GET YOUR POINT.
DON'T TAKE IT PERSONALLY, SUPERMAN. I'M SURE YOU'RE VERY EFFECTIVE IN METROPOLIS, BUT GOTHAM HAS ITS OWN RULES.
NOW, IF YOU'LL EXCUSE US, I BELIEVE WE HAVE A SHORT STAY IN A COZY LITTLE CELL SCHEDULED WHILE YOU TWO KEEP LOOKING FOR OUR BOSS AND THAT KIDNAPPED BILLIONAIRE.
HAPPY HUNTING, SUPER-SAPS!
NICE TO MEET YOU, BIG GUY.

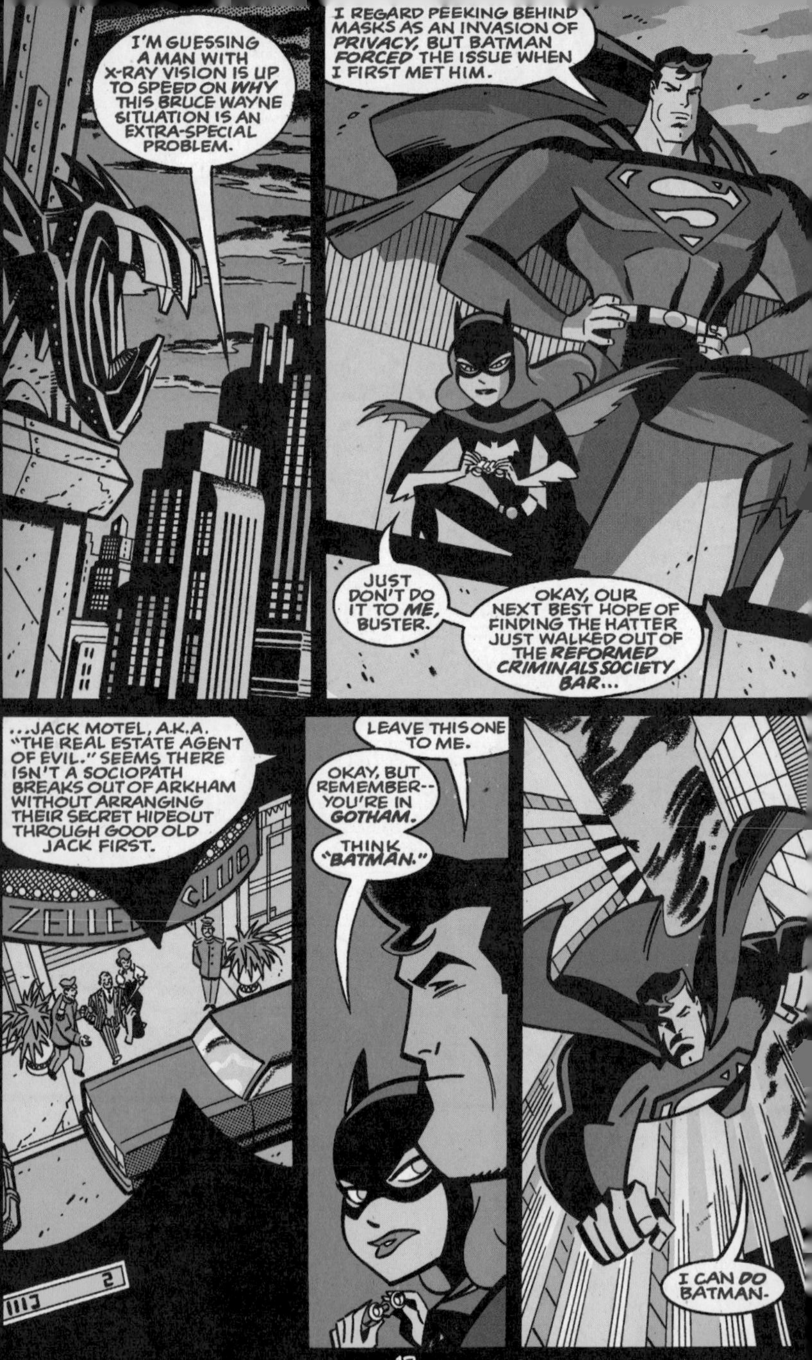
I'M GUESSING A MAN WITH X-RAY VISION IS UP TO SPEED ON WHY THIS BRUCE WAYNE SITUATION IS AN EXTRA-SPECIAL PROBLEM.
I REGARD PEEKING BEHIND MASKS AS AN INVASION OF PRIVACY, BUT BATMAN FORCED THE ISSUE WHEN I FIRST MET HIM.
JUST DON'T DO IT TO ME, BUSTER.
OKAY, OUR NEXT BEST HOPE OF FINDING THE HATTER JUST WALKED OUT OF THE REFORMED CRIMINALS SOCIETY BAR...
...JACK MOTEL, A.K.A. "THE REAL ESTATE AGENT OF EVIL." SEEMS THERE ISN'T A SOCIOPATH BREAKS OUT OF ARKHAM WITHOUT ARRANGING THEIR SECRET HIDEOUT THROUGH GOOD OLD JACK FIRST.
CLUB
LEAVE THIS ONE TO ME.
OKAY, BUT REMEMBER-- YOU'RE IN GOTHAM.
THINK "BATMAN."
I CAN DO BATMAN.

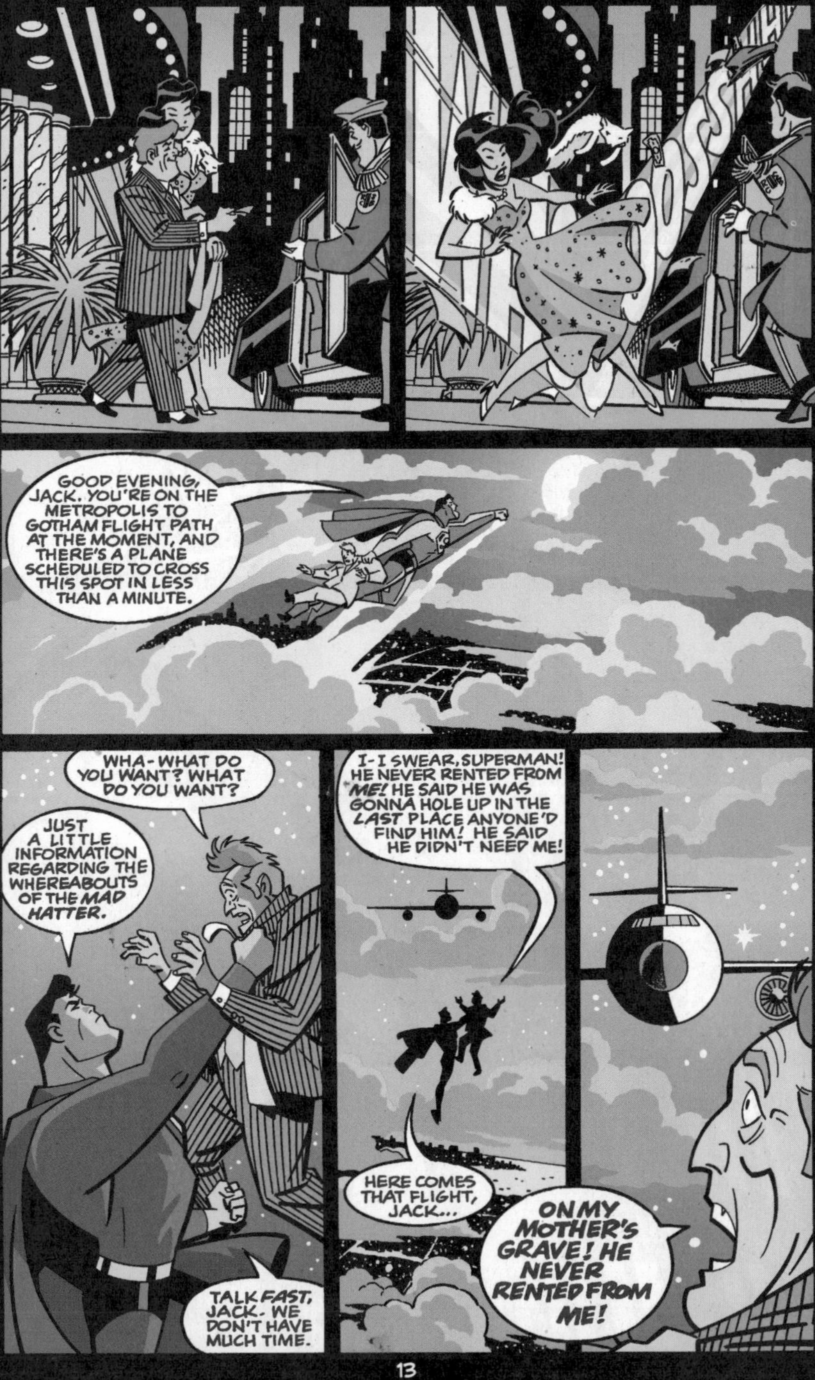
GOOD EVENING, JACK. YOU'RE ON THE METROPOLIS TO GOTHAM FLIGHT PATH AT THE MOMENT, AND THERE'S A PLANE SCHEDULED TO CROSS THIS SPOT IN LESS THAN A MINUTE.
WHA-WHAT DO YOU WANT? WHAT DO YOU WANT?
JUST A LITTLE INFORMATION REGARDING THE WHEREABOUTS OF THE MAD HATTER.
TALK FAST, JACK. WE DON'T HAVE MUCH TIME.
I-I SWEAR, SUPERMAN! HE NEVER RENTED FROM ME! HE SAID HE WAS GONNA HOLE UP IN THE LAST PLACE ANYONE'D FIND HIM! HE SAID HE DIDN'T NEED ME!
HERE COMES THAT FLIGHT, JACK...
ON MY MOTHER'S GRAVE! HE NEVER RENTED FROM ME!

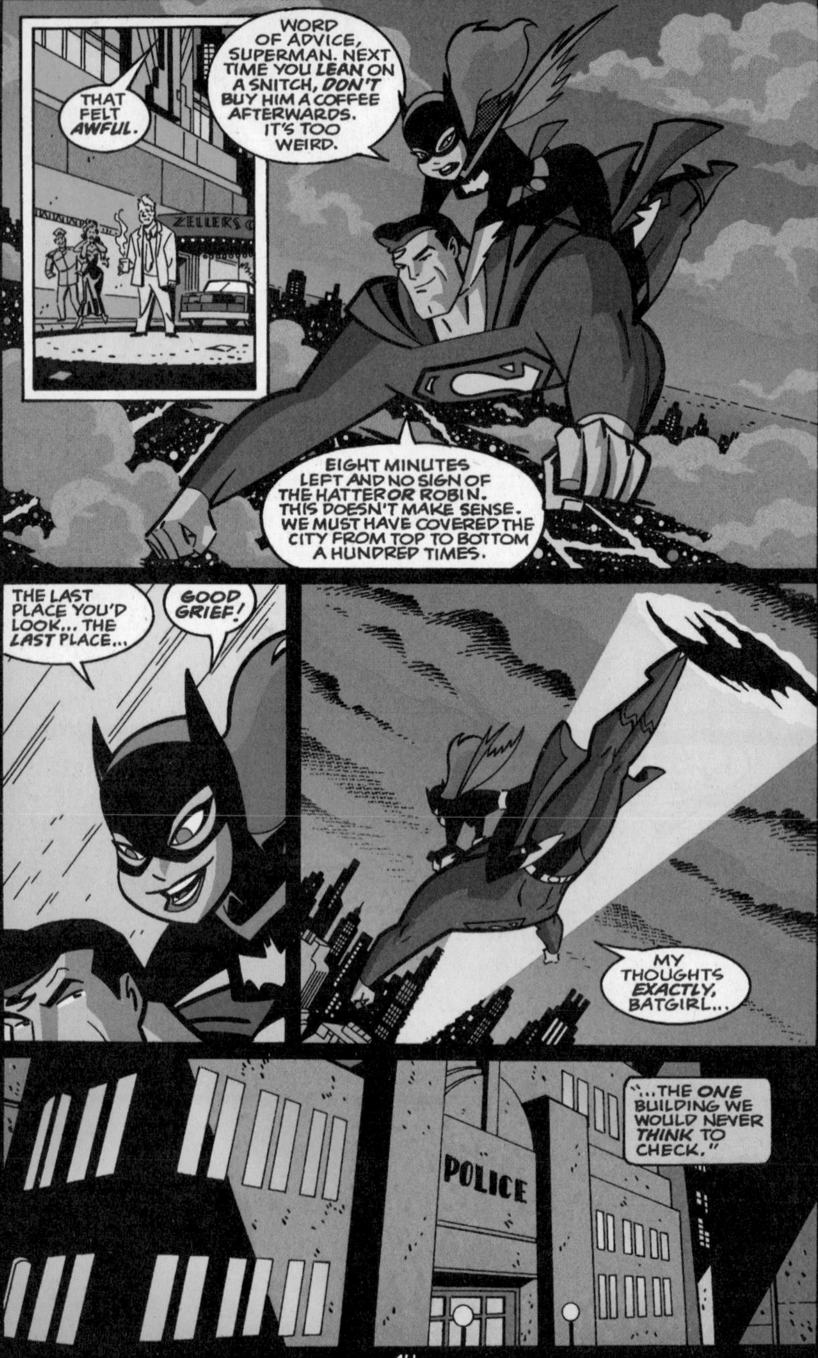
THAT FELT AWFUL.
WORD OF ADVICE, SUPERMAN. NEXT TIME YOU LEAN ON A SNITCH, DON'T BUY HIM A COFFEE AFTERWARDS. IT'S TOO WEIRD.
ZELLERS
EIGHT MINUTES LEFT AND NO SIGN OF THE HATTER OR ROBIN. THIS DOESN'T MAKE SENSE. WE MUST HAVE COVERED THE CITY FROM TOP TO BOTTOM A HUNDRED TIMES.
THE LAST PLACE YOU'D LOOK... THE LAST PLACE...
GOOD GRIEF!
MY THOUGHTS EXACTLY, BATGIRL...
"...THE ONE BUILDING WE WOULD NEVER THINK TO CHECK."
POLICE

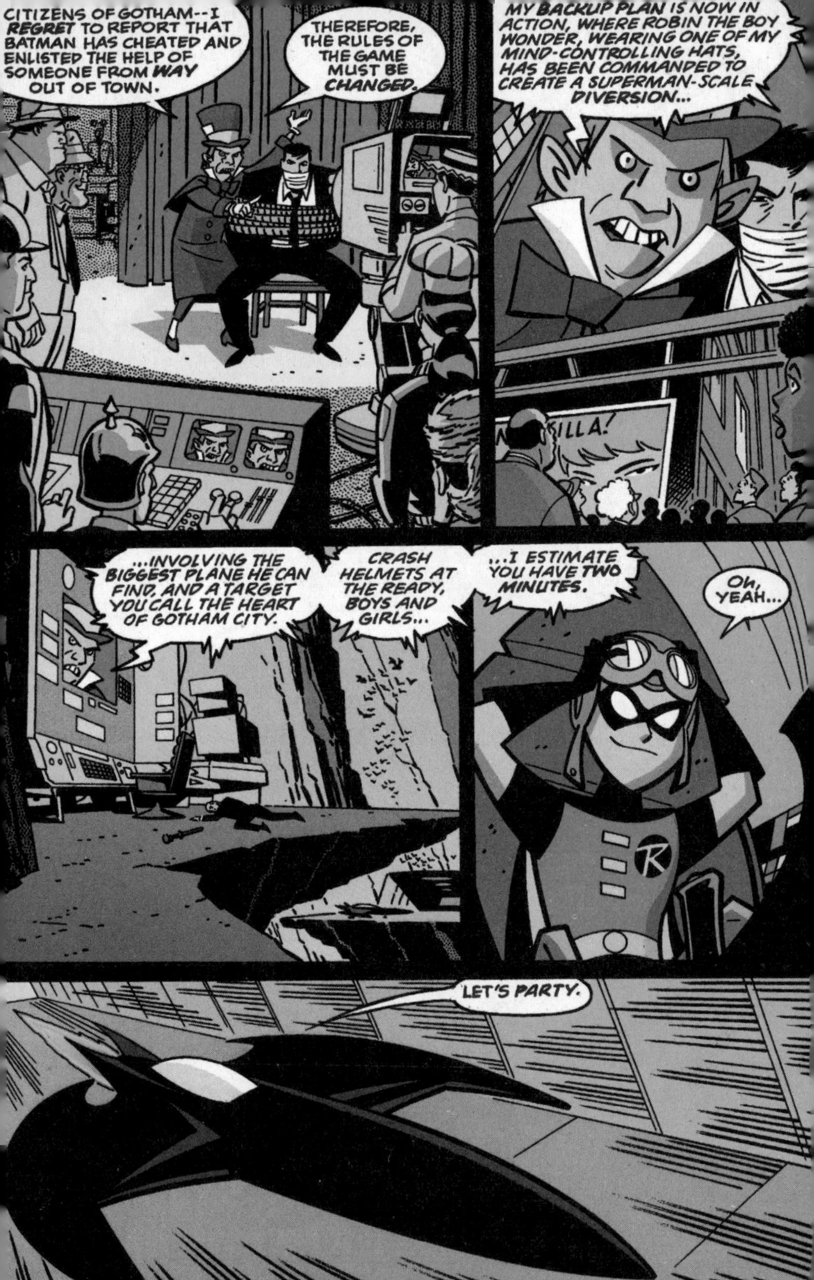
CITIZENS OF GOTHAM--I REGRET TO REPORT THAT BATMAN HAS CHEATED AND ENLISTED THE HELP OF SOMEONE FROM WAY OUT OF TOWN.
THEREFORE, THE RULES OF THE GAME MUST BE CHANGED.
MY BACKUP PLAN IS NOW IN ACTION, WHERE ROBIN THE BOY WONDER, WEARING ONE OF MY MIND-CONTROLLING HATS, HAS BEEN COMMANDED TO CREATE A SUPERMAN-SCALE DIVERSION...
ILLA!
...INVOLVING THE BIGGEST PLANE HE CAN FIND, AND A TARGET YOU CALL THE HEART OF GOTHAM CITY.
CRASH HELMETS AT THE READY, BOYS AND GIRLS...
...I ESTIMATE YOU HAVE TWO MINUTES.
Oh, YEAH...
LET'S PARTY.

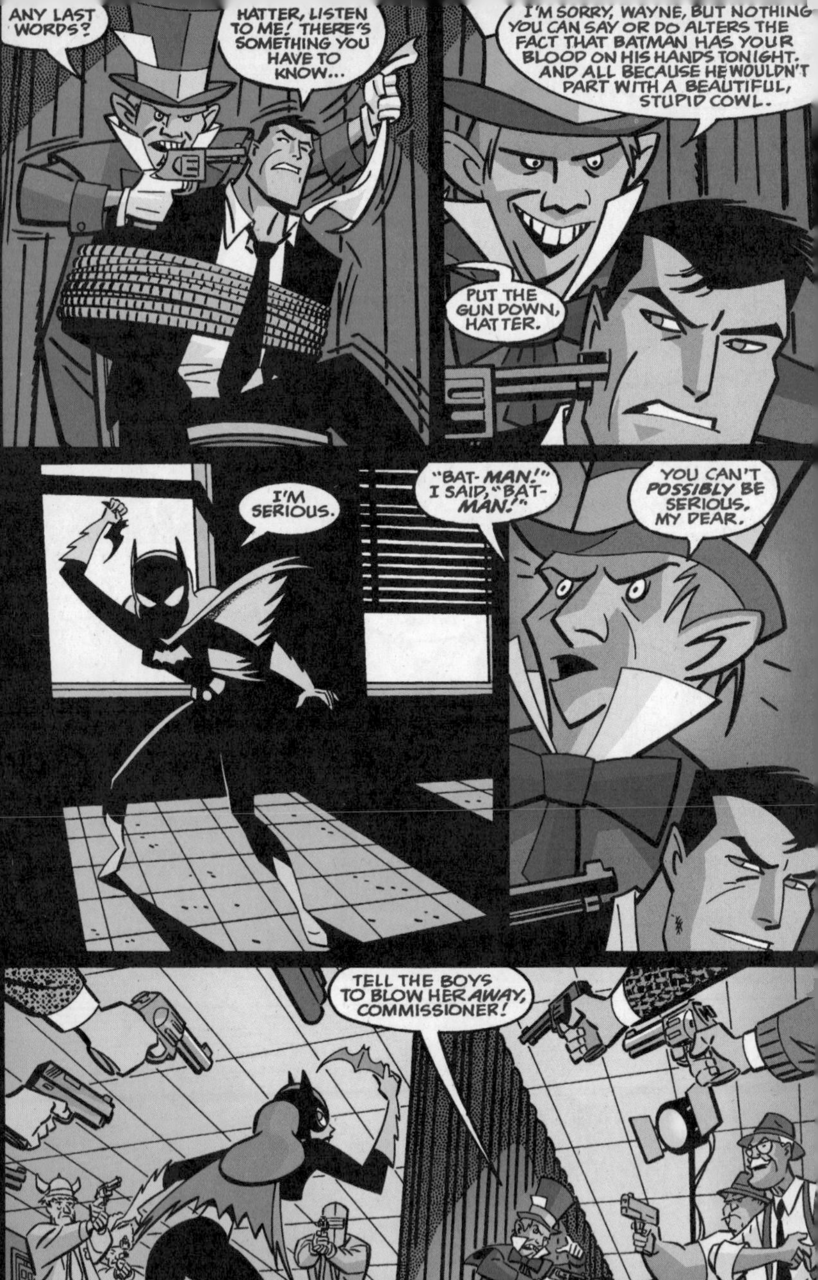
ANY LAST WORDS?
HATTER, LISTEN TO ME! THERE'S SOMETHING YOU HAVE TO KNOW...
I'M SORRY, WAYNE, BUT NOTHING YOU CAN SAY OR DO ALTERS THE FACT THAT BATMAN HAS YOUR BLOOD ON HIS HANDS TONIGHT. AND ALL BECAUSE HE WOULDN'T PART WITH A BEAUTIFUL, STUPID COWL.
PUT THE GUN DOWN, HATTER.
I'M SERIOUS.
"BAT-MAN!" I SAID, "BAT-MAN!"
YOU CAN'T POSSIBLY BE SERIOUS, MY DEAR.
TELL THE BOYS TO BLOW HER AWAY, COMMISSIONER!

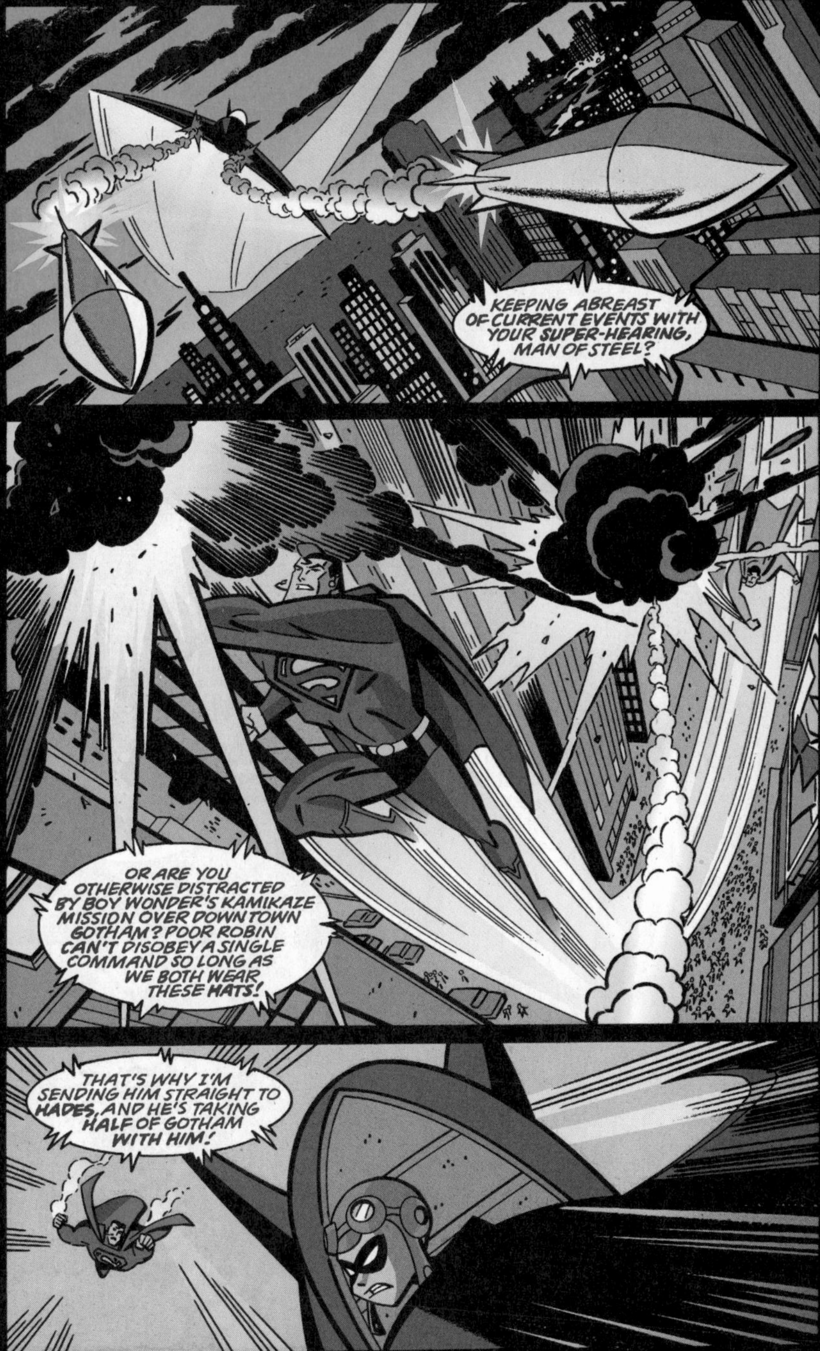
KEEPING ABREAST OF CURRENT EVENTS WITH YOUR SUPER-HEARING, MAN OF STEEL?
OR ARE YOU OTHERWISE DISTRACTED BY BOY WONDER'S KAMIKAZE MISSION OVER DOWNTOWN GOTHAM? POOR ROBIN CAN'T DISOBEY A SINGLE COMMAND SO LONG AS WE BOTH WEAR THESE HATS!
THAT'S WHY I'M SENDING HIM STRAIGHT TO HADES, AND HE'S TAKING HALF OF GOTHAM WITH HIM!

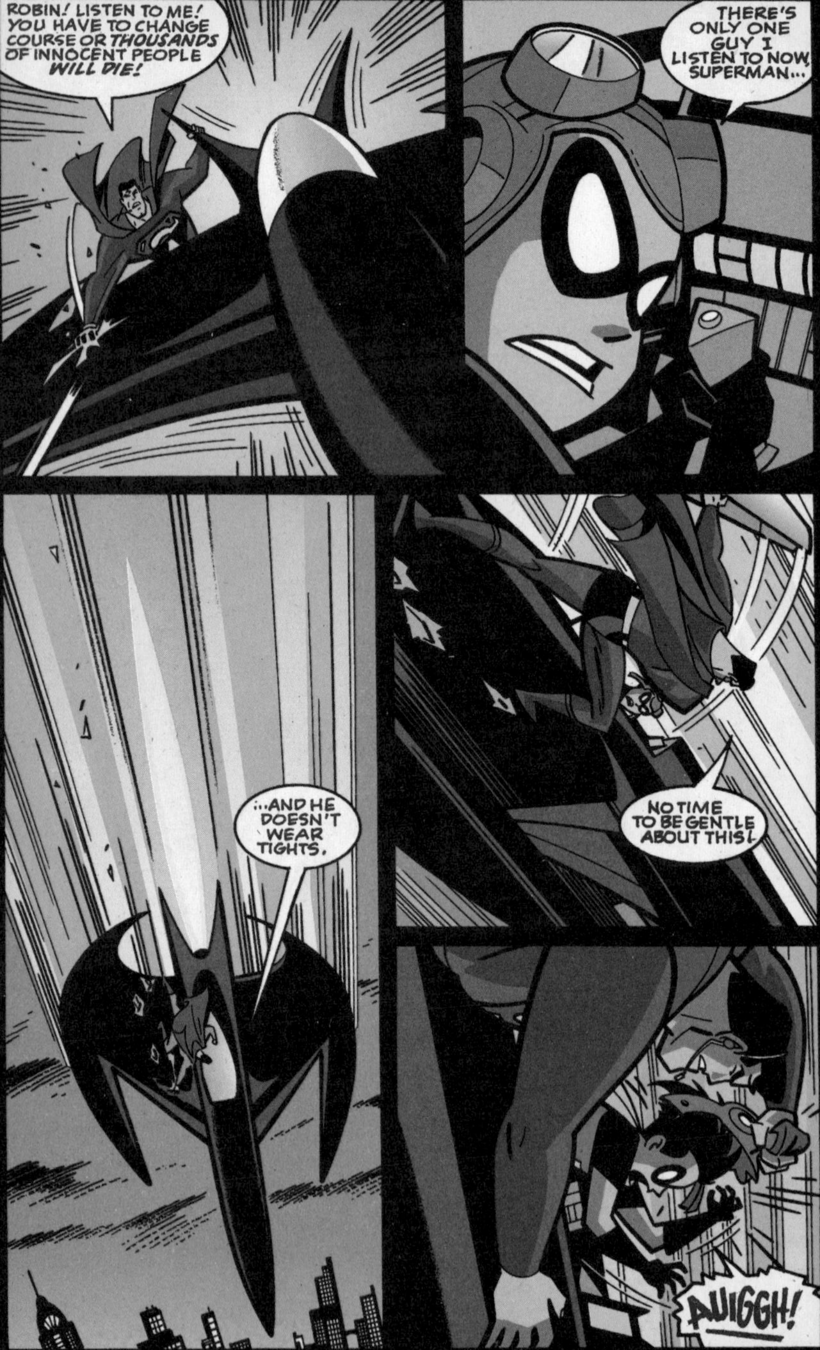
ROBIN! LISTEN TO ME! YOU HAVE TO CHANGE COURSE OR THOUSANDS OF INNOCENT PEOPLE WILL DIE!
THERE'S ONLY ONE GUY I LISTEN TO NOW, SUPERMAN...
...AND HE DOESN'T WEAR TIGHTS.
NO TIME TO BE GENTLE ABOUT THIS!
AUIGGH!

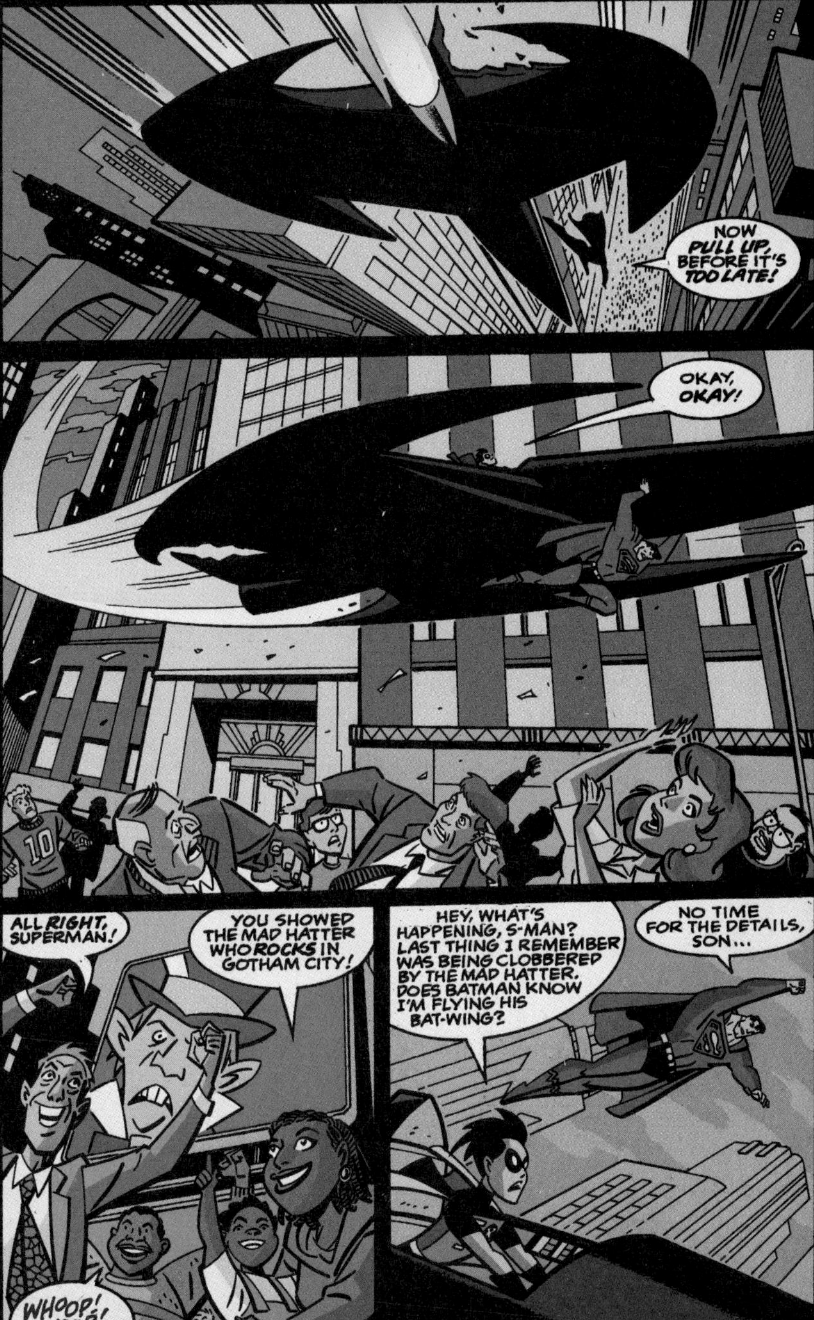
NOW PULL UP, BEFORE IT'S TOO LATE!
OKAY, OKAY!
ALL RIGHT, SUPERMAN!
YOU SHOWED THE MAD HATTER WHO ROCKS IN GOTHAM CITY!
WHOOP! WHOOP! WHOOP!
HEY, WHAT'S HAPPENING, S-MAN? LAST THING I REMEMBER WAS BEING CLOBBERED BY THE MAD HATTER. DOES BATMAN KNOW I'M FLYING HIS BAT-WING?
NO TIME FOR THE DETAILS, SON...

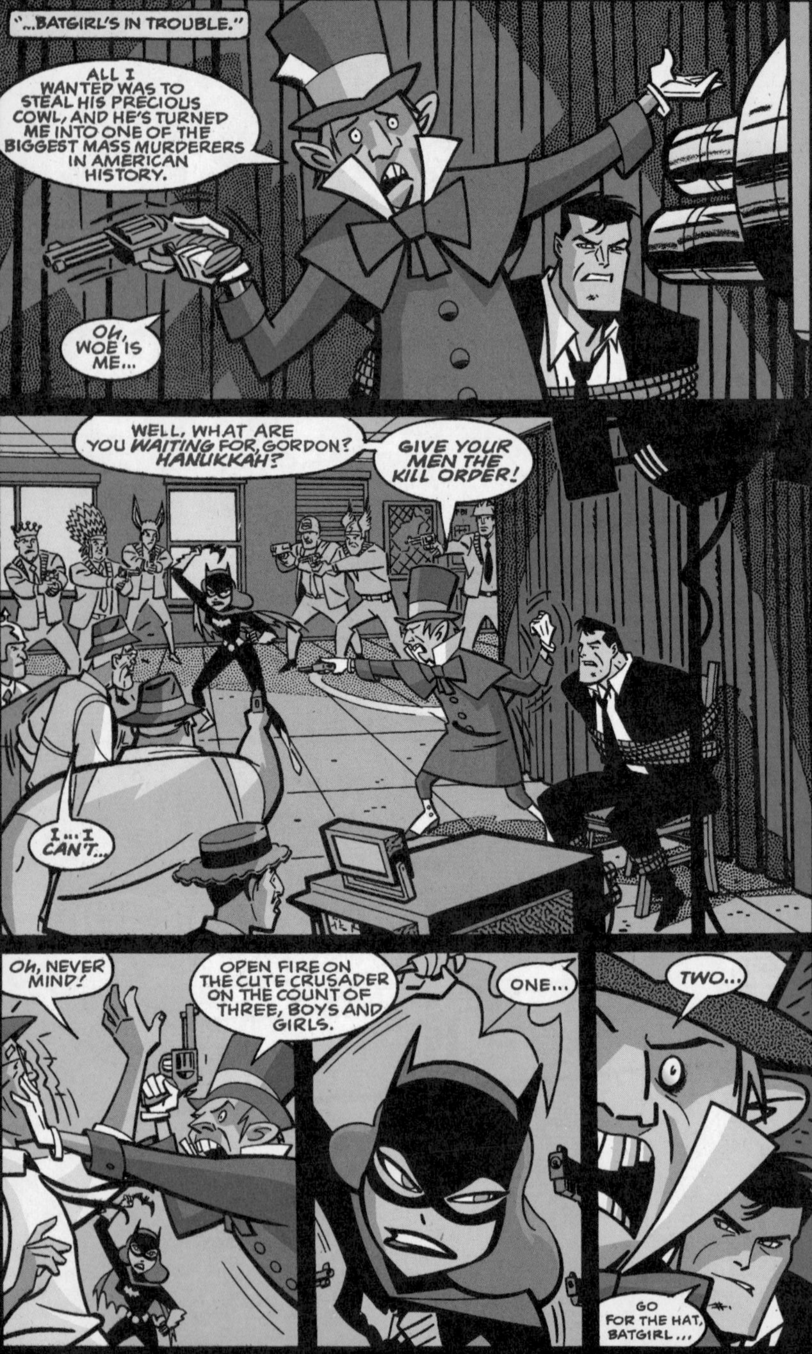
"...BATGIRL'S IN TROUBLE."
ALL I WANTED WAS TO STEAL HIS PRECIOUS COWL, AND HE'S TURNED ME INTO ONE OF THE BIGGEST MASS MURDERERS IN AMERICAN HISTORY.
OH, WOE IS ME...
WELL, WHAT ARE YOU WAITING FOR, GORDON? HANUKKAH?
GIVE YOUR MEN THE KILL ORDER!
I...I CAN'T...
OH, NEVER MIND!
OPEN FIRE ON THE CUTE CRUSADER ON THE COUNT OF THREE, BOYS AND GIRLS.
ONE...
TWO...
GO FOR THE HAT, BATGIRL...

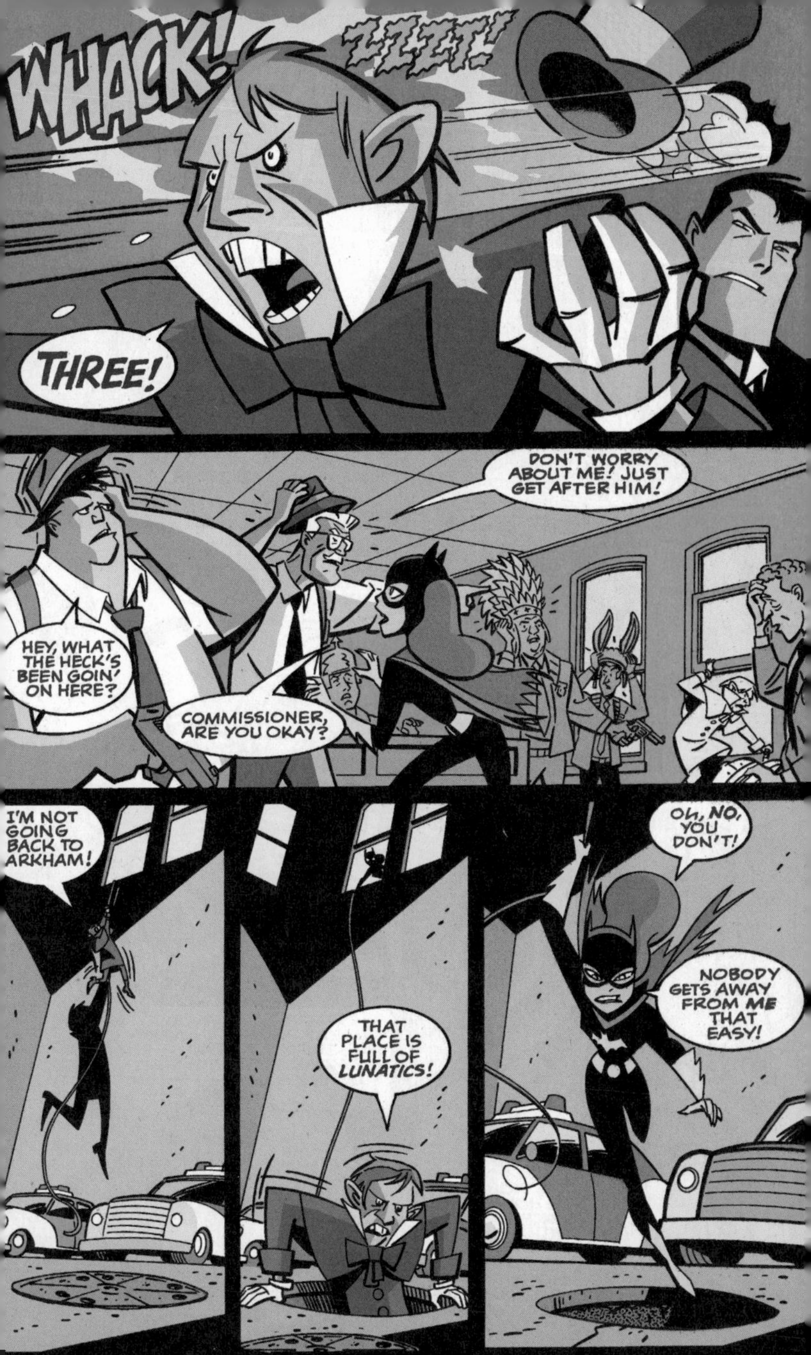

WHACK!
ZZZT!
THREE!
DON'T WORRY ABOUT ME! JUST GET AFTER HIM!
HEY, WHAT THE HECK'S BEEN GOIN' ON HERE?
COMMISSIONER, ARE YOU OKAY?
I'M NOT GOING BACK TO ARKHAM!
THAT PLACE IS FULL OF *LUNATICS*!
OH, *NO*, YOU DON'T!
NOBODY GETS AWAY FROM *ME* THAT EASY!

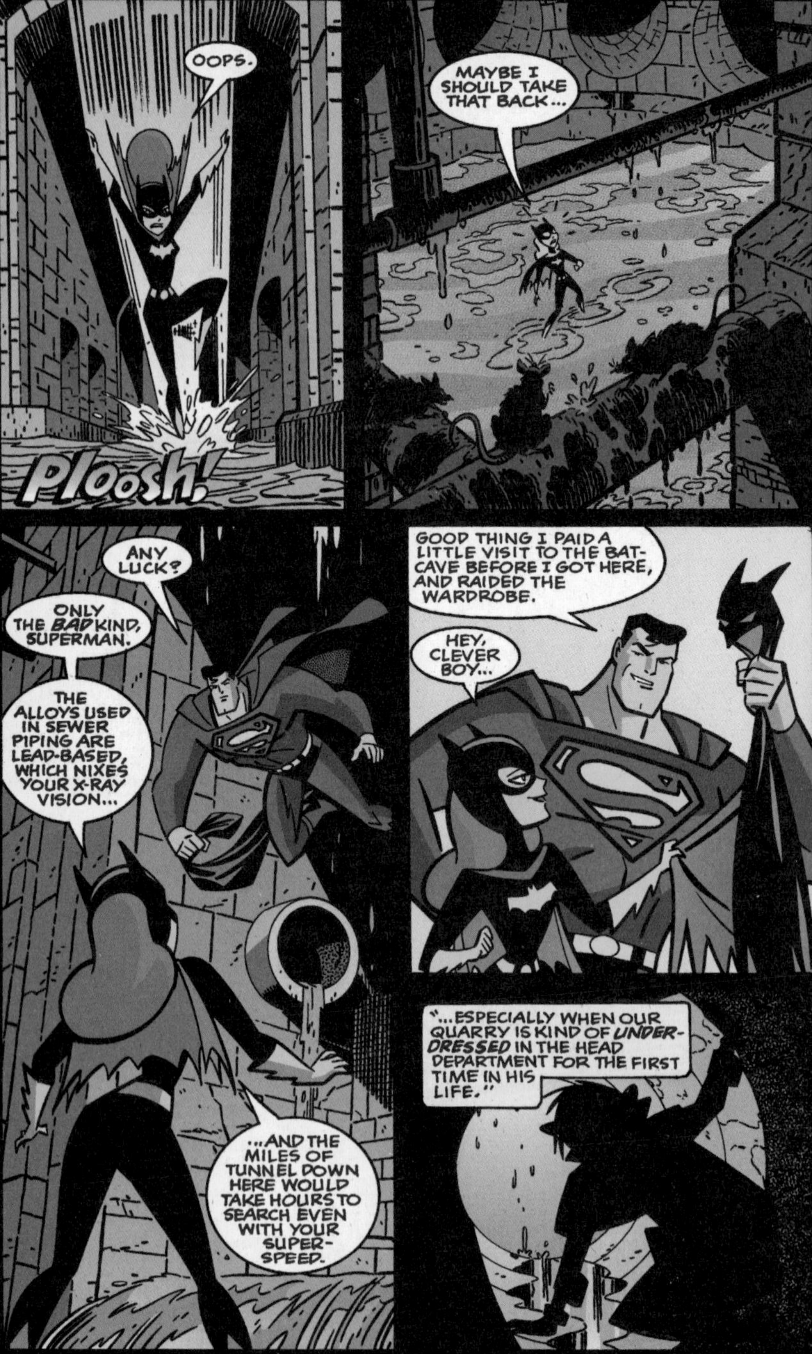
OOPS.
PLOOSH!
MAYBE I SHOULD TAKE THAT BACK...
ANY LUCK?
ONLY THE *BAD* KIND, SUPERMAN.
THE ALLOYS USED IN SEWER PIPING ARE LEAD-BASED, WHICH NIXES YOUR X-RAY VISION...
...AND THE MILES OF TUNNEL DOWN HERE WOULD TAKE HOURS TO SEARCH EVEN WITH YOUR SUPER-SPEED.
GOOD THING I PAID A LITTLE VISIT TO THE BAT-CAVE BEFORE I GOT HERE, AND RAIDED THE WARDROBE.
HEY, CLEVER BOY...
"...ESPECIALLY WHEN OUR QUARRY IS KIND OF *UNDER-DRESSED* IN THE HEAD DEPARTMENT FOR THE FIRST TIME IN HIS LIFE."

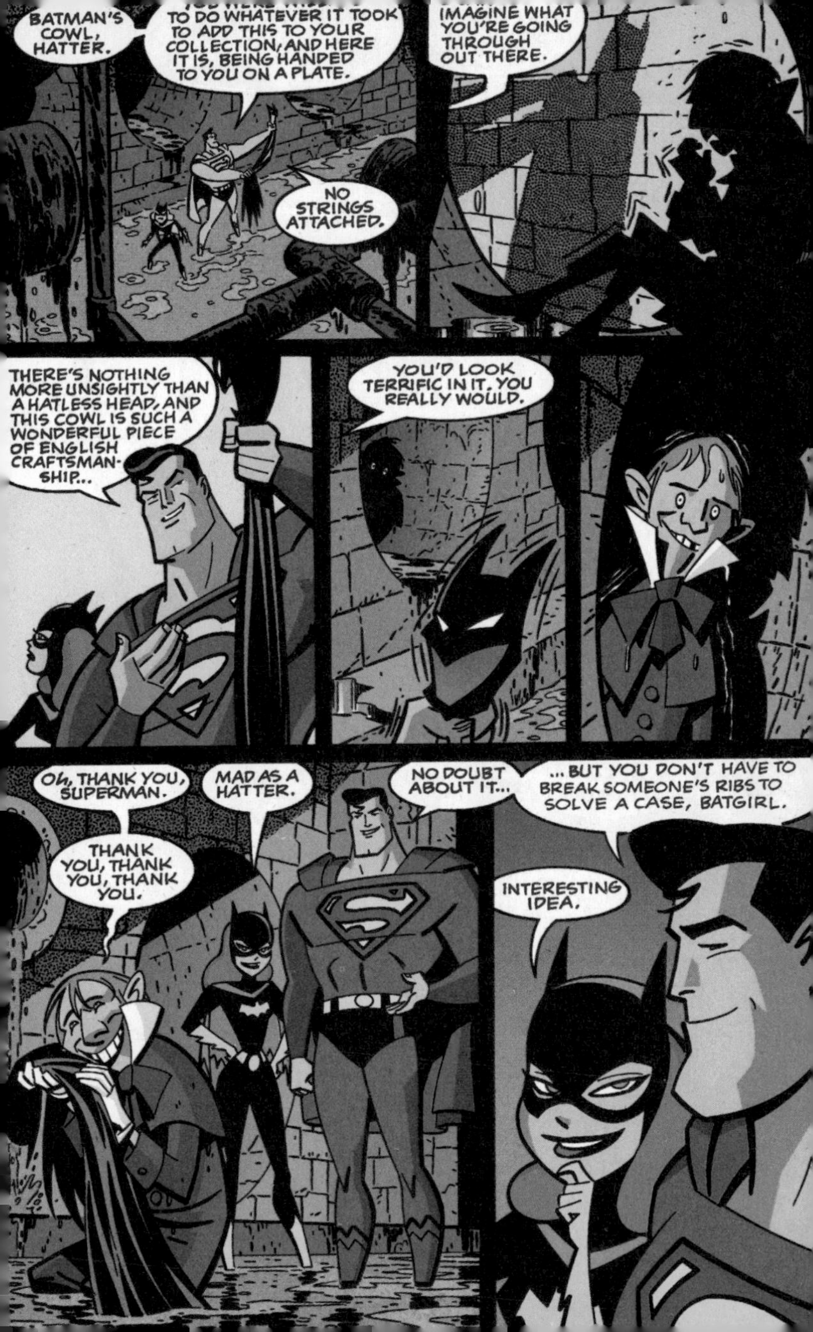
BATMAN'S COWL, HATTER.
TO DO WHATEVER IT TOOK TO ADD THIS TO YOUR COLLECTION, AND HERE IT IS, BEING HANDED TO YOU ON A PLATE.
NO STRINGS ATTACHED.
IMAGINE WHAT YOU'RE GOING THROUGH OUT THERE.
THERE'S NOTHING MORE UNSIGHTLY THAN A HATLESS HEAD, AND THIS COWL IS SUCH A WONDERFUL PIECE OF ENGLISH CRAFTSMAN-SHIP...
YOU'D LOOK TERRIFIC IN IT. YOU REALLY WOULD.
OH, THANK YOU, SUPERMAN.
THANK YOU, THANK YOU, THANK YOU.
MAD AS A HATTER.
NO DOUBT ABOUT IT...
... BUT YOU DON'T HAVE TO BREAK SOMEONE'S RIBS TO SOLVE A CASE, BATGIRL.
INTERESTING IDEA.

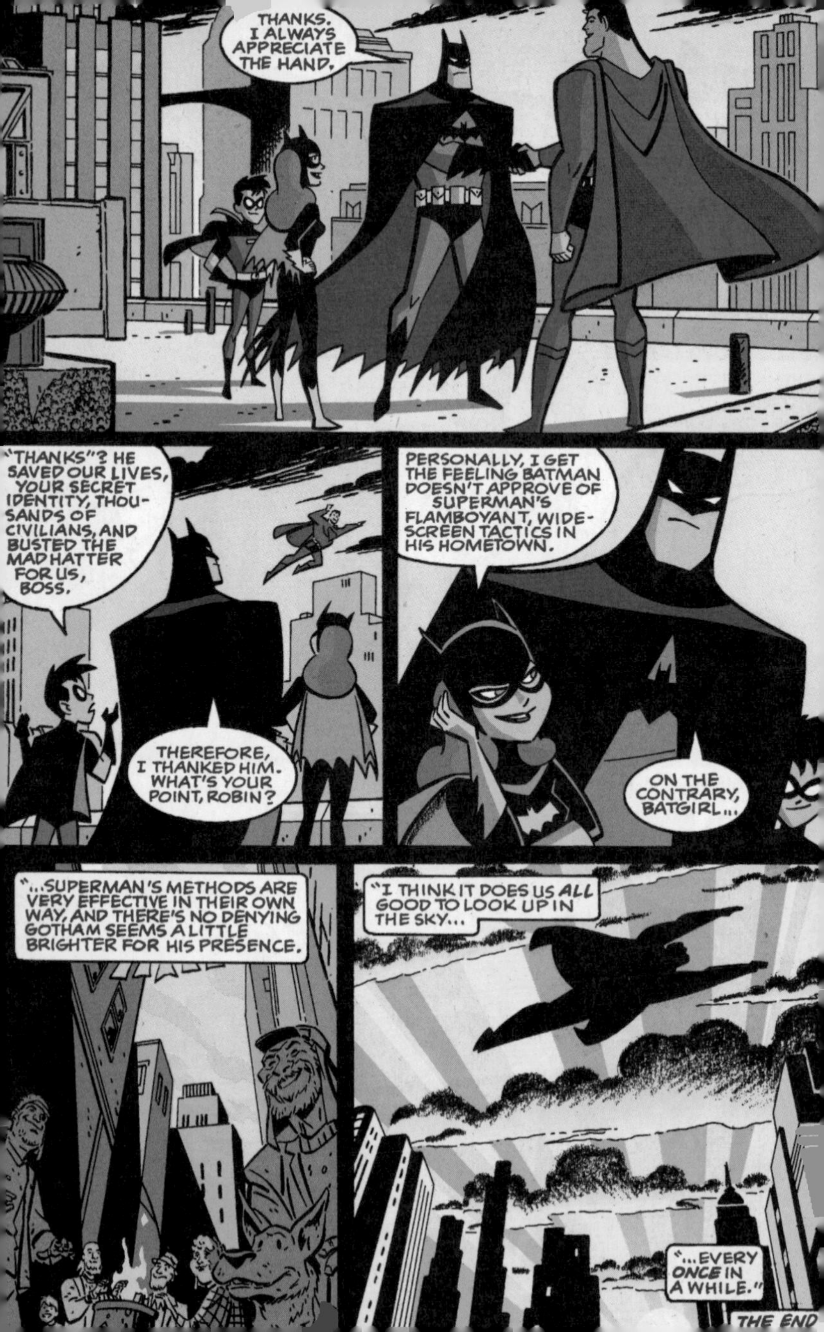
THANKS. I ALWAYS APPRECIATE THE HAND.
"THANKS"? HE SAVED OUR LIVES, YOUR SECRET IDENTITY, THOUSANDS OF CIVILIANS, AND BUSTED THE MAD HATTER FOR US, BOSS.
THEREFORE, I THANKED HIM. WHAT'S YOUR POINT, ROBIN?
PERSONALLY, I GET THE FEELING BATMAN DOESN'T APPROVE OF SUPERMAN'S FLAMBOYANT, WIDE-SCREEN TACTICS IN HIS HOMETOWN.
ON THE CONTRARY, BATGIRL...
"...SUPERMAN'S METHODS ARE VERY EFFECTIVE IN THEIR OWN WAY, AND THERE'S NO DENYING GOTHAM SEEMS A LITTLE BRIGHTER FOR HIS PRESENCE.
"I THINK IT DOES US ALL GOOD TO LOOK UP IN THE SKY...
"...EVERY ONCE IN A WHILE."
THE END

Yesterday's MAN of TOMORROW

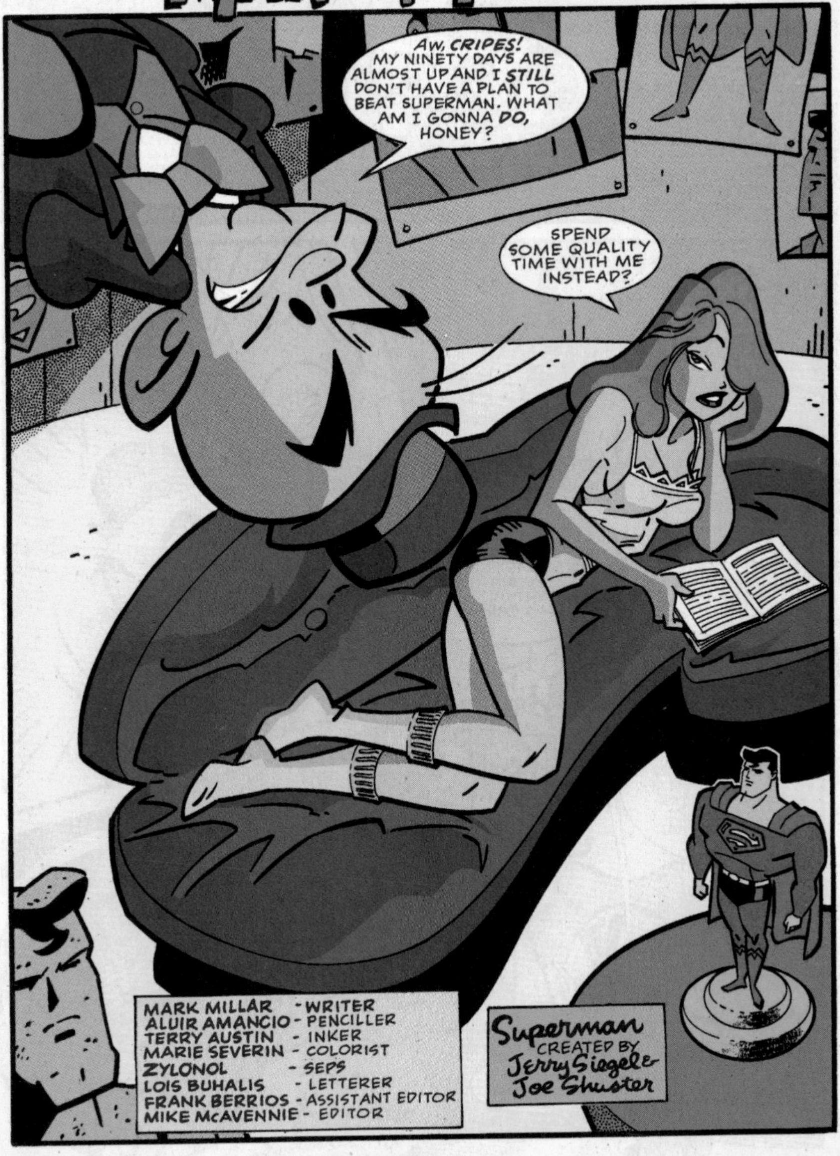
AW, CRIPES! MY NINETY DAYS ARE ALMOST UP AND I STILL DON'T HAVE A PLAN TO BEAT SUPERMAN. WHAT AM I GONNA DO, HONEY?
SPEND SOME QUALITY TIME WITH ME INSTEAD?
MARK MILLAR - WRITER
ALUIR AMANCIO - PENCILLER
TERRY AUSTIN - INKER
MARIE SEVERIN - COLORIST
ZYLONOL - SEPS
LOIS BUHALIS - LETTERER
FRANK BERRIOS - ASSISTANT EDITOR
MIKE McAVENNIE - EDITOR
Superman CREATED BY Jerry Siegel & Joe Shuster

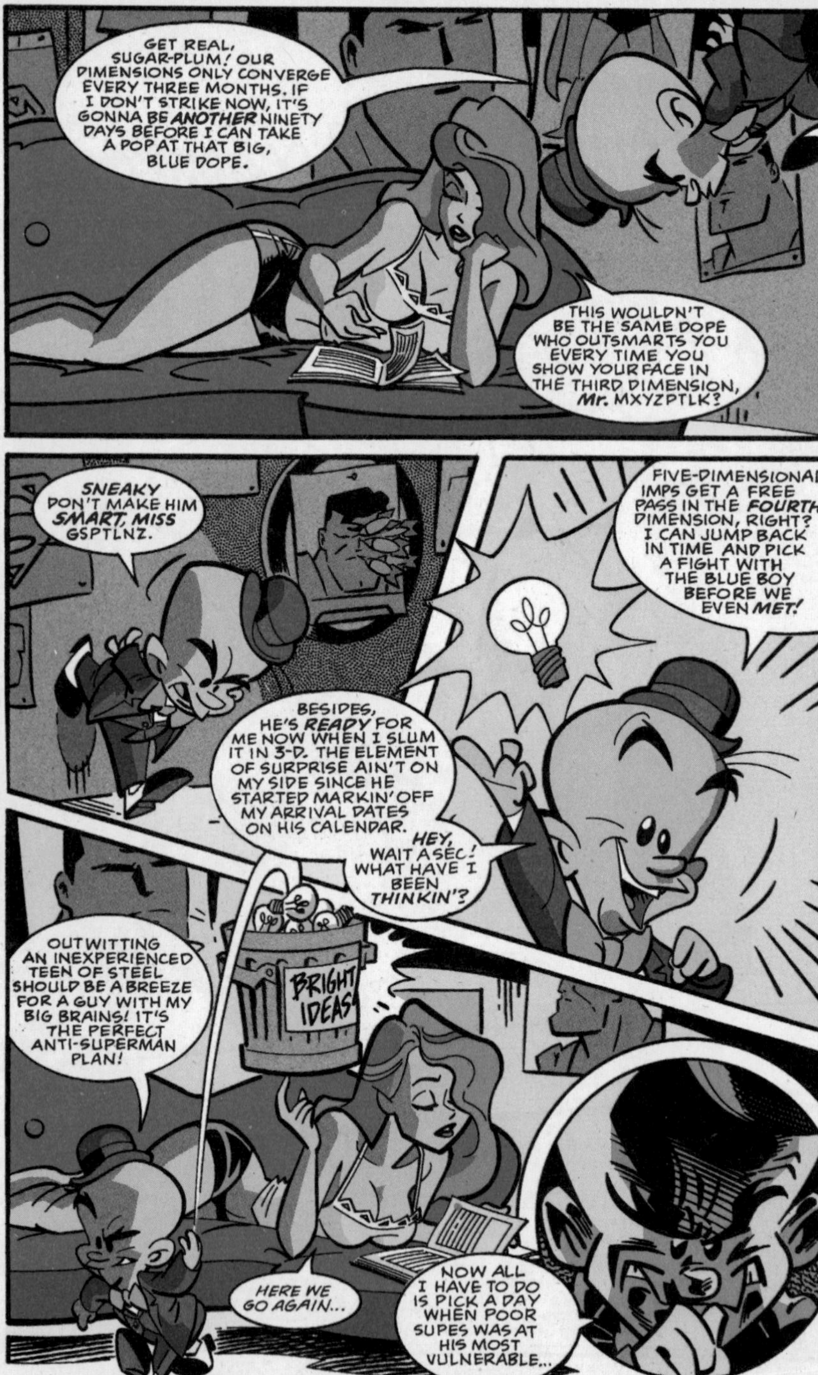
GET REAL, SUGAR-PLUM! OUR DIMENSIONS ONLY CONVERGE EVERY THREE MONTHS. IF I DON'T STRIKE NOW, IT'S GONNA BE *ANOTHER* NINETY DAYS BEFORE I CAN TAKE A POP AT THAT BIG, BLUE DOPE.
THIS WOULDN'T BE THE SAME DOPE WHO OUTSMARTS YOU EVERY TIME YOU SHOW YOUR FACE IN THE THIRD DIMENSION, *Mr.* MXYZPTLK?
SNEAKY DON'T MAKE HIM *SMART, MISS* GSPTLNZ.
FIVE-DIMENSIONAL IMPS GET A FREE PASS IN THE *FOURTH* DIMENSION, RIGHT? I CAN JUMP BACK IN TIME AND PICK A FIGHT WITH THE BLUE BOY BEFORE WE EVEN *MET!*
BESIDES, HE'S *READY* FOR ME NOW WHEN I SLUM IT IN 3-D. THE ELEMENT OF SURPRISE AIN'T ON MY SIDE SINCE HE STARTED MARKIN' OFF MY ARRIVAL DATES ON HIS CALENDAR.
HEY, WAIT A SEC! WHAT HAVE I BEEN *THINKIN'*?
BRIGHT IDEAS
OUTWITTING AN INEXPERIENCED TEEN OF STEEL SHOULD BE A BREEZE FOR A GUY WITH MY BIG BRAINS! IT'S THE PERFECT ANTI-SUPERMAN PLAN!
HERE WE GO AGAIN...
NOW ALL I HAVE TO DO IS PICK A DAY WHEN POOR SUPES WAS AT HIS MOST VULNERABLE...

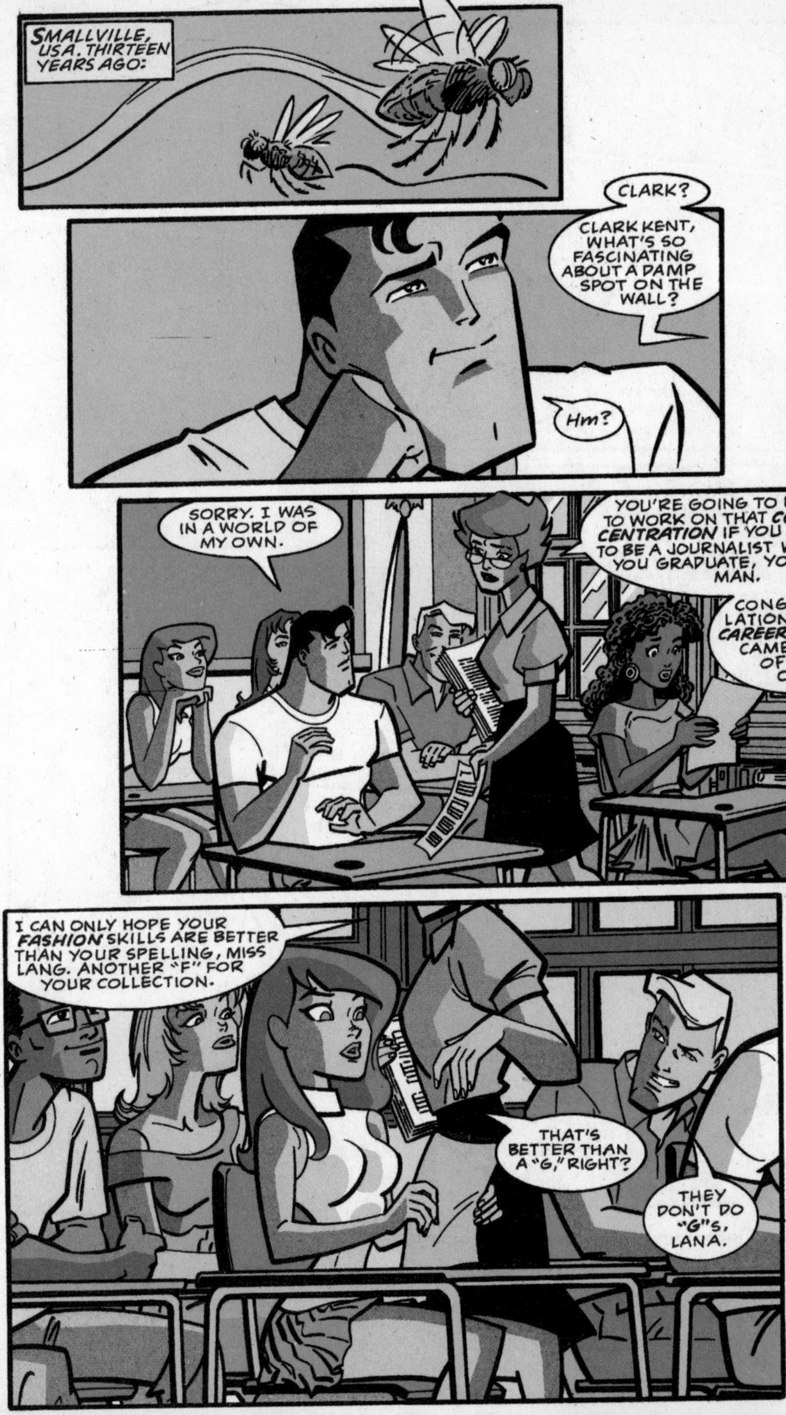
SMALLVILLE, USA. THIRTEEN YEARS AGO:
CLARK?
CLARK KENT, WHAT'S SO FASCINATING ABOUT A DAMP SPOT ON THE WALL?
Hm?
SORRY. I WAS IN A WORLD OF MY OWN.
YOU'RE GOING TO HAVE TO WORK ON THAT CONCENTRATION IF YOU WANT TO BE A JOURNALIST WHEN YOU GRADUATE, YOUNG MAN.
CONGRATULATIONS. YOUR CAREER PAPER CAME TOP OF THE CLASS.
I CAN ONLY HOPE YOUR FASHION SKILLS ARE BETTER THAN YOUR SPELLING, MISS LANG. ANOTHER "F" FOR YOUR COLLECTION.
THAT'S BETTER THAN A "G," RIGHT?
THEY DON'T DO "G"S, LANA.

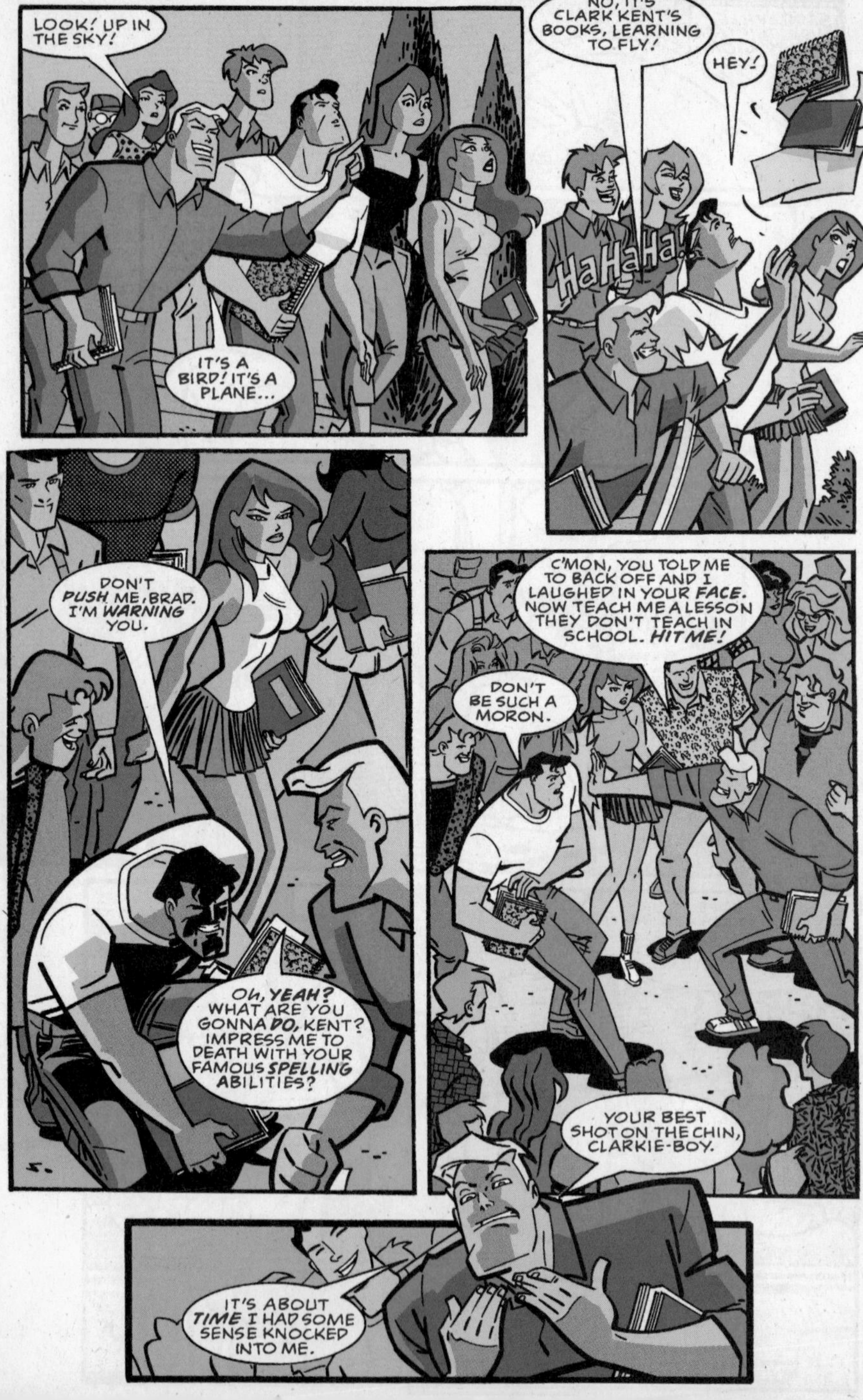
LOOK! UP IN THE SKY!
IT'S A BIRD! IT'S A PLANE...
NO, IT'S CLARK KENT'S BOOKS, LEARNING TO FLY!
HEY!
HaHaHaHa!
DON'T PUSH ME, BRAD. I'M WARNING YOU.
Oh, YEAH? WHAT ARE YOU GONNA DO, KENT? IMPRESS ME TO DEATH WITH YOUR FAMOUS SPELLING ABILITIES?
C'MON, YOU TOLD ME TO BACK OFF AND I LAUGHED IN YOUR FACE. NOW TEACH ME A LESSON THEY DON'T TEACH IN SCHOOL. HIT ME!
DON'T BE SUCH A MORON.
YOUR BEST SHOT ON THE CHIN, CLARKIE-BOY.
IT'S ABOUT TIME I HAD SOME SENSE KNOCKED INTO ME.

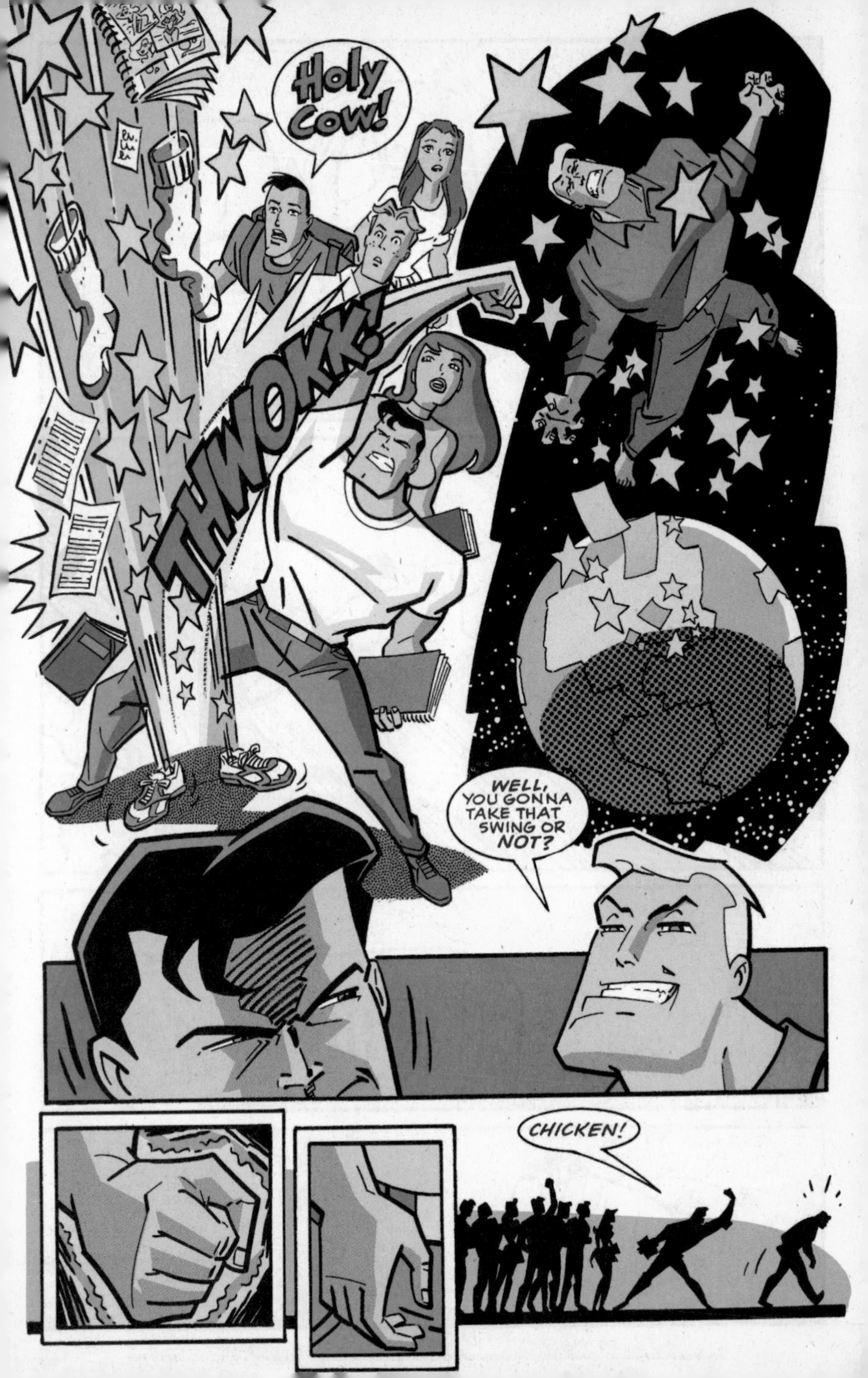
Holy Cow!
THWOKK!
WELL, YOU GONNA TAKE THAT SWING OR NOT?
CHICKEN!

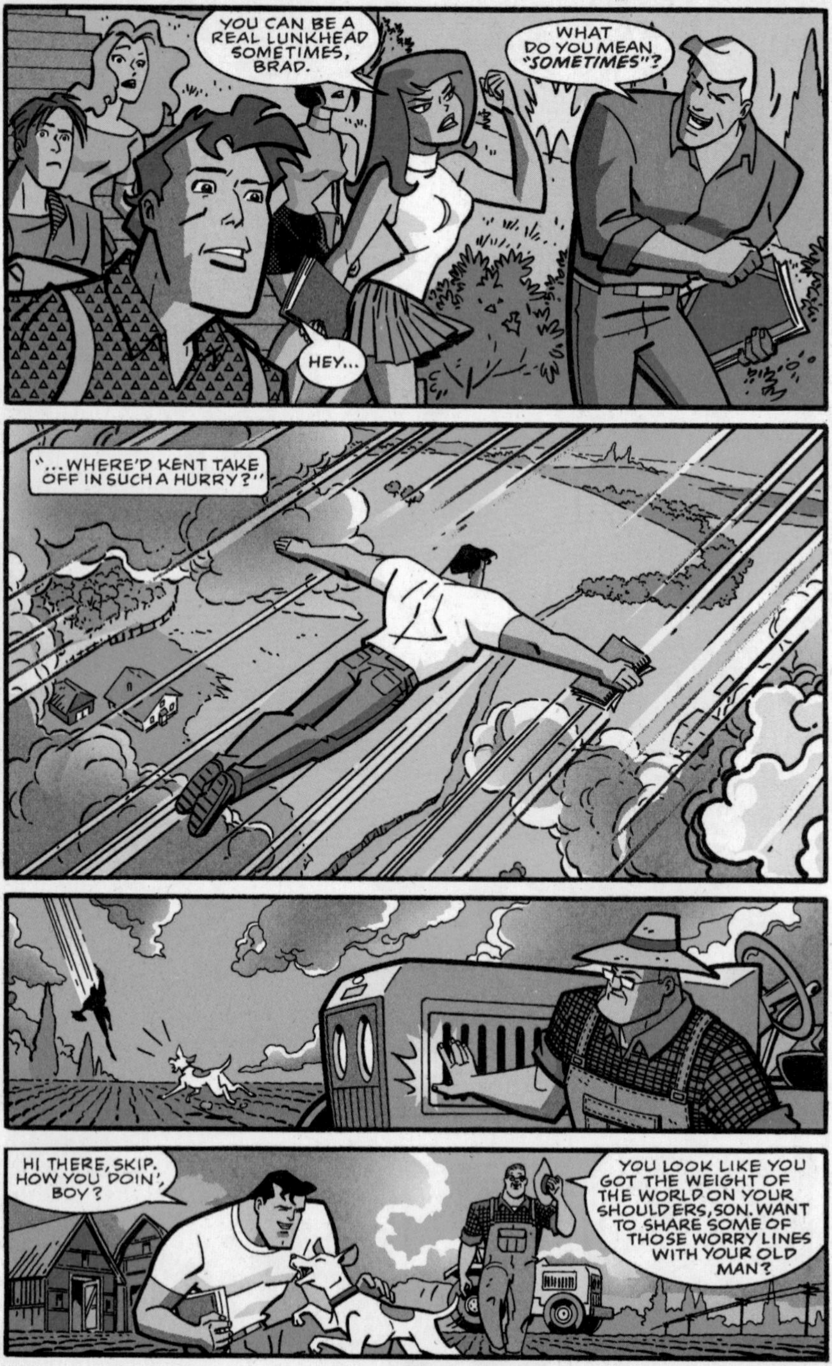
YOU CAN BE A REAL LUNKHEAD SOMETIMES, BRAD.
WHAT DO YOU MEAN "SOMETIMES"?
HEY...
"...WHERE'D KENT TAKE OFF IN SUCH A HURRY?"
HI THERE, SKIP. HOW YOU DOIN', BOY?
YOU LOOK LIKE YOU GOT THE WEIGHT OF THE WORLD ON YOUR SHOULDERS, SON. WANT TO SHARE SOME OF THOSE WORRY LINES WITH YOUR OLD MAN?

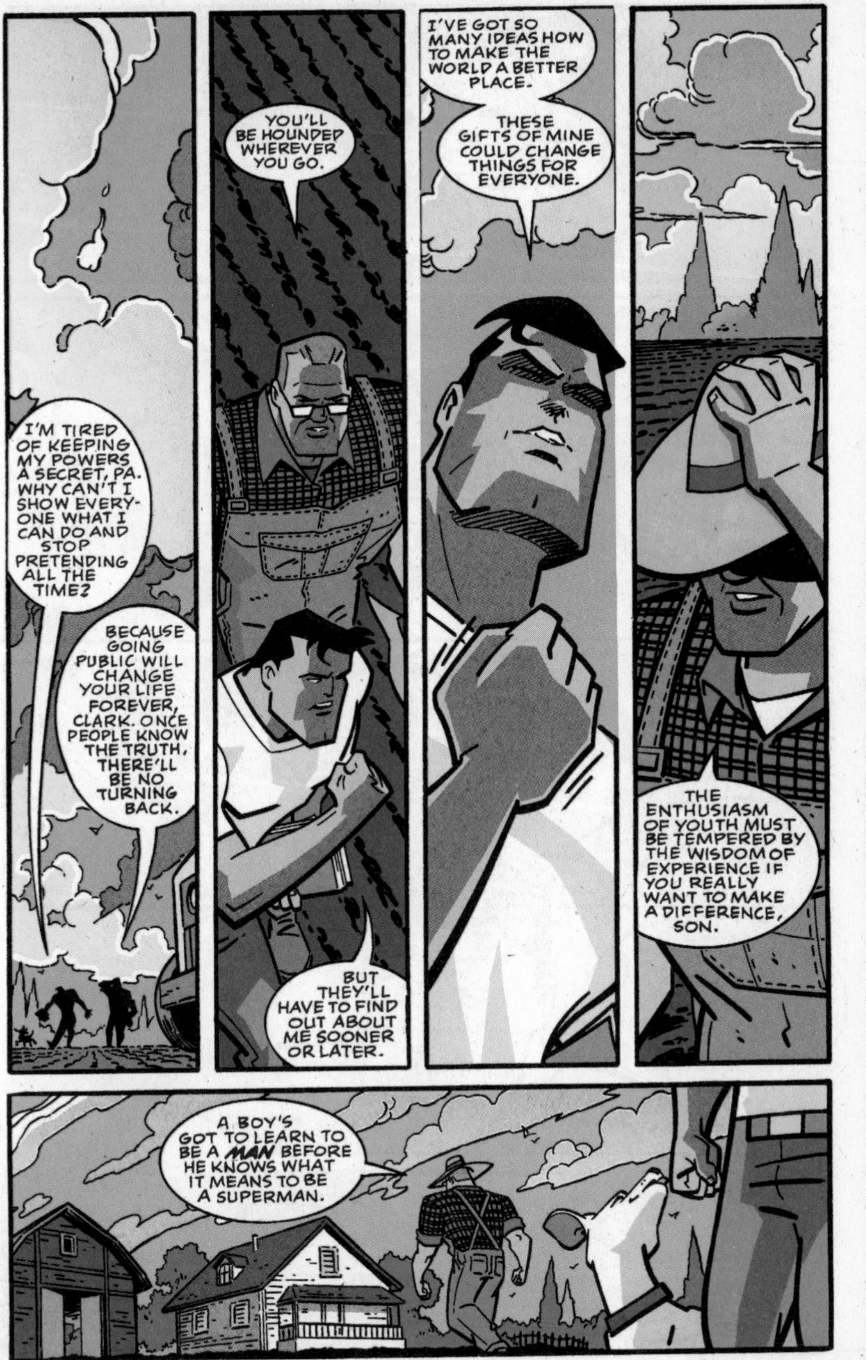
I'M TIRED OF KEEPING MY POWERS A SECRET, PA. WHY CAN'T I SHOW EVERYONE WHAT I CAN DO AND STOP PRETENDING ALL THE TIME?
BECAUSE GOING PUBLIC WILL CHANGE YOUR LIFE FOREVER, CLARK. ONCE PEOPLE KNOW THE TRUTH, THERE'LL BE NO TURNING BACK.
YOU'LL BE HOUNDED WHEREVER YOU GO.
BUT THEY'LL HAVE TO FIND OUT ABOUT ME SOONER OR LATER.
I'VE GOT SO MANY IDEAS HOW TO MAKE THE WORLD A BETTER PLACE.
THESE GIFTS OF MINE COULD CHANGE THINGS FOR EVERYONE.
THE ENTHUSIASM OF YOUTH MUST BE TEMPERED BY THE WISDOM OF EXPERIENCE IF YOU REALLY WANT TO MAKE A DIFFERENCE, SON.
A BOY'S GOT TO LEARN TO BE A ***MAN*** BEFORE HE KNOWS WHAT IT MEANS TO BE A SUPERMAN.

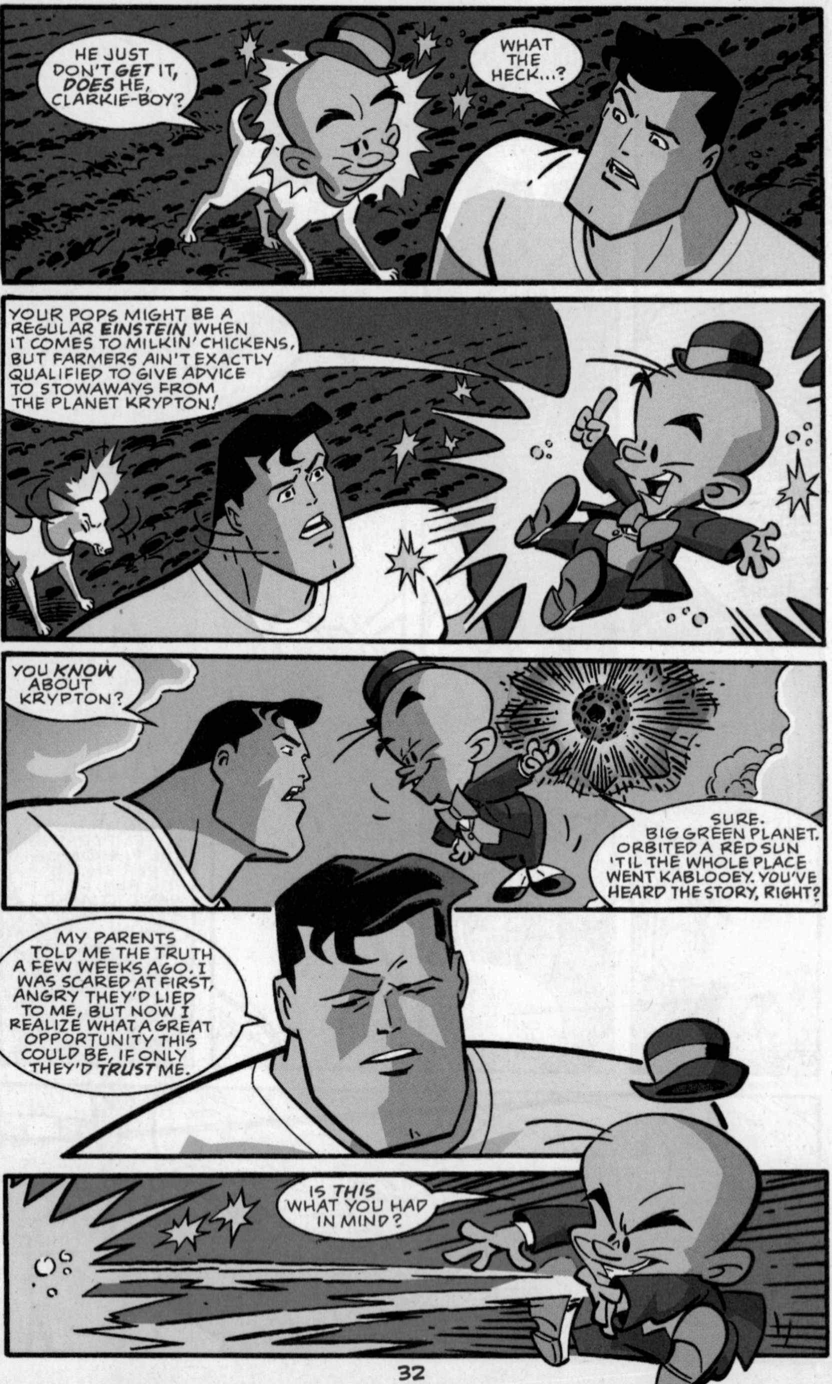

HE JUST DON'T GET IT, DOES HE, CLARKIE-BOY?
WHAT THE HECK...?
YOUR POPS MIGHT BE A REGULAR EINSTEIN WHEN IT COMES TO MILKIN' CHICKENS, BUT FARMERS AIN'T EXACTLY QUALIFIED TO GIVE ADVICE TO STOWAWAYS FROM THE PLANET KRYPTON!
YOU KNOW ABOUT KRYPTON?
SURE. BIG GREEN PLANET. ORBITED A RED SUN 'TIL THE WHOLE PLACE WENT KABLOOEY. YOU'VE HEARD THE STORY, RIGHT?
MY PARENTS TOLD ME THE TRUTH A FEW WEEKS AGO. I WAS SCARED AT FIRST, ANGRY THEY'D LIED TO ME, BUT NOW I REALIZE WHAT A GREAT OPPORTUNITY THIS COULD BE, IF ONLY THEY'D TRUST ME.
IS THIS WHAT YOU HAD IN MIND?

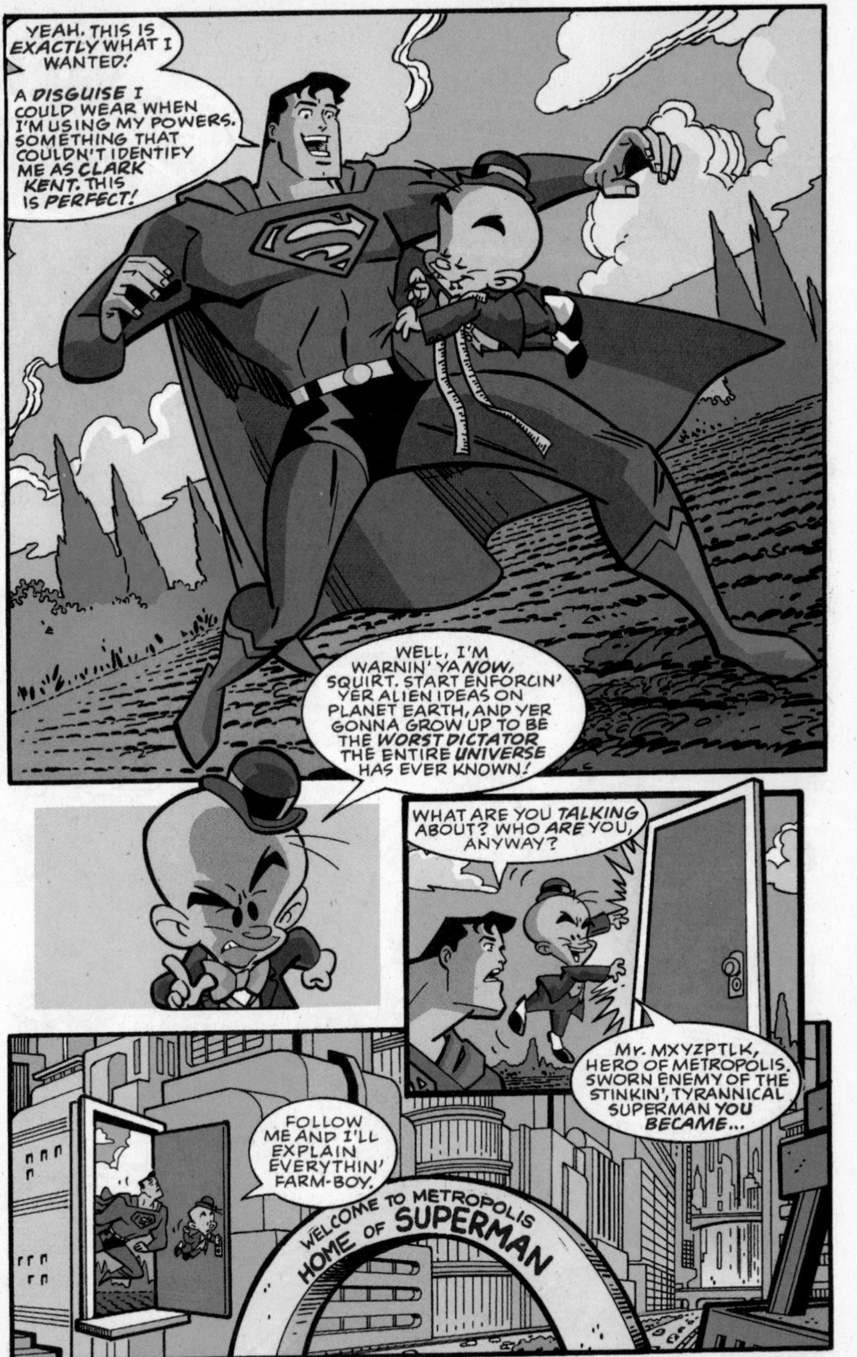
YEAH. THIS IS EXACTLY WHAT I WANTED!
A DISGUISE I COULD WEAR WHEN I'M USING MY POWERS. SOMETHING THAT COULDN'T IDENTIFY ME AS CLARK KENT. THIS IS PERFECT!
WELL, I'M WARNIN' YA NOW, SQUIRT. START ENFORCIN' YER ALIEN IDEAS ON PLANET EARTH, AND YER GONNA GROW UP TO BE THE WORST DICTATOR THE ENTIRE UNIVERSE HAS EVER KNOWN!
WHAT ARE YOU TALKING ABOUT? WHO ARE YOU, ANYWAY?
Mr. MXYZPTLK, HERO OF METROPOLIS. SWORN ENEMY OF THE STINKIN', TYRANNICAL SUPERMAN YOU BECAME...
FOLLOW ME AND I'LL EXPLAIN EVERYTHIN' FARM-BOY.
WELCOME TO METROPOLIS
HOME OF SUPERMAN

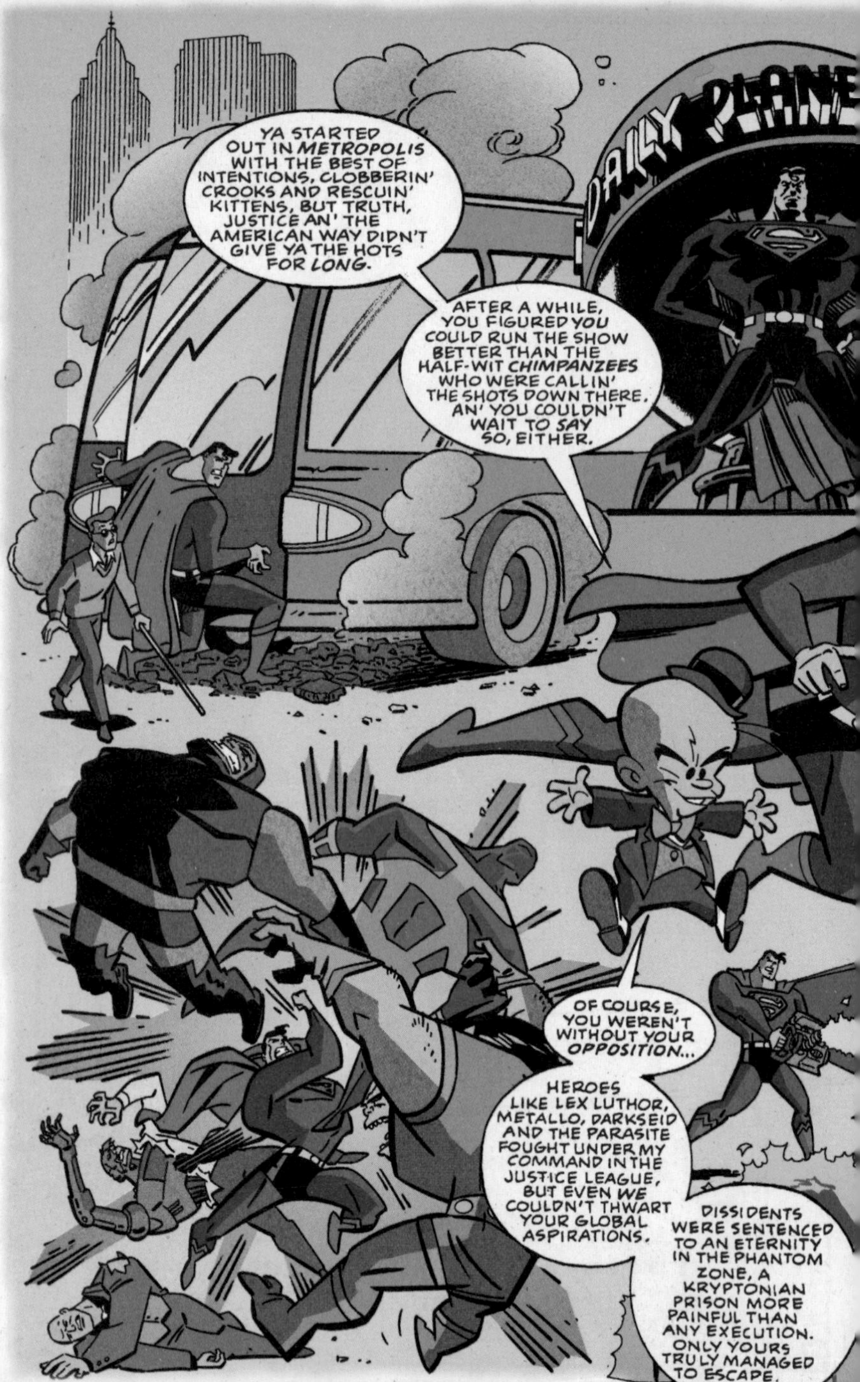
YA STARTED OUT IN METROPOLIS WITH THE BEST OF INTENTIONS, CLOBBERIN' CROOKS AND RESCUIN' KITTENS, BUT TRUTH, JUSTICE AN' THE AMERICAN WAY DIDN'T GIVE YA THE HOTS FOR LONG.
AFTER A WHILE, YOU FIGURED YOU COULD RUN THE SHOW BETTER THAN THE HALF-WIT CHIMPANZEES WHO WERE CALLIN' THE SHOTS DOWN THERE. AN' YOU COULDN'T WAIT TO SAY SO, EITHER.
DAILY PLANE
OF COURSE, YOU WEREN'T WITHOUT YOUR OPPOSITION...
HEROES LIKE LEX LUTHOR, METALLO, DARKSEID AND THE PARASITE FOUGHT UNDER MY COMMAND IN THE JUSTICE LEAGUE, BUT EVEN WE COULDN'T THWART YOUR GLOBAL ASPIRATIONS.
DISSIDENTS WERE SENTENCED TO AN ETERNITY IN THE PHANTOM ZONE, A KRYPTONIAN PRISON MORE PAINFUL THAN ANY EXECUTION. ONLY YOURS TRULY MANAGED TO ESCAPE.

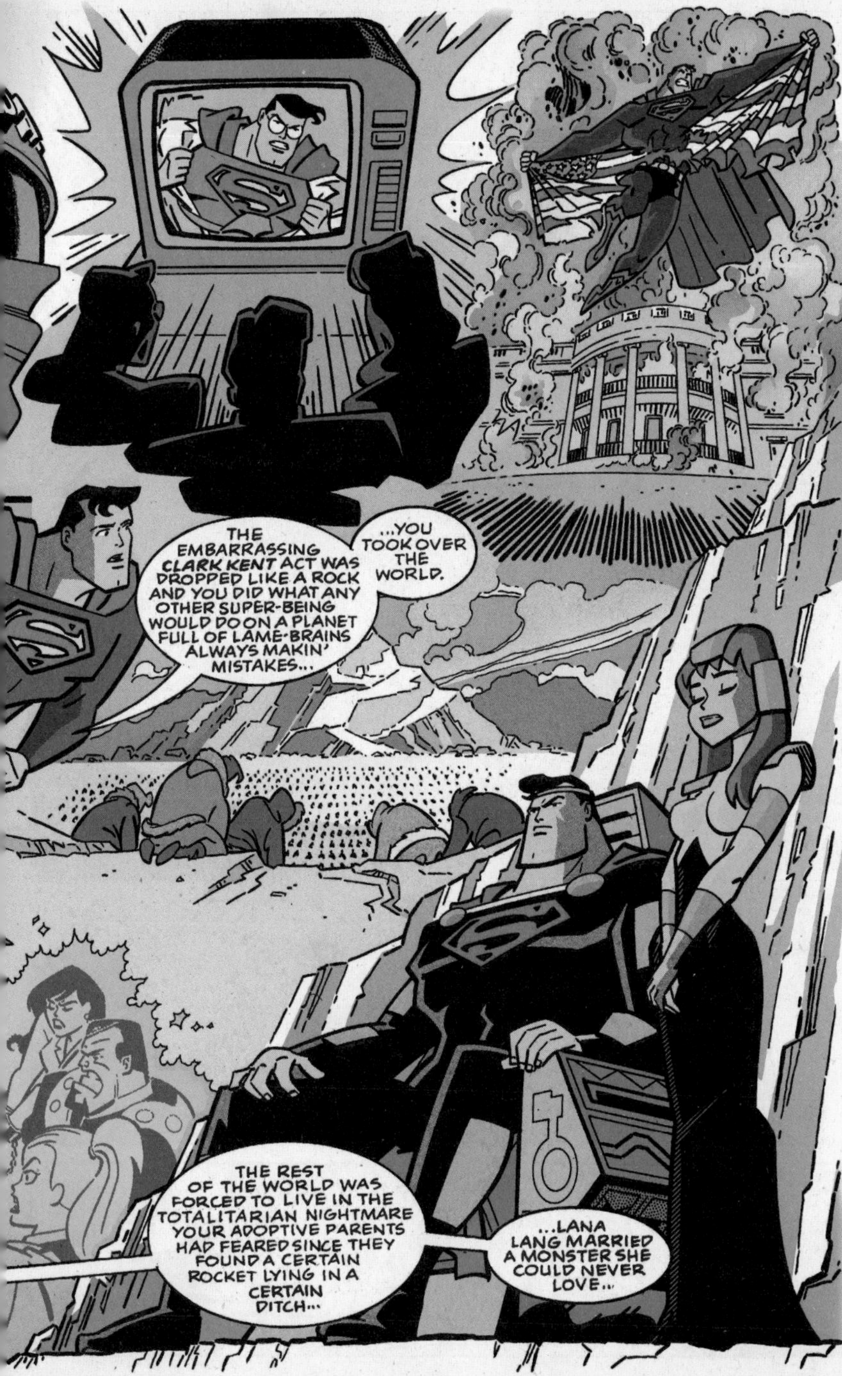
THE EMBARRASSING CLARK KENT ACT WAS DROPPED LIKE A ROCK AND YOU DID WHAT ANY OTHER SUPER-BEING WOULD DO ON A PLANET FULL OF LAME-BRAINS ALWAYS MAKIN' MISTAKES...
...YOU TOOK OVER THE WORLD.
THE REST OF THE WORLD WAS FORCED TO LIVE IN THE TOTALITARIAN NIGHTMARE YOUR ADOPTIVE PARENTS HAD FEARED SINCE THEY FOUND A CERTAIN ROCKET LYING IN A CERTAIN DITCH...
...LANA LANG MARRIED A MONSTER SHE COULD NEVER LOVE...

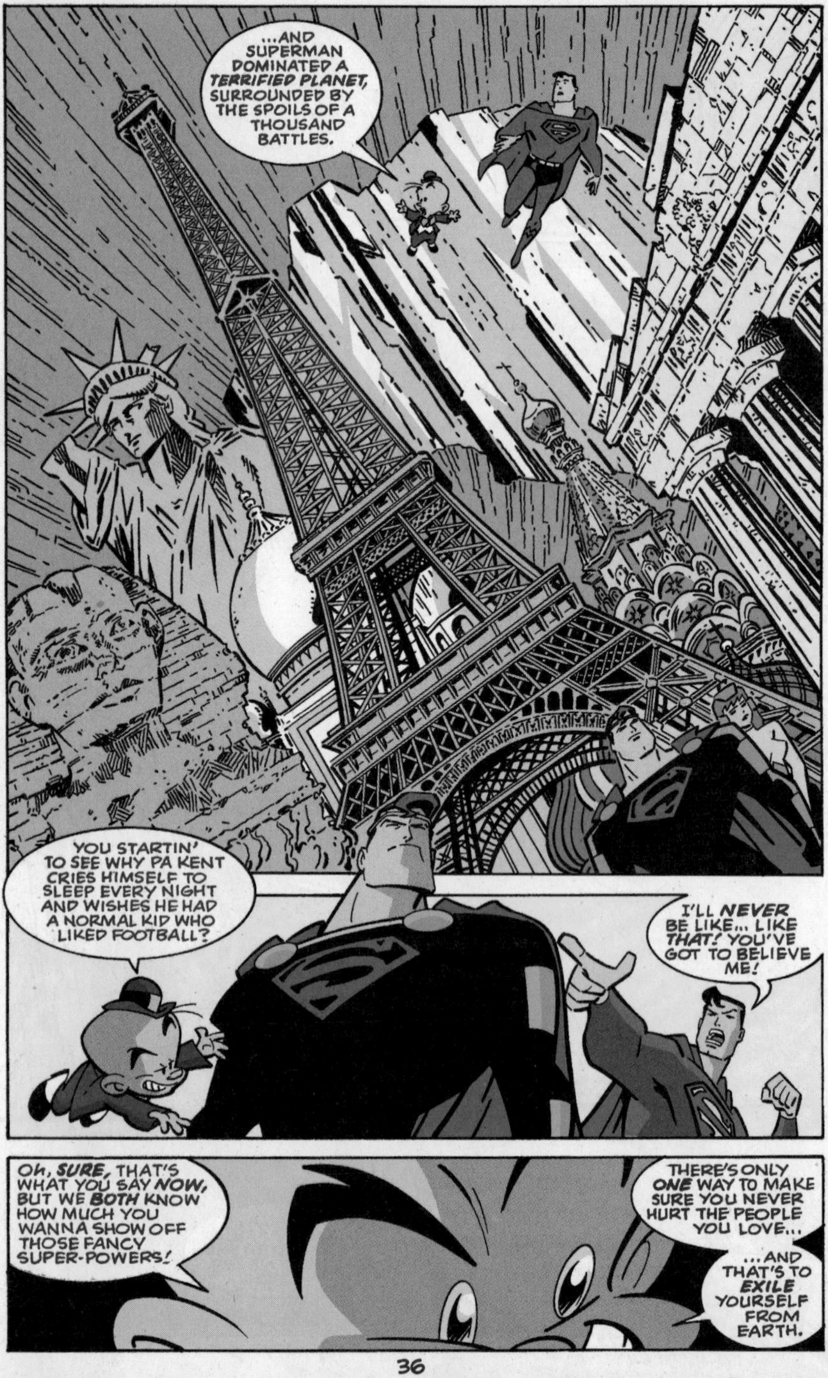
...AND SUPERMAN DOMINATED A TERRIFIED PLANET, SURROUNDED BY THE SPOILS OF A THOUSAND BATTLES.
YOU STARTIN' TO SEE WHY PA KENT CRIES HIMSELF TO SLEEP EVERY NIGHT AND WISHES HE HAD A NORMAL KID WHO LIKED FOOTBALL?
I'LL NEVER BE LIKE... LIKE THAT! YOU'VE GOT TO BELIEVE ME!
Oh, SURE, THAT'S WHAT YOU SAY NOW, BUT WE BOTH KNOW HOW MUCH YOU WANNA SHOW OFF THOSE FANCY SUPER-POWERS!
THERE'S ONLY ONE WAY TO MAKE SURE YOU NEVER HURT THE PEOPLE YOU LOVE...
...AND THAT'S TO EXILE YOURSELF FROM EARTH.

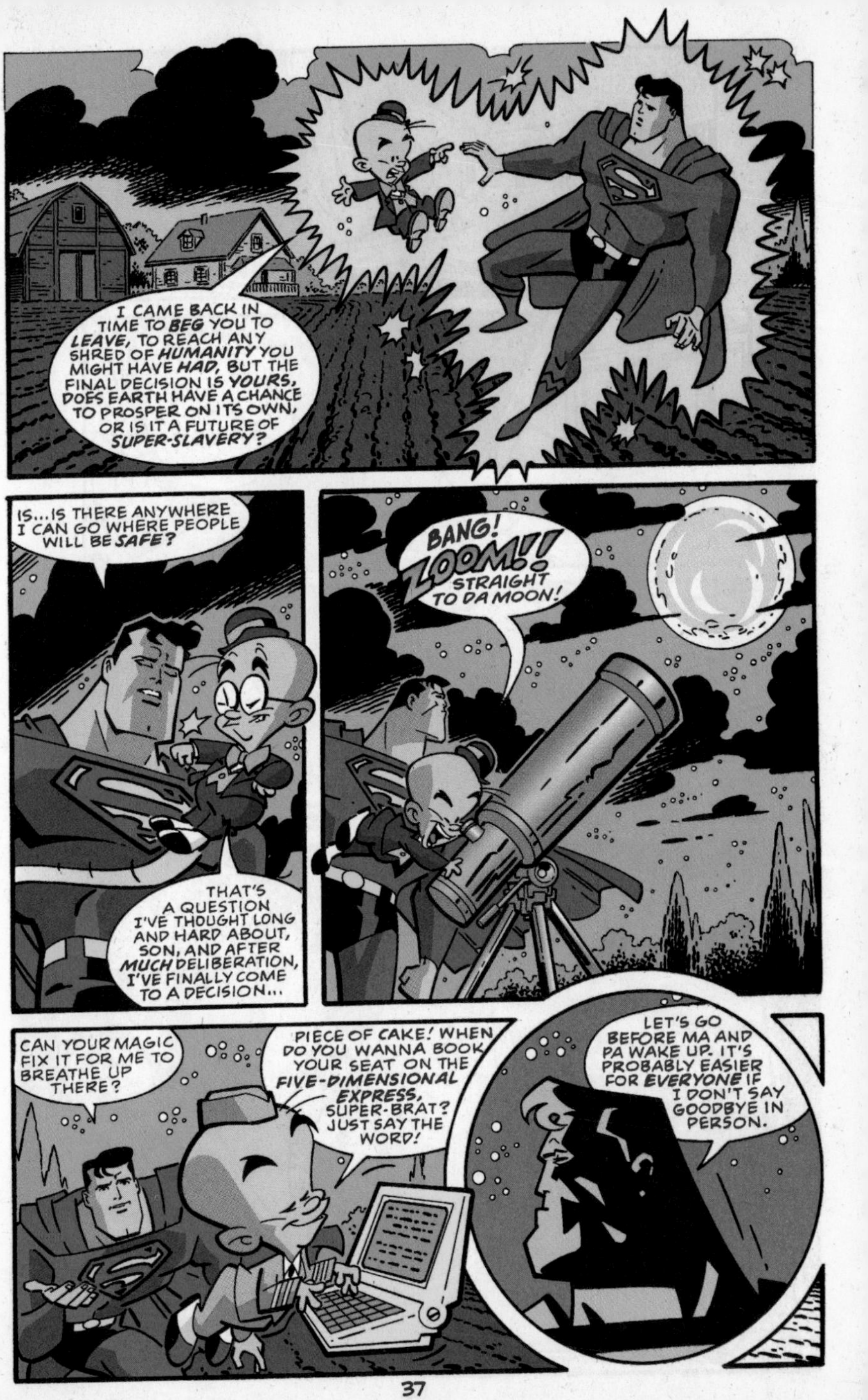
I CAME BACK IN TIME TO BEG YOU TO LEAVE, TO REACH ANY SHRED OF HUMANITY YOU MIGHT HAVE HAD, BUT THE FINAL DECISION IS YOURS. DOES EARTH HAVE A CHANCE TO PROSPER ON ITS OWN, OR IS IT A FUTURE OF SUPER-SLAVERY?
IS... IS THERE ANYWHERE I CAN GO WHERE PEOPLE WILL BE SAFE?
THAT'S A QUESTION I'VE THOUGHT LONG AND HARD ABOUT, SON, AND AFTER MUCH DELIBERATION, I'VE FINALLY COME TO A DECISION...
BANG! ZOOM!! STRAIGHT TO DA MOON!
CAN YOUR MAGIC FIX IT FOR ME TO BREATHE UP THERE?
PIECE OF CAKE! WHEN DO YOU WANNA BOOK YOUR SEAT ON THE FIVE-DIMENSIONAL EXPRESS, SUPER-BRAT? JUST SAY THE WORD!
LET'S GO BEFORE MA AND PA WAKE UP. IT'S PROBABLY EASIER FOR EVERYONE IF I DON'T SAY GOODBYE IN PERSON.

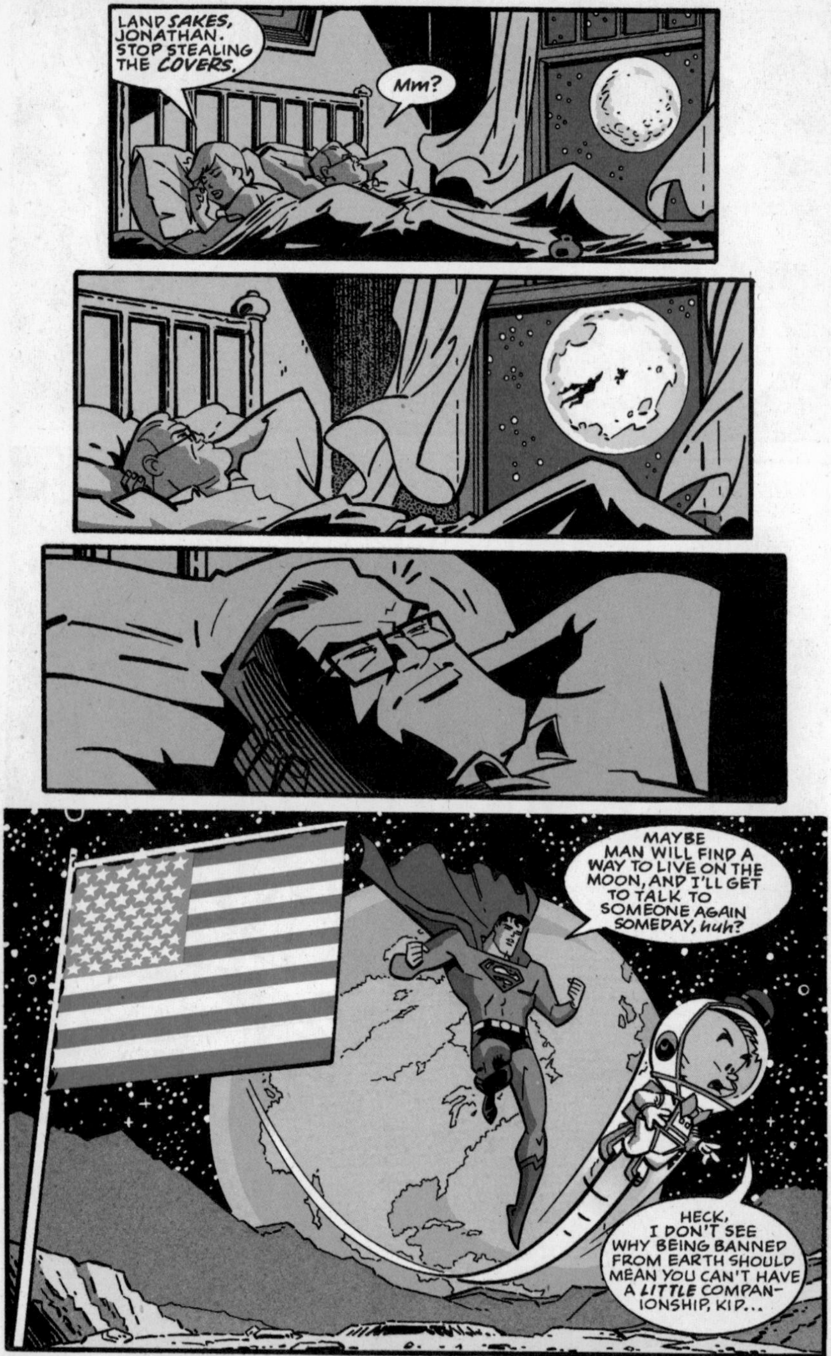
LAND SAKES, JONATHAN. STOP STEALING THE COVERS.
Mm?
MAYBE MAN WILL FIND A WAY TO LIVE ON THE MOON, AND I'LL GET TO TALK TO SOMEONE AGAIN SOMEDAY, huh?
HECK, I DON'T SEE WHY BEING BANNED FROM EARTH SHOULD MEAN YOU CAN'T HAVE A LITTLE COMPANIONSHIP, KID...

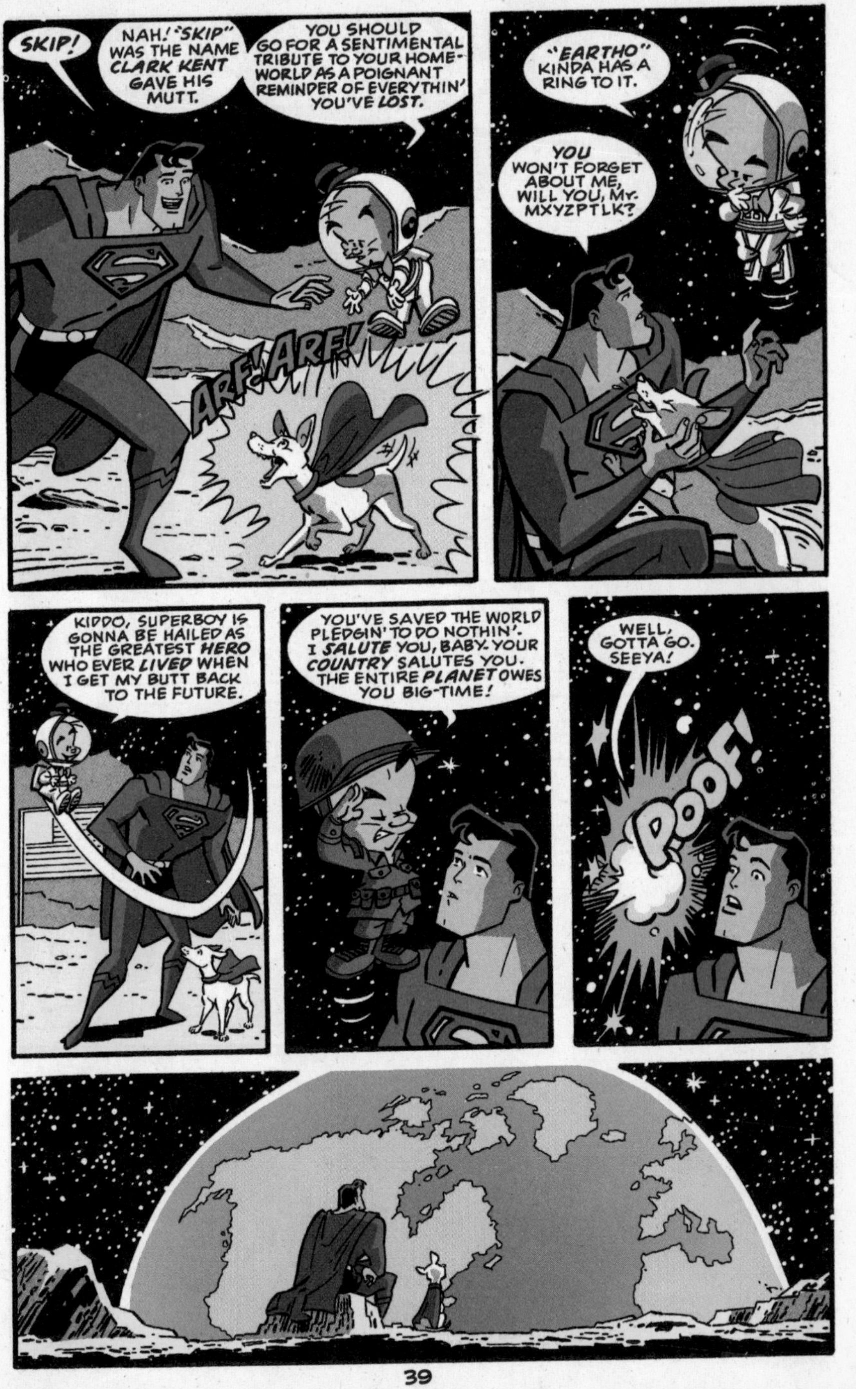

SKIP!
NAH! "SKIP" WAS THE NAME CLARK KENT GAVE HIS MUTT.
YOU SHOULD GO FOR A SENTIMENTAL TRIBUTE TO YOUR HOME-WORLD AS A POIGNANT REMINDER OF EVERYTHIN' YOU'VE LOST.
ARF! ARF!
"EARTHO" KINDA HAS A RING TO IT.
YOU WON'T FORGET ABOUT ME, WILL YOU, MR. MXYZPTLK?
KIDDO, SUPERBOY IS GONNA BE HAILED AS THE GREATEST HERO WHO EVER LIVED WHEN I GET MY BUTT BACK TO THE FUTURE.
YOU'VE SAVED THE WORLD PLEDGIN' TO DO NOTHIN'. I SALUTE YOU, BABY. YOUR COUNTRY SALUTES YOU. THE ENTIRE PLANET OWES YOU BIG-TIME!
WELL, GOTTA GO. SEEYA!
POOF!

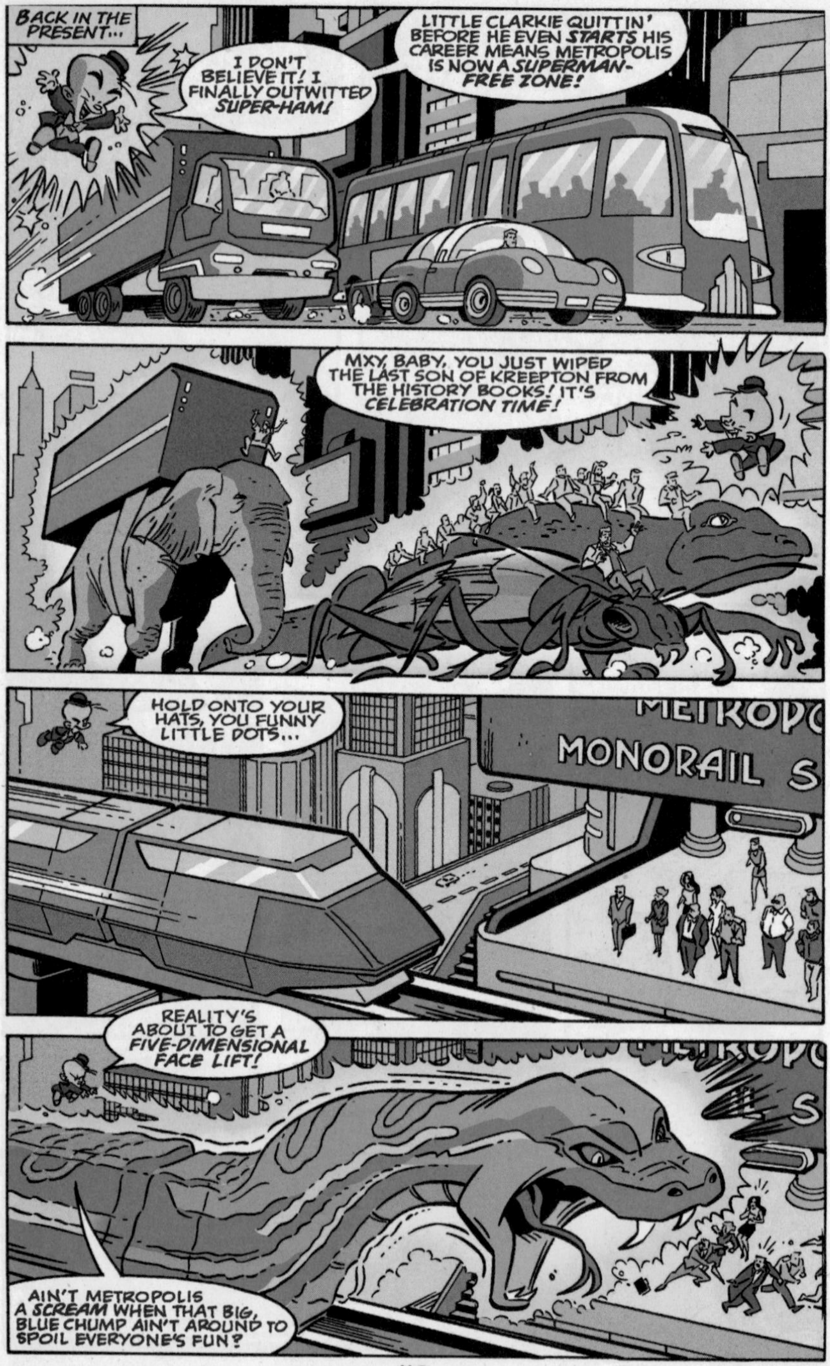
BACK IN THE PRESENT...
I DON'T BELIEVE IT! I FINALLY OUTWITTED SUPER-HAM!
LITTLE CLARKIE QUITTIN' BEFORE HE EVEN STARTS HIS CAREER MEANS METROPOLIS IS NOW A SUPERMAN-FREE ZONE!
MXY, BABY, YOU JUST WIPED THE LAST SON OF KREEPTON FROM THE HISTORY BOOKS! IT'S CELEBRATION TIME!
HOLD ONTO YOUR HATS, YOU FUNNY LITTLE DOTS...
MONORAIL S
REALITY'S ABOUT TO GET A FIVE-DIMENSIONAL FACE LIFT!
AIN'T METROPOLIS A SCREAM WHEN THAT BIG, BLUE CHUMP AIN'T AROUND TO SPOIL EVERYONE'S FUN?

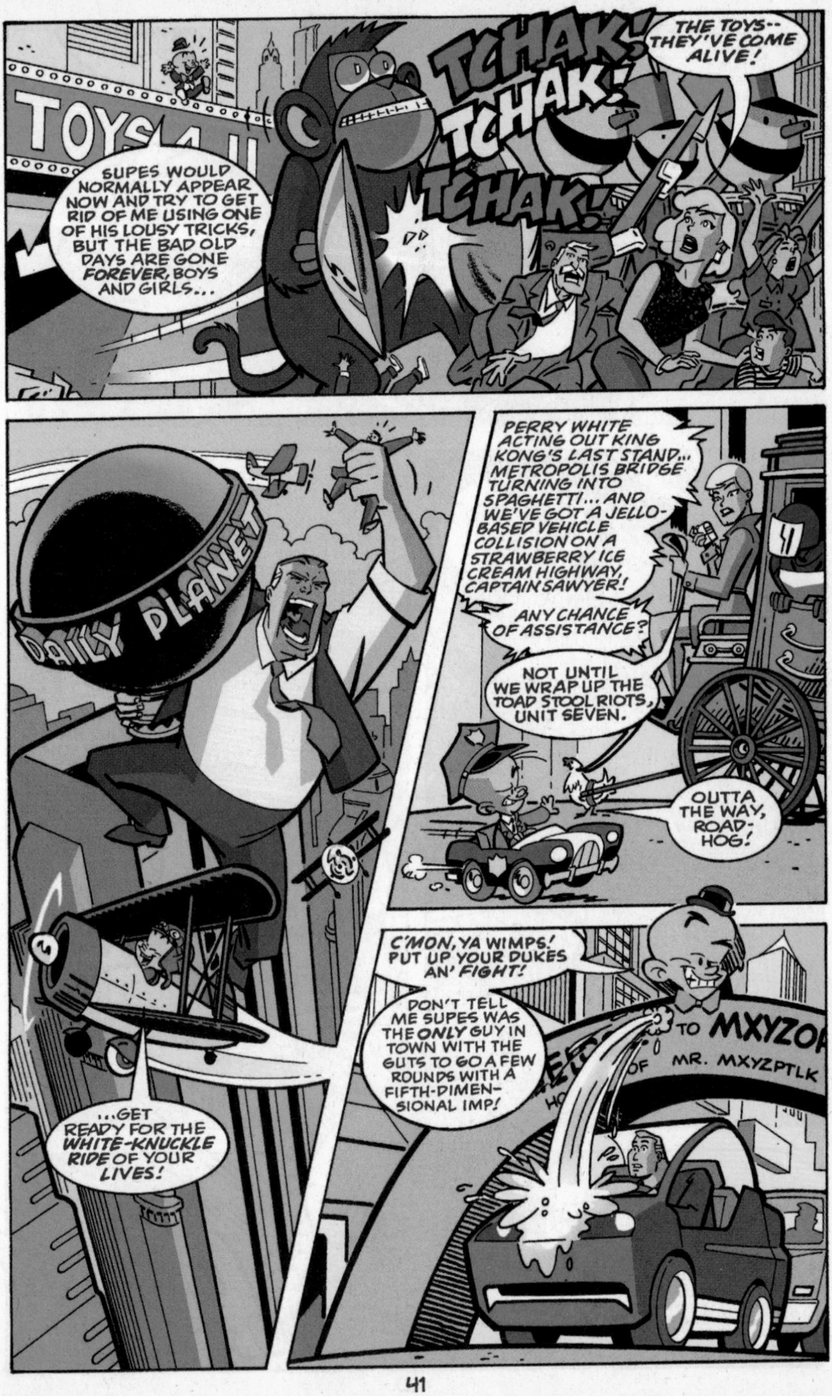
TOYS 4 U
TCHAK! TCHAK! TCHAK!
THE TOYS-- THEY'VE COME ALIVE!
SUPES WOULD NORMALLY APPEAR NOW AND TRY TO GET RID OF ME USING ONE OF HIS LOUSY TRICKS, BUT THE BAD OLD DAYS ARE GONE FOREVER, BOYS AND GIRLS...
DAILY PLANET
...GET READY FOR THE WHITE-KNUCKLE RIDE OF YOUR LIVES!
PERRY WHITE ACTING OUT KING KONG'S LAST STAND... METROPOLIS BRIDGE TURNING INTO SPAGHETTI... AND WE'VE GOT A JELLO-BASED VEHICLE COLLISION ON A STRAWBERRY ICE CREAM HIGHWAY, CAPTAIN SAWYER!
ANY CHANCE OF ASSISTANCE?
NOT UNTIL WE WRAP UP THE TOAD STOOL RIOTS, UNIT SEVEN.
OUTTA THE WAY, ROAD-HOG!
C'MON, YA WIMPS! PUT UP YOUR DUKES AN' FIGHT!
DON'T TELL ME SUPES WAS THE ONLY GUY IN TOWN WITH THE GUTS TO GO A FEW ROUNDS WITH A FIFTH-DIMENSIONAL IMP!
TO MXYZOP
OF MR. MXYZPTLK

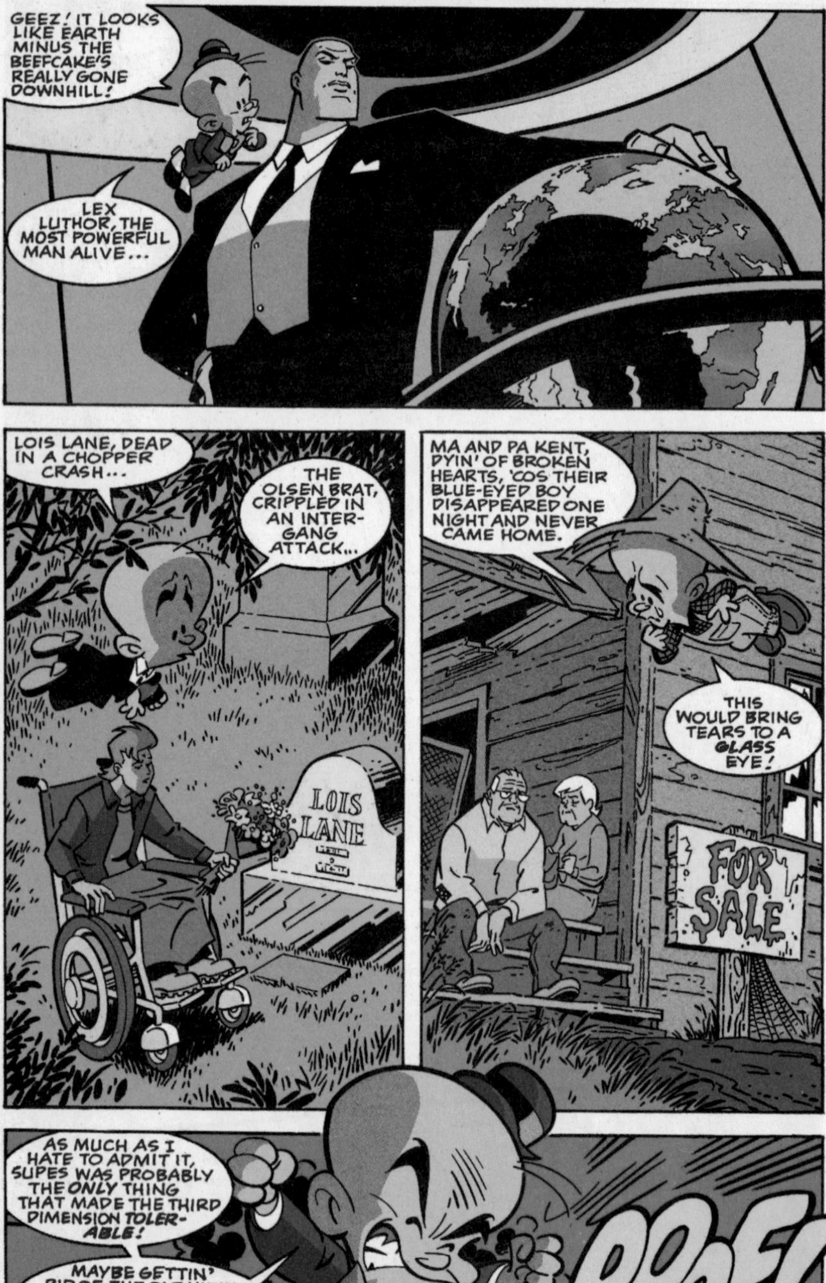
GEEZ! IT LOOKS LIKE EARTH MINUS THE BEEFCAKE'S REALLY GONE DOWNHILL!
LEX LUTHOR, THE MOST POWERFUL MAN ALIVE...
LOIS LANE, DEAD IN A CHOPPER CRASH...
THE OLSEN BRAT, CRIPPLED IN AN INTER-GANG ATTACK...
LOIS LANE
MA AND PA KENT, DYIN' OF BROKEN HEARTS, 'COS THEIR BLUE-EYED BOY DISAPPEARED ONE NIGHT AND NEVER CAME HOME.
THIS WOULD BRING TEARS TO A GLASS EYE!
FOR SALE
AS MUCH AS I HATE TO ADMIT IT, SUPES WAS PROBABLY THE ONLY THING THAT MADE THE THIRD DIMENSION TOLER-ABLE!
MAYBE GETTIN' RID OF THE OLD HUNK IN TRUNKS WASN'T SUCH A SMART IDEA, AFTER ALL.
POOF!

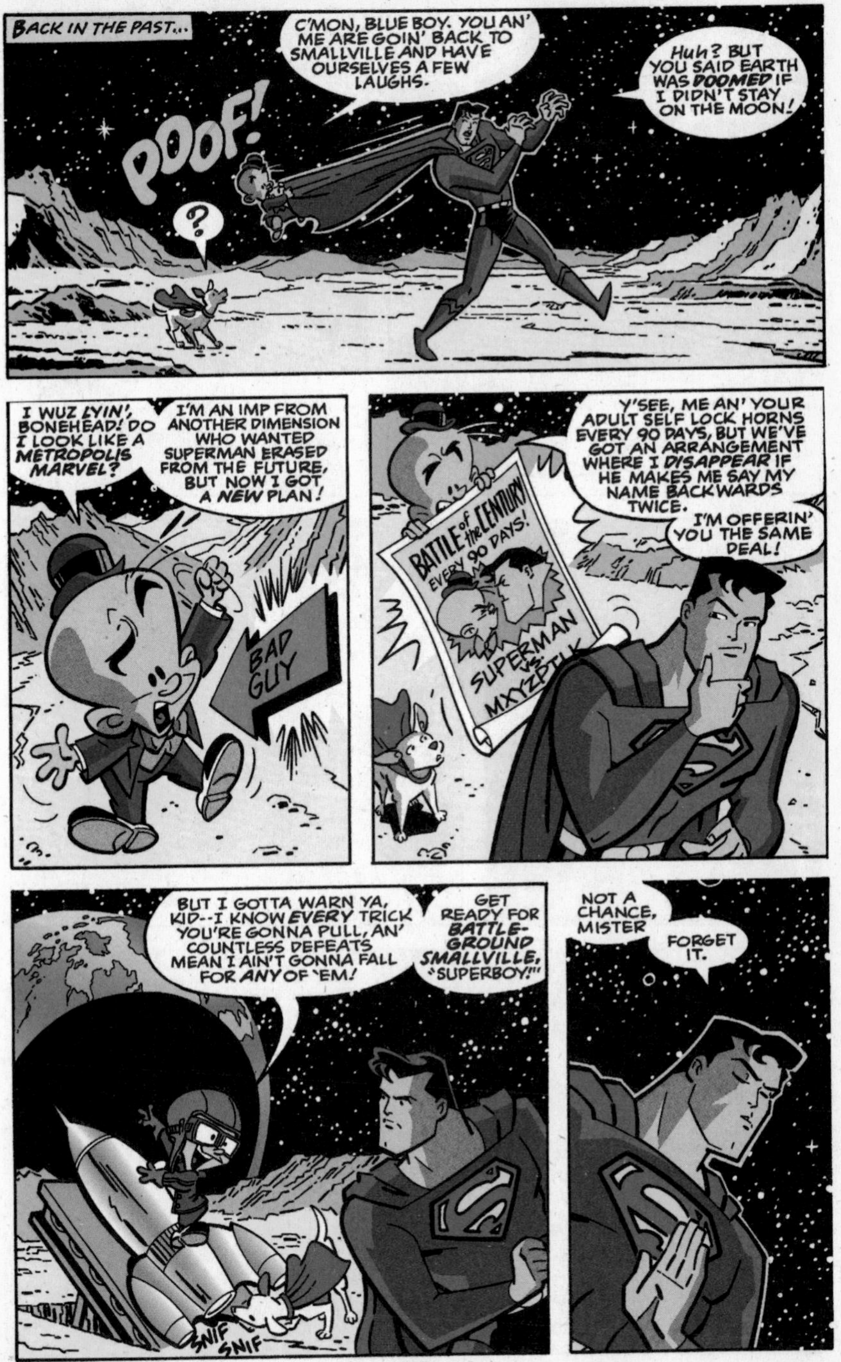
BACK IN THE PAST...
C'MON, BLUE BOY. YOU AN' ME ARE GOIN' BACK TO SMALLVILLE AND HAVE OURSELVES A FEW LAUGHS.
POOF!
Huh? BUT YOU SAID EARTH WAS DOOMED IF I DIDN'T STAY ON THE MOON!
?
I WUZ LYIN', BONEHEAD! DO I LOOK LIKE A METROPOLIS MARVEL?
I'M AN IMP FROM ANOTHER DIMENSION WHO WANTED SUPERMAN ERASED FROM THE FUTURE, BUT NOW I GOT A NEW PLAN!
BAD GUY
Y'SEE, ME AN' YOUR ADULT SELF LOCK HORNS EVERY 90 DAYS, BUT WE'VE GOT AN ARRANGEMENT WHERE I DISAPPEAR IF HE MAKES ME SAY MY NAME BACKWARDS TWICE.
I'M OFFERIN' YOU THE SAME DEAL!
BATTLE of the CENTURY EVERY 90 DAYS!
SUPERMAN VS. MXYZPTLK
BUT I GOTTA WARN YA, KID--I KNOW EVERY TRICK YOU'RE GONNA PULL, AN' COUNTLESS DEFEATS MEAN I AIN'T GONNA FALL FOR ANY OF 'EM!
GET READY FOR BATTLE-GROUND SMALLVILLE, "SUPERBOY!"
SNIF SNIF
NOT A CHANCE, MISTER
FORGET IT.

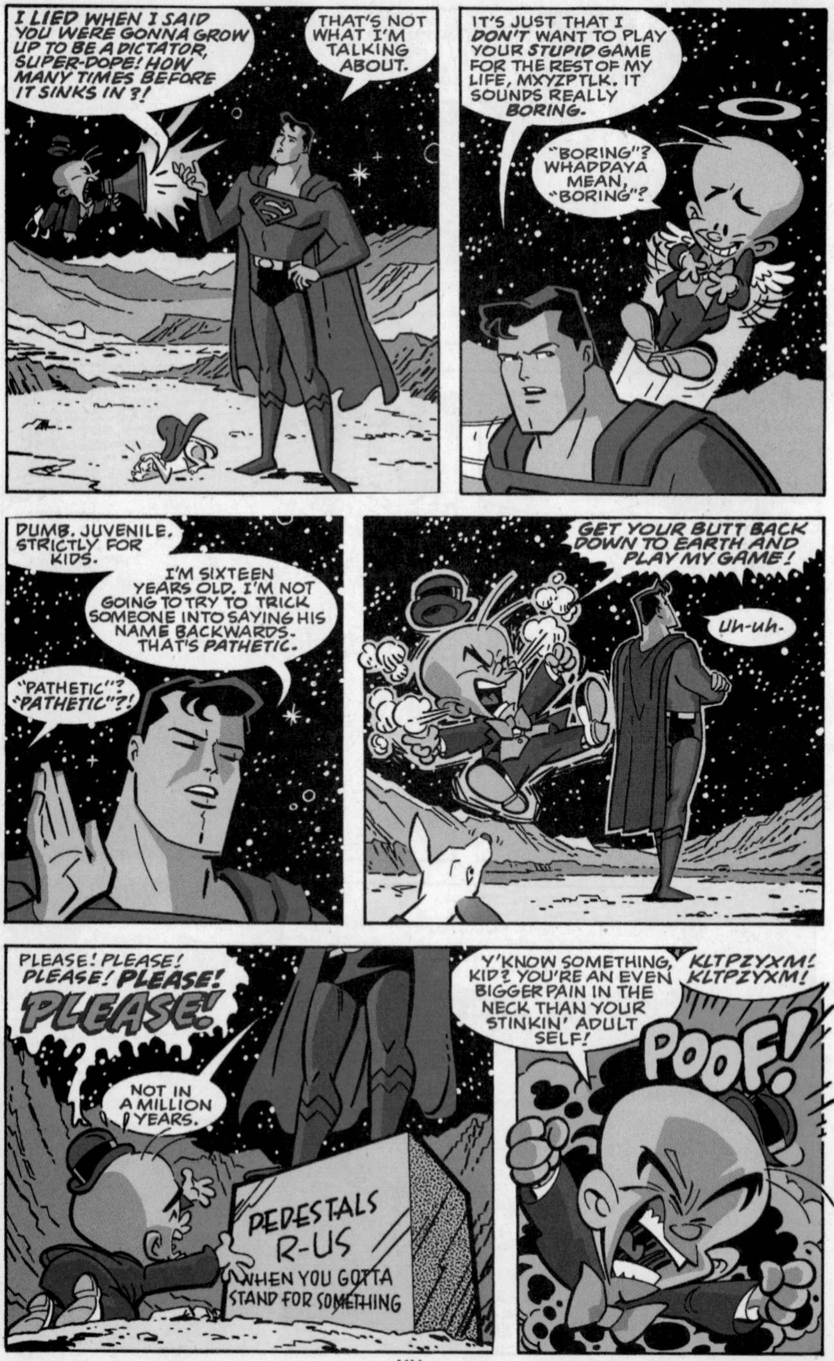

I LIED WHEN I SAID YOU WERE GONNA GROW UP TO BE A DICTATOR, SUPER-DOPE! HOW MANY TIMES BEFORE IT SINKS IN ?!
THAT'S NOT WHAT I'M TALKING ABOUT.
IT'S JUST THAT I DON'T WANT TO PLAY YOUR STUPID GAME FOR THE REST OF MY LIFE, MXYZPTLK. IT SOUNDS REALLY BORING.
"BORING"? WHADDAYA MEAN, "BORING"?
DUMB. JUVENILE. STRICTLY FOR KIDS.
I'M SIXTEEN YEARS OLD. I'M NOT GOING TO TRY TO TRICK SOMEONE INTO SAYING HIS NAME BACKWARDS. THAT'S PATHETIC.
"PATHETIC"? "PATHETIC"?!
GET YOUR BUTT BACK DOWN TO EARTH AND PLAY MY GAME!
Uh-uh.
PLEASE! PLEASE! PLEASE! PLEASE!
PLEASE!
NOT IN A MILLION YEARS.
PEDESTALS R-US
WHEN YOU GOTTA STAND FOR SOMETHING
Y'KNOW SOMETHING, KID? YOU'RE AN EVEN BIGGER PAIN IN THE NECK THAN YOUR STINKIN' ADULT SELF!
KLTPZYXM! KLTPZYXM!
POOF!

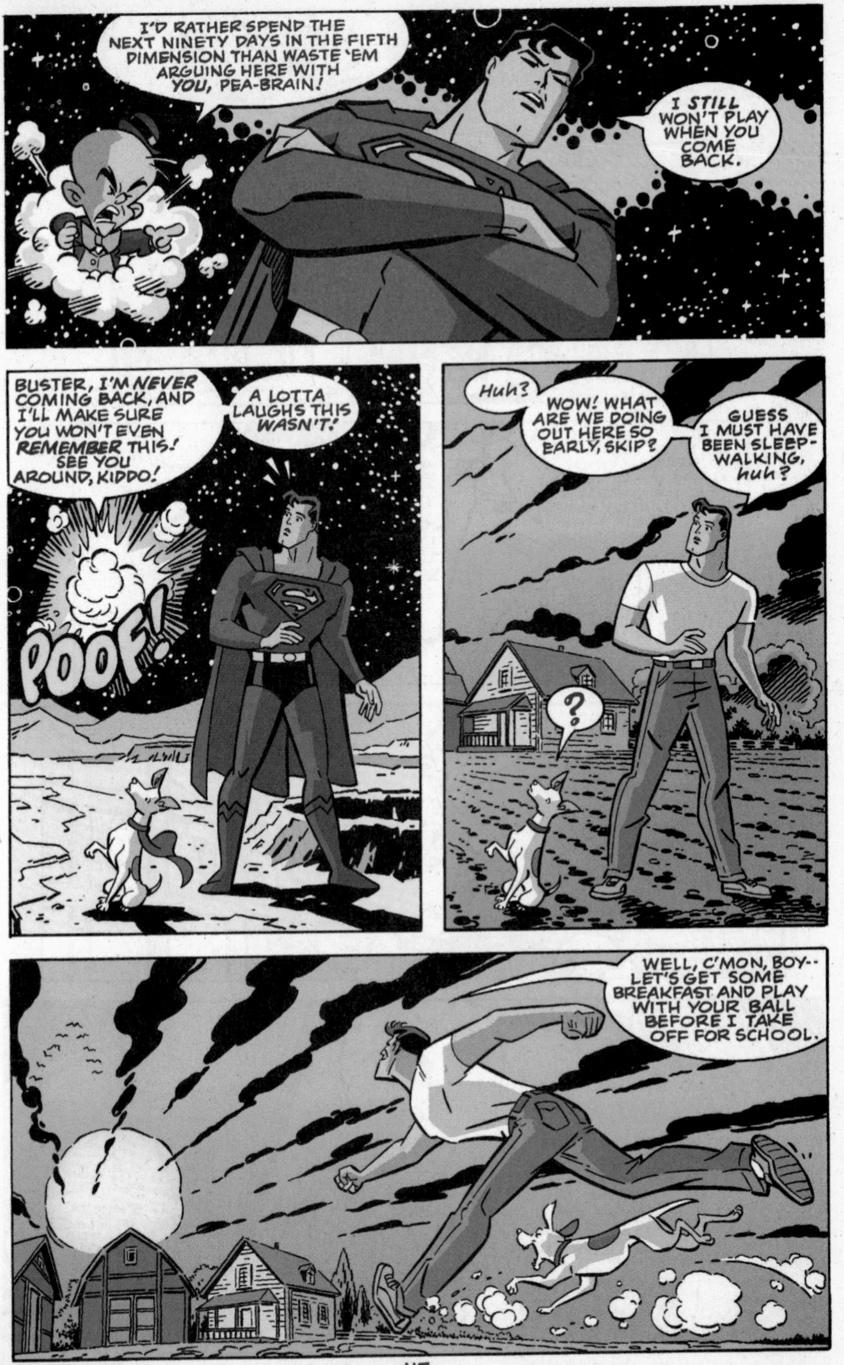
I'D RATHER SPEND THE NEXT NINETY DAYS IN THE FIFTH DIMENSION THAN WASTE 'EM ARGUING HERE WITH YOU, PEA-BRAIN!
I STILL WON'T PLAY WHEN YOU COME BACK.
BUSTER, I'M NEVER COMING BACK, AND I'LL MAKE SURE YOU WON'T EVEN REMEMBER THIS! SEE YOU AROUND, KIDDO!
A LOTTA LAUGHS THIS WASN'T!
POOF!
Huh?
WOW! WHAT ARE WE DOING OUT HERE SO EARLY, SKIP?
GUESS I MUST HAVE BEEN SLEEP-WALKING, huh?
?
WELL, C'MON, BOY-- LET'S GET SOME BREAKFAST AND PLAY WITH YOUR BALL BEFORE I TAKE OFF FOR SCHOOL.

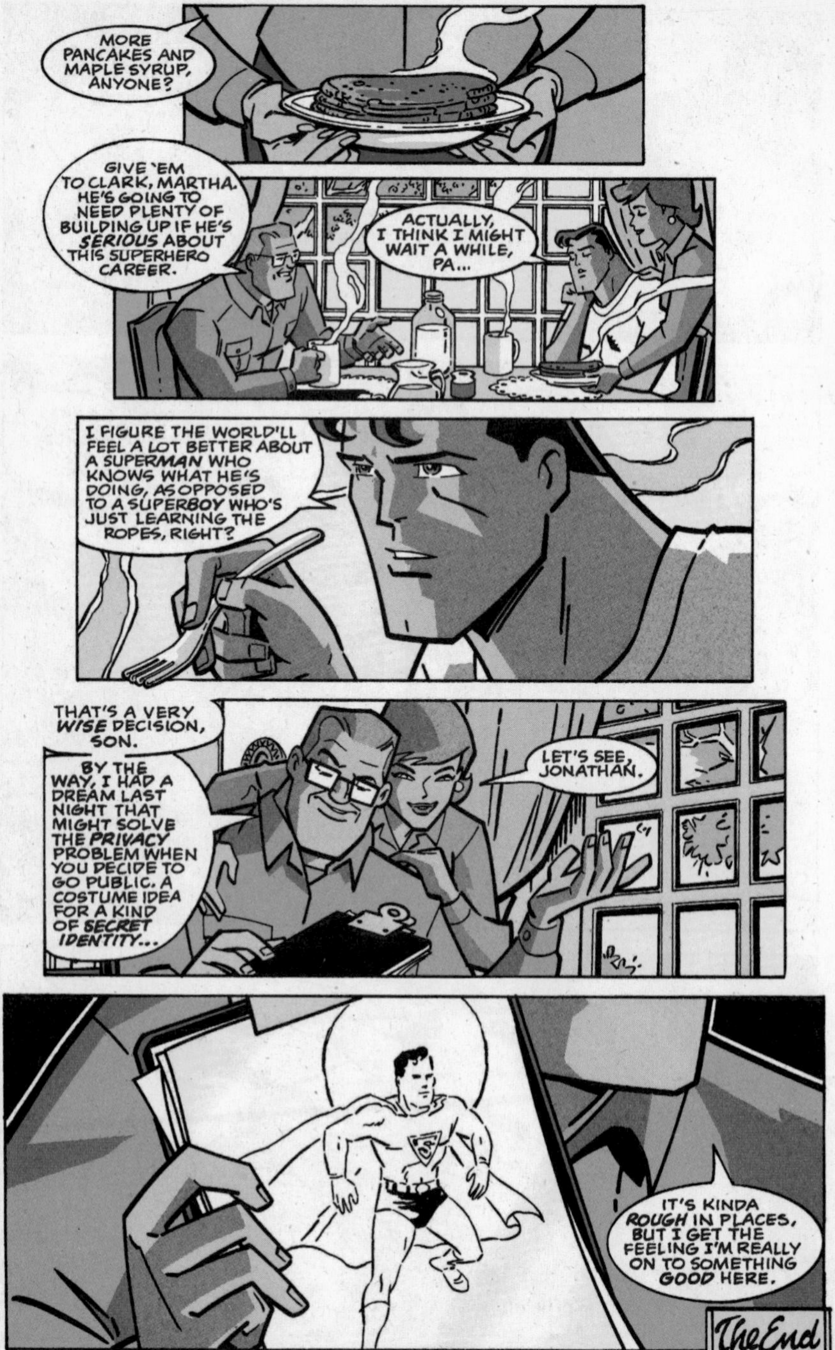
MORE PANCAKES AND MAPLE SYRUP, ANYONE?
GIVE 'EM TO CLARK, MARTHA. HE'S GOING TO NEED PLENTY OF BUILDING UP IF HE'S SERIOUS ABOUT THIS SUPERHERO CAREER.
ACTUALLY, I THINK I MIGHT WAIT A WHILE, PA...
I FIGURE THE WORLD'LL FEEL A LOT BETTER ABOUT A SUPERMAN WHO KNOWS WHAT HE'S DOING, AS OPPOSED TO A SUPERBOY WHO'S JUST LEARNING THE ROPES, RIGHT?
THAT'S A VERY WISE DECISION, SON.
BY THE WAY, I HAD A DREAM LAST NIGHT THAT MIGHT SOLVE THE PRIVACY PROBLEM WHEN YOU DECIDE TO GO PUBLIC. A COSTUME IDEA FOR A KIND OF SECRET IDENTITY...
LET'S SEE, JONATHAN.
IT'S KINDA ROUGH IN PLACES, BUT I GET THE FEELING I'M REALLY ON TO SOMETHING GOOD HERE.
The End

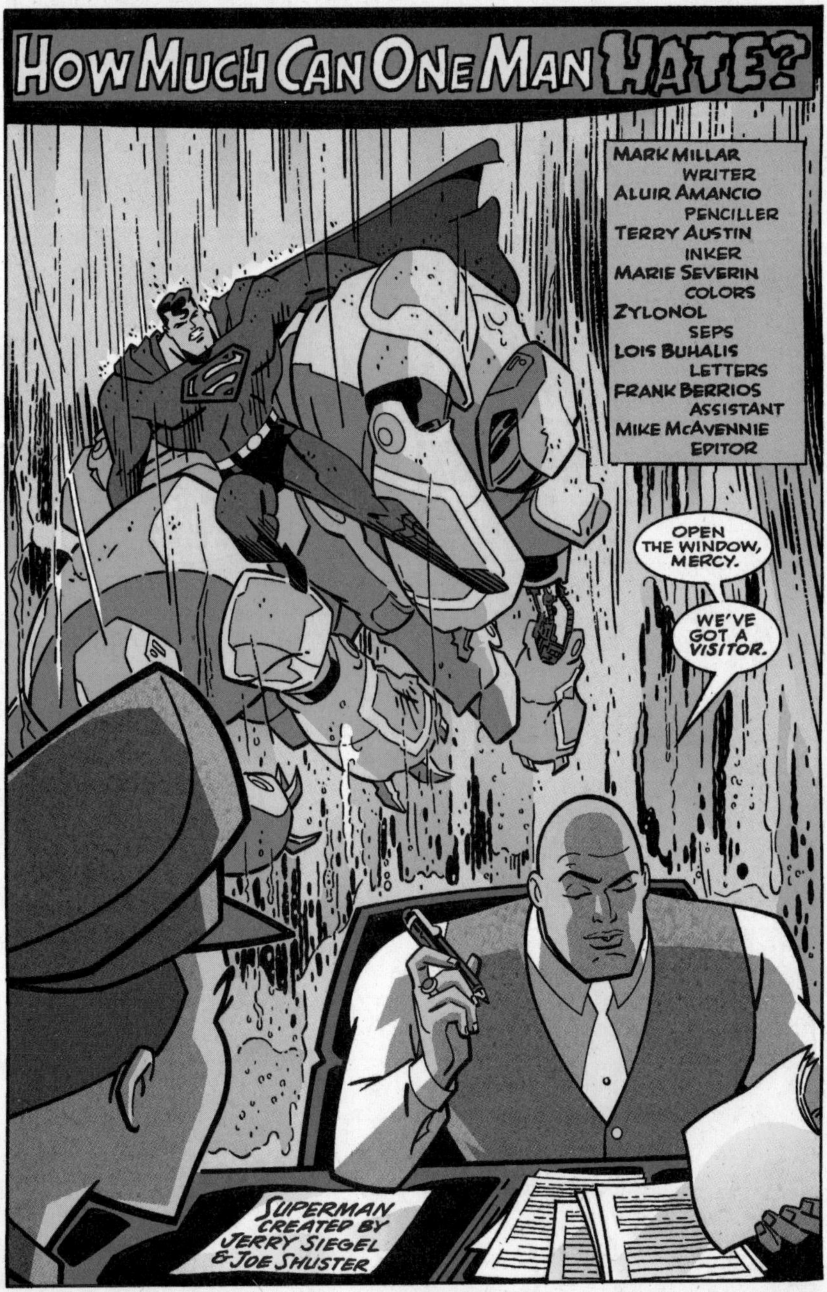
HOW MUCH CAN ONE MAN HATE?
MARK MILLAR WRITER
ALUIR AMANCIO PENCILLER
TERRY AUSTIN INKER
MARIE SEVERIN COLORS
ZYLONOL SEPS
LOIS BUHALIS LETTERS
FRANK BERRIOS ASSISTANT
MIKE McAVENNIE EDITOR
OPEN THE WINDOW, MERCY.
WE'VE GOT A VISITOR.
SUPERMAN CREATED BY JERRY SIEGEL & JOE SHUSTER

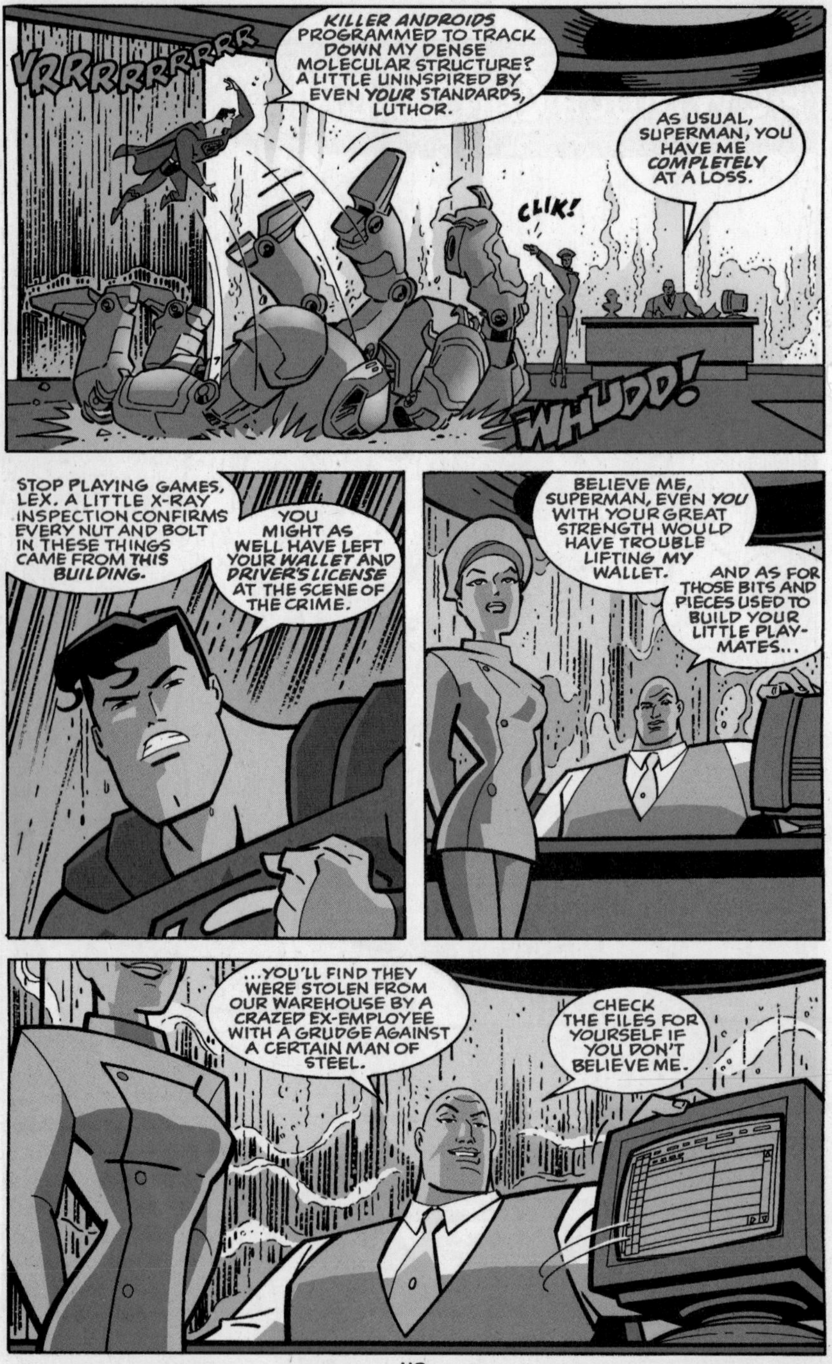
VRRRRRRRRRR
KILLER ANDROIDS PROGRAMMED TO TRACK DOWN MY DENSE MOLECULAR STRUCTURE? A LITTLE UNINSPIRED BY EVEN YOUR STANDARDS, LUTHOR.
AS USUAL, SUPERMAN, YOU HAVE ME COMPLETELY AT A LOSS.
CLIK!
WHUDD!
STOP PLAYING GAMES, LEX. A LITTLE X-RAY INSPECTION CONFIRMS EVERY NUT AND BOLT IN THESE THINGS CAME FROM THIS BUILDING.
YOU MIGHT AS WELL HAVE LEFT YOUR WALLET AND DRIVER'S LICENSE AT THE SCENE OF THE CRIME.
BELIEVE ME, SUPERMAN, EVEN YOU WITH YOUR GREAT STRENGTH WOULD HAVE TROUBLE LIFTING MY WALLET.
AND AS FOR THOSE BITS AND PIECES USED TO BUILD YOUR LITTLE PLAY-MATES...
...YOU'LL FIND THEY WERE STOLEN FROM OUR WAREHOUSE BY A CRAZED EX-EMPLOYEE WITH A GRUDGE AGAINST A CERTAIN MAN OF STEEL.
CHECK THE FILES FOR YOURSELF IF YOU DON'T BELIEVE ME.

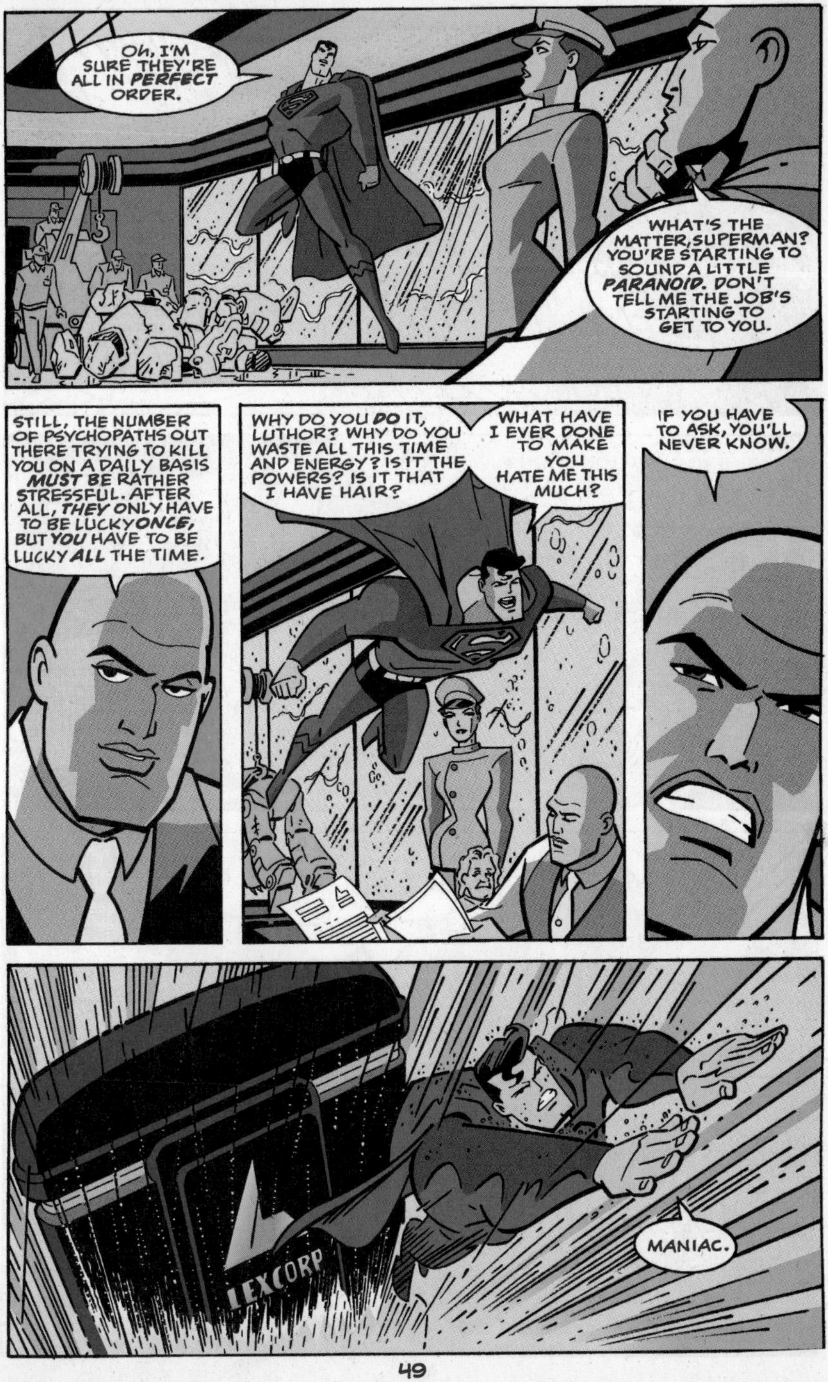
OH, I'M SURE THEY'RE ALL IN *PERFECT* ORDER.
WHAT'S THE MATTER, SUPERMAN? YOU'RE STARTING TO SOUND A LITTLE *PARANOID.* DON'T TELL ME THE JOB'S STARTING TO GET TO YOU.
STILL, THE NUMBER OF PSYCHOPATHS OUT THERE TRYING TO KILL YOU ON A DAILY BASIS *MUST* BE RATHER STRESSFUL. AFTER ALL, *THEY* ONLY HAVE TO BE LUCKY *ONCE,* BUT *YOU* HAVE TO BE LUCKY *ALL* THE TIME.
WHY DO YOU *DO* IT, LUTHOR? WHY DO YOU WASTE ALL THIS TIME AND ENERGY? IS IT THE POWERS? IS IT THAT I HAVE HAIR?
WHAT HAVE I EVER DONE TO MAKE YOU HATE ME THIS MUCH?
IF YOU HAVE TO ASK, YOU'LL NEVER KNOW.
LEXCORP
MANIAC.

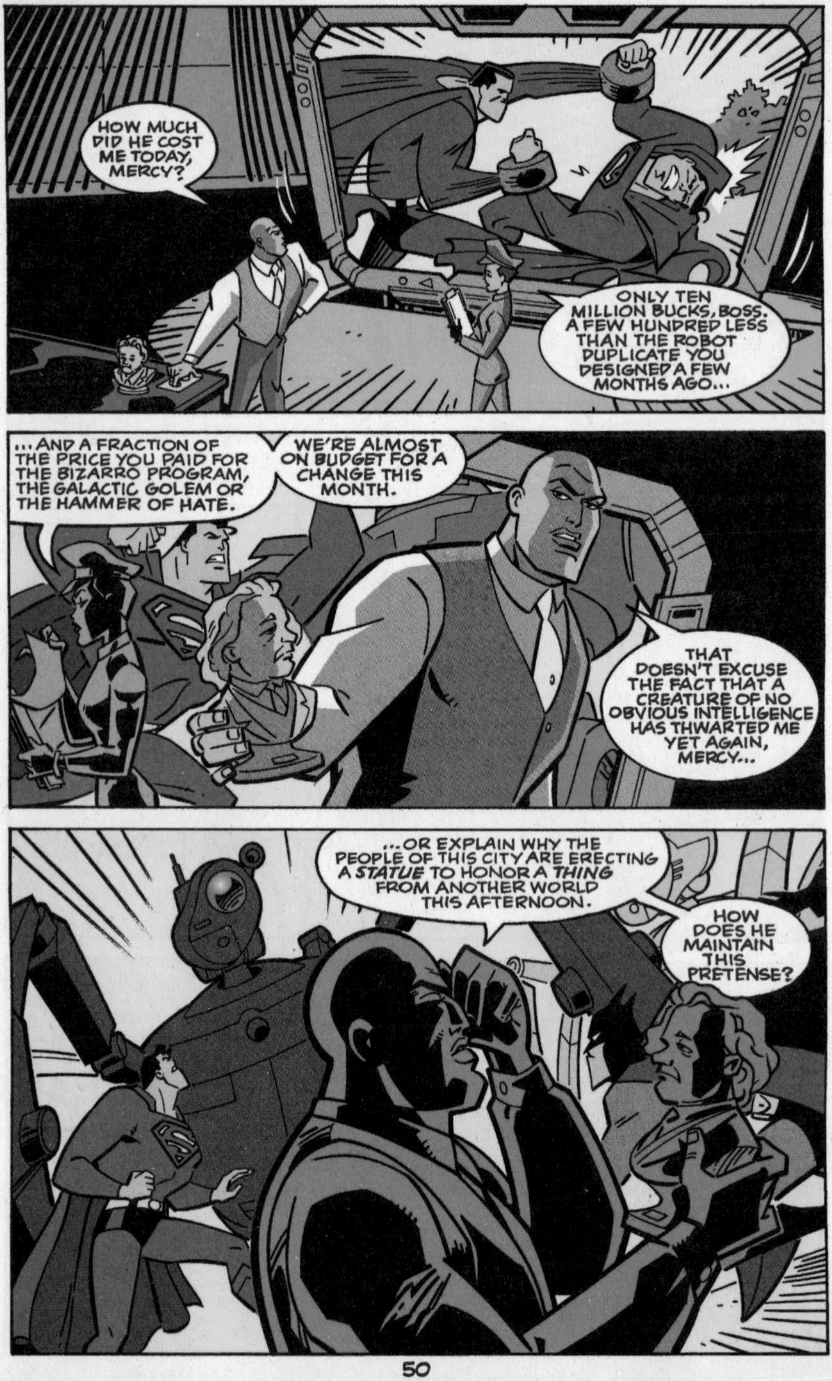
HOW MUCH DID HE COST ME TODAY, MERCY?
ONLY TEN MILLION BUCKS, BOSS. A FEW HUNDRED LESS THAN THE ROBOT DUPLICATE YOU DESIGNED A FEW MONTHS AGO...
...AND A FRACTION OF THE PRICE YOU PAID FOR THE BIZARRO PROGRAM, THE GALACTIC GOLEM OR THE HAMMER OF HATE.
WE'RE ALMOST ON BUDGET FOR A CHANGE THIS MONTH.
THAT DOESN'T EXCUSE THE FACT THAT A CREATURE OF NO OBVIOUS INTELLIGENCE HAS THWARTED ME YET AGAIN, MERCY...
...OR EXPLAIN WHY THE PEOPLE OF THIS CITY ARE ERECTING A STATUE TO HONOR A THING FROM ANOTHER WORLD THIS AFTERNOON.
HOW DOES HE MAINTAIN THIS PRETENSE?

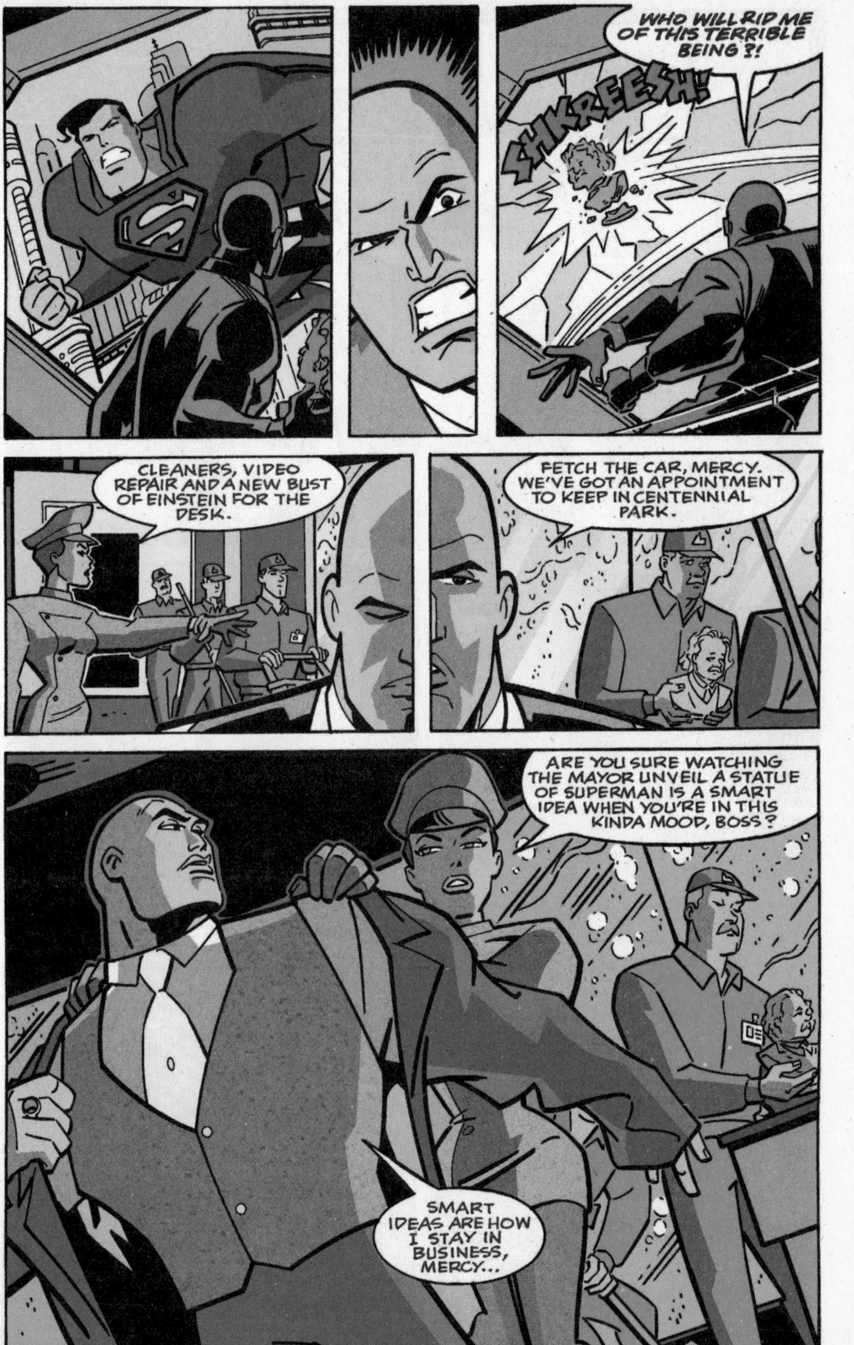
WHO WILL RID ME OF THIS TERRIBLE BEING ?!
SHKREESH!
CLEANERS, VIDEO REPAIR AND A NEW BUST OF EINSTEIN FOR THE DESK.
FETCH THE CAR, MERCY. WE'VE GOT AN APPOINTMENT TO KEEP IN CENTENNIAL PARK.
ARE YOU SURE WATCHING THE MAYOR UNVEIL A STATUE OF SUPERMAN IS A SMART IDEA WHEN YOU'RE IN THIS KINDA MOOD, BOSS?
SMART IDEAS ARE HOW I STAY IN BUSINESS, MERCY...

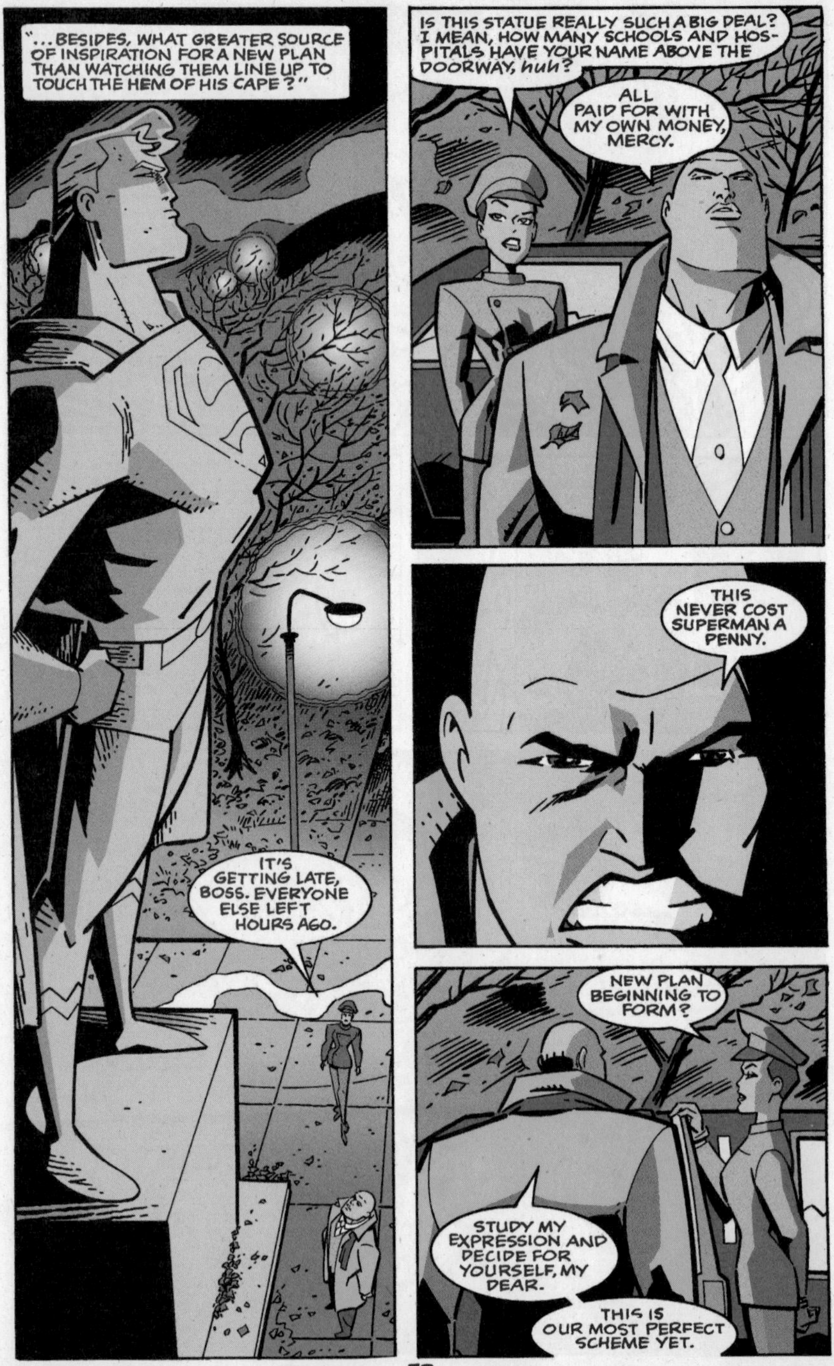
"... BESIDES, WHAT GREATER SOURCE OF INSPIRATION FOR A NEW PLAN THAN WATCHING THEM LINE UP TO TOUCH THE HEM OF HIS CAPE?"
IT'S GETTING LATE, BOSS. EVERYONE ELSE LEFT HOURS AGO.
IS THIS STATUE REALLY SUCH A BIG DEAL? I MEAN, HOW MANY SCHOOLS AND HOSPITALS HAVE YOUR NAME ABOVE THE DOORWAY, *huh*?
ALL PAID FOR WITH MY OWN MONEY, MERCY.
THIS NEVER COST SUPERMAN A PENNY.
NEW PLAN BEGINNING TO FORM?
STUDY MY EXPRESSION AND DECIDE FOR YOURSELF, MY DEAR.
THIS IS OUR MOST PERFECT SCHEME YET.

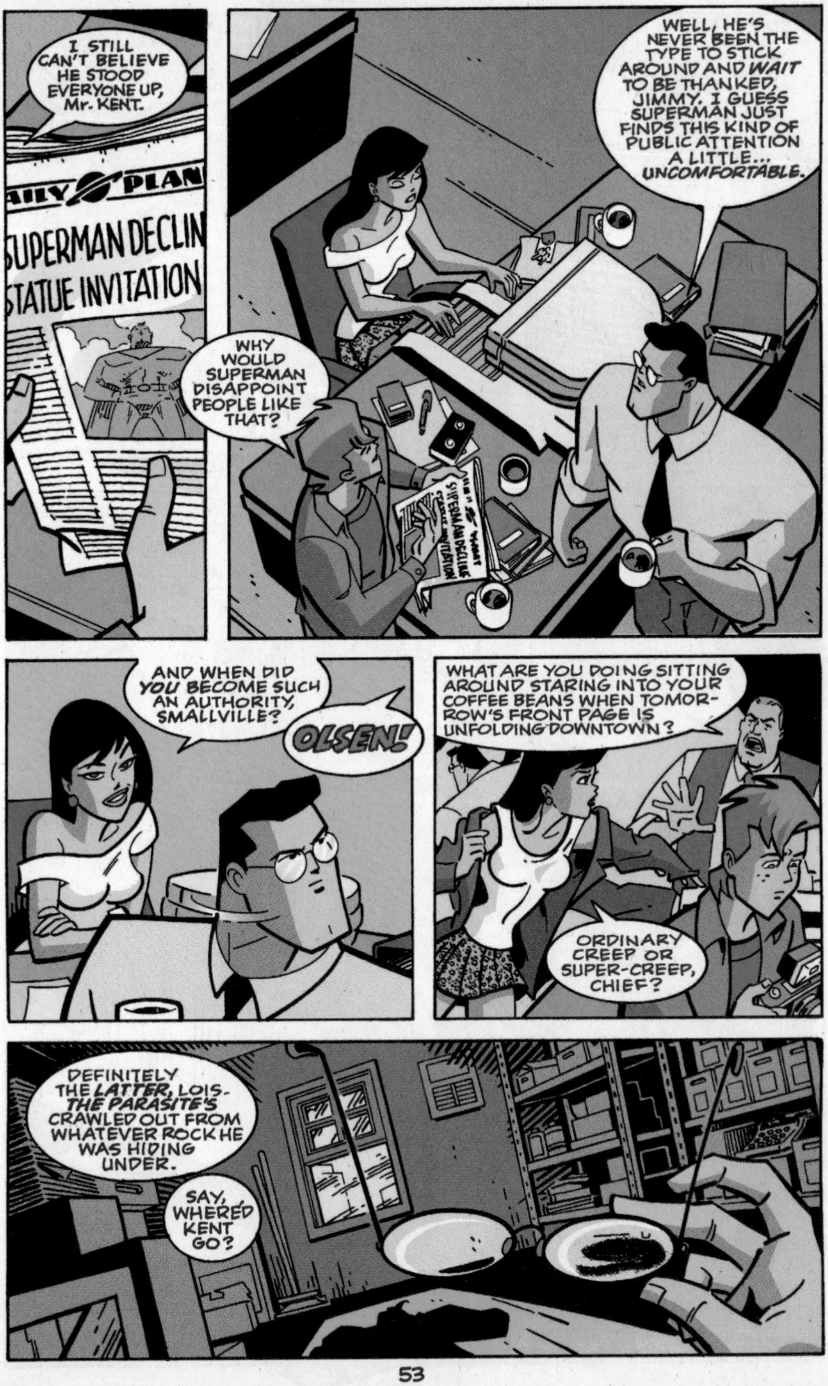
I STILL CAN'T BELIEVE HE STOOD EVERYONE UP, Mr. KENT.
AILY PLAN
SUPERMAN DECLIN
STATUE INVITATION
WELL, HE'S NEVER BEEN THE TYPE TO STICK AROUND AND *WAIT* TO BE THANKED, JIMMY. I GUESS SUPERMAN JUST FINDS THIS KIND OF PUBLIC ATTENTION A LITTLE... *UNCOMFORTABLE.*
WHY WOULD SUPERMAN DISAPPOINT PEOPLE LIKE THAT?
SUPERMAN DECLINE STATUE INVITATION
AND WHEN DID *YOU* BECOME SUCH AN AUTHORITY, SMALLVILLE?
OLSEN!
WHAT ARE YOU DOING SITTING AROUND STARING INTO YOUR COFFEE BEANS WHEN TOMORROW'S FRONT PAGE IS UNFOLDING DOWNTOWN?
ORDINARY CREEP OR SUPER-CREEP, CHIEF?
DEFINITELY THE *LATTER,* LOIS. *THE PARASITE'S* CRAWLED OUT FROM WHATEVER ROCK HE WAS HIDING UNDER.
SAY, WHERE'D KENT GO?

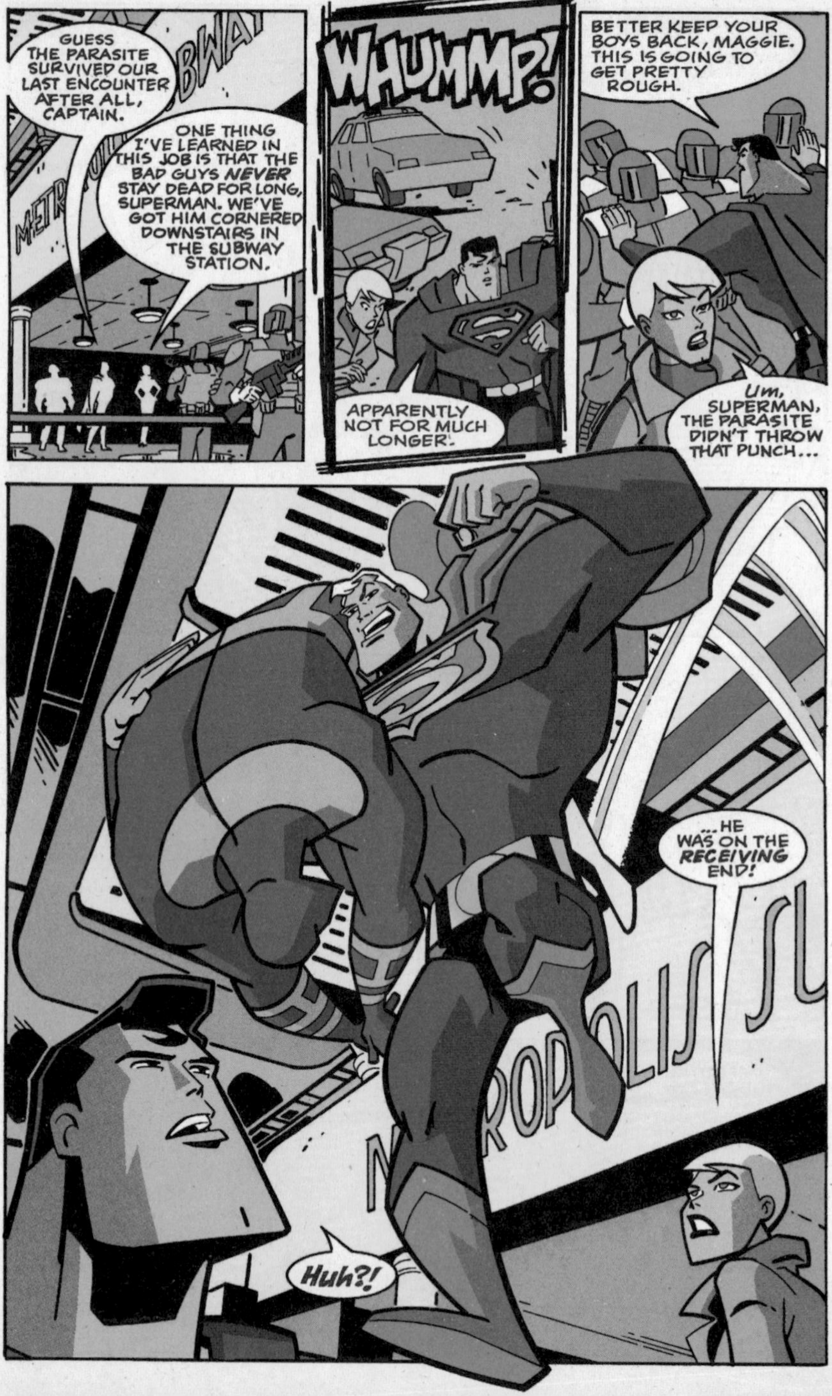
GUESS THE PARASITE SURVIVED OUR LAST ENCOUNTER AFTER ALL, CAPTAIN.
ONE THING I'VE LEARNED IN THIS JOB IS THAT THE BAD GUYS NEVER STAY DEAD FOR LONG, SUPERMAN. WE'VE GOT HIM CORNERED DOWNSTAIRS IN THE SUBWAY STATION.
WHUMMP!
APPARENTLY NOT FOR MUCH LONGER.
BETTER KEEP YOUR BOYS BACK, MAGGIE. THIS IS GOING TO GET PRETTY ROUGH.
Um, SUPERMAN, THE PARASITE DIDN'T THROW THAT PUNCH...
...HE WAS ON THE RECEIVING END!
Huh?!

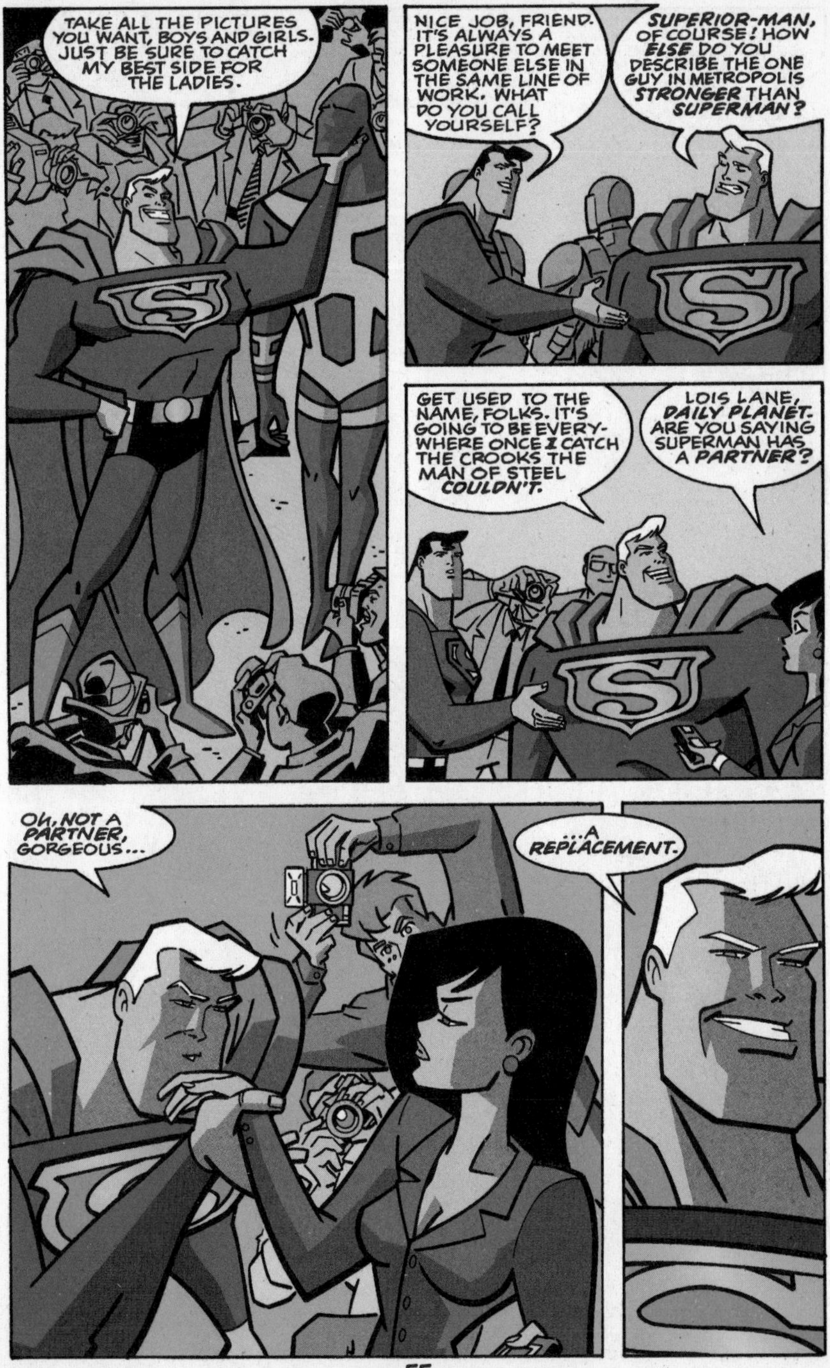
TAKE ALL THE PICTURES YOU WANT, BOYS AND GIRLS. JUST BE SURE TO CATCH MY BEST SIDE FOR THE LADIES.
NICE JOB, FRIEND. IT'S ALWAYS A PLEASURE TO MEET SOMEONE ELSE IN THE SAME LINE OF WORK. WHAT DO YOU CALL YOURSELF?
SUPERIOR-MAN, OF COURSE! HOW ELSE DO YOU DESCRIBE THE ONE GUY IN METROPOLIS STRONGER THAN SUPERMAN?
GET USED TO THE NAME, FOLKS. IT'S GOING TO BE EVERYWHERE ONCE I CATCH THE CROOKS THE MAN OF STEEL COULDN'T.
LOIS LANE, DAILY PLANET. ARE YOU SAYING SUPERMAN HAS A PARTNER?
OH, NOT A PARTNER, GORGEOUS...
...A REPLACEMENT.

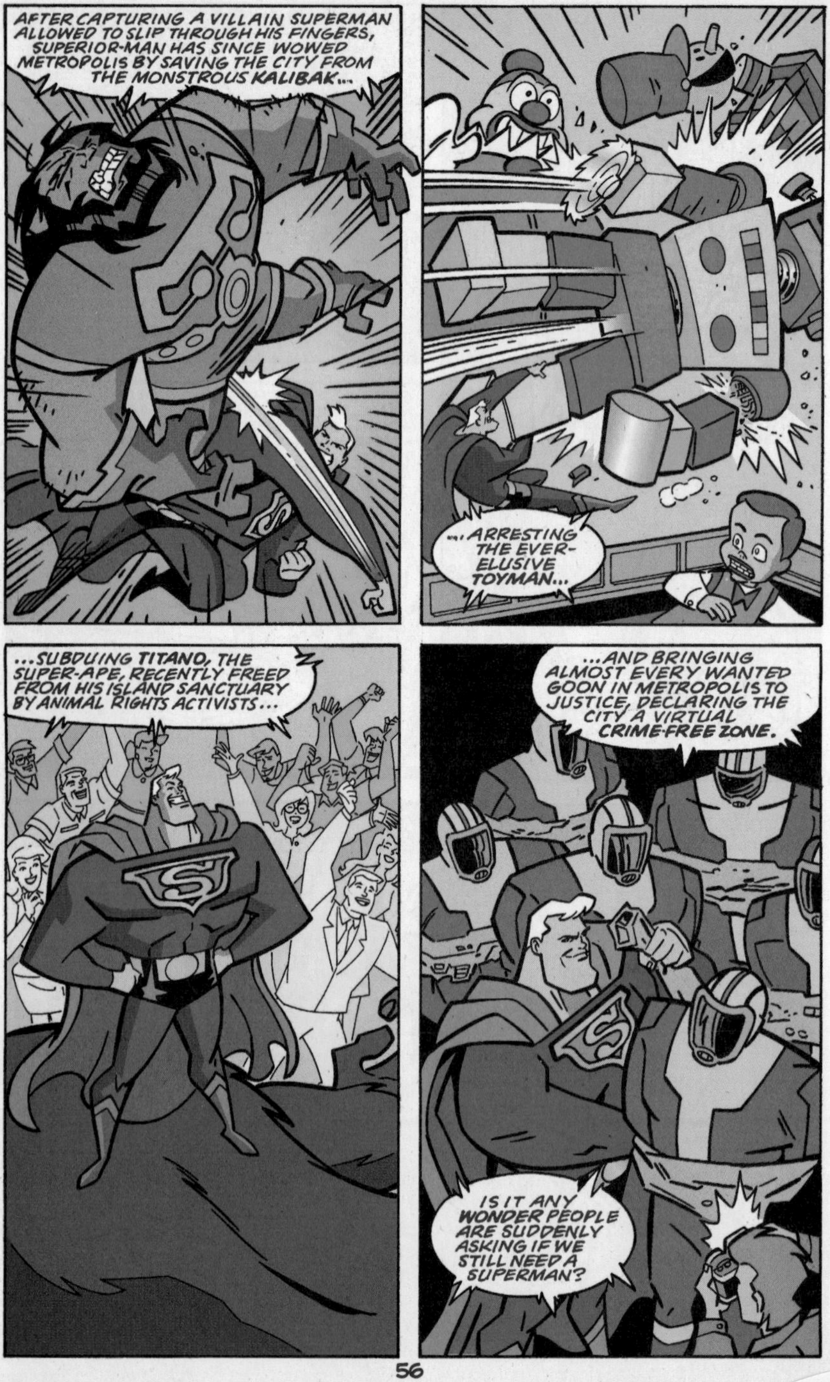
AFTER CAPTURING A VILLAIN SUPERMAN ALLOWED TO SLIP THROUGH HIS FINGERS, SUPERIOR-MAN HAS SINCE WOWED METROPOLIS BY SAVING THE CITY FROM THE MONSTROUS KALIBAK...
...ARRESTING THE EVER-ELUSIVE TOYMAN...
...SUBDUING TITANO, THE SUPER-APE, RECENTLY FREED FROM HIS ISLAND SANCTUARY BY ANIMAL RIGHTS ACTIVISTS...
...AND BRINGING ALMOST EVERY WANTED GOON IN METROPOLIS TO JUSTICE, DECLARING THE CITY A VIRTUAL CRIME-FREE ZONE.
IS IT ANY WONDER PEOPLE ARE SUDDENLY ASKING IF WE STILL NEED A SUPERMAN?

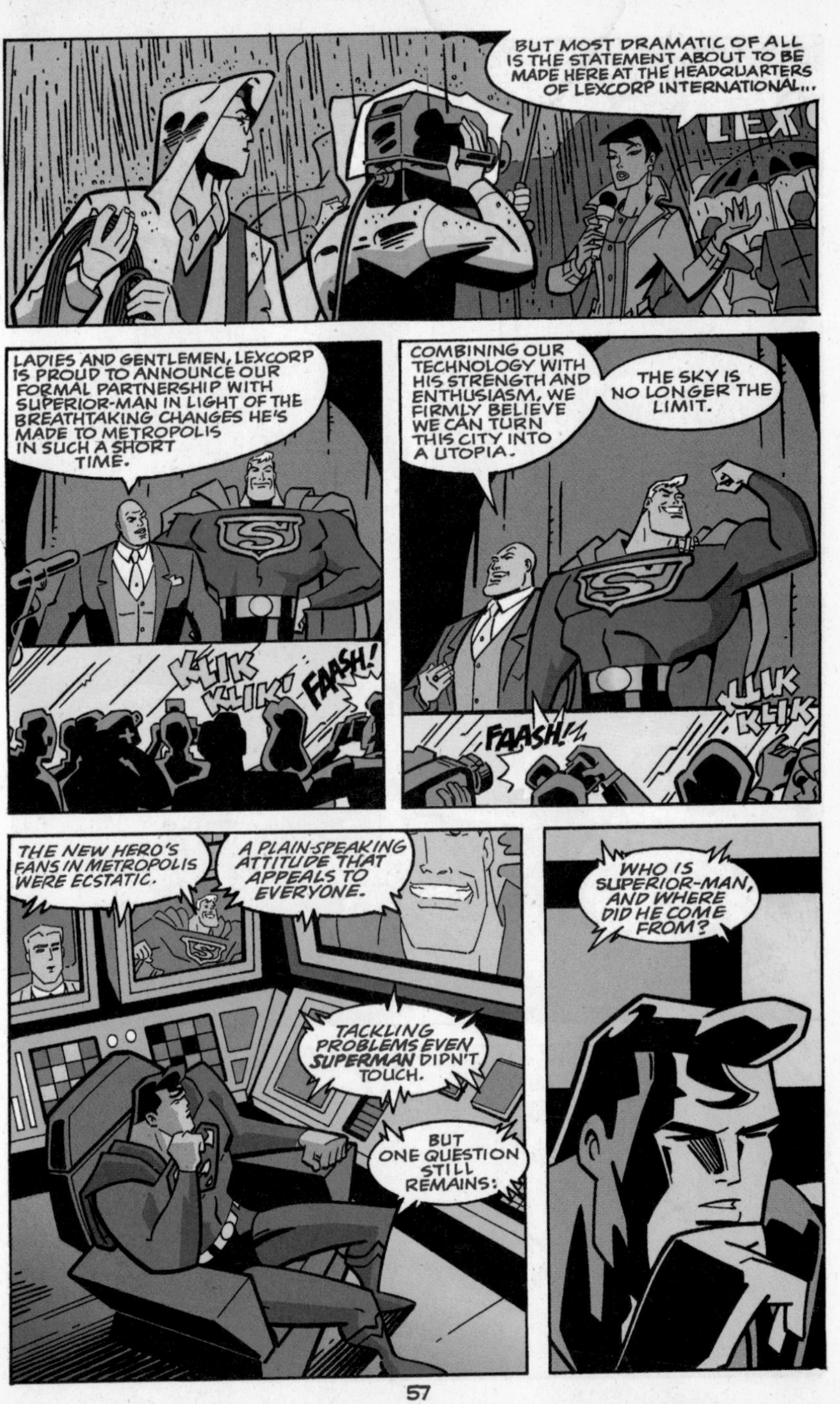

BUT MOST DRAMATIC OF ALL IS THE STATEMENT ABOUT TO BE MADE HERE AT THE HEADQUARTERS OF LEXCORP INTERNATIONAL...
LADIES AND GENTLEMEN, LEXCORP IS PROUD TO ANNOUNCE OUR FORMAL PARTNERSHIP WITH SUPERIOR-MAN IN LIGHT OF THE BREATHTAKING CHANGES HE'S MADE TO METROPOLIS IN SUCH A SHORT TIME.
KLIK KLIK!
FAASH!
COMBINING OUR TECHNOLOGY WITH HIS STRENGTH AND ENTHUSIASM, WE FIRMLY BELIEVE WE CAN TURN THIS CITY INTO A UTOPIA.
THE SKY IS NO LONGER THE LIMIT.
KLIK KLIK
FAASH!
THE NEW HERO'S FANS IN METROPOLIS WERE ECSTATIC.
A PLAIN-SPEAKING ATTITUDE THAT APPEALS TO EVERYONE.
TACKLING PROBLEMS EVEN SUPERMAN DIDN'T TOUCH.
BUT ONE QUESTION STILL REMAINS:
WHO IS SUPERIOR-MAN, AND WHERE DID HE COME FROM?

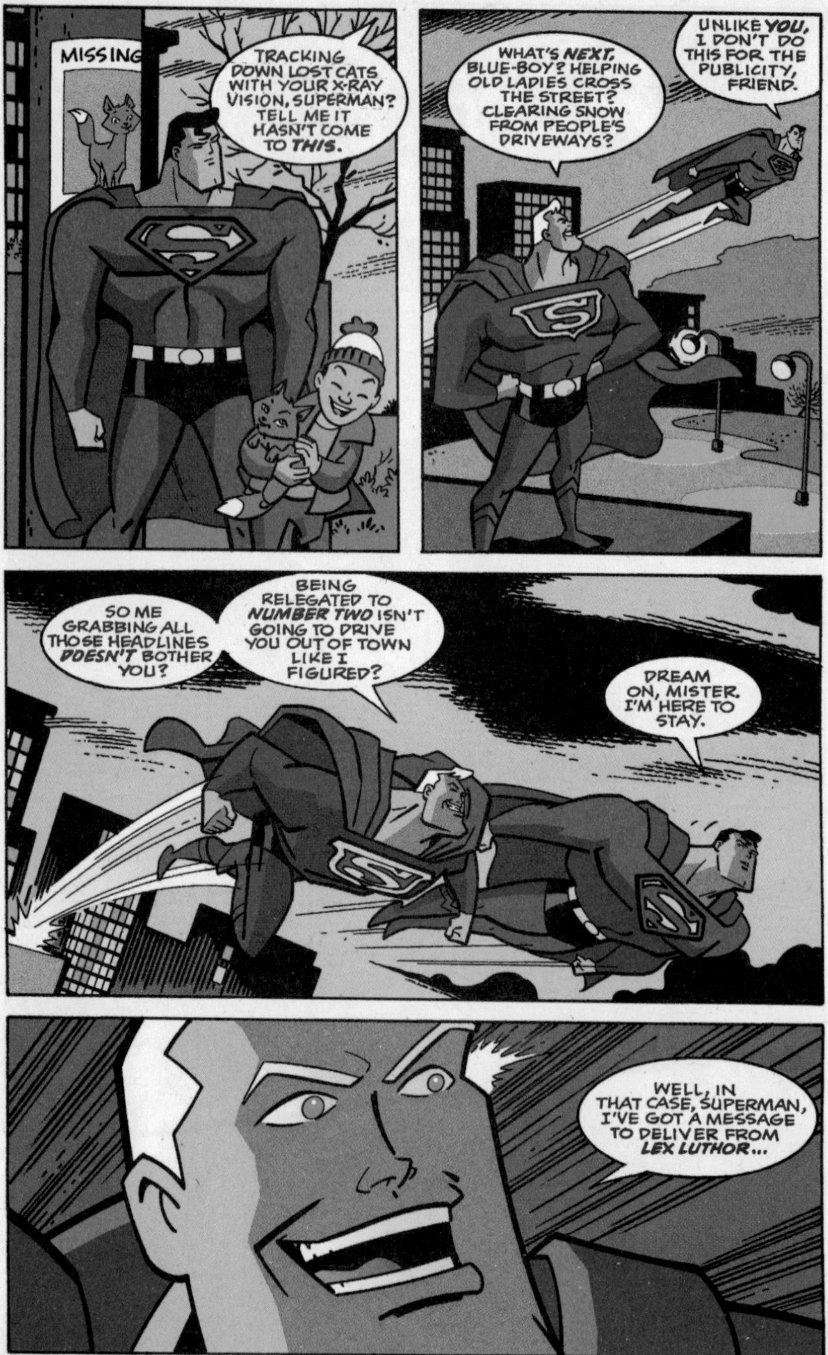
MISSING
TRACKING DOWN LOST CATS WITH YOUR X-RAY VISION, SUPERMAN? TELL ME IT HASN'T COME TO THIS.
WHAT'S NEXT, BLUE-BOY? HELPING OLD LADIES CROSS THE STREET? CLEARING SNOW FROM PEOPLE'S DRIVEWAYS?
UNLIKE YOU, I DON'T DO THIS FOR THE PUBLICITY, FRIEND.
SO ME GRABBING ALL THOSE HEADLINES DOESN'T BOTHER YOU?
BEING RELEGATED TO NUMBER TWO ISN'T GOING TO DRIVE YOU OUT OF TOWN LIKE I FIGURED?
DREAM ON, MISTER. I'M HERE TO STAY.
WELL, IN THAT CASE, SUPERMAN, I'VE GOT A MESSAGE TO DELIVER FROM LEX LUTHOR...

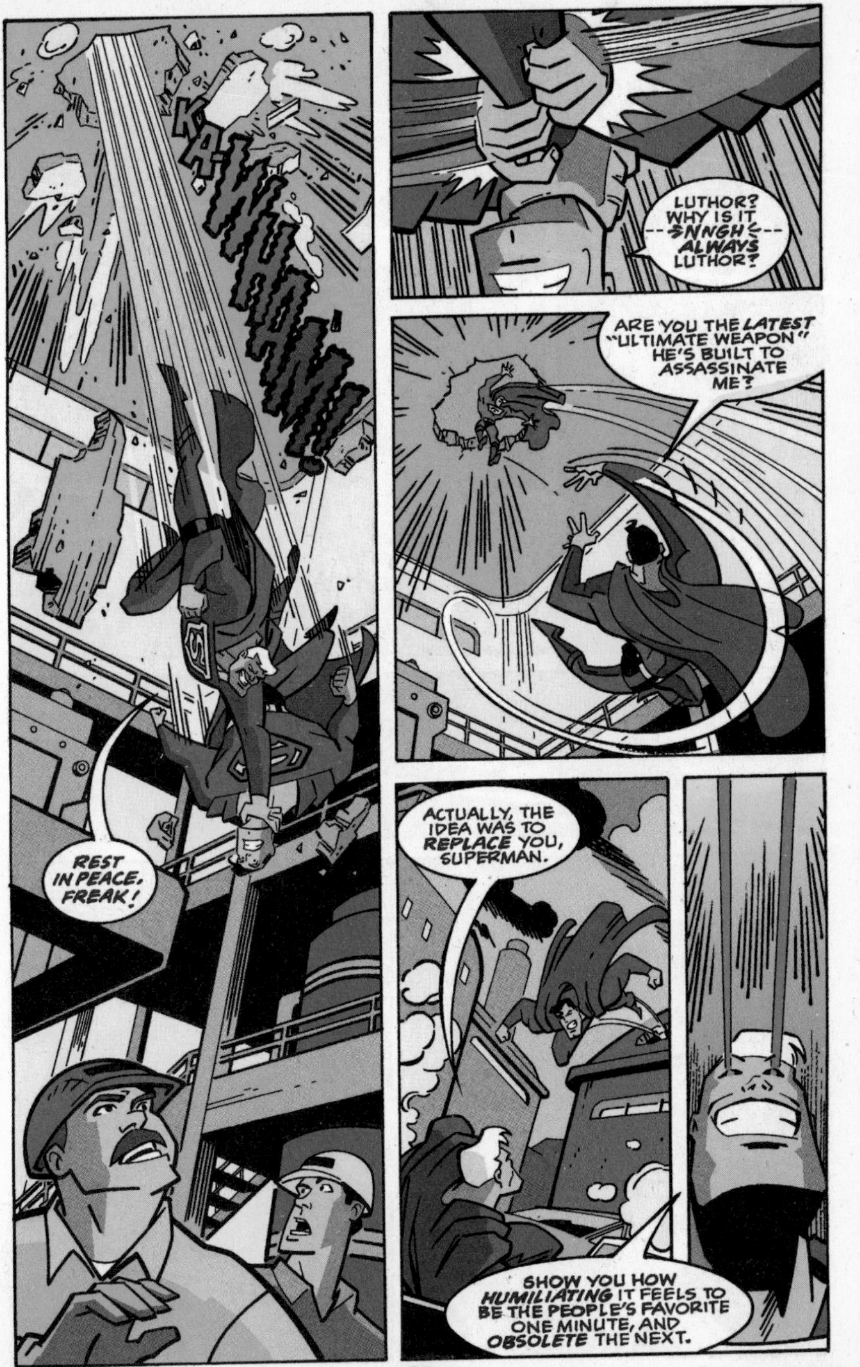
KA-WHAWHAM!
REST IN PEACE, FREAK!
LUTHOR? WHY IS IT --SNNGH-- ALWAYS LUTHOR?
ARE YOU THE LATEST "ULTIMATE WEAPON" HE'S BUILT TO ASSASSINATE ME?
ACTUALLY, THE IDEA WAS TO REPLACE YOU, SUPERMAN.
SHOW YOU HOW HUMILIATING IT FEELS TO BE THE PEOPLE'S FAVORITE ONE MINUTE, AND OBSOLETE THE NEXT.

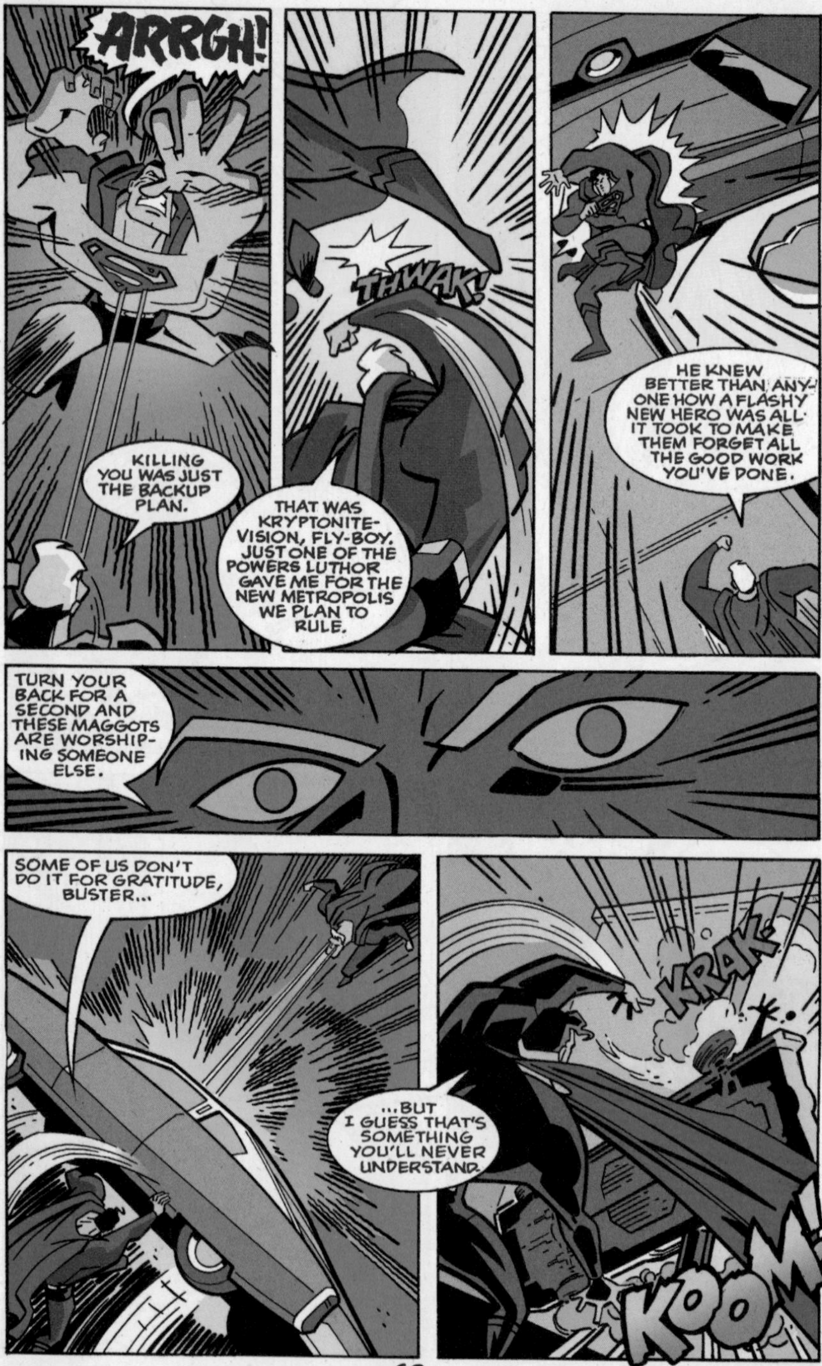
ARRGH!
KILLING YOU WAS JUST THE BACKUP PLAN.
THWAK!
THAT WAS KRYPTONITE-VISION, FLY-BOY. JUST ONE OF THE POWERS LUTHOR GAVE ME FOR THE NEW METROPOLIS WE PLAN TO RULE.
HE KNEW BETTER THAN ANY-ONE HOW A FLASHY NEW HERO WAS ALL IT TOOK TO MAKE THEM FORGET ALL THE GOOD WORK YOU'VE DONE.
TURN YOUR BACK FOR A SECOND AND THESE MAGGOTS ARE WORSHIP-ING SOMEONE ELSE.
SOME OF US DON'T DO IT FOR GRATITUDE, BUSTER...
...BUT I GUESS THAT'S SOMETHING YOU'LL NEVER UNDERSTAND.
KRAK
KOOM

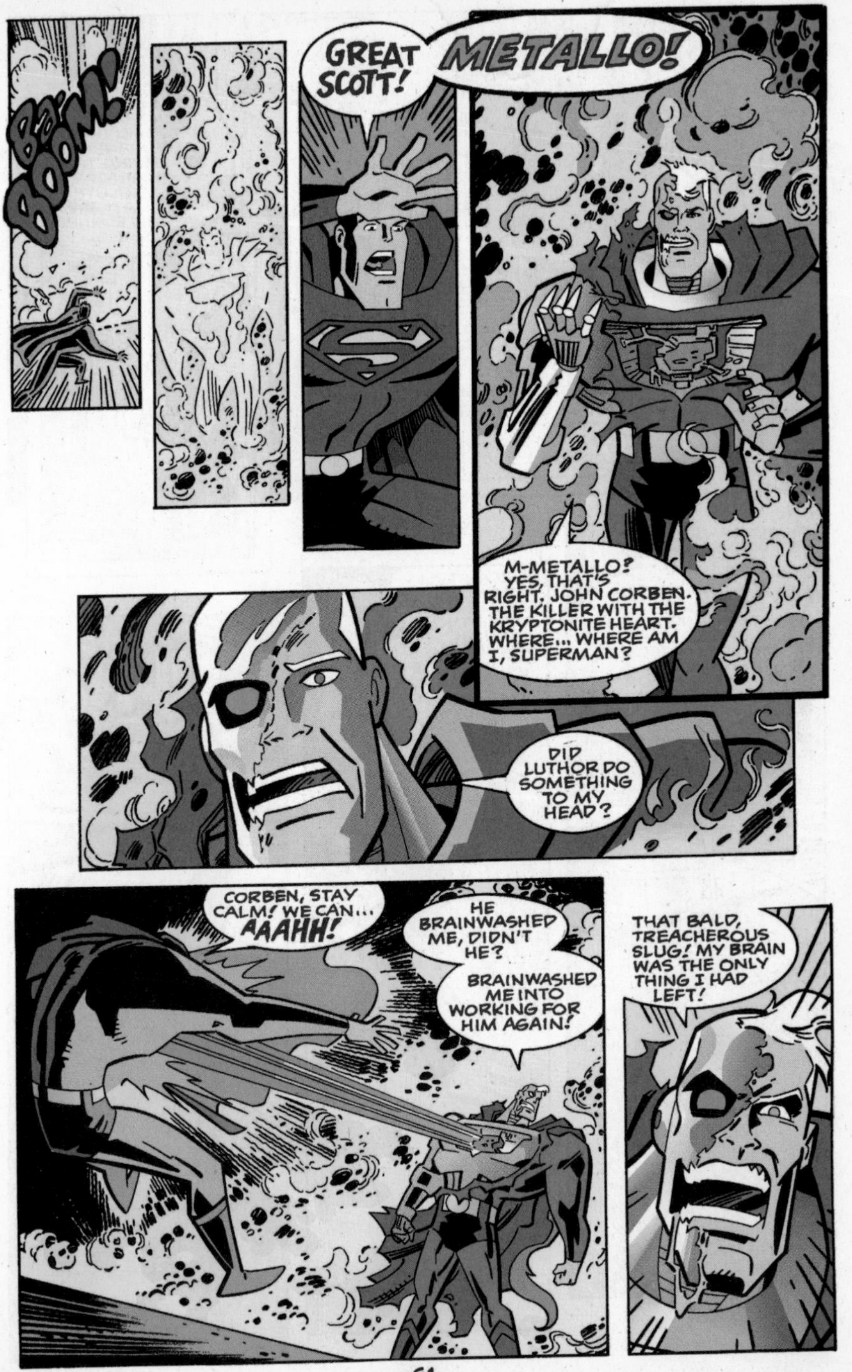
BA-BOOM!
GREAT SCOTT!
METALLO!
M-METALLO? YES, THAT'S RIGHT. JOHN CORBEN. THE KILLER WITH THE KRYPTONITE HEART. WHERE... WHERE AM I, SUPERMAN?
DID LUTHOR DO SOMETHING TO MY HEAD?
CORBEN, STAY CALM! WE CAN... AAAHH!
HE BRAINWASHED ME, DIDN'T HE?
BRAINWASHED ME INTO WORKING FOR HIM AGAIN!
THAT BALD, TREACHEROUS SLUG! MY BRAIN WAS THE ONLY THING I HAD LEFT!

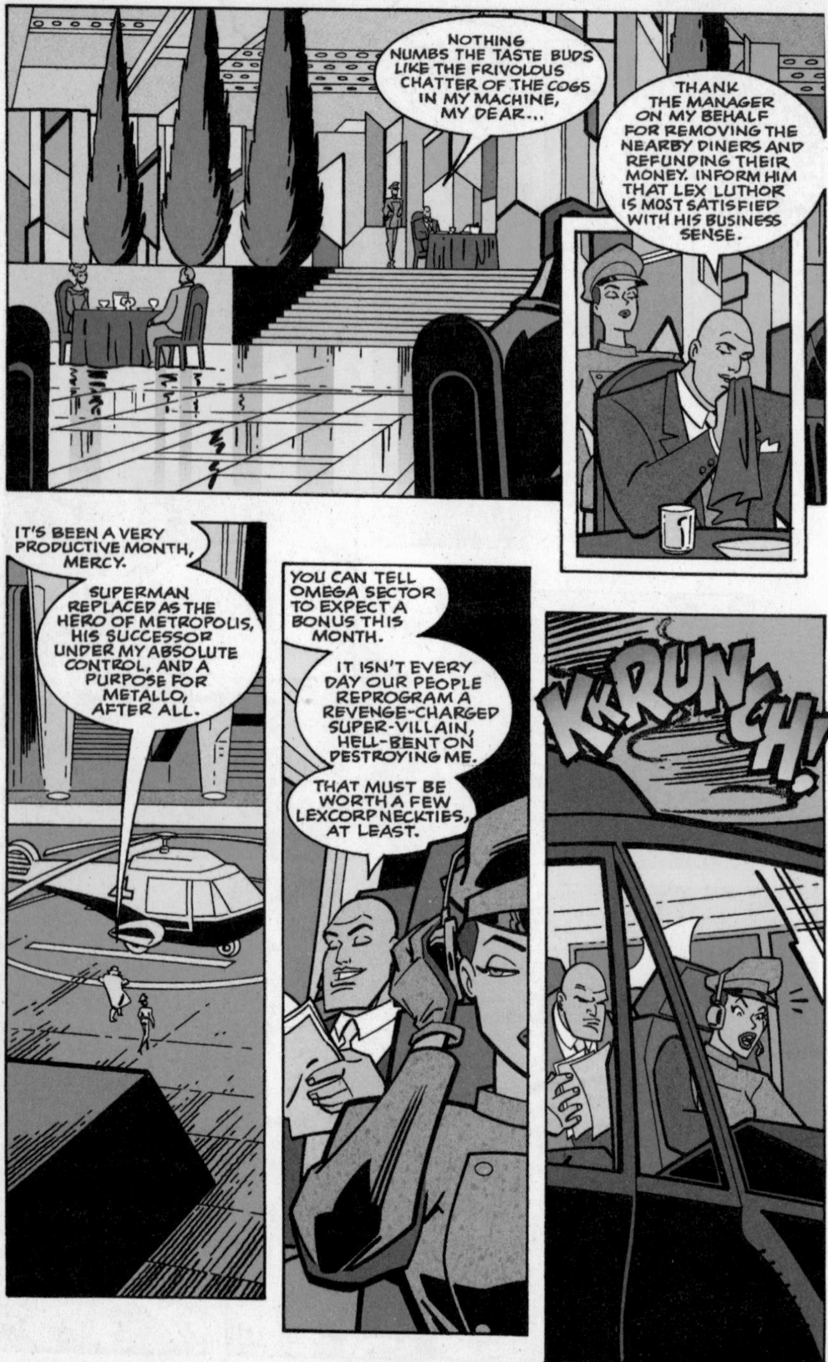
NOTHING NUMBS THE TASTE BUDS LIKE THE FRIVOLOUS CHATTER OF THE COGS IN MY MACHINE, MY DEAR...
THANK THE MANAGER ON MY BEHALF FOR REMOVING THE NEARBY DINERS AND REFUNDING THEIR MONEY. INFORM HIM THAT LEX LUTHOR IS MOST SATISFIED WITH HIS BUSINESS SENSE.
IT'S BEEN A VERY PRODUCTIVE MONTH, MERCY.
SUPERMAN REPLACED AS THE HERO OF METROPOLIS, HIS SUCCESSOR UNDER MY ABSOLUTE CONTROL, AND A PURPOSE FOR METALLO, AFTER ALL.
YOU CAN TELL OMEGA SECTOR TO EXPECT A BONUS THIS MONTH.
IT ISN'T EVERY DAY OUR PEOPLE REPROGRAM A REVENGE-CHARGED SUPER-VILLAIN, HELL-BENT ON DESTROYING ME.
THAT MUST BE WORTH A FEW LEXCORP NECKTIES, AT LEAST.
K-KRUNCH!

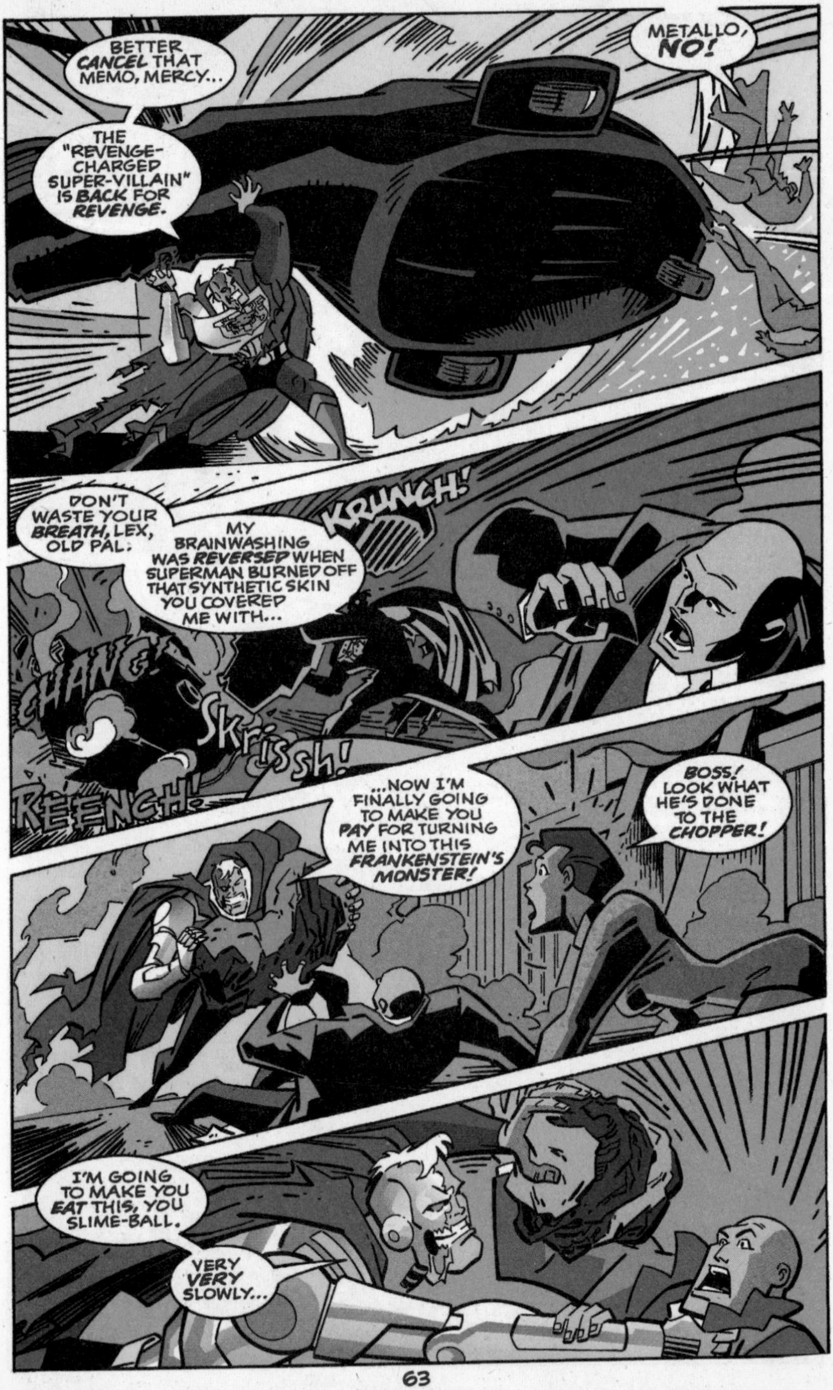

BETTER CANCEL THAT MEMO, MERCY...
METALLO, NO!
THE "REVENGE-CHARGED SUPER-VILLAIN" IS BACK FOR REVENGE.
DON'T WASTE YOUR BREATH, LEX, OLD PAL.
KRUNCH!
MY BRAINWASHING WAS REVERSED WHEN SUPERMAN BURNED OFF THAT SYNTHETIC SKIN YOU COVERED ME WITH...
CHANG!
Skrissh!
REENCH!
...NOW I'M FINALLY GOING TO MAKE YOU PAY FOR TURNING ME INTO THIS FRANKENSTEIN'S MONSTER!
BOSS! LOOK WHAT HE'S DONE TO THE CHOPPER!
I'M GOING TO MAKE YOU EAT THIS, YOU SLIME-BALL.
VERY VERY SLOWLY...

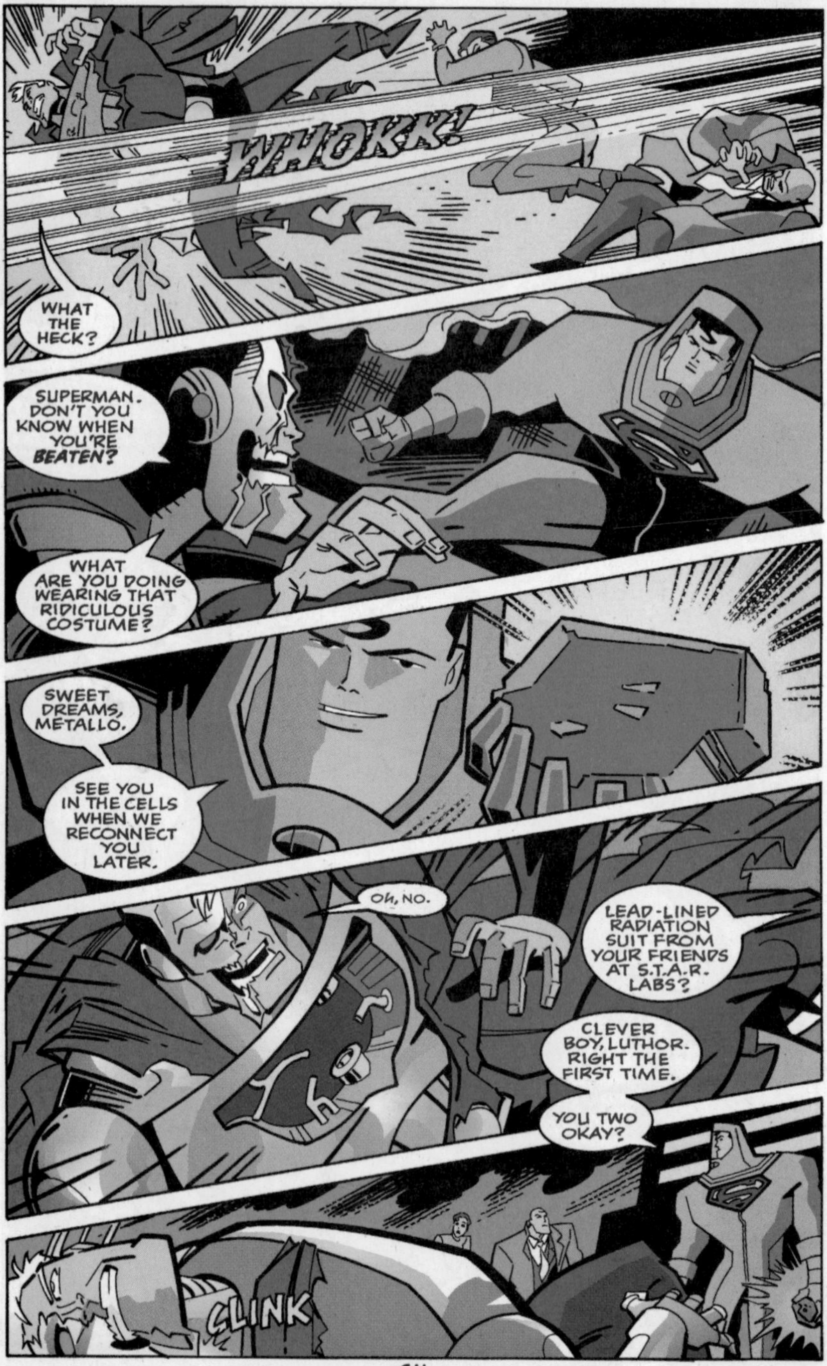
WHOKK!
WHAT THE HECK?
SUPERMAN. DON'T YOU KNOW WHEN YOU'RE *BEATEN?*
WHAT ARE YOU DOING WEARING THAT RIDICULOUS COSTUME?
SWEET DREAMS, METALLO.
SEE YOU IN THE CELLS WHEN WE RECONNECT YOU LATER.
OH, NO.
LEAD-LINED RADIATION SUIT FROM YOUR FRIENDS AT S.T.A.R. LABS?
CLEVER BOY, LUTHOR. RIGHT THE FIRST TIME.
YOU TWO OKAY?
CLINK

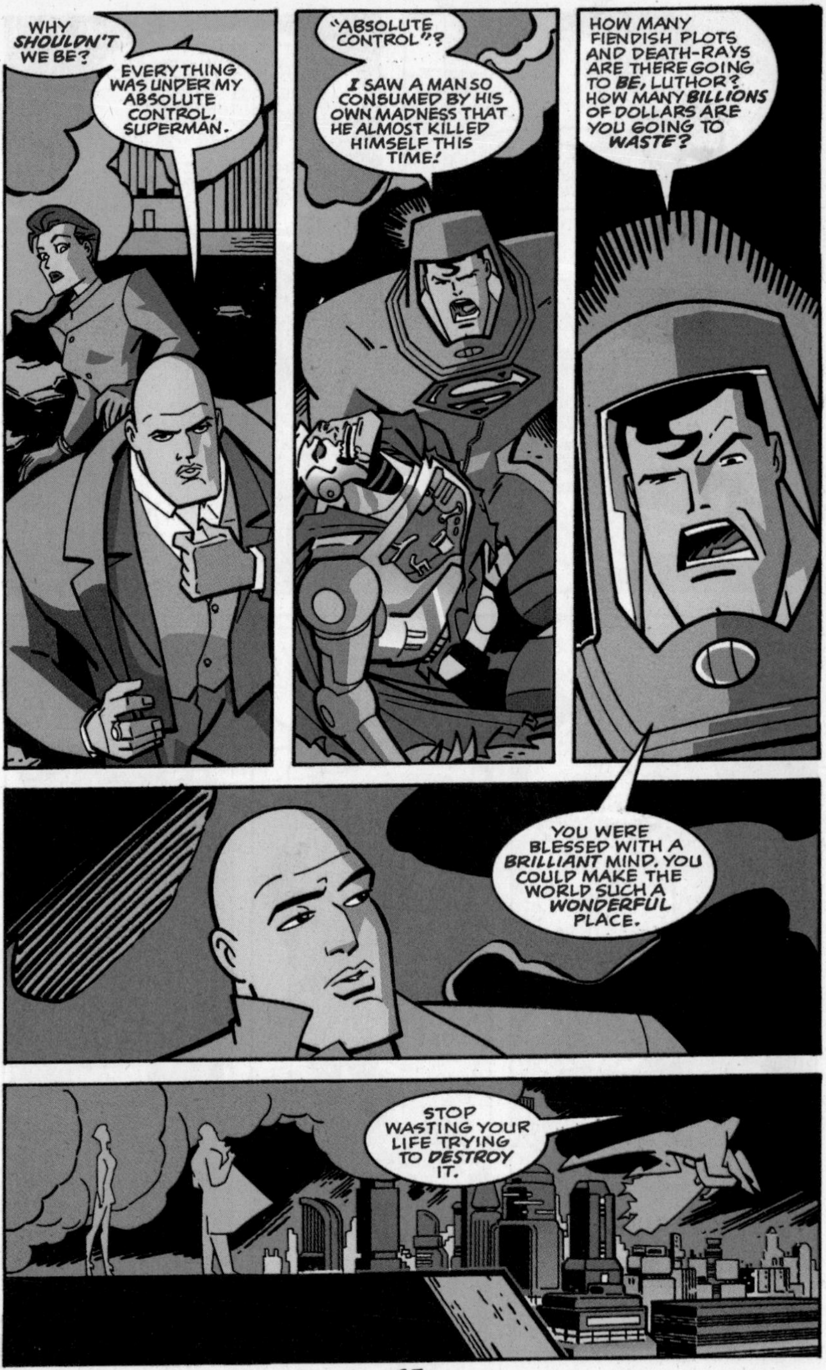
WHY SHOULDN'T WE BE?
EVERYTHING WAS UNDER MY ABSOLUTE CONTROL, SUPERMAN.
"ABSOLUTE CONTROL"?
I SAW A MAN SO CONSUMED BY HIS OWN MADNESS THAT HE ALMOST KILLED HIMSELF THIS TIME!
HOW MANY FIENDISH PLOTS AND DEATH-RAYS ARE THERE GOING TO BE, LUTHOR? HOW MANY BILLIONS OF DOLLARS ARE YOU GOING TO WASTE?
YOU WERE BLESSED WITH A BRILLIANT MIND. YOU COULD MAKE THE WORLD SUCH A WONDERFUL PLACE.
STOP WASTING YOUR LIFE TRYING TO DESTROY IT.

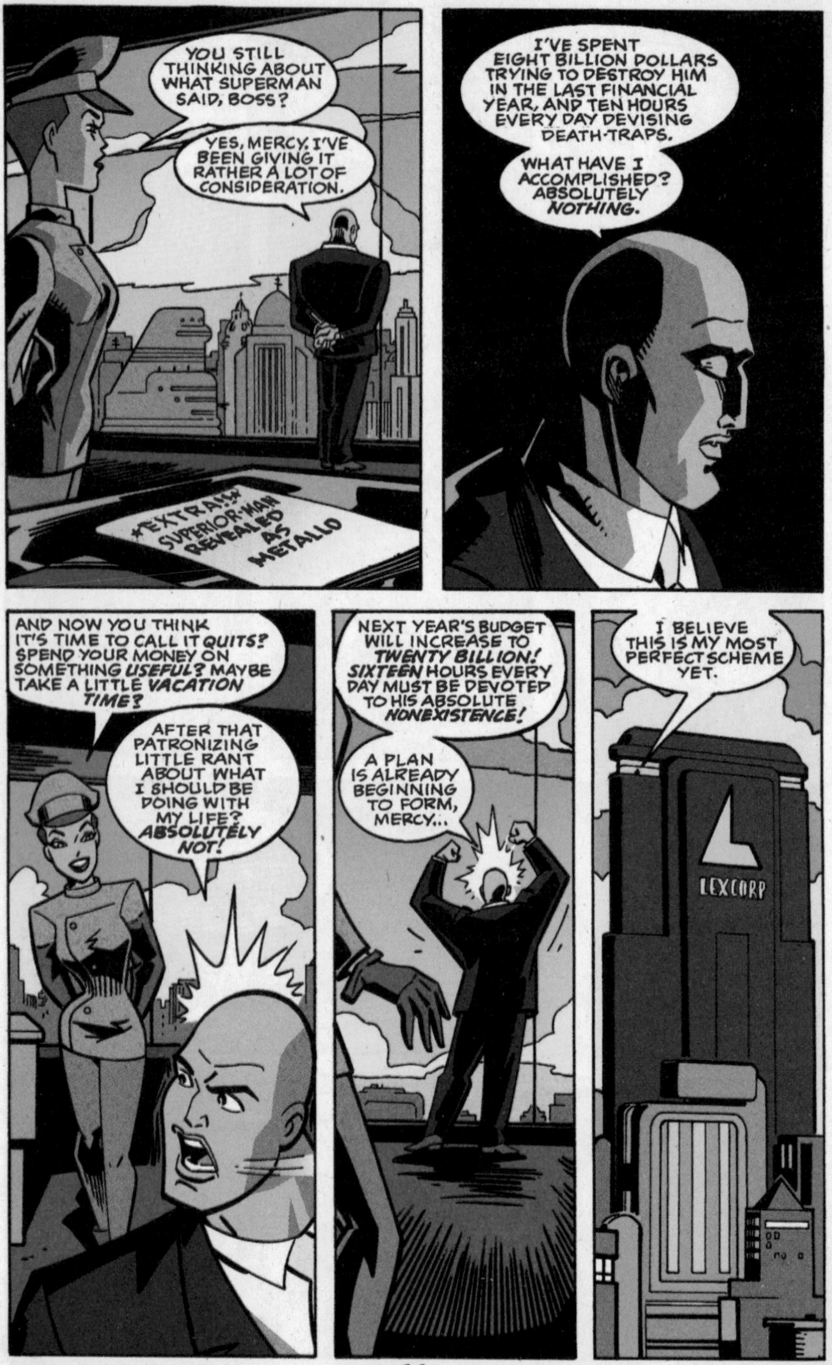
YOU STILL THINKING ABOUT WHAT SUPERMAN SAID, BOSS?
YES, MERCY. I'VE BEEN GIVING IT RATHER A LOT OF CONSIDERATION.
EXTRA!!! SUPERIOR-MAN REVEALED AS METALLO
I'VE SPENT EIGHT BILLION DOLLARS TRYING TO DESTROY HIM IN THE LAST FINANCIAL YEAR, AND TEN HOURS EVERY DAY DEVISING DEATH-TRAPS.
WHAT HAVE I ACCOMPLISHED? ABSOLUTELY *NOTHING*.
AND NOW YOU THINK IT'S TIME TO CALL IT *QUITS?* SPEND YOUR MONEY ON SOMETHING *USEFUL?* MAYBE TAKE A LITTLE *VACATION TIME?*
AFTER THAT PATRONIZING LITTLE RANT ABOUT WHAT I SHOULD BE DOING WITH MY LIFE? *ABSOLUTELY NOT!*
NEXT YEAR'S BUDGET WILL INCREASE TO *TWENTY BILLION! SIXTEEN* HOURS EVERY DAY MUST BE DEVOTED TO HIS ABSOLUTE *NONEXISTENCE!*
A PLAN IS ALREADY BEGINNING TO FORM, MERCY...
I BELIEVE THIS IS MY MOST PERFECT SCHEME YET.
LEXCORP

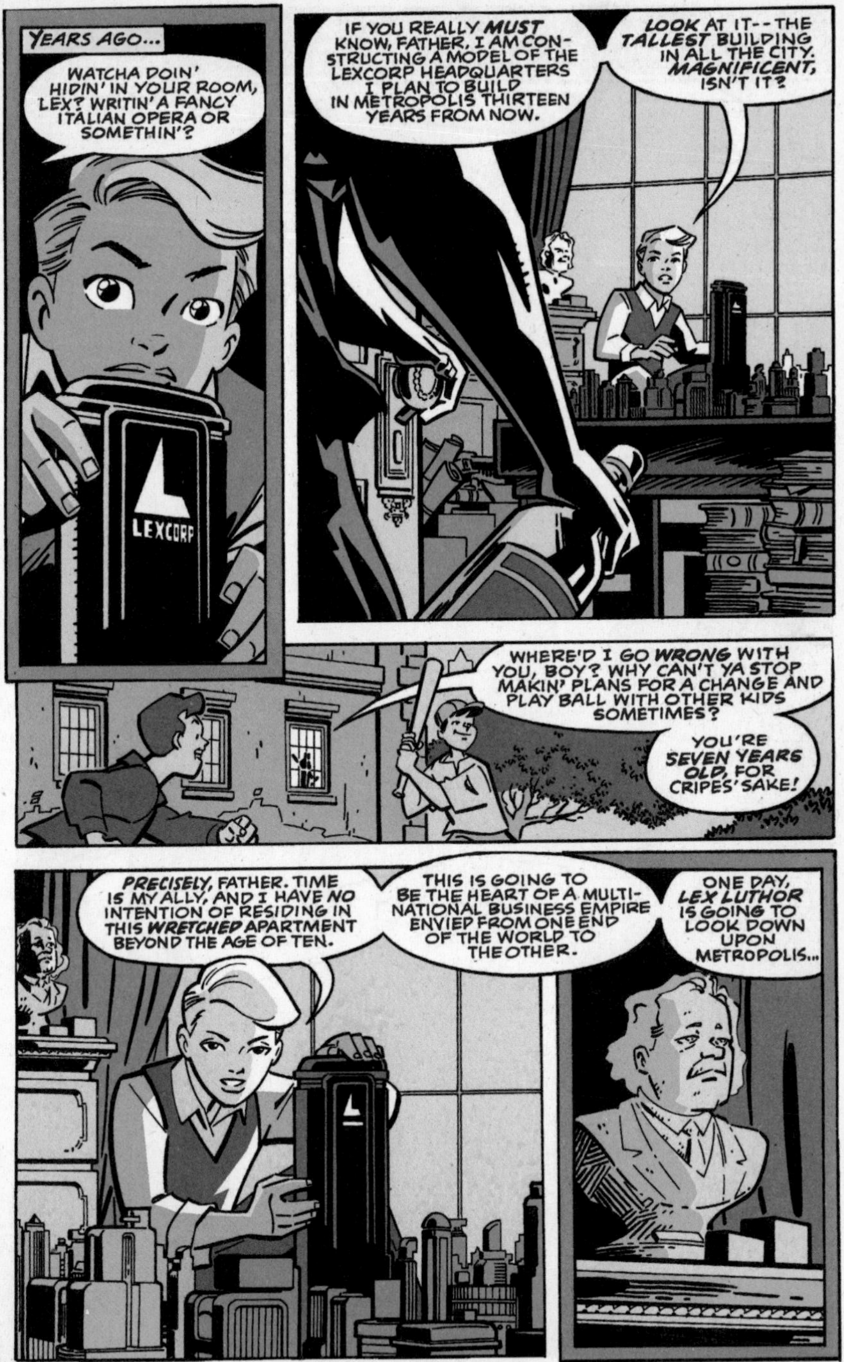
YEARS AGO...
WATCHA DOIN' HIDIN' IN YOUR ROOM, LEX? WRITIN' A FANCY ITALIAN OPERA OR SOMETHIN'?
LEXCORP
IF YOU REALLY MUST KNOW, FATHER, I AM CONSTRUCTING A MODEL OF THE LEXCORP HEADQUARTERS I PLAN TO BUILD IN METROPOLIS THIRTEEN YEARS FROM NOW.
LOOK AT IT--THE TALLEST BUILDING IN ALL THE CITY. MAGNIFICENT, ISN'T IT?
WHERE'D I GO WRONG WITH YOU, BOY? WHY CAN'T YA STOP MAKIN' PLANS FOR A CHANGE AND PLAY BALL WITH OTHER KIDS SOMETIMES?
YOU'RE SEVEN YEARS OLD, FOR CRIPES' SAKE!
PRECISELY, FATHER. TIME IS MY ALLY, AND I HAVE NO INTENTION OF RESIDING IN THIS WRETCHED APARTMENT BEYOND THE AGE OF TEN.
THIS IS GOING TO BE THE HEART OF A MULTINATIONAL BUSINESS EMPIRE ENVIED FROM ONE END OF THE WORLD TO THE OTHER.
ONE DAY, LEX LUTHOR IS GOING TO LOOK DOWN UPON METROPOLIS...

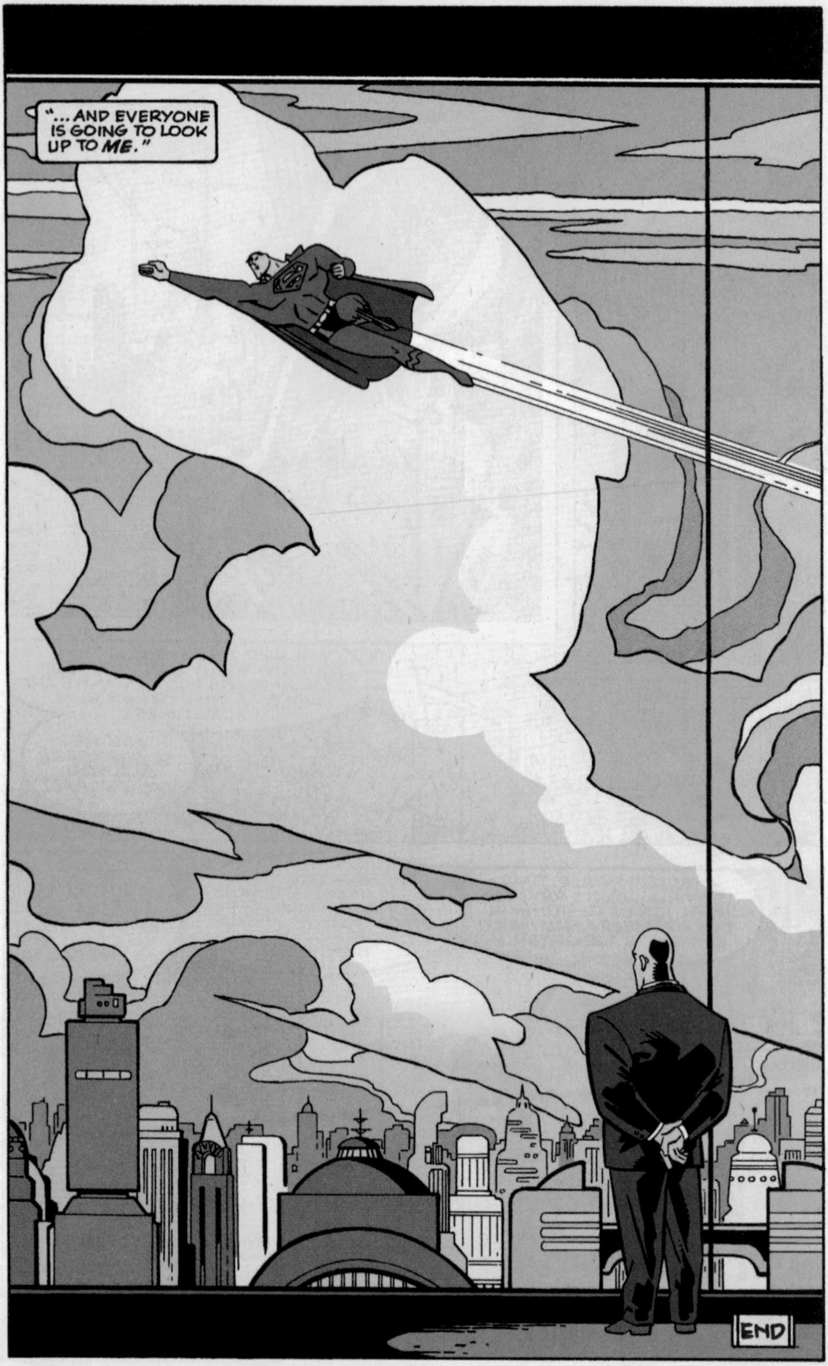
"...AND EVERYONE IS GOING TO LOOK UP TO *ME*."
END

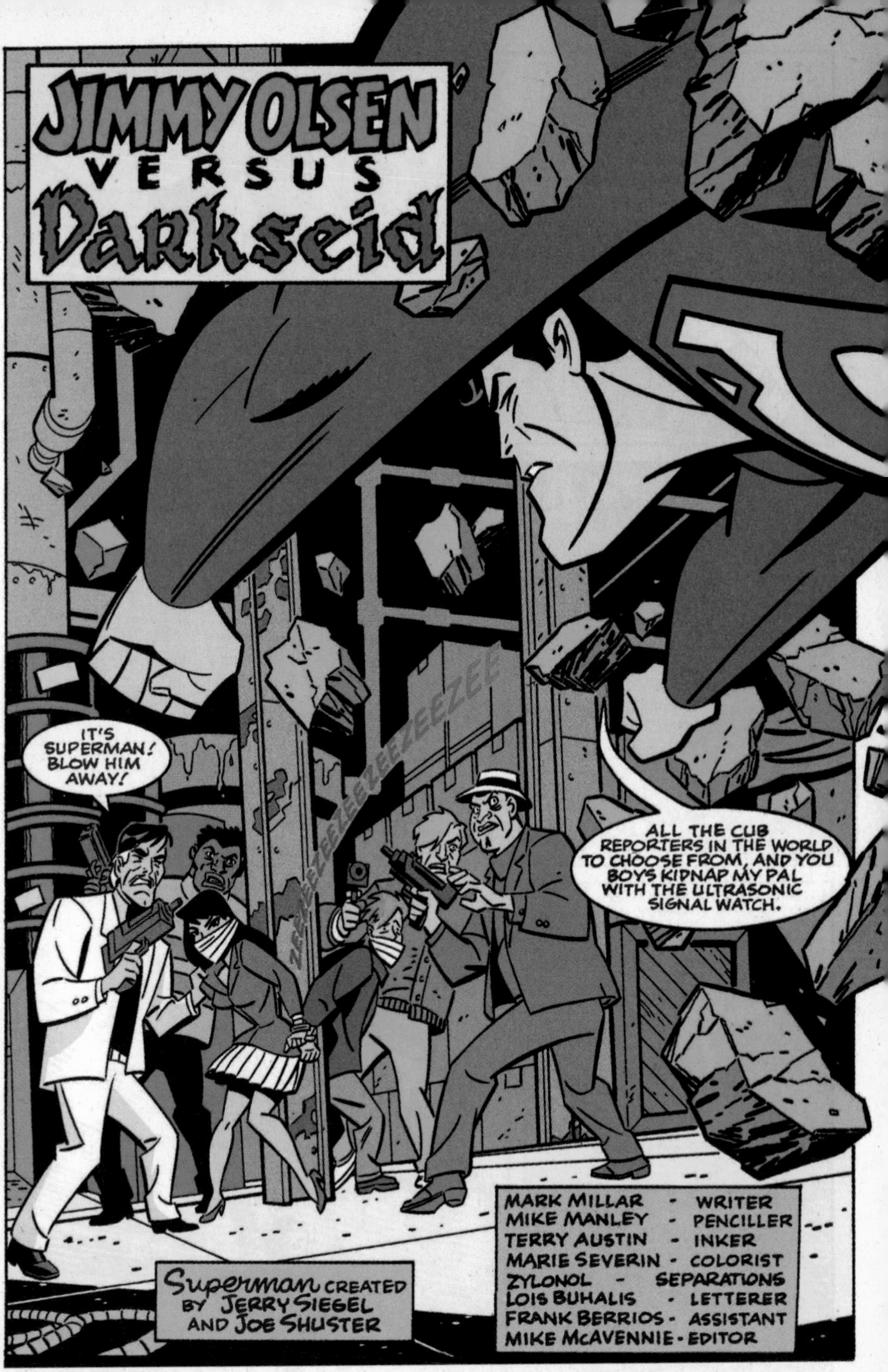
JIMMY OLSEN VERSUS Darkseid
IT'S SUPERMAN! BLOW HIM AWAY!
ZEEEEEZEEZEEZEEZEEZEE
ALL THE CUB REPORTERS IN THE WORLD TO CHOOSE FROM, AND YOU BOYS KIDNAP MY PAL WITH THE ULTRASONIC SIGNAL WATCH.
Superman CREATED BY JERRY SIEGEL AND JOE SHUSTER
MARK MILLAR - WRITER
MIKE MANLEY - PENCILLER
TERRY AUSTIN - INKER
MARIE SEVERIN - COLORIST
ZYLONOL - SEPARATIONS
LOIS BUHALIS - LETTERER
FRANK BERRIOS - ASSISTANT
MIKE McAVENNIE - EDITOR

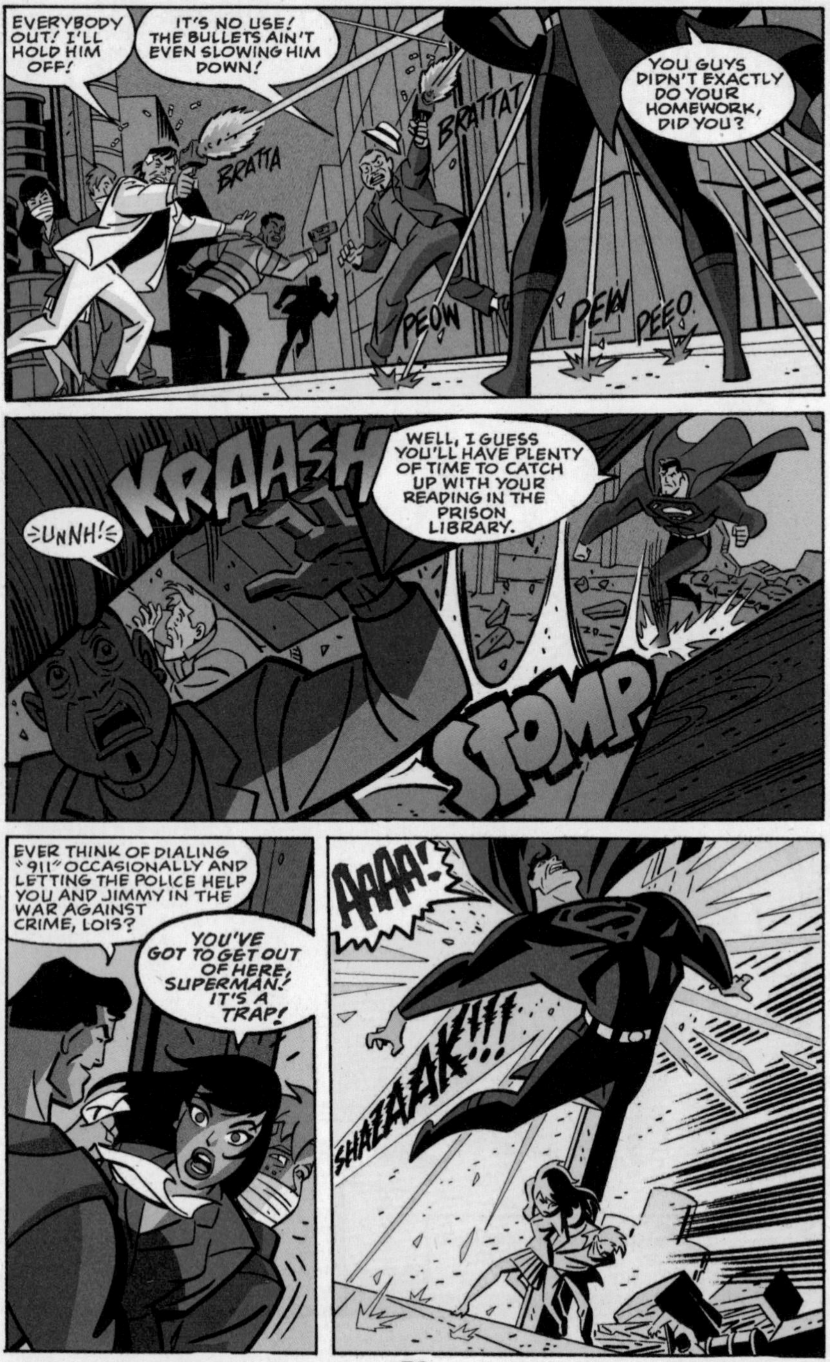
EVERYBODY OUT! I'LL HOLD HIM OFF!
IT'S NO USE! THE BULLETS AIN'T EVEN SLOWING HIM DOWN!
BRATTA
BRATTAT
YOU GUYS DIDN'T EXACTLY DO YOUR HOMEWORK, DID YOU?
PEOW
PEW
PEEO
KRAASH
UNNH!
WELL, I GUESS YOU'LL HAVE PLENTY OF TIME TO CATCH UP WITH YOUR READING IN THE PRISON LIBRARY.
STOMP
EVER THINK OF DIALING "911" OCCASIONALLY AND LETTING THE POLICE HELP YOU AND JIMMY IN THE WAR AGAINST CRIME, LOIS?
YOU'VE GOT TO GET OUT OF HERE, SUPERMAN! IT'S A TRAP!
AAAA!
SHZAAAK!!!

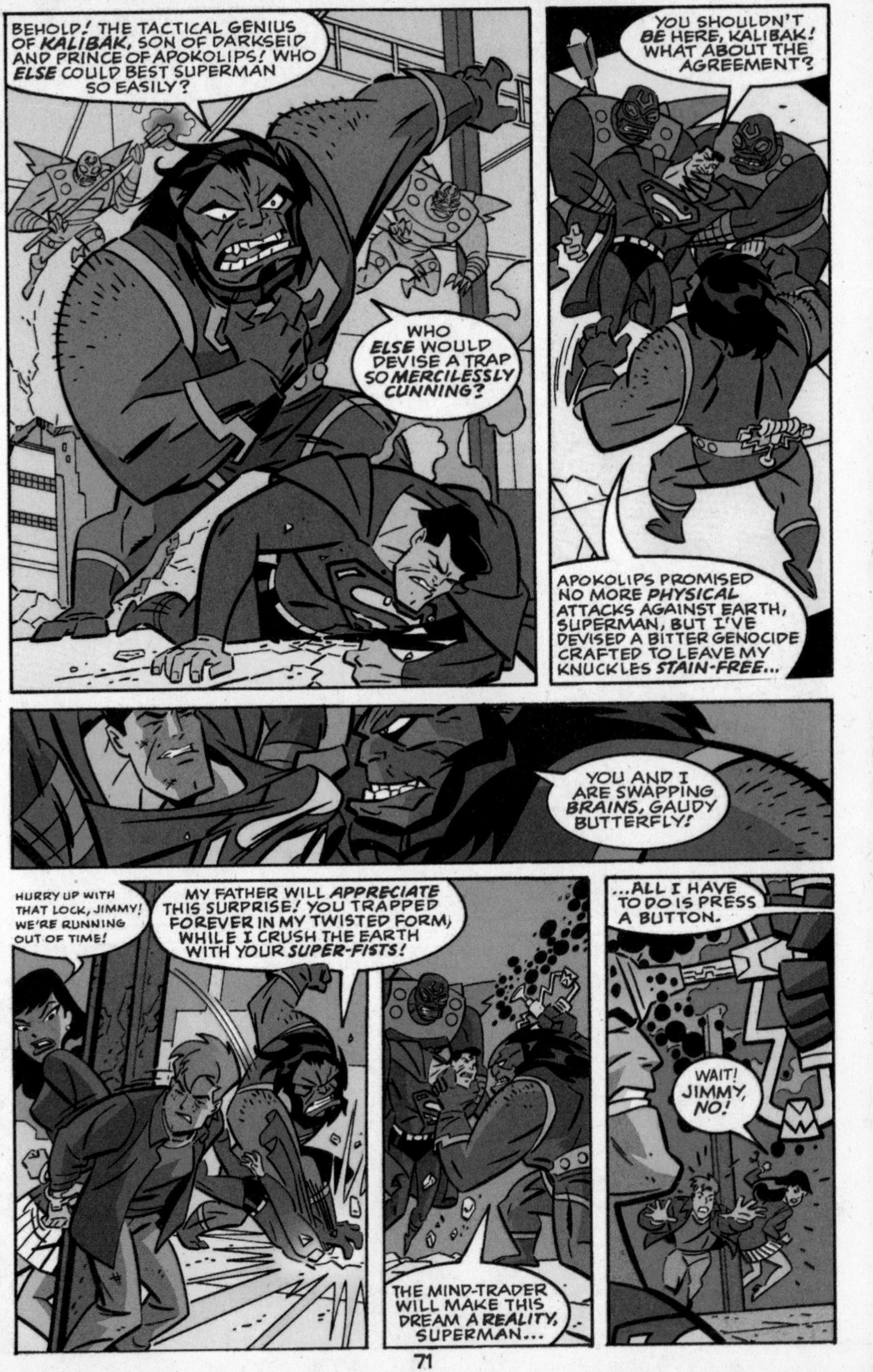
BEHOLD! THE TACTICAL GENIUS OF KALIBAK, SON OF DARKSEID AND PRINCE OF APOKOLIPS! WHO ELSE COULD BEST SUPERMAN SO EASILY?
WHO ELSE WOULD DEVISE A TRAP SO MERCILESSLY CUNNING?
YOU SHOULDN'T BE HERE, KALIBAK! WHAT ABOUT THE AGREEMENT?
APOKOLIPS PROMISED NO MORE PHYSICAL ATTACKS AGAINST EARTH, SUPERMAN, BUT I'VE DEVISED A BITTER GENOCIDE CRAFTED TO LEAVE MY KNUCKLES STAIN-FREE...
YOU AND I ARE SWAPPING BRAINS, GAUDY BUTTERFLY!
HURRY UP WITH THAT LOCK, JIMMY! WE'RE RUNNING OUT OF TIME!
MY FATHER WILL APPRECIATE THIS SURPRISE! YOU TRAPPED FOREVER IN MY TWISTED FORM, WHILE I CRUSH THE EARTH WITH YOUR SUPER-FISTS!
THE MIND-TRADER WILL MAKE THIS DREAM A REALITY, SUPERMAN...
...ALL I HAVE TO DO IS PRESS A BUTTON.
WAIT! JIMMY, NO!

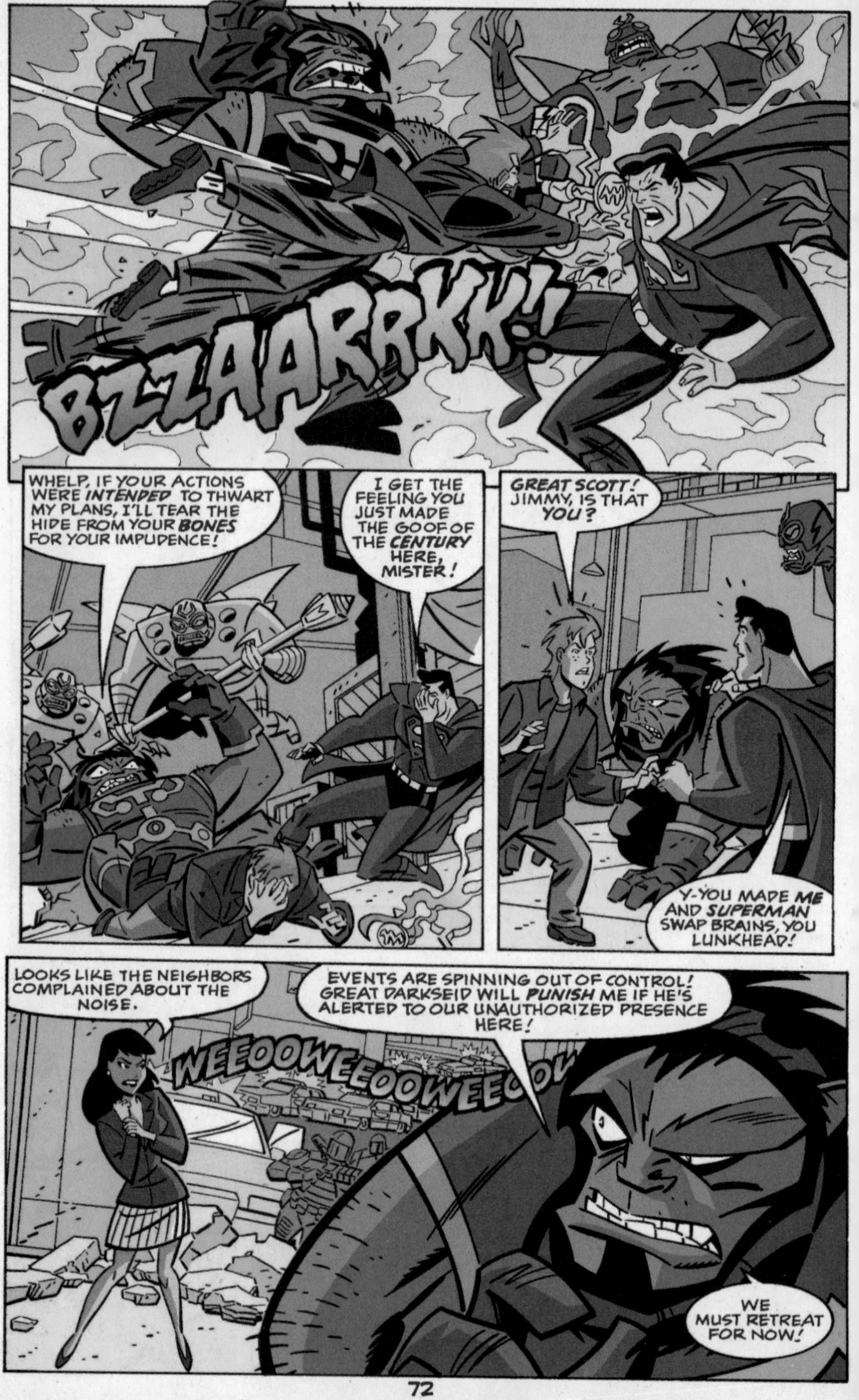
BZZAARRKK!!
WHELP, IF YOUR ACTIONS WERE INTENDED TO THWART MY PLANS, I'LL TEAR THE HIDE FROM YOUR BONES FOR YOUR IMPUDENCE!
I GET THE FEELING YOU JUST MADE THE GOOF OF THE CENTURY HERE, MISTER!
GREAT SCOTT! JIMMY, IS THAT YOU?
Y-YOU MADE ME AND SUPERMAN SWAP BRAINS, YOU LUNKHEAD!
LOOKS LIKE THE NEIGHBORS COMPLAINED ABOUT THE NOISE.
EVENTS ARE SPINNING OUT OF CONTROL! GREAT DARKSEID WILL PUNISH ME IF HE'S ALERTED TO OUR UNAUTHORIZED PRESENCE HERE!
WEEOOWEEOOWEEOO
WE MUST RETREAT FOR NOW!

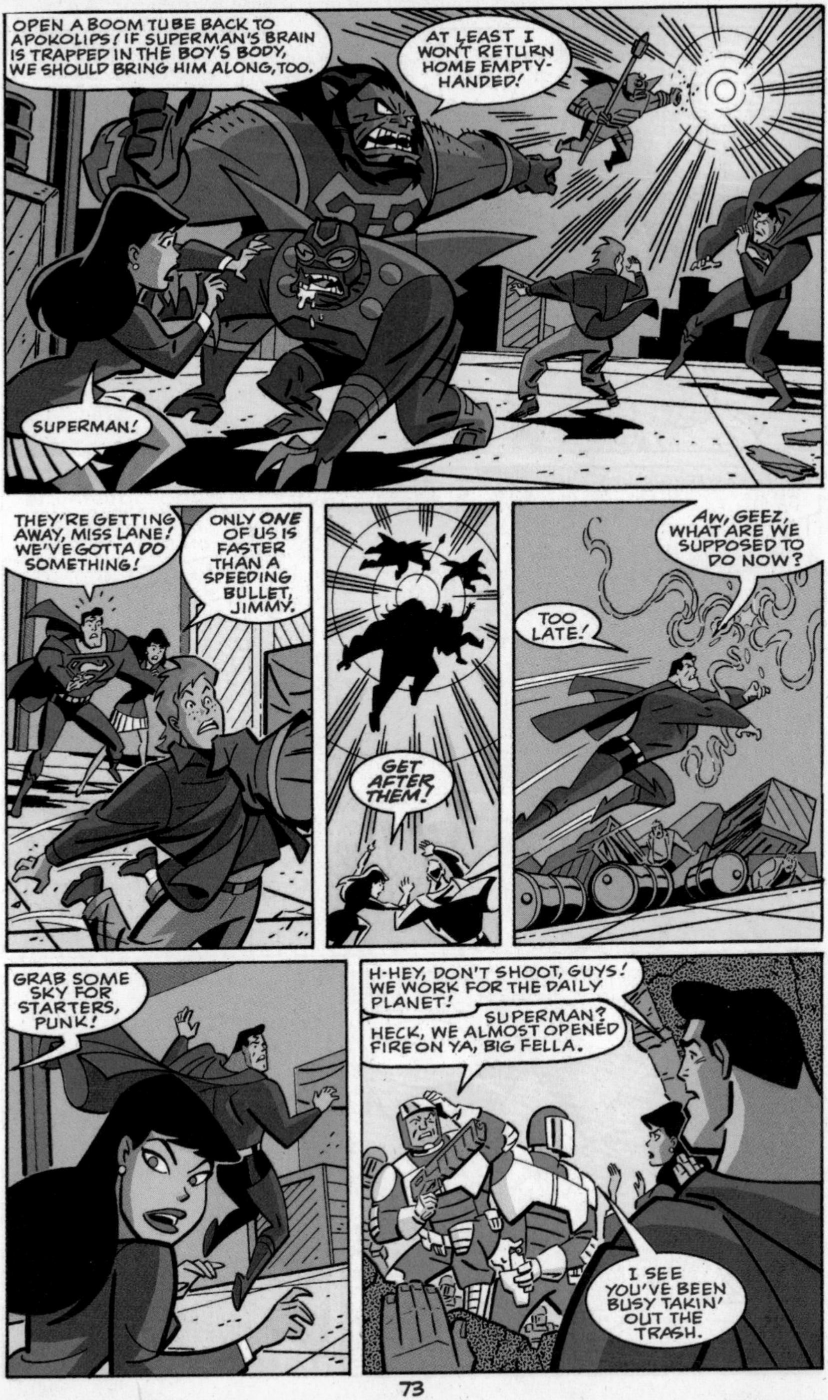

OPEN A BOOM TUBE BACK TO APOKOLIPS! IF SUPERMAN'S BRAIN IS TRAPPED IN THE BOY'S BODY, WE SHOULD BRING HIM ALONG, TOO.
AT LEAST I WON'T RETURN HOME EMPTY-HANDED!
SUPERMAN!
THEY'RE GETTING AWAY, MISS LANE! WE'VE GOTTA DO SOMETHING!
ONLY ONE OF US IS FASTER THAN A SPEEDING BULLET, JIMMY.
GET AFTER THEM!
AW, GEEZ, WHAT ARE WE SUPPOSED TO DO NOW?
TOO LATE!
GRAB SOME SKY FOR STARTERS, PUNK!
H-HEY, DON'T SHOOT, GUYS! WE WORK FOR THE DAILY PLANET!
SUPERMAN? HECK, WE ALMOST OPENED FIRE ON YA, BIG FELLA.
I SEE YOU'VE BEEN BUSY TAKIN' OUT THE TRASH.

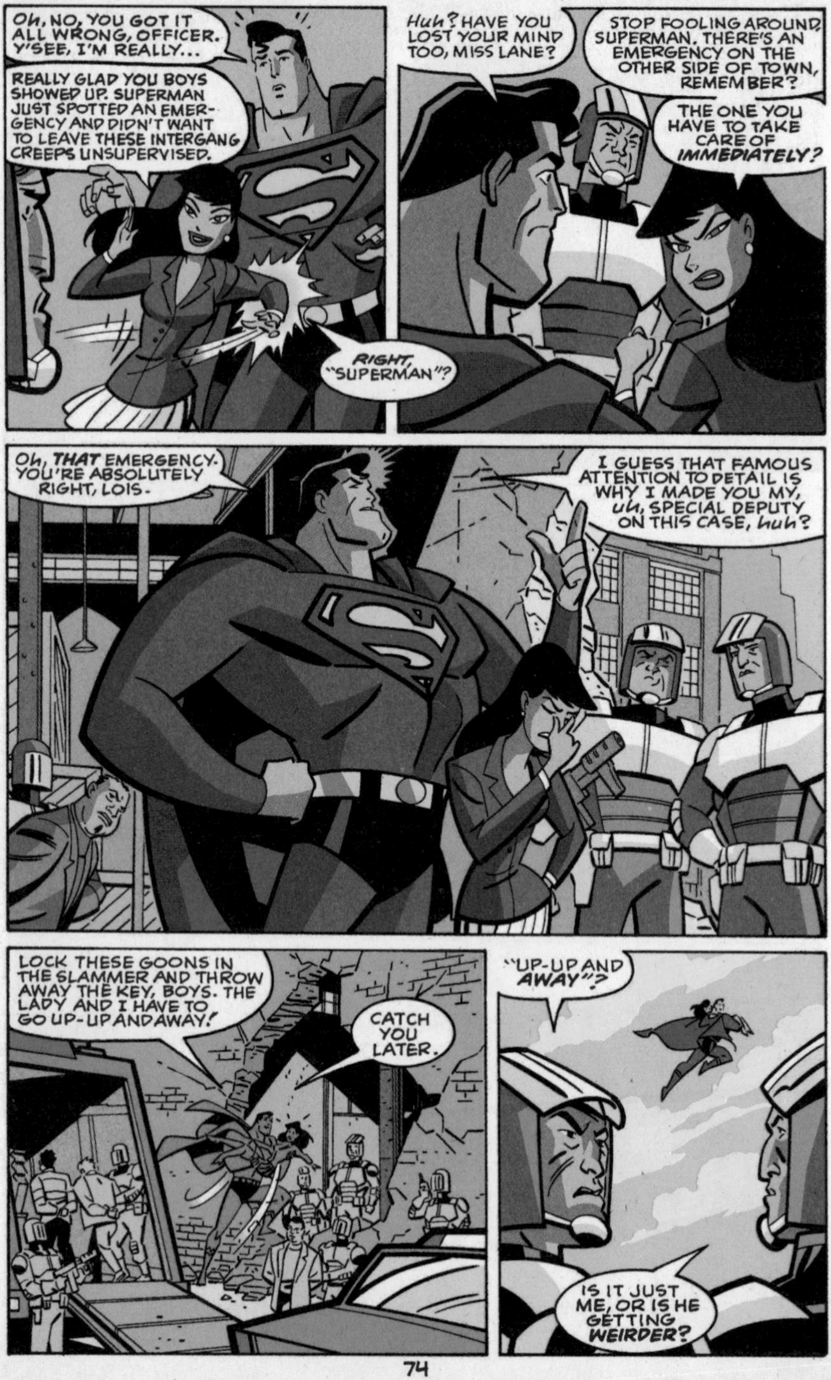
OH, NO, YOU GOT IT ALL WRONG, OFFICER. Y'SEE, I'M REALLY...
REALLY GLAD YOU BOYS SHOWED UP. SUPERMAN JUST SPOTTED AN EMERGENCY AND DIDN'T WANT TO LEAVE THESE INTERGANG CREEPS UNSUPERVISED.
RIGHT, "SUPERMAN"?
HUH? HAVE YOU LOST YOUR MIND TOO, MISS LANE?
STOP FOOLING AROUND, SUPERMAN. THERE'S AN EMERGENCY ON THE OTHER SIDE OF TOWN, REMEMBER?
THE ONE YOU HAVE TO TAKE CARE OF IMMEDIATELY?
OH, THAT EMERGENCY. YOU'RE ABSOLUTELY RIGHT, LOIS.
I GUESS THAT FAMOUS ATTENTION TO DETAIL IS WHY I MADE YOU MY, UH, SPECIAL DEPUTY ON THIS CASE, HUH?
LOCK THESE GOONS IN THE SLAMMER AND THROW AWAY THE KEY, BOYS. THE LADY AND I HAVE TO GO UP-UP AND AWAY!
CATCH YOU LATER.
"UP-UP AND AWAY"?
IS IT JUST ME, OR IS HE GETTING WEIRDER?

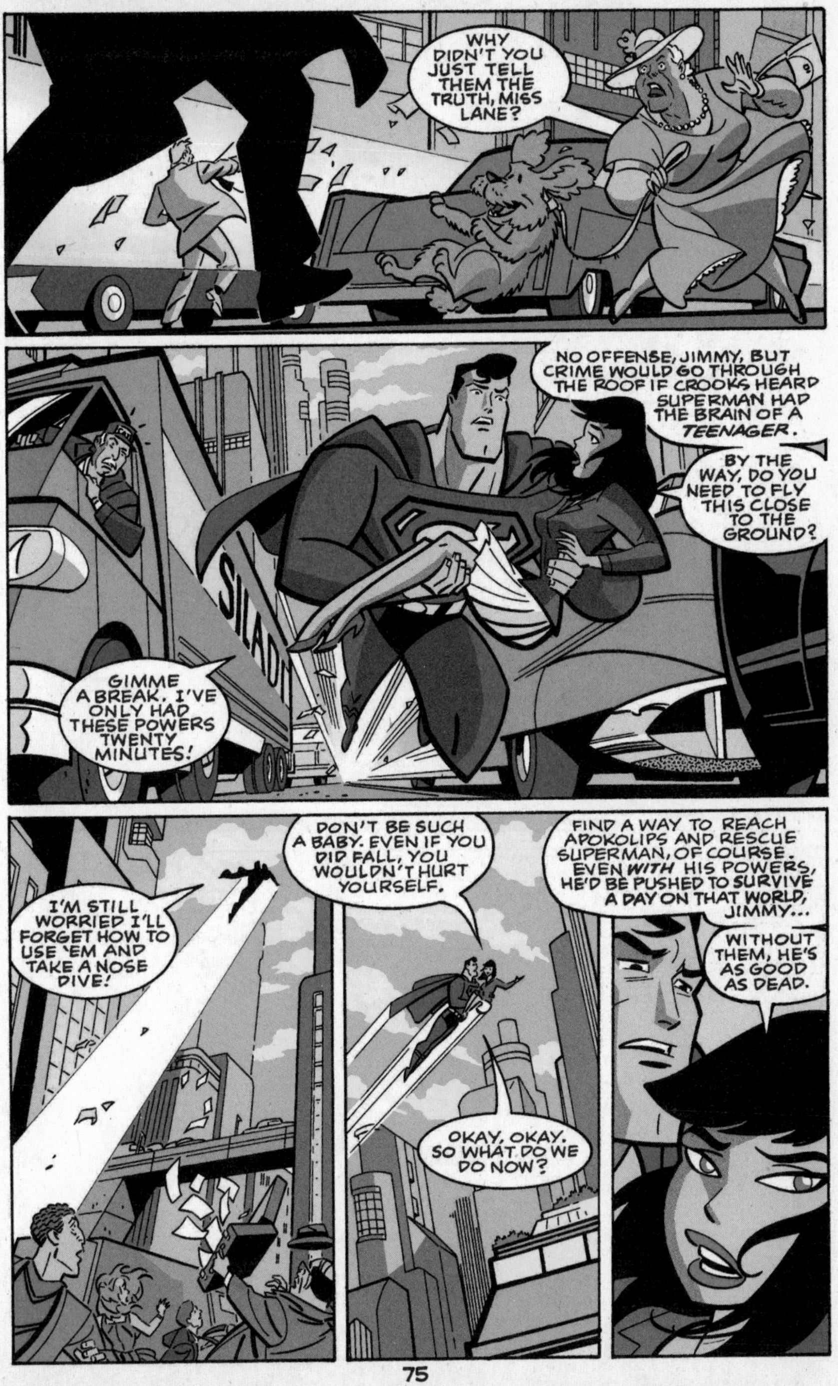
WHY DIDN'T YOU JUST TELL THEM THE TRUTH, MISS LANE?
NO OFFENSE, JIMMY, BUT CRIME WOULD GO THROUGH THE ROOF IF CROOKS HEARD SUPERMAN HAD THE BRAIN OF A TEENAGER.
BY THE WAY, DO YOU NEED TO FLY THIS CLOSE TO THE GROUND?
GIMME A BREAK. I'VE ONLY HAD THESE POWERS TWENTY MINUTES!
SILADI
I'M STILL WORRIED I'LL FORGET HOW TO USE 'EM AND TAKE A NOSE DIVE!
DON'T BE SUCH A BABY. EVEN IF YOU DID FALL, YOU WOULDN'T HURT YOURSELF.
OKAY, OKAY. SO WHAT DO WE DO NOW?
FIND A WAY TO REACH APOKOLIPS AND RESCUE SUPERMAN, OF COURSE. EVEN WITH HIS POWERS, HE'D BE PUSHED TO SURVIVE A DAY ON THAT WORLD, JIMMY...
WITHOUT THEM, HE'S AS GOOD AS DEAD.

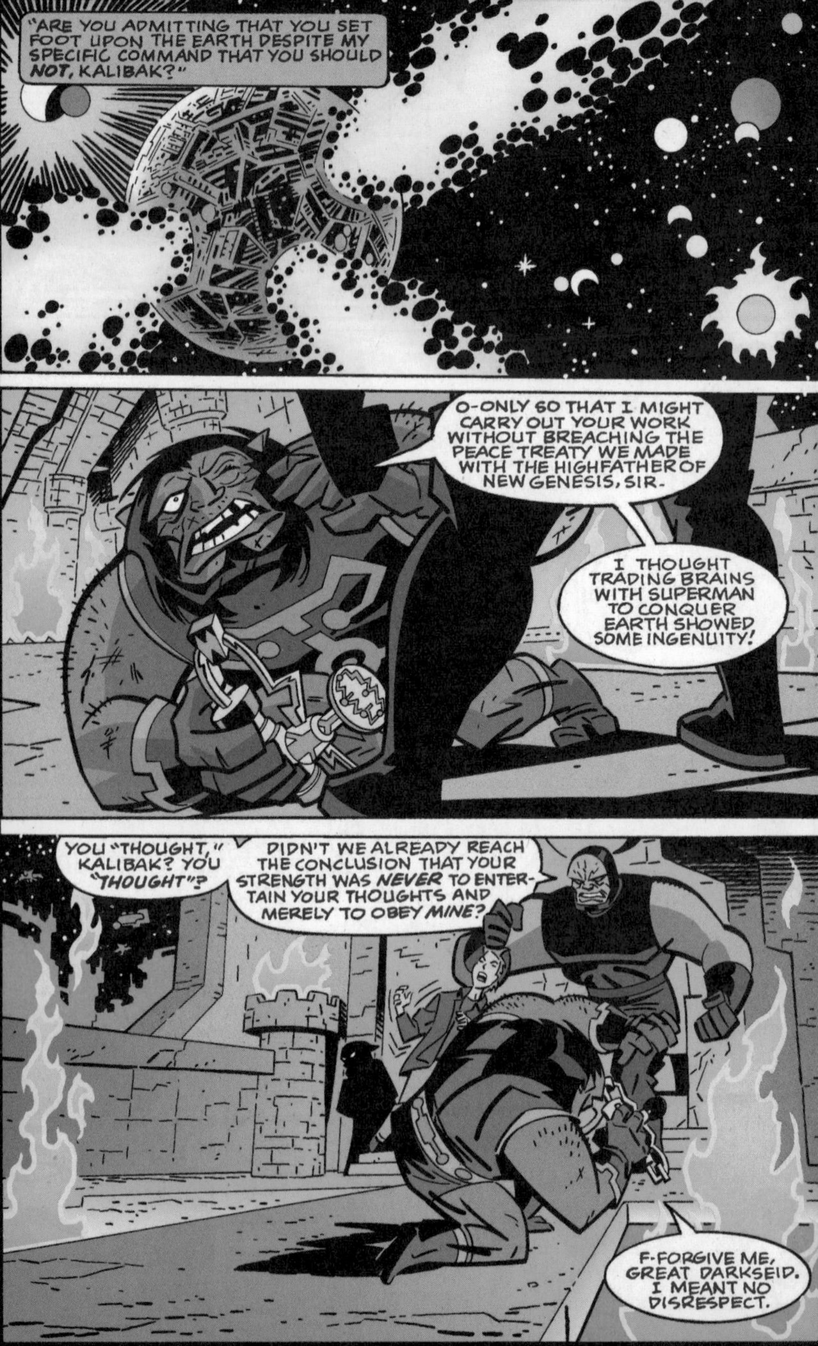
"ARE YOU ADMITTING THAT YOU SET FOOT UPON THE EARTH DESPITE MY SPECIFIC COMMAND THAT YOU SHOULD NOT, KALIBAK?"
O-ONLY SO THAT I MIGHT CARRY OUT YOUR WORK WITHOUT BREACHING THE PEACE TREATY WE MADE WITH THE HIGHFATHER OF NEW GENESIS, SIR.
I THOUGHT TRADING BRAINS WITH SUPERMAN TO CONQUER EARTH SHOWED SOME INGENUITY!
YOU "THOUGHT," KALIBAK? YOU "THOUGHT"?
DIDN'T WE ALREADY REACH THE CONCLUSION THAT YOUR STRENGTH WAS NEVER TO ENTERTAIN YOUR THOUGHTS AND MERELY TO OBEY MINE?
F-FORGIVE ME, GREAT DARKSEID. I MEANT NO DISRESPECT.

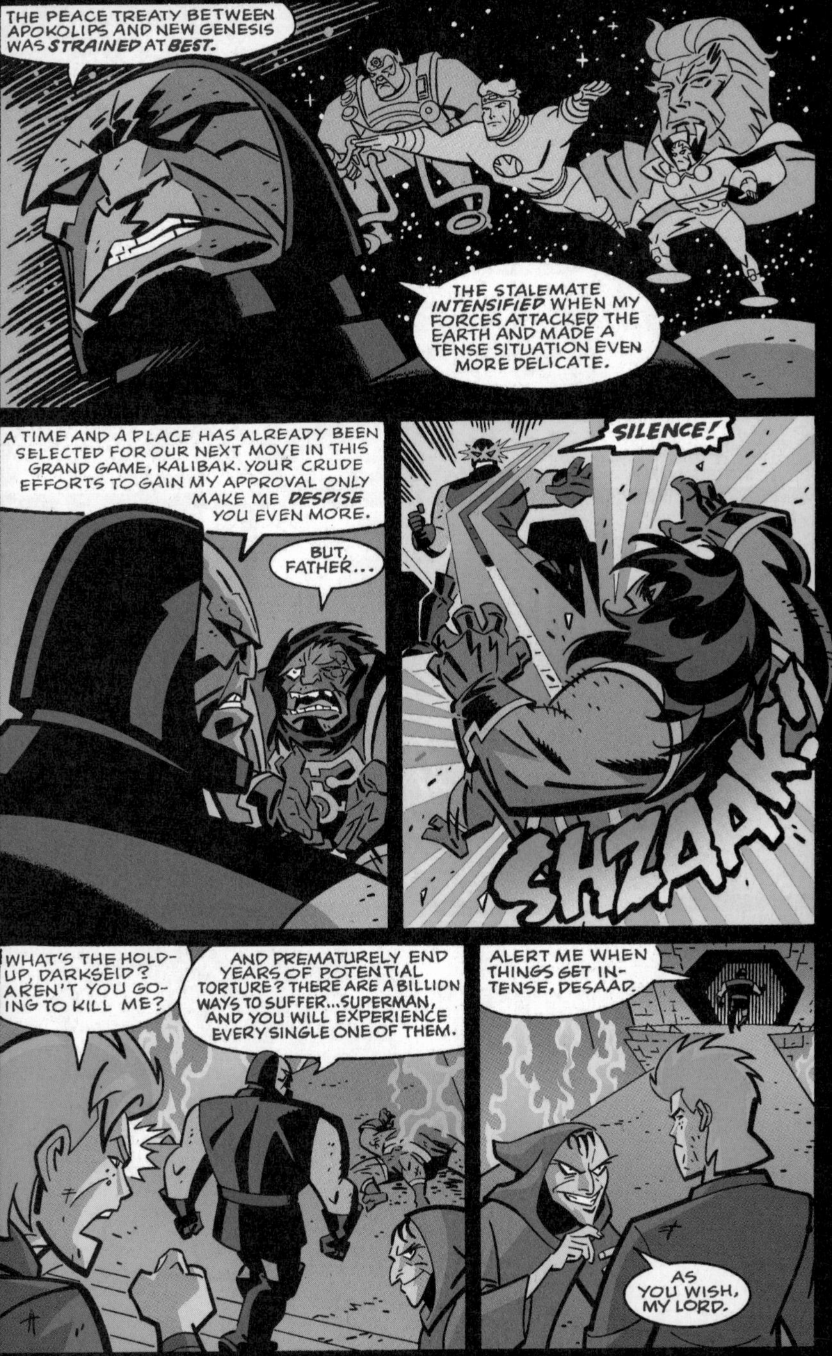

THE PEACE TREATY BETWEEN APOKOLIPS AND NEW GENESIS WAS STRAINED AT BEST.
THE STALEMATE INTENSIFIED WHEN MY FORCES ATTACKED THE EARTH AND MADE A TENSE SITUATION EVEN MORE DELICATE.
A TIME AND A PLACE HAS ALREADY BEEN SELECTED FOR OUR NEXT MOVE IN THIS GRAND GAME, KALIBAK. YOUR CRUDE EFFORTS TO GAIN MY APPROVAL ONLY MAKE ME DESPISE YOU EVEN MORE.
BUT, FATHER...
SILENCE!
SHZAAK!
WHAT'S THE HOLD-UP, DARKSEID? AREN'T YOU GOING TO KILL ME?
AND PREMATURELY END YEARS OF POTENTIAL TORTURE? THERE ARE A BILLION WAYS TO SUFFER...SUPERMAN, AND YOU WILL EXPERIENCE EVERY SINGLE ONE OF THEM.
ALERT ME WHEN THINGS GET INTENSE, DESAAD.
AS YOU WISH, MY LORD.

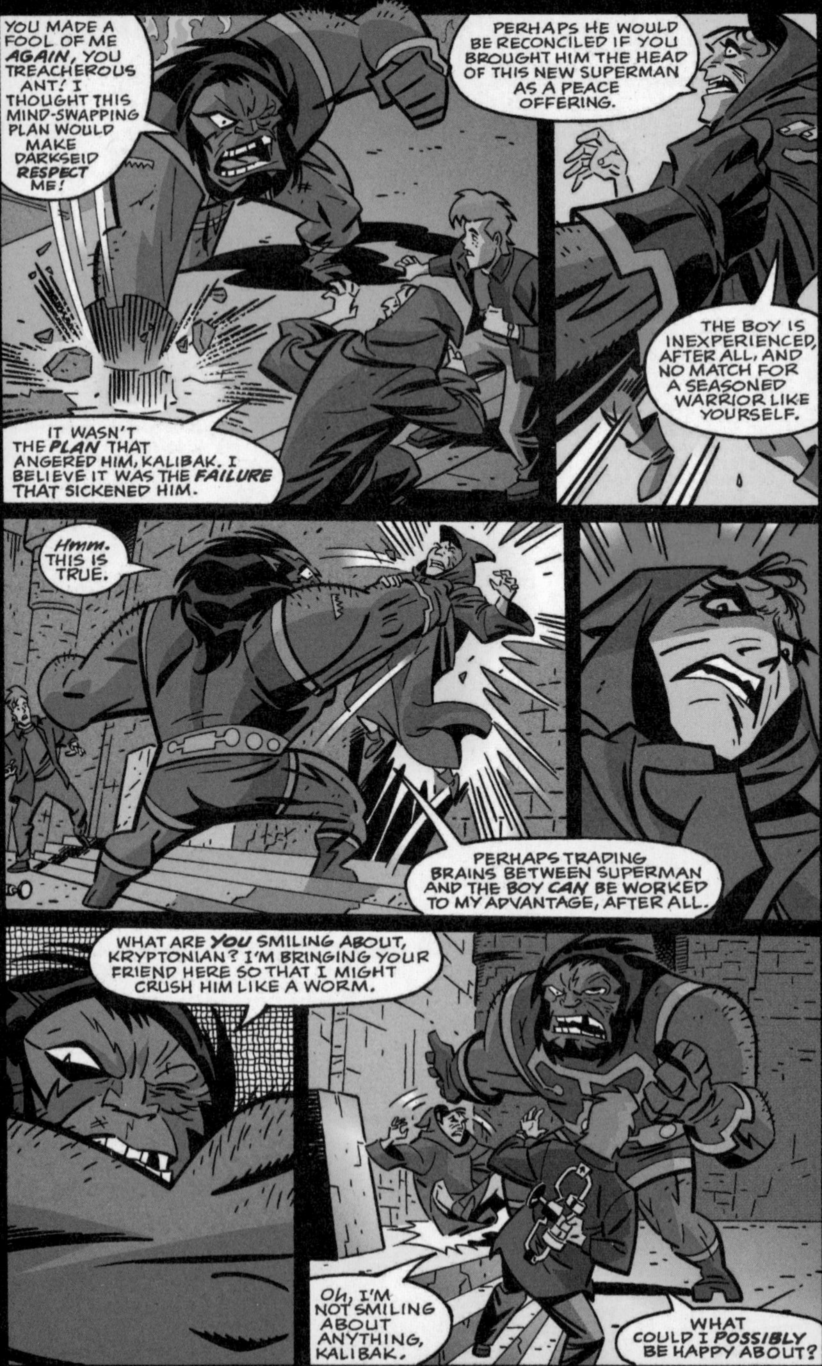
YOU MADE A FOOL OF ME AGAIN, YOU TREACHEROUS ANT! I THOUGHT THIS MIND-SWAPPING PLAN WOULD MAKE DARKSEID RESPECT ME!
IT WASN'T THE PLAN THAT ANGERED HIM, KALIBAK. I BELIEVE IT WAS THE FAILURE THAT SICKENED HIM.
PERHAPS HE WOULD BE RECONCILED IF YOU BROUGHT HIM THE HEAD OF THIS NEW SUPERMAN AS A PEACE OFFERING.
THE BOY IS INEXPERIENCED, AFTER ALL, AND NO MATCH FOR A SEASONED WARRIOR LIKE YOURSELF.
Hmm. THIS IS TRUE.
PERHAPS TRADING BRAINS BETWEEN SUPERMAN AND THE BOY CAN BE WORKED TO MY ADVANTAGE, AFTER ALL.
WHAT ARE YOU SMILING ABOUT, KRYPTONIAN? I'M BRINGING YOUR FRIEND HERE SO THAT I MIGHT CRUSH HIM LIKE A WORM.
Oh, I'M NOT SMILING ABOUT ANYTHING, KALIBAK.
WHAT COULD I POSSIBLY BE HAPPY ABOUT?

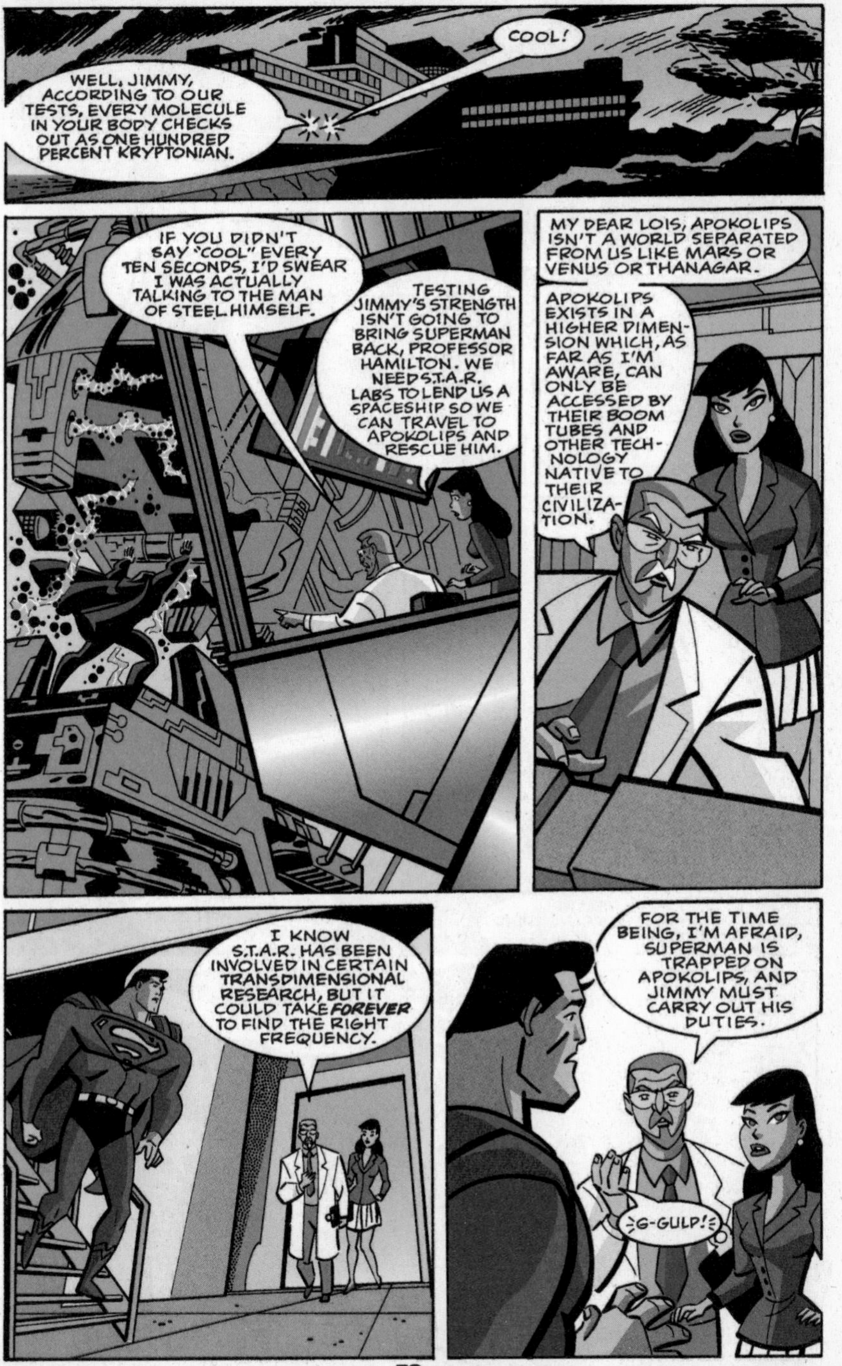
WELL, JIMMY, ACCORDING TO OUR TESTS, EVERY MOLECULE IN YOUR BODY CHECKS OUT AS ONE HUNDRED PERCENT KRYPTONIAN.
COOL!
IF YOU DIDN'T SAY "COOL" EVERY TEN SECONDS, I'D SWEAR I WAS ACTUALLY TALKING TO THE MAN OF STEEL HIMSELF.
TESTING JIMMY'S STRENGTH ISN'T GOING TO BRING SUPERMAN BACK, PROFESSOR HAMILTON. WE NEED S.T.A.R. LABS TO LEND US A SPACESHIP SO WE CAN TRAVEL TO APOKOLIPS AND RESCUE HIM.
MY DEAR LOIS, APOKOLIPS ISN'T A WORLD SEPARATED FROM US LIKE MARS OR VENUS OR THANAGAR.
APOKOLIPS EXISTS IN A HIGHER DIMENSION WHICH, AS FAR AS I'M AWARE, CAN ONLY BE ACCESSED BY THEIR BOOM TUBES AND OTHER TECHNOLOGY NATIVE TO THEIR CIVILIZATION.
I KNOW S.T.A.R. HAS BEEN INVOLVED IN CERTAIN TRANSDIMENSIONAL RESEARCH, BUT IT COULD TAKE *FOREVER* TO FIND THE RIGHT FREQUENCY.
FOR THE TIME BEING, I'M AFRAID, SUPERMAN IS TRAPPED ON APOKOLIPS, AND JIMMY MUST CARRY OUT HIS DUTIES.
G-GULP!

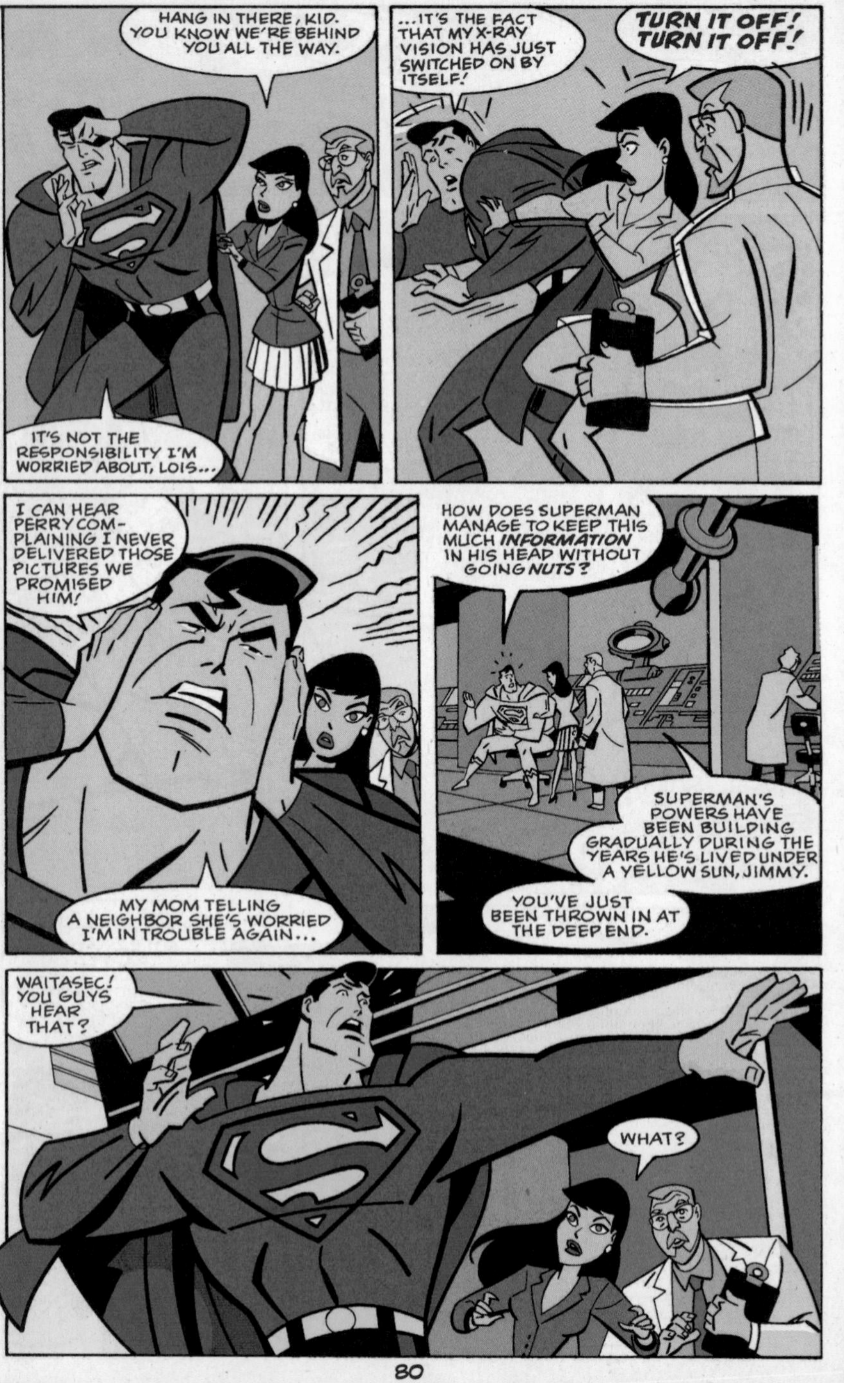
HANG IN THERE, KID. YOU KNOW WE'RE BEHIND YOU ALL THE WAY.
IT'S NOT THE RESPONSIBILITY I'M WORRIED ABOUT, LOIS...
...IT'S THE FACT THAT MY X-RAY VISION HAS JUST SWITCHED ON BY ITSELF!
TURN IT OFF! TURN IT OFF!
I CAN HEAR PERRY COM-PLAINING I NEVER DELIVERED THOSE PICTURES WE PROMISED HIM!
MY MOM TELLING A NEIGHBOR SHE'S WORRIED I'M IN TROUBLE AGAIN...
HOW DOES SUPERMAN MANAGE TO KEEP THIS MUCH INFORMATION IN HIS HEAD WITHOUT GOING NUTS?
SUPERMAN'S POWERS HAVE BEEN BUILDING GRADUALLY DURING THE YEARS HE'S LIVED UNDER A YELLOW SUN, JIMMY.
YOU'VE JUST BEEN THROWN IN AT THE DEEP END.
WAITASEC! YOU GUYS HEAR THAT?
WHAT?

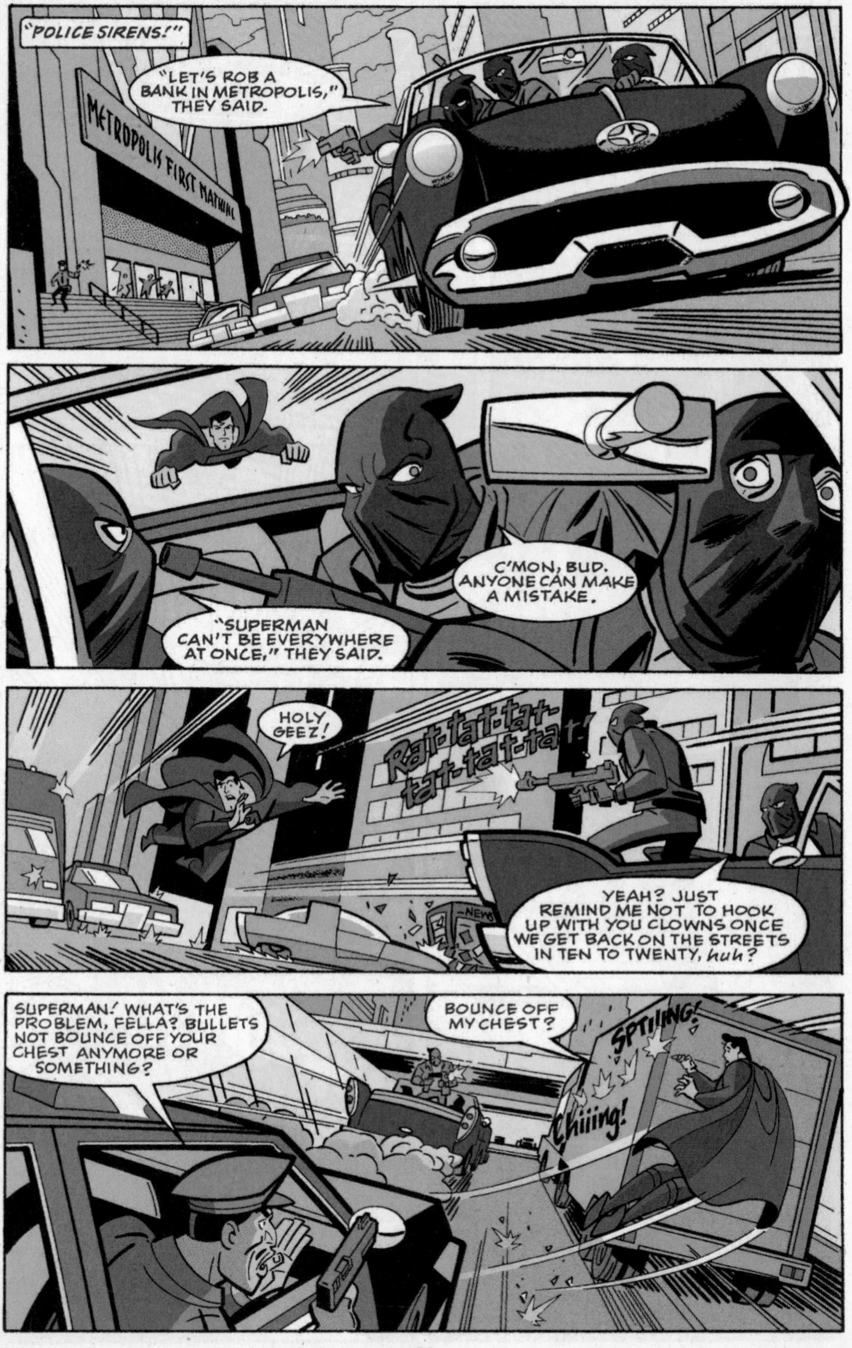
"POLICE SIRENS!"
"LET'S ROB A BANK IN METROPOLIS," THEY SAID.
METROPOLIS FIRST NATIONAL
"SUPERMAN CAN'T BE EVERYWHERE AT ONCE," THEY SAID.
C'MON, BUD. ANYONE CAN MAKE A MISTAKE.
HOLY GEEZ!
Rat-tat-tat-tat-tat-tat-tat!
YEAH? JUST REMIND ME NOT TO HOOK UP WITH YOU CLOWNS ONCE WE GET BACK ON THE STREETS IN TEN TO TWENTY, huh?
SUPERMAN! WHAT'S THE PROBLEM, FELLA? BULLETS NOT BOUNCE OFF YOUR CHEST ANYMORE OR SOMETHING?
BOUNCE OFF MY CHEST?
SPTIIING!
Chiiing!

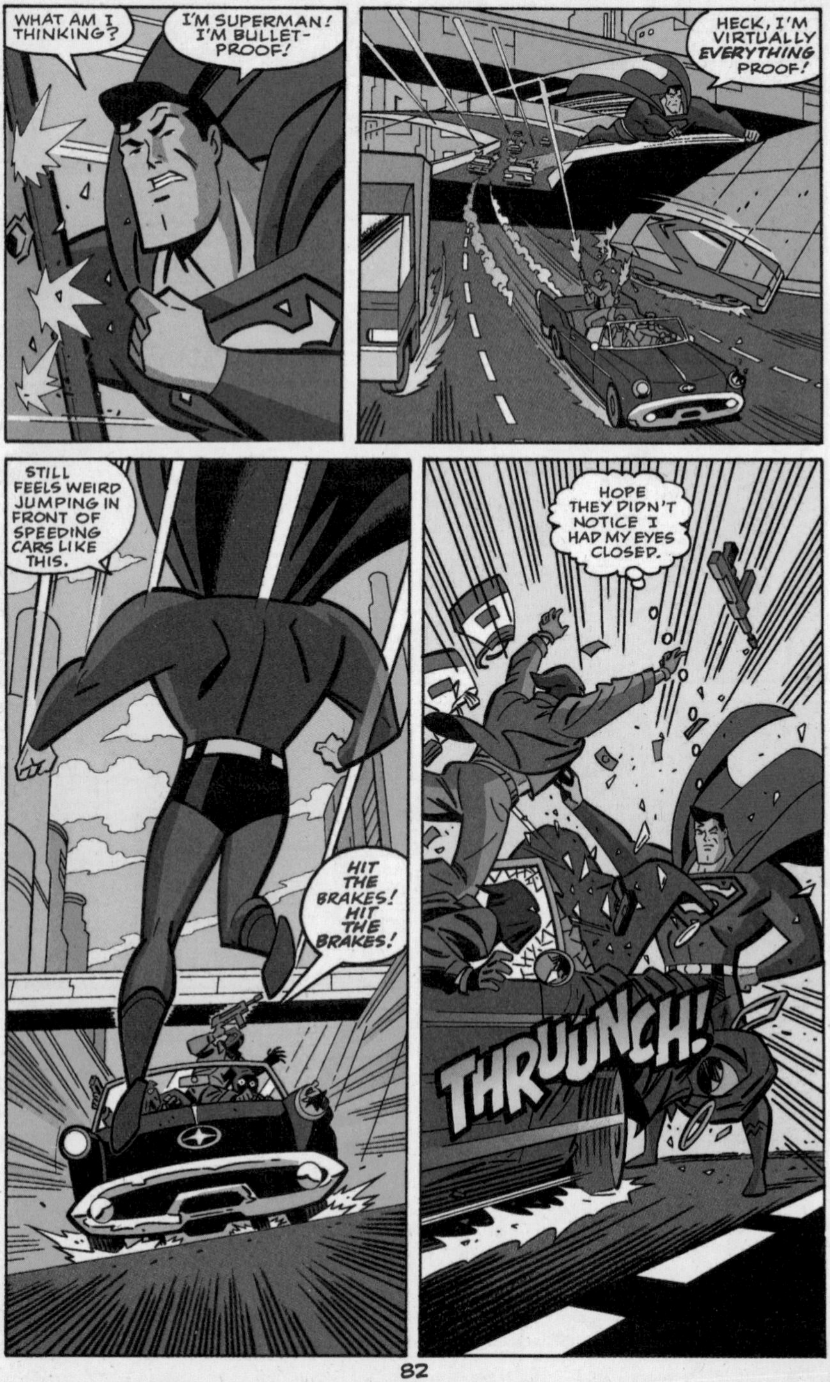
WHAT AM I THINKING?
I'M SUPERMAN! I'M BULLET-PROOF!
HECK, I'M VIRTUALLY EVERYTHING PROOF!
STILL FEELS WEIRD JUMPING IN FRONT OF SPEEDING CARS LIKE THIS.
HIT THE BRAKES! HIT THE BRAKES!
HOPE THEY DIDN'T NOTICE I HAD MY EYES CLOSED.
THRUUNCH!

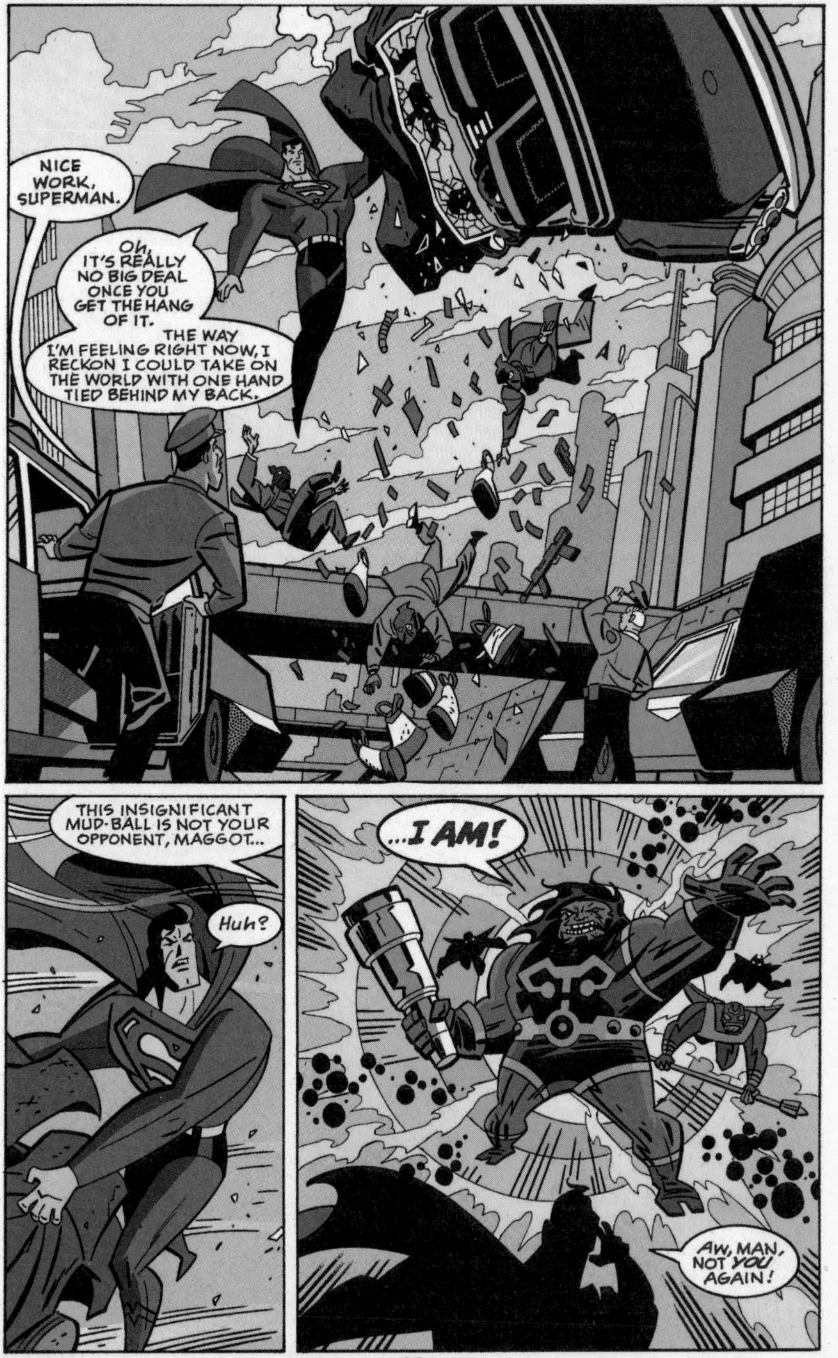
NICE WORK, SUPERMAN.
Oh, IT'S REALLY NO BIG DEAL ONCE YOU GET THE HANG OF IT.
THE WAY I'M FEELING RIGHT NOW, I RECKON I COULD TAKE ON THE WORLD WITH ONE HAND TIED BEHIND MY BACK.
THIS INSIGNIFICANT MUD-BALL IS NOT YOUR OPPONENT, MAGGOT...
Huh?
...I AM!
AW, MAN, NOT *YOU* AGAIN!

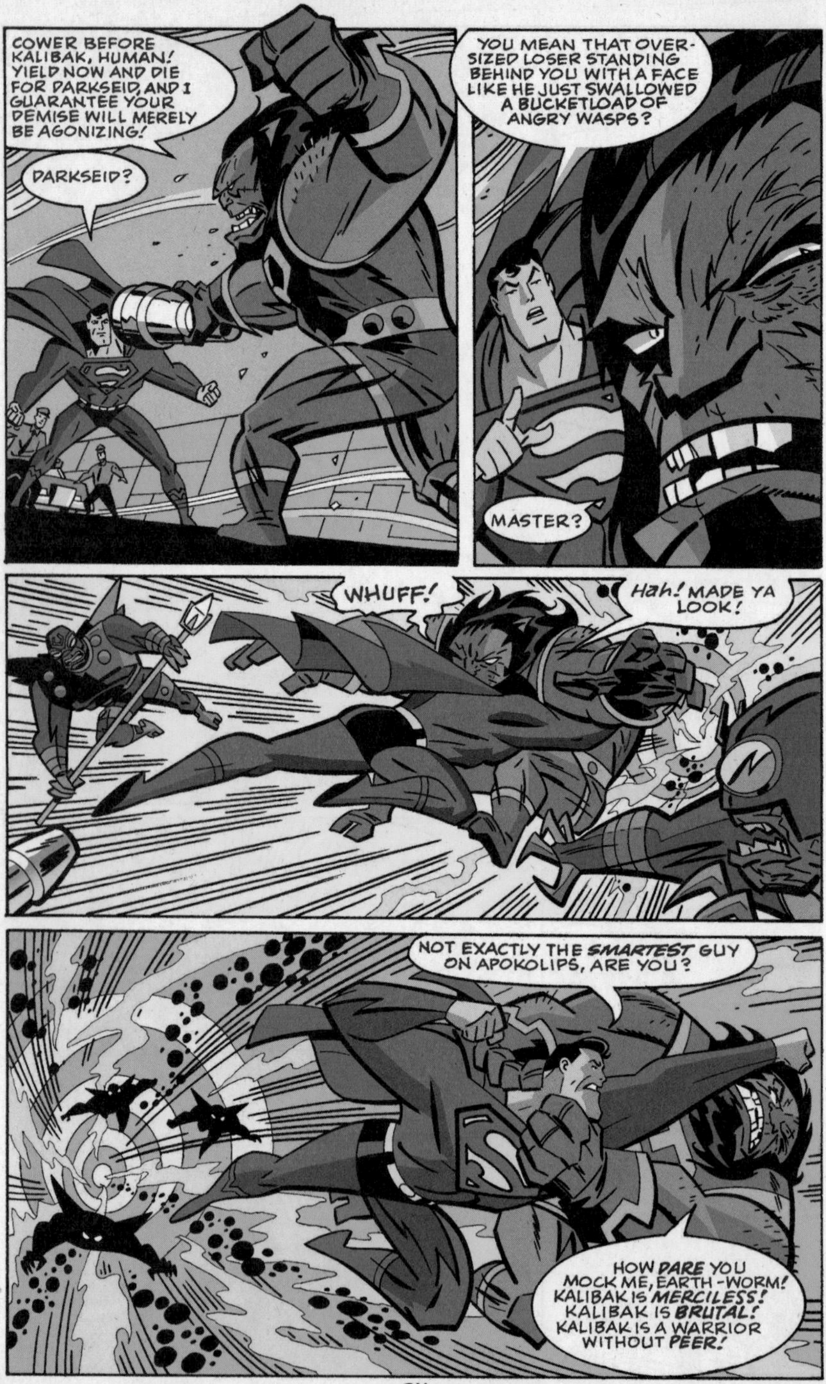
COWER BEFORE KALIBAK, HUMAN! YIELD NOW AND DIE FOR DARKSEID, AND I GUARANTEE YOUR DEMISE WILL MERELY BE AGONIZING!
DARKSEID?
YOU MEAN THAT OVER-SIZED LOSER STANDING BEHIND YOU WITH A FACE LIKE HE JUST SWALLOWED A BUCKETLOAD OF ANGRY WASPS?
MASTER?
WHUFF!
Hah! MADE YA LOOK!
NOT EXACTLY THE SMARTEST GUY ON APOKOLIPS, ARE YOU?
HOW DARE YOU MOCK ME, EARTH-WORM! KALIBAK IS MERCILESS! KALIBAK IS BRUTAL! KALIBAK IS A WARRIOR WITHOUT PEER!

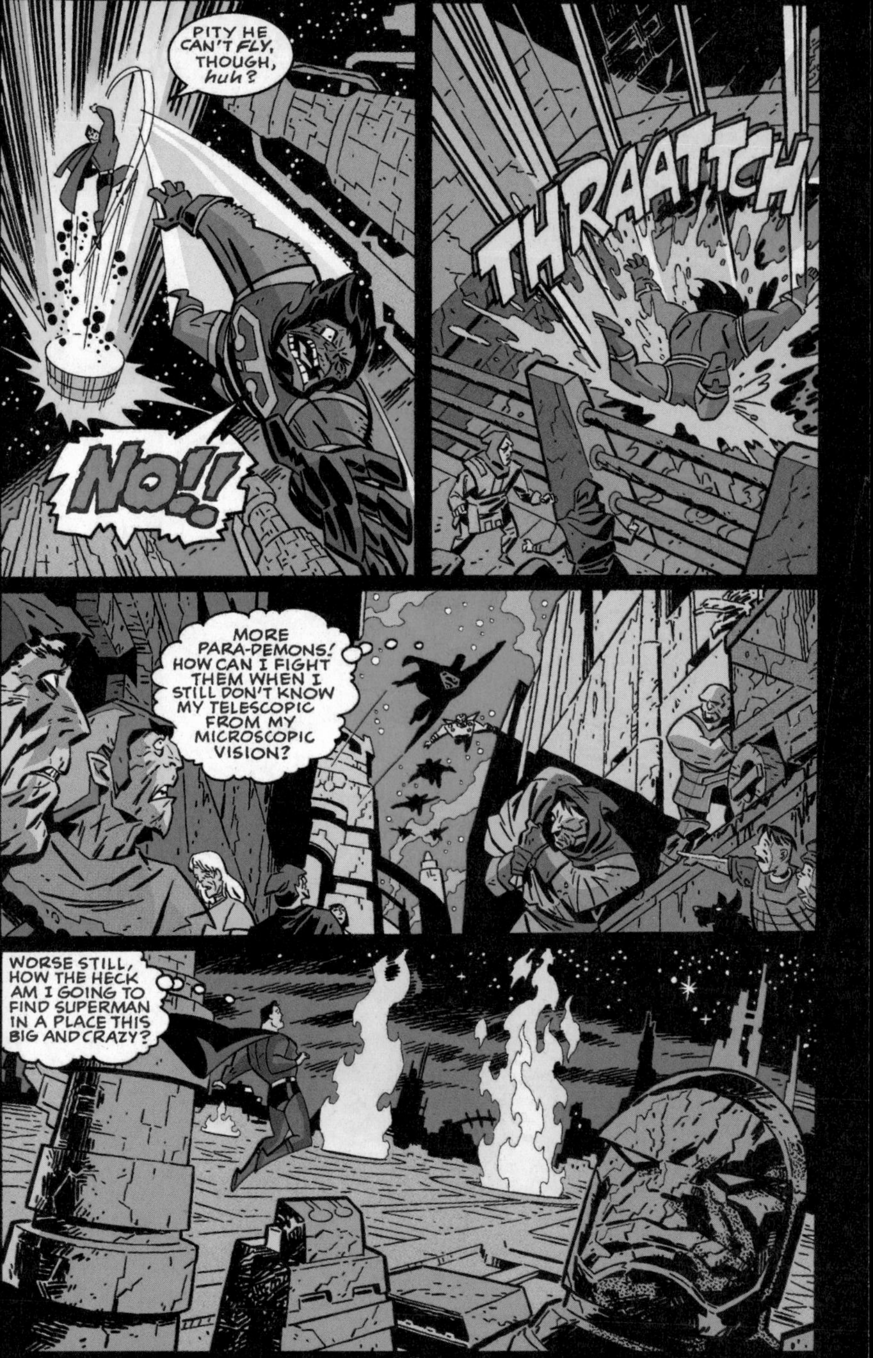
PITY HE CAN'T FLY, THOUGH, huh?
NO!!
THRAATTCH
MORE PARA-DEMONS! HOW CAN I FIGHT THEM WHEN I STILL DON'T KNOW MY TELESCOPIC FROM MY MICROSCOPIC VISION?
WORSE STILL, HOW THE HECK AM I GOING TO FIND SUPERMAN IN A PLACE THIS BIG AND CRAZY?

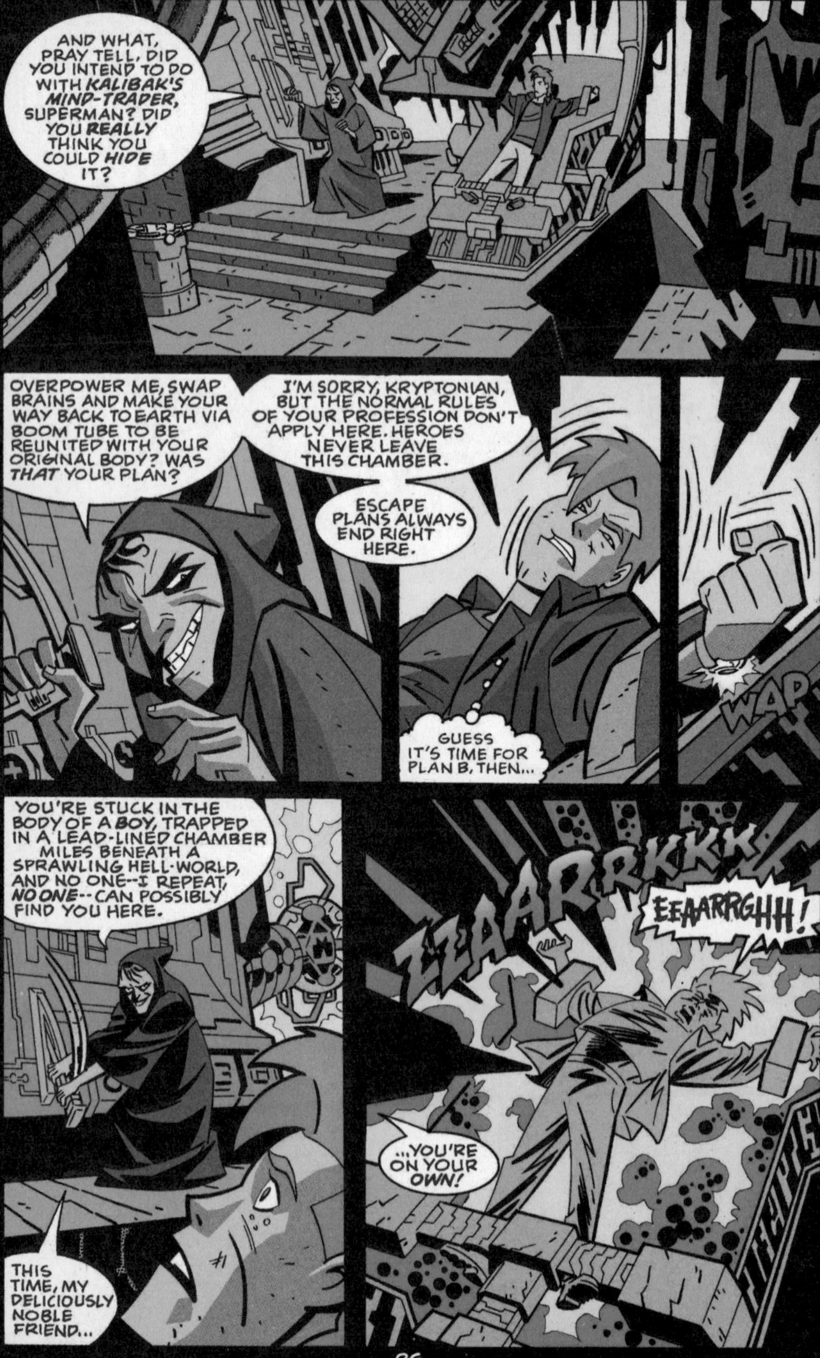

AND WHAT, PRAY TELL, DID YOU INTEND TO DO WITH KALIBAK'S MIND-TRADER, SUPERMAN? DID YOU REALLY THINK YOU COULD HIDE IT?
OVERPOWER ME, SWAP BRAINS AND MAKE YOUR WAY BACK TO EARTH VIA BOOM TUBE TO BE REUNITED WITH YOUR ORIGINAL BODY? WAS THAT YOUR PLAN?
I'M SORRY, KRYPTONIAN, BUT THE NORMAL RULES OF YOUR PROFESSION DON'T APPLY HERE. HEROES NEVER LEAVE THIS CHAMBER.
ESCAPE PLANS ALWAYS END RIGHT HERE.
GUESS IT'S TIME FOR PLAN B, THEN...
WAP
YOU'RE STUCK IN THE BODY OF A BOY, TRAPPED IN A LEAD-LINED CHAMBER MILES BENEATH A SPRAWLING HELL-WORLD, AND NO ONE--I REPEAT, NO ONE--CAN POSSIBLY FIND YOU HERE.
THIS TIME, MY DELICIOUSLY NOBLE FRIEND...
ZZAARRKKK
EEAARRGHH!
...YOU'RE ON YOUR OWN!

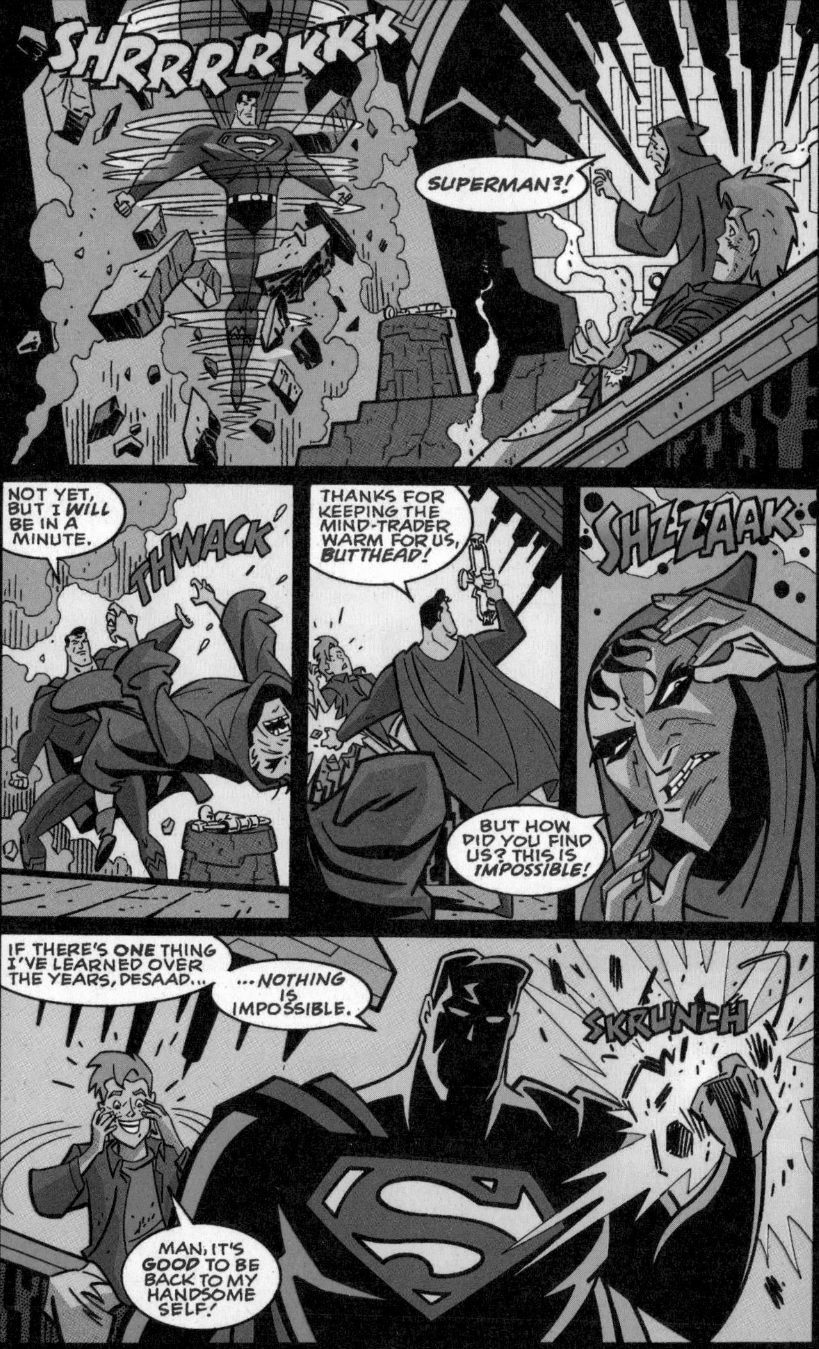

SHRRRRKKK
SUPERMAN?!
NOT YET, BUT I WILL BE IN A MINUTE.
THWACK
THANKS FOR KEEPING THE MIND-TRADER WARM FOR US, BUTTHEAD!
SHZZAAK
BUT HOW DID YOU FIND US? THIS IS IMPOSSIBLE!
IF THERE'S ONE THING I'VE LEARNED OVER THE YEARS, DESAAD...
...NOTHING IS IMPOSSIBLE.
SKRUNCH
MAN, IT'S GOOD TO BE BACK TO MY HANDSOME SELF!

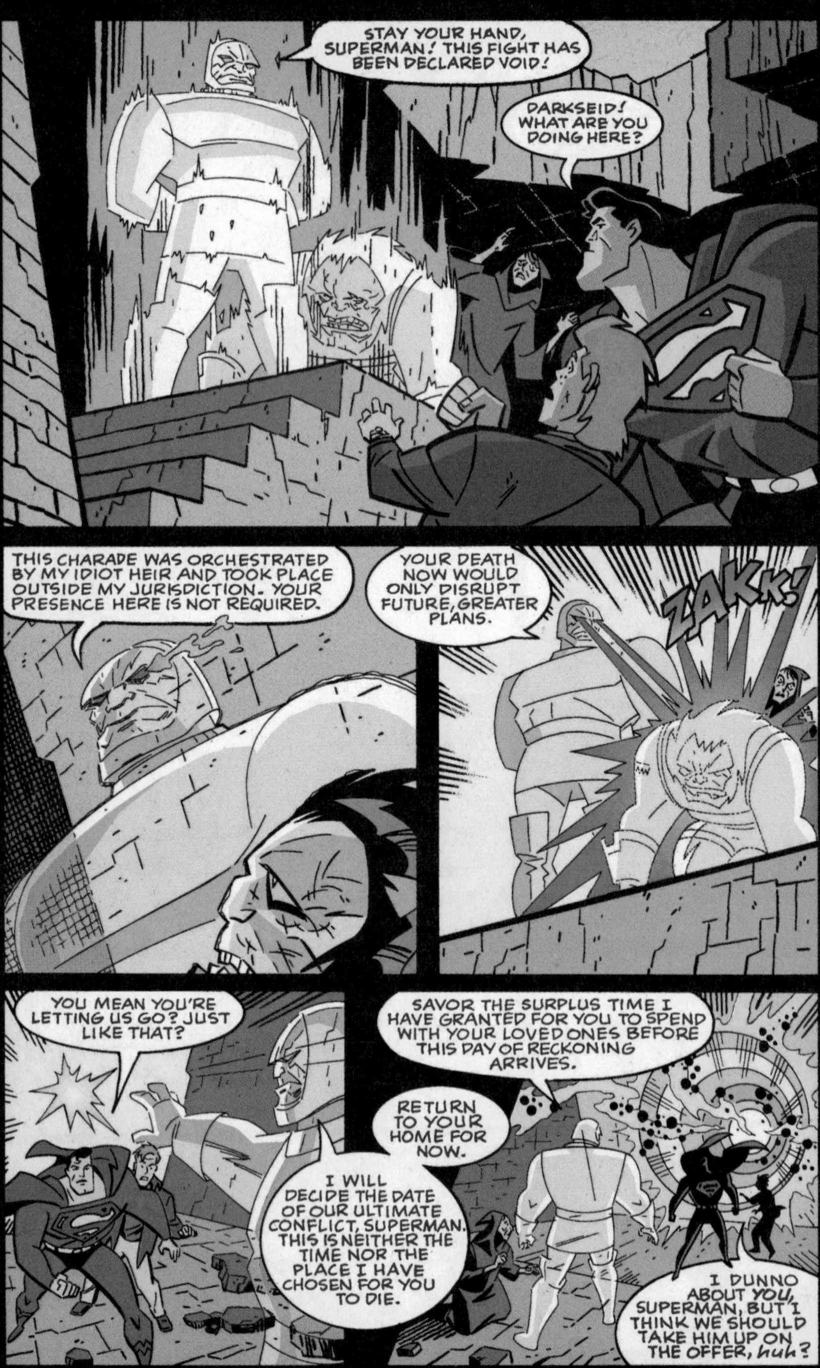
STAY YOUR HAND, SUPERMAN! THIS FIGHT HAS BEEN DECLARED VOID!
DARKSEID! WHAT ARE YOU DOING HERE?
THIS CHARADE WAS ORCHESTRATED BY MY IDIOT HEIR AND TOOK PLACE OUTSIDE MY JURISDICTION. YOUR PRESENCE HERE IS NOT REQUIRED.
YOUR DEATH NOW WOULD ONLY DISRUPT FUTURE, GREATER PLANS.
ZAKK!
YOU MEAN YOU'RE LETTING US GO? JUST LIKE THAT?
I WILL DECIDE THE DATE OF OUR ULTIMATE CONFLICT, SUPERMAN. THIS IS NEITHER THE TIME NOR THE PLACE I HAVE CHOSEN FOR YOU TO DIE.
SAVOR THE SURPLUS TIME I HAVE GRANTED FOR YOU TO SPEND WITH YOUR LOVED ONES BEFORE THIS DAY OF RECKONING ARRIVES.
RETURN TO YOUR HOME FOR NOW.
I DUNNO ABOUT *YOU*, SUPERMAN, BUT I THINK WE SHOULD TAKE HIM UP ON THE OFFER, *huh*?

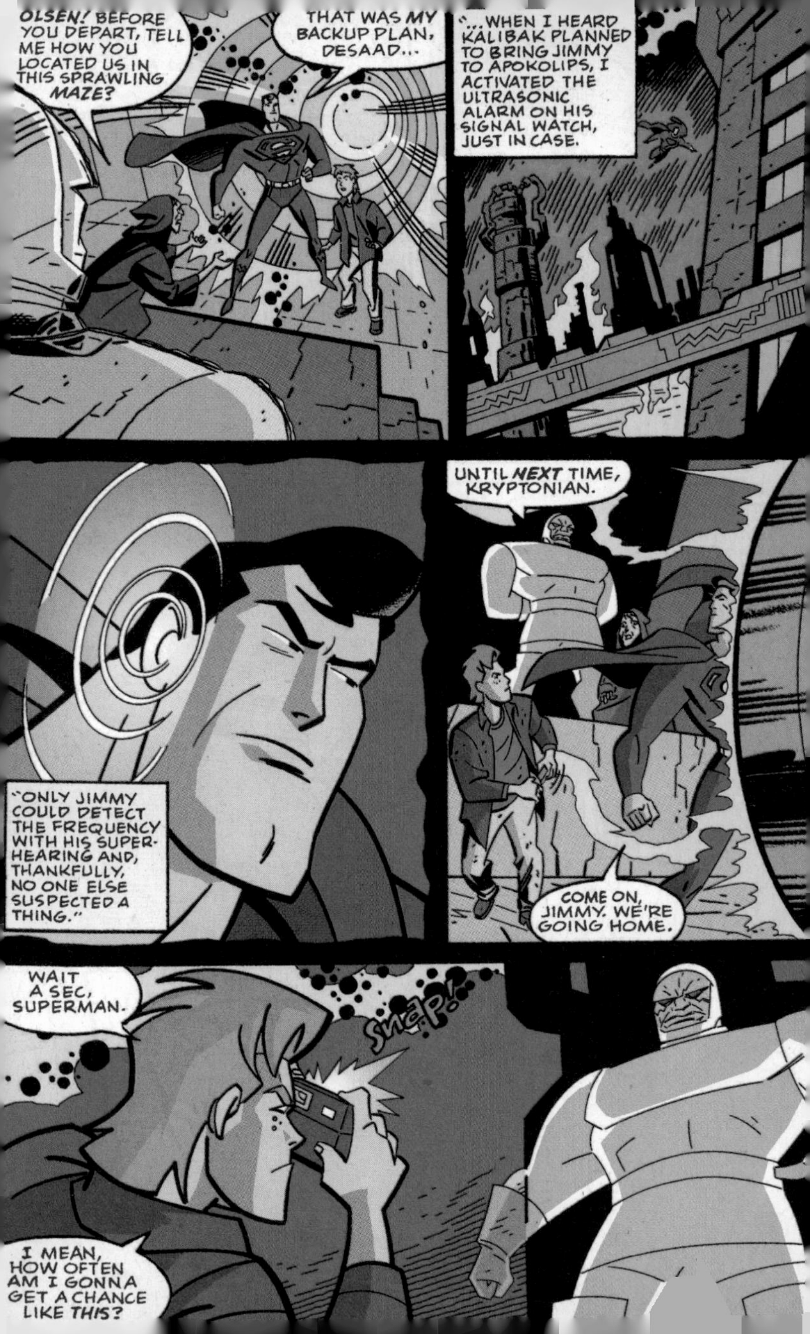
OLSEN! BEFORE YOU DEPART, TELL ME HOW YOU LOCATED US IN THIS SPRAWLING MAZE?
THAT WAS MY BACKUP PLAN, DESAAD...
"...WHEN I HEARD KALIBAK PLANNED TO BRING JIMMY TO APOKOLIPS, I ACTIVATED THE ULTRASONIC ALARM ON HIS SIGNAL WATCH, JUST IN CASE.
"ONLY JIMMY COULD DETECT THE FREQUENCY WITH HIS SUPER-HEARING AND, THANKFULLY, NO ONE ELSE SUSPECTED A THING."
UNTIL NEXT TIME, KRYPTONIAN.
COME ON, JIMMY. WE'RE GOING HOME.
WAIT A SEC, SUPERMAN.
SNAP!
I MEAN, HOW OFTEN AM I GONNA GET A CHANCE LIKE THIS?

CUB REPORTER
...HES APOKOLIPS PLOT
BY JAMES OLSEN AND ??? C. KENT

WELL, OLSEN, I'VE GOT TO HAND IT TO YOU, SON...

...IT'S NOT EVERY DAY THE PLANET RUNS A PHOTO OF AN ALIEN DICTATOR FROM ANOTHER DIMENSION ON OUR FRONT PAGE.

WHAT DID THE METROPOLIS EAGLE LEAD WITH THIS MORNING, KENT?

JUST THE METROPOLOTTO WINNING NUMBERS AND A RUMOR LEX LUTHOR IS CONSIDERING A WIG, CHIEF.

≈A-hem≈

S-SOMETHING *WRONG*, MISS LANE?

YOU *BET* THERE IS, BUSTER. THIS STARTED OUT AS *OUR* STORY. HOW DID *SMALLVILLE* END UP WITH THE BY-LINE?

THREE SODAS, TWO CHEESEBURGERS AND A LARGE FRIES, LOIS.

YOU GREEDY LITTLE SKUNK! I OUGHT TO PUNCH YOUR LIGHTS OUT!

SORRY, MISS LANE.

WOULD YOU BELIEVE I WASN'T *MYSELF* AT THE TIME?

End

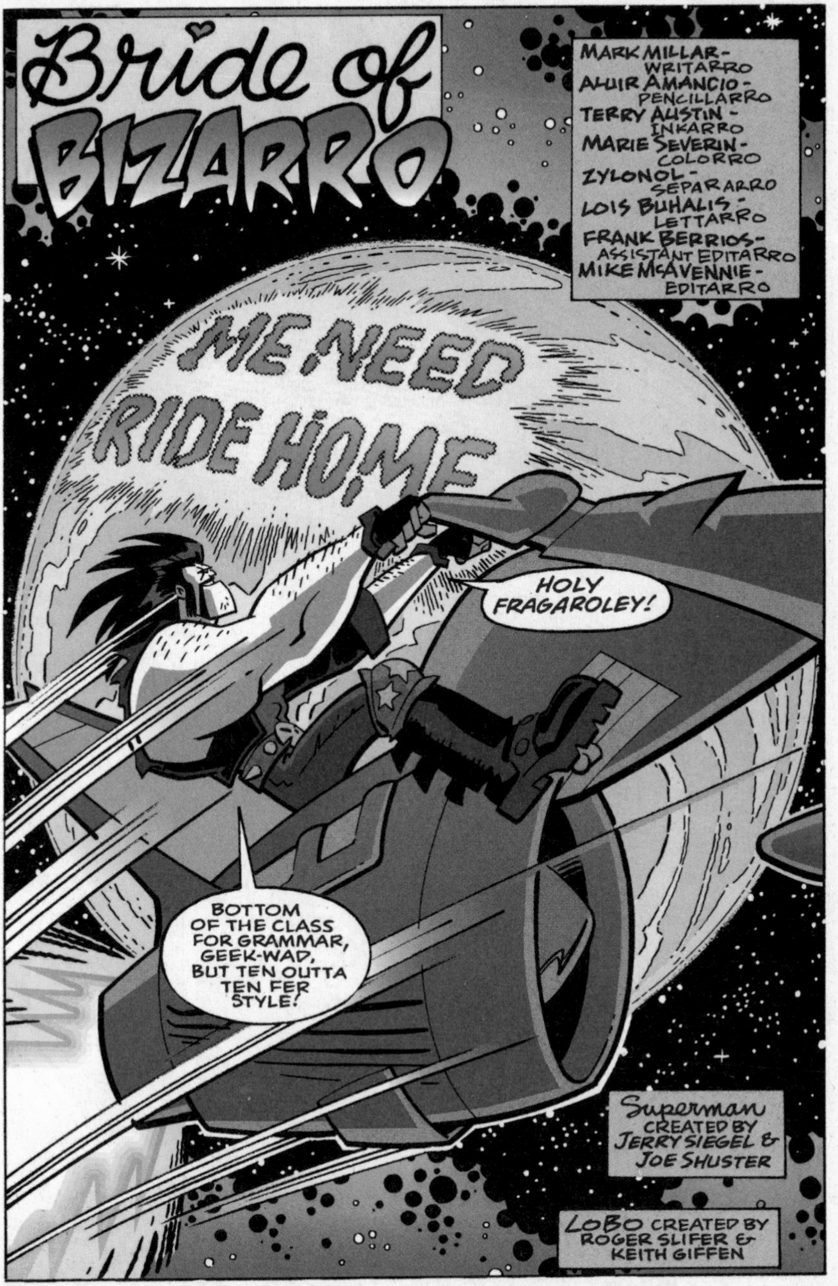

Bride of BIZARRO
MARK MILLAR - WRITARRO
ALUIR AMANCIO - PENCILLARRO
TERRY AUSTIN - INKARRO
MARIE SEVERIN - COLORRO
ZYLONOL - SEPARARRO
LOIS BUHALIS - LETTARRO
FRANK BERRIOS - ASSISTANT EDITARRO
MIKE McAVENNIE - EDITARRO
ME NEED RIDE HOME
HOLY FRAGAROLEY!
BOTTOM OF THE CLASS FOR GRAMMAR, GEEK-WAD, BUT TEN OUTTA TEN FER STYLE!
Superman CREATED BY JERRY SIEGEL & JOE SHUSTER
LOBO CREATED BY ROGER SLIFER & KEITH GIFFEN

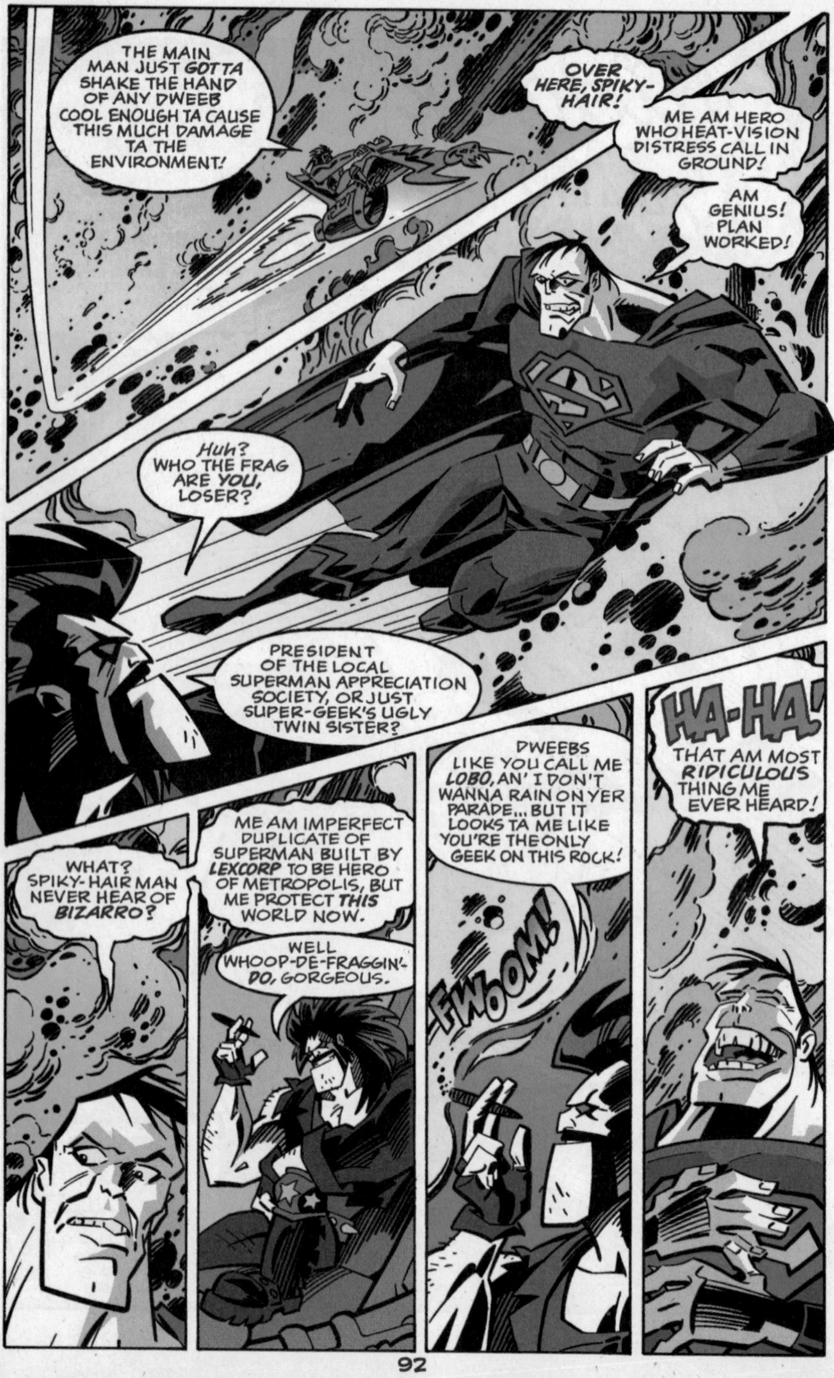
THE MAIN MAN JUST GOTTA SHAKE THE HAND OF ANY DWEEB COOL ENOUGH TA CAUSE THIS MUCH DAMAGE TA THE ENVIRONMENT!
OVER HERE, SPIKY-HAIR!
ME AM HERO WHO HEAT-VISION DISTRESS CALL IN GROUND!
AM GENIUS! PLAN WORKED!
Huh? WHO THE FRAG ARE YOU, LOSER?
PRESIDENT OF THE LOCAL SUPERMAN APPRECIATION SOCIETY, OR JUST SUPER-GEEK'S UGLY TWIN SISTER?
WHAT? SPIKY-HAIR MAN NEVER HEAR OF BIZARRO?
ME AM IMPERFECT DUPLICATE OF SUPERMAN BUILT BY LEXCORP TO BE HERO OF METROPOLIS, BUT ME PROTECT THIS WORLD NOW.
WELL WHOOP-DE-FRAGGIN'-DO, GORGEOUS.
DWEEBS LIKE YOU CALL ME LOBO, AN' I DON'T WANNA RAIN ON YER PARADE... BUT IT LOOKS TA ME LIKE YOU'RE THE ONLY GEEK ON THIS ROCK!
FWOOM!
HA-HA!
THAT AM MOST RIDICULOUS THING ME EVER HEARD!

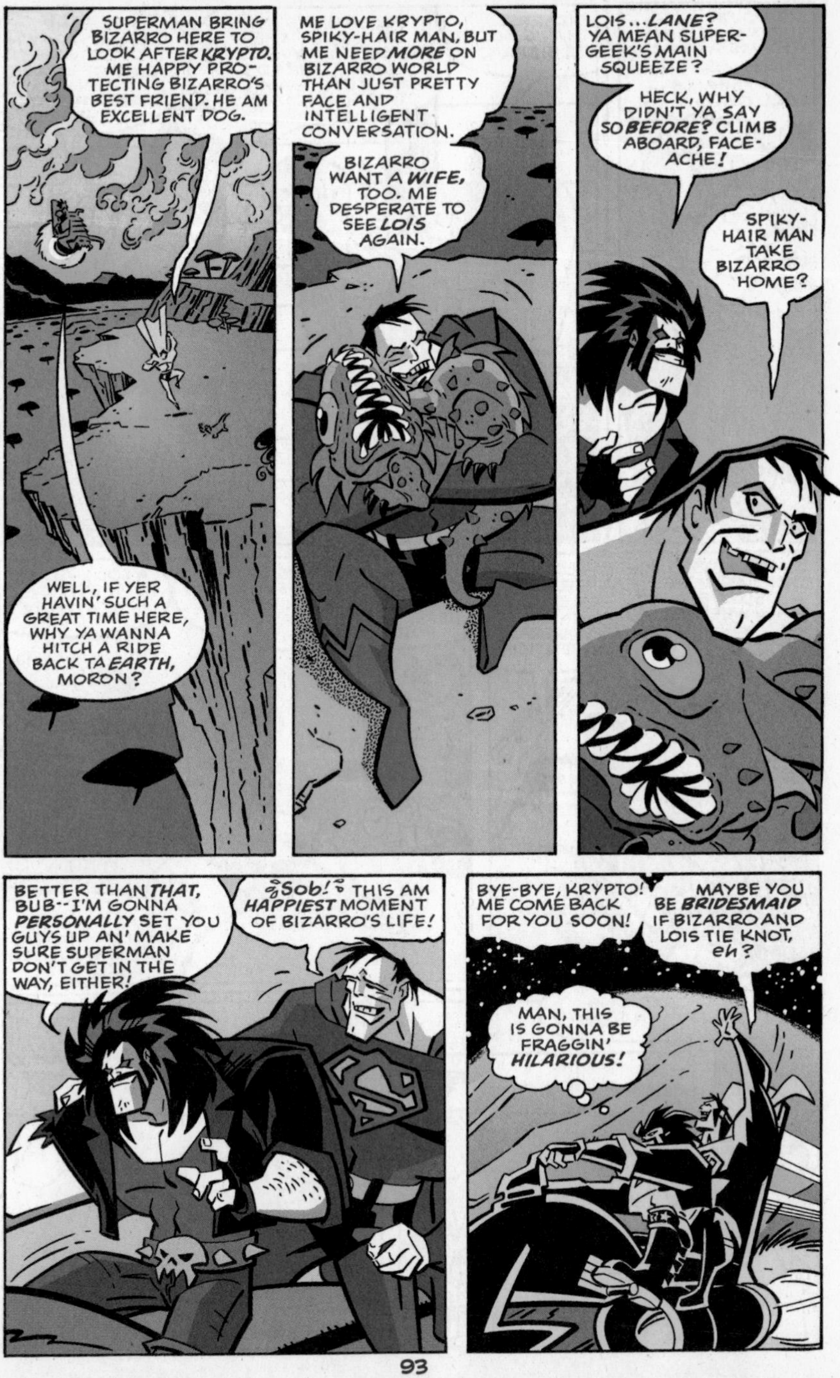
SUPERMAN BRING BIZARRO HERE TO LOOK AFTER *KRYPTO*. ME HAPPY PROTECTING BIZARRO'S BEST FRIEND. HE AM EXCELLENT DOG.
WELL, IF YER HAVIN' SUCH A GREAT TIME HERE, WHY YA WANNA HITCH A RIDE BACK TA *EARTH*, MORON?
ME LOVE KRYPTO, SPIKY-HAIR MAN, BUT ME NEED *MORE* ON BIZARRO WORLD THAN JUST PRETTY FACE AND INTELLIGENT CONVERSATION.
BIZARRO WANT A *WIFE*, TOO. ME DESPERATE TO SEE *LOIS* AGAIN.
LOIS...*LANE*? YA MEAN SUPER-GEEK'S MAIN SQUEEZE?
HECK, WHY DIDN'T YA SAY SO *BEFORE*? CLIMB ABOARD, FACE-ACHE!
SPIKY-HAIR MAN TAKE BIZARRO HOME?
BETTER THAN *THAT*, BUB--I'M GONNA *PERSONALLY* SET YOU GUYS UP AN' MAKE SURE SUPERMAN DON'T GET IN THE WAY, EITHER!
Sob! THIS AM *HAPPIEST* MOMENT OF BIZARRO'S LIFE!
BYE-BYE, KRYPTO! ME COME BACK FOR YOU SOON!
MAYBE YOU BE *BRIDESMAID* IF BIZARRO AND LOIS TIE KNOT, eh?
MAN, THIS IS GONNA BE FRAGGIN' *HILARIOUS*!

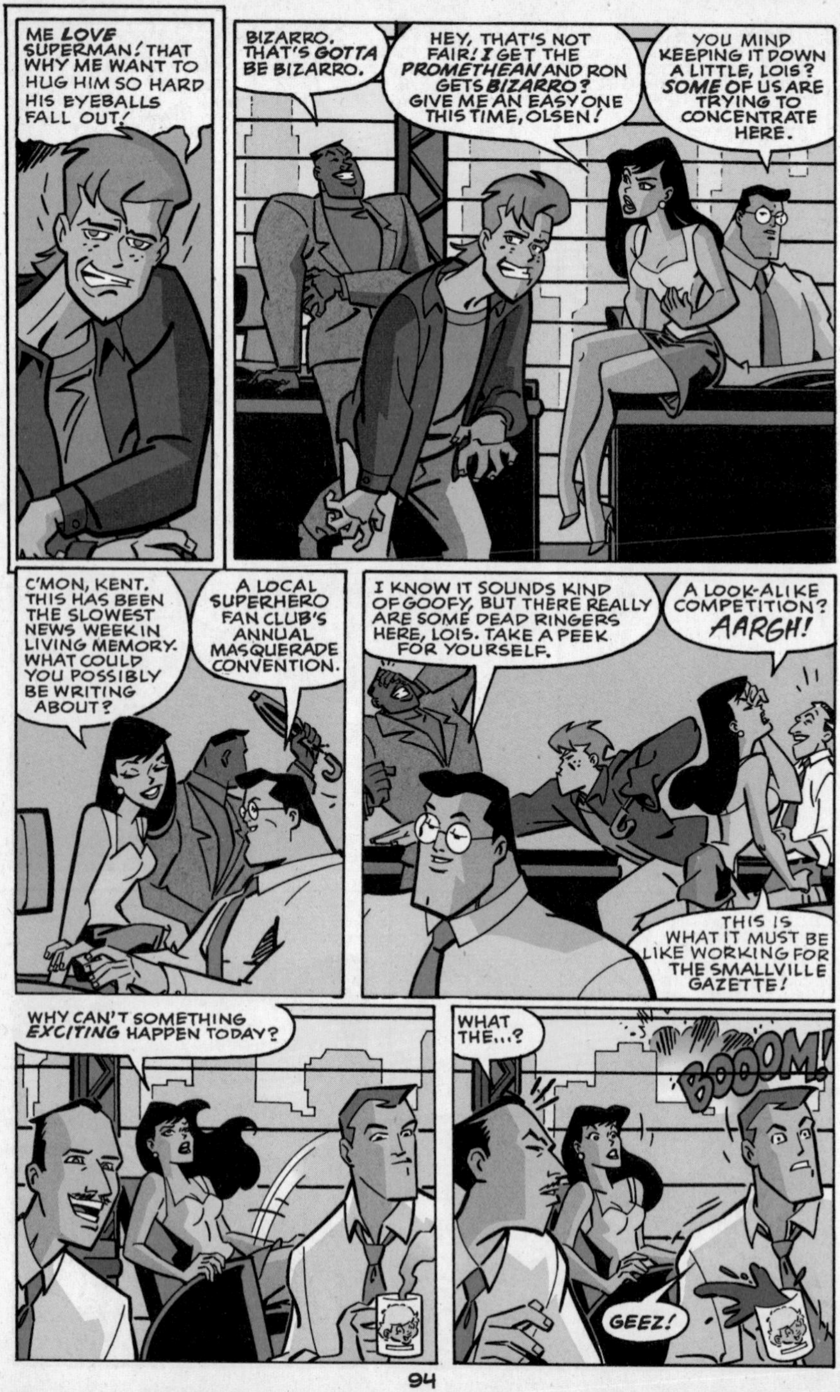

ME *LOVE* SUPERMAN! THAT WHY ME WANT TO HUG HIM SO HARD HIS EYEBALLS FALL OUT!
BIZARRO. THAT'S *GOTTA* BE BIZARRO.
HEY, THAT'S NOT FAIR! *I* GET THE *PROMETHEAN* AND RON GETS *BIZARRO?* GIVE ME AN EASY ONE THIS TIME, OLSEN!
YOU MIND KEEPING IT DOWN A LITTLE, LOIS? *SOME* OF US ARE TRYING TO CONCENTRATE HERE.
C'MON, KENT. THIS HAS BEEN THE SLOWEST NEWS WEEK IN LIVING MEMORY. WHAT COULD YOU POSSIBLY BE WRITING ABOUT?
A LOCAL SUPERHERO FAN CLUB'S ANNUAL MASQUERADE CONVENTION.
I KNOW IT SOUNDS KIND OF GOOFY, BUT THERE REALLY ARE SOME DEAD RINGERS HERE, LOIS. TAKE A PEEK FOR YOURSELF.
A LOOK-ALIKE COMPETITION? *AARGH!*
THIS IS WHAT IT MUST BE LIKE WORKING FOR THE SMALLVILLE GAZETTE!
WHY CAN'T SOMETHING *EXCITING* HAPPEN TODAY?
WHAT THE...?
BOOOM!
GEEZ!

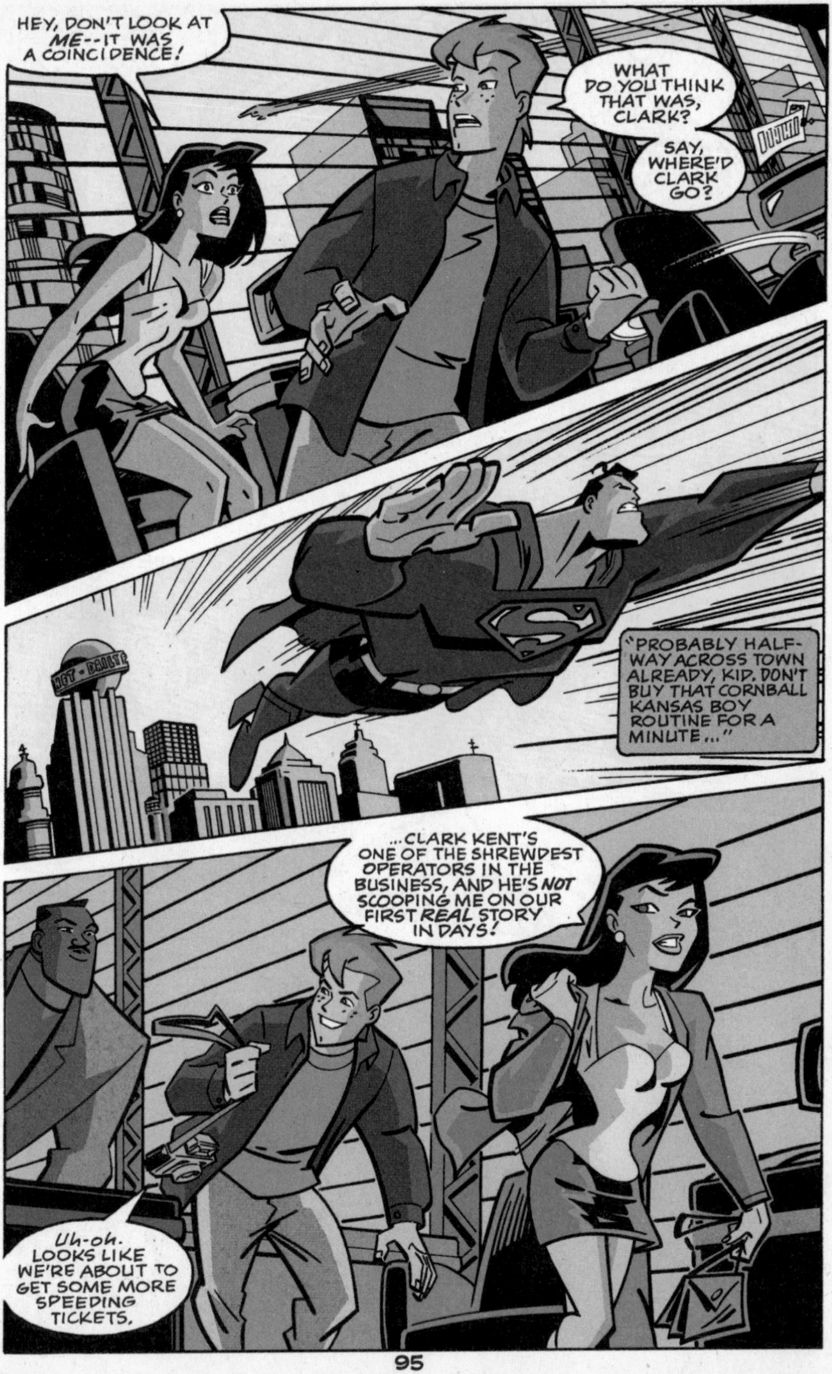
HEY, DON'T LOOK AT ME--IT WAS A COINCIDENCE!
WHAT DO YOU THINK THAT WAS, CLARK?
SAY, WHERE'D CLARK GO?
"PROBABLY HALF-WAY ACROSS TOWN ALREADY, KID. DON'T BUY THAT CORNBALL KANSAS BOY ROUTINE FOR A MINUTE..."
...CLARK KENT'S ONE OF THE SHREWDEST OPERATORS IN THE BUSINESS, AND HE'S NOT SCOOPING ME ON OUR FIRST REAL STORY IN DAYS!
Uh-oh. LOOKS LIKE WE'RE ABOUT TO GET SOME MORE SPEEDING TICKETS.

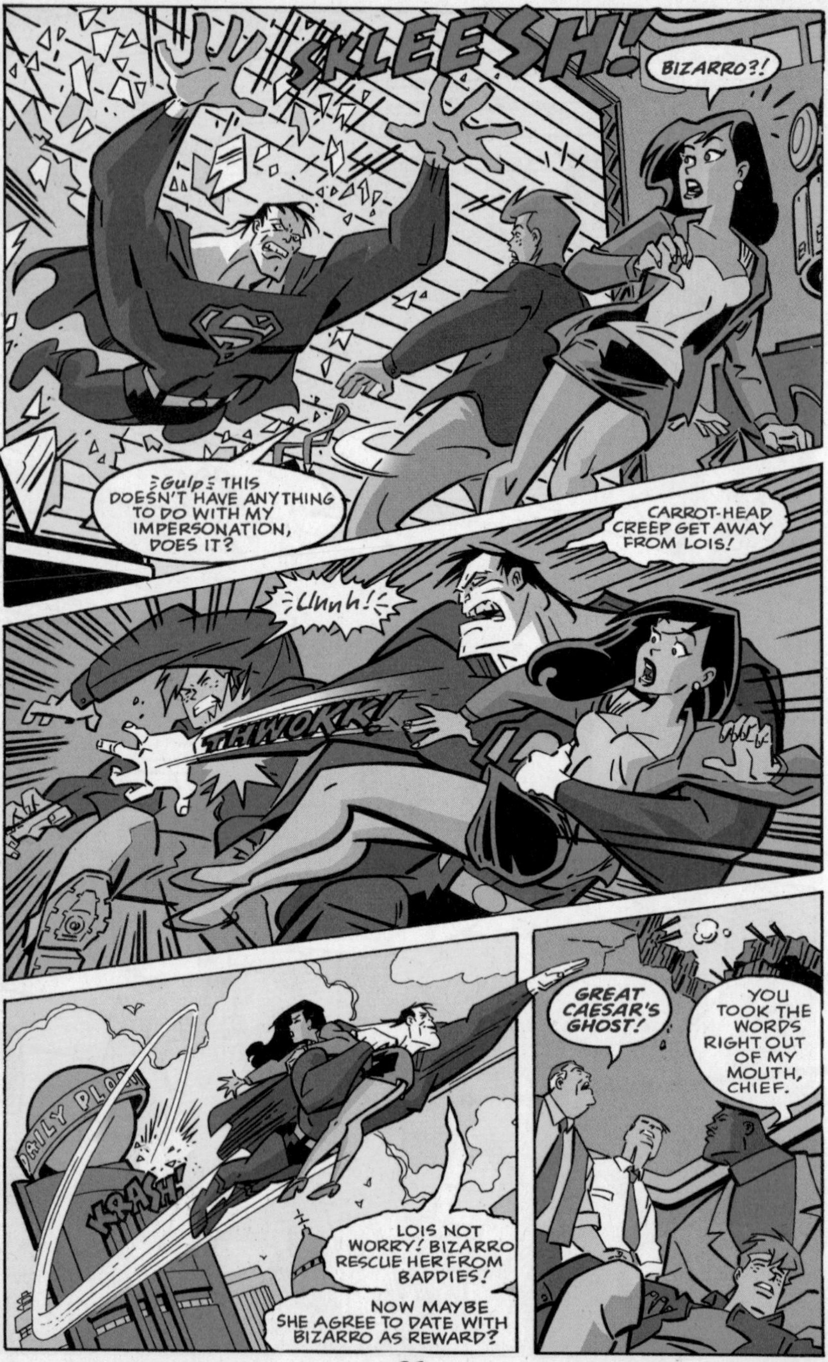
SKLEESH!
BIZARRO?!
Gulp THIS DOESN'T HAVE ANYTHING TO DO WITH MY IMPERSONATION, DOES IT?
CARROT-HEAD CREEP GET AWAY FROM LOIS!
Unnh!
THWOKK!
DAILY PLANET
KRASH!
LOIS NOT WORRY! BIZARRO RESCUE HER FROM BADDIES!
NOW MAYBE SHE AGREE TO DATE WITH BIZARRO AS REWARD?
GREAT CAESAR'S GHOST!
YOU TOOK THE WORDS RIGHT OUT OF MY MOUTH, CHIEF.

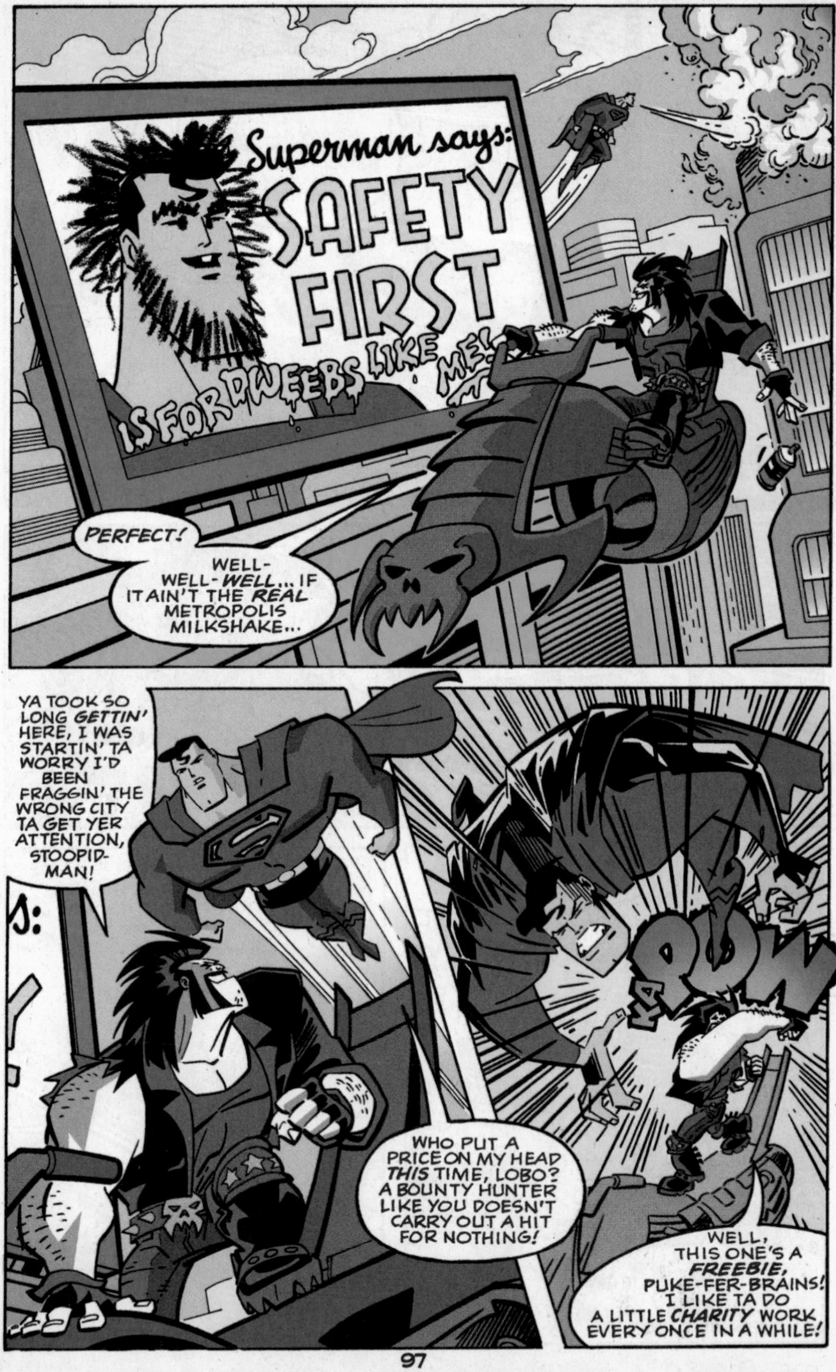
Superman says:
SAFETY FIRST
IS FOR DWEEBS LIKE ME!
PERFECT!
WELL-WELL-WELL... IF IT AIN'T THE REAL METROPOLIS MILKSHAKE...
YA TOOK SO LONG GETTIN' HERE, I WAS STARTIN' TA WORRY I'D BEEN FRAGGIN' THE WRONG CITY TA GET YER ATTENTION, STOOPID-MAN!
WHO PUT A PRICE ON MY HEAD THIS TIME, LOBO? A BOUNTY HUNTER LIKE YOU DOESN'T CARRY OUT A HIT FOR NOTHING!
KA-POW
WELL, THIS ONE'S A FREEBIE, PUKE-FER-BRAINS! I LIKE TA DO A LITTLE CHARITY WORK EVERY ONCE IN A WHILE!

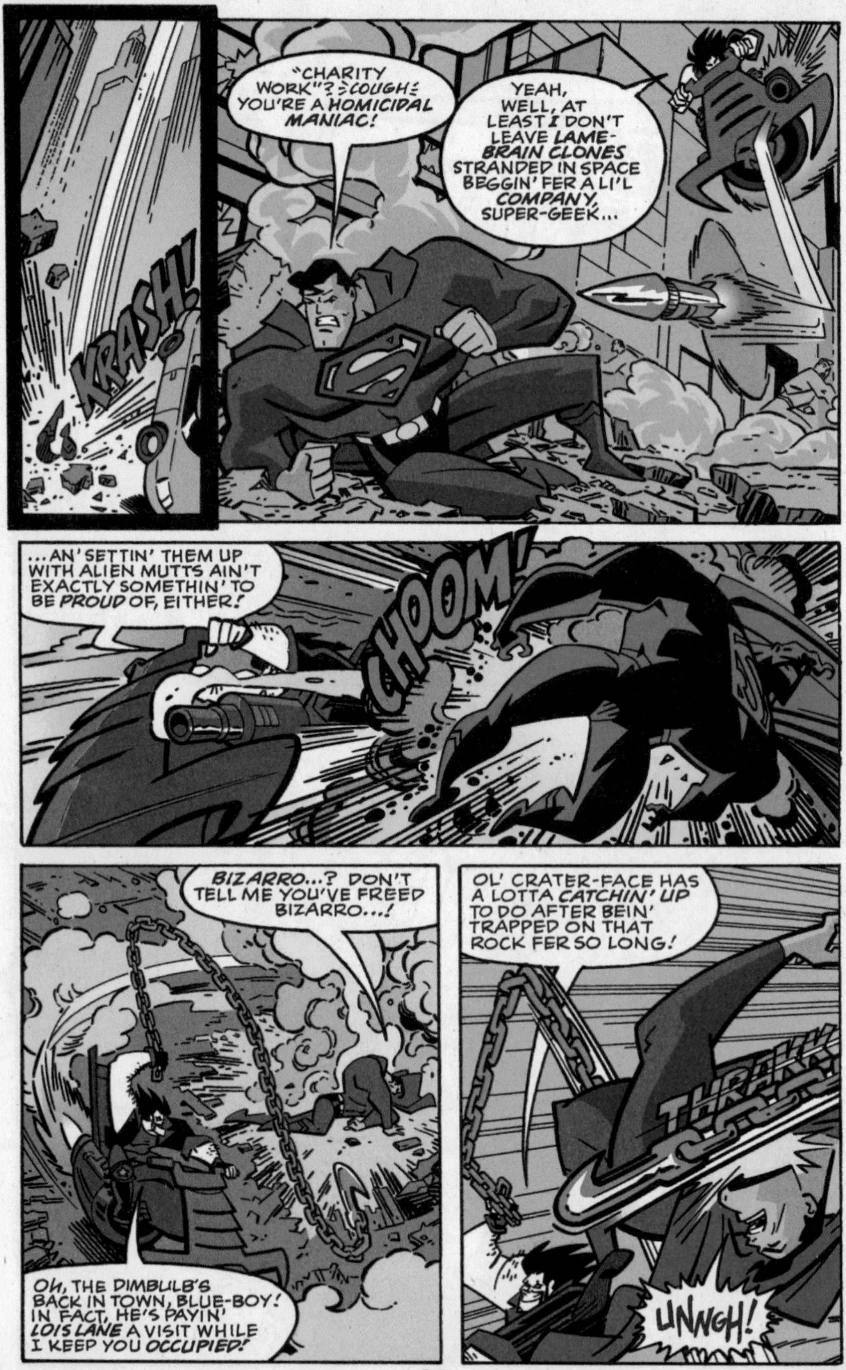

"CHARITY WORK"? ≡COUGH≡ YOU'RE A HOMICIDAL MANIAC!
YEAH, WELL, AT LEAST I DON'T LEAVE LAME-BRAIN CLONES STRANDED IN SPACE BEGGIN' FER A LI'L COMPANY, SUPER-GEEK...
KRASH!
...AN' SETTIN' THEM UP WITH ALIEN MUTTS AIN'T EXACTLY SOMETHIN' TO BE PROUD OF, EITHER!
CHOOOM!
BIZARRO...? DON'T TELL ME YOU'VE FREED BIZARRO...!
OH, THE DIMBULB'S BACK IN TOWN, BLUE-BOY! IN FACT, HE'S PAYIN' LOIS LANE A VISIT WHILE I KEEP YOU OCCUPIED!
OL' CRATER-FACE HAS A LOTTA CATCHIN' UP TO DO AFTER BEIN' TRAPPED ON THAT ROCK FER SO LONG!
UNNGH!

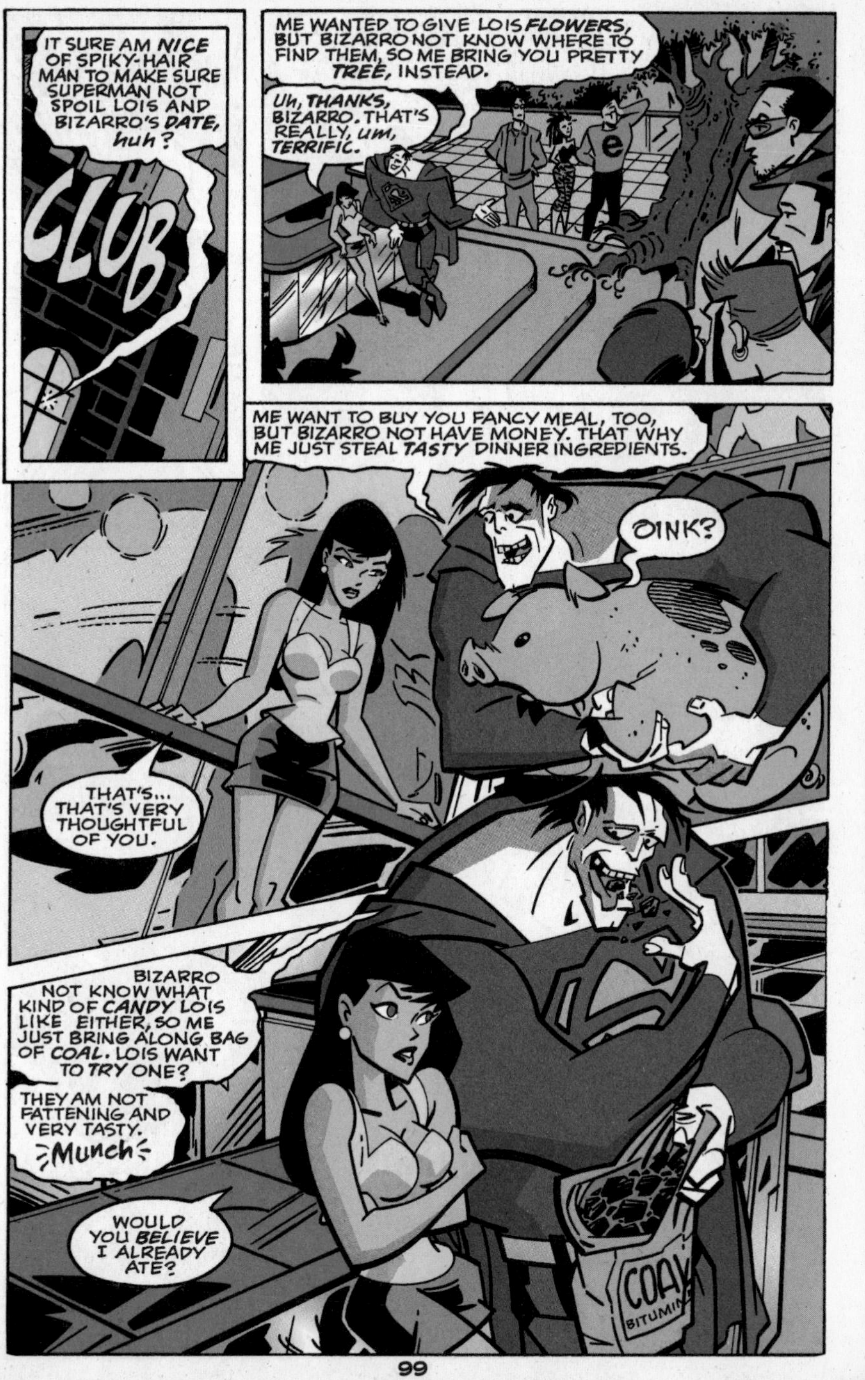
IT SURE AM NICE OF SPIKY-HAIR MAN TO MAKE SURE SUPERMAN NOT SPOIL LOIS AND BIZARRO'S DATE, huh?
CLUB
ME WANTED TO GIVE LOIS FLOWERS, BUT BIZARRO NOT KNOW WHERE TO FIND THEM, SO ME BRING YOU PRETTY TREE, INSTEAD.
Uh, THANKS, BIZARRO. THAT'S REALLY, um, TERRIFIC.
ME WANT TO BUY YOU FANCY MEAL, TOO, BUT BIZARRO NOT HAVE MONEY. THAT WHY ME JUST STEAL TASTY DINNER INGREDIENTS.
OINK?
THAT'S... THAT'S VERY THOUGHTFUL OF YOU.
BIZARRO NOT KNOW WHAT KIND OF CANDY LOIS LIKE EITHER, SO ME JUST BRING ALONG BAG OF COAL. LOIS WANT TO TRY ONE?
THEY AM NOT FATTENING AND VERY TASTY.
Munch
WOULD YOU BELIEVE I ALREADY ATE?
COAL
BITUMIN

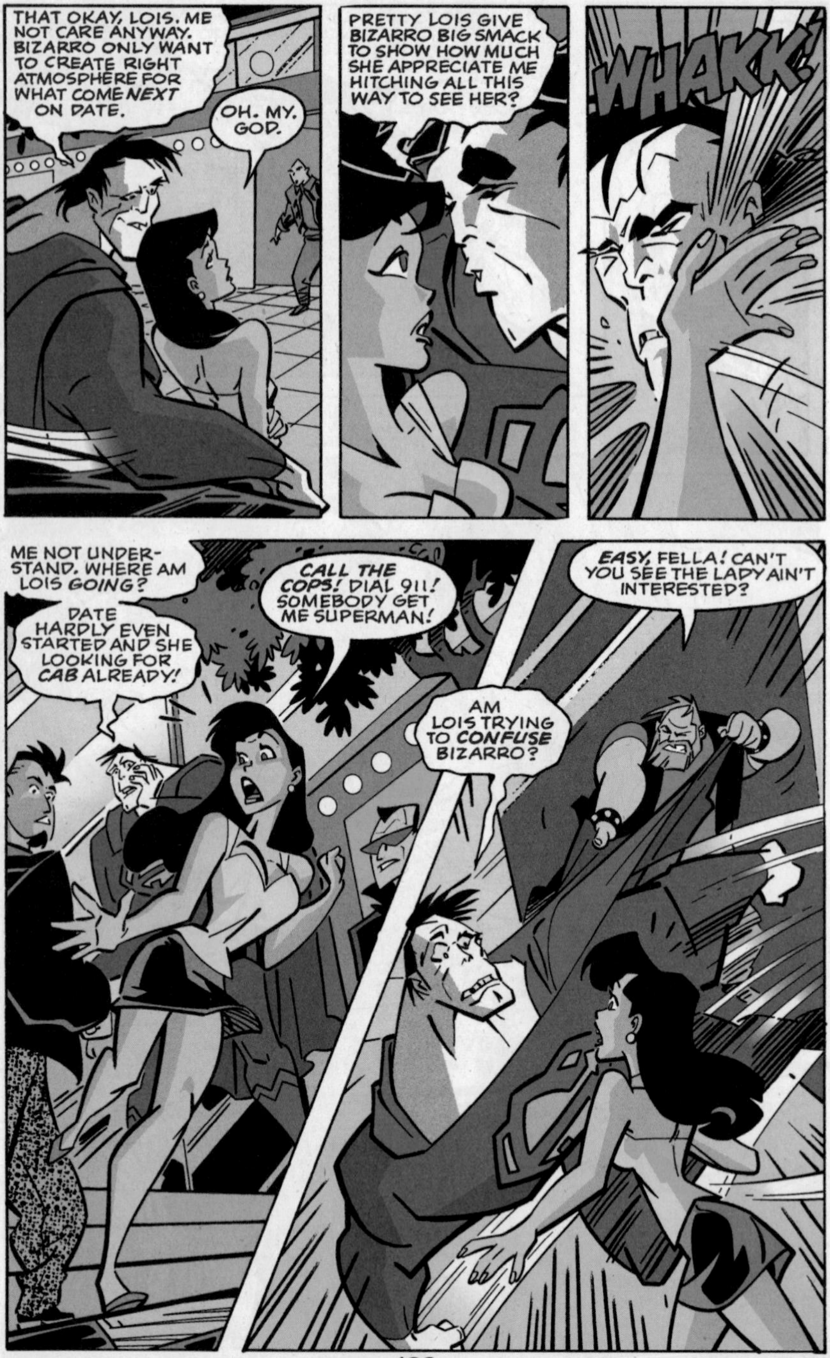
THAT OKAY, LOIS. ME NOT CARE ANYWAY. BIZARRO ONLY WANT TO CREATE RIGHT ATMOSPHERE FOR WHAT COME *NEXT* ON DATE.
OH. MY. GOD.
PRETTY LOIS GIVE BIZARRO BIG SMACK TO SHOW HOW MUCH SHE APPRECIATE ME HITCHING ALL THIS WAY TO SEE HER?
WHAKK!
ME NOT UNDER-STAND. WHERE AM LOIS *GOING*?
DATE HARDLY EVEN STARTED AND SHE LOOKING FOR *CAB* ALREADY!
CALL THE COPS! DIAL 911! SOMEBODY GET ME SUPERMAN!
AM LOIS TRYING TO *CONFUSE* BIZARRO?
EASY, FELLA! CAN'T YOU SEE THE LADY AIN'T INTERESTED?

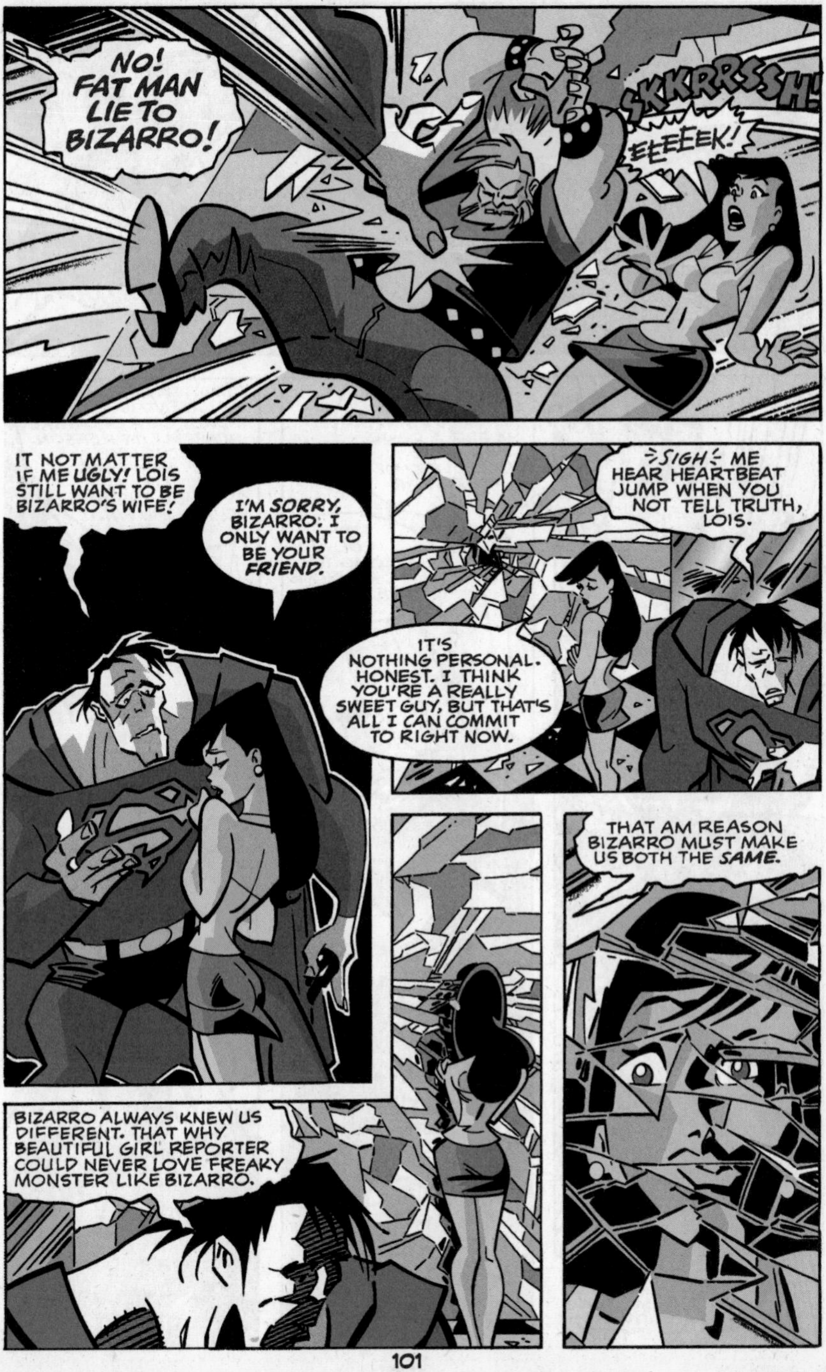
NO! FAT MAN LIE TO BIZARRO!
SKKRRSSH!
EEEEEK!
IT NOT MATTER IF ME UGLY! LOIS STILL WANT TO BE BIZARRO'S WIFE!
I'M SORRY, BIZARRO. I ONLY WANT TO BE YOUR FRIEND.
IT'S NOTHING PERSONAL. HONEST. I THINK YOU'RE A REALLY SWEET GUY, BUT THAT'S ALL I CAN COMMIT TO RIGHT NOW.
SIGH ME HEAR HEARTBEAT JUMP WHEN YOU NOT TELL TRUTH, LOIS.
BIZARRO ALWAYS KNEW US DIFFERENT. THAT WHY BEAUTIFUL GIRL REPORTER COULD NEVER LOVE FREAKY MONSTER LIKE BIZARRO.
THAT AM REASON BIZARRO MUST MAKE US BOTH THE SAME.

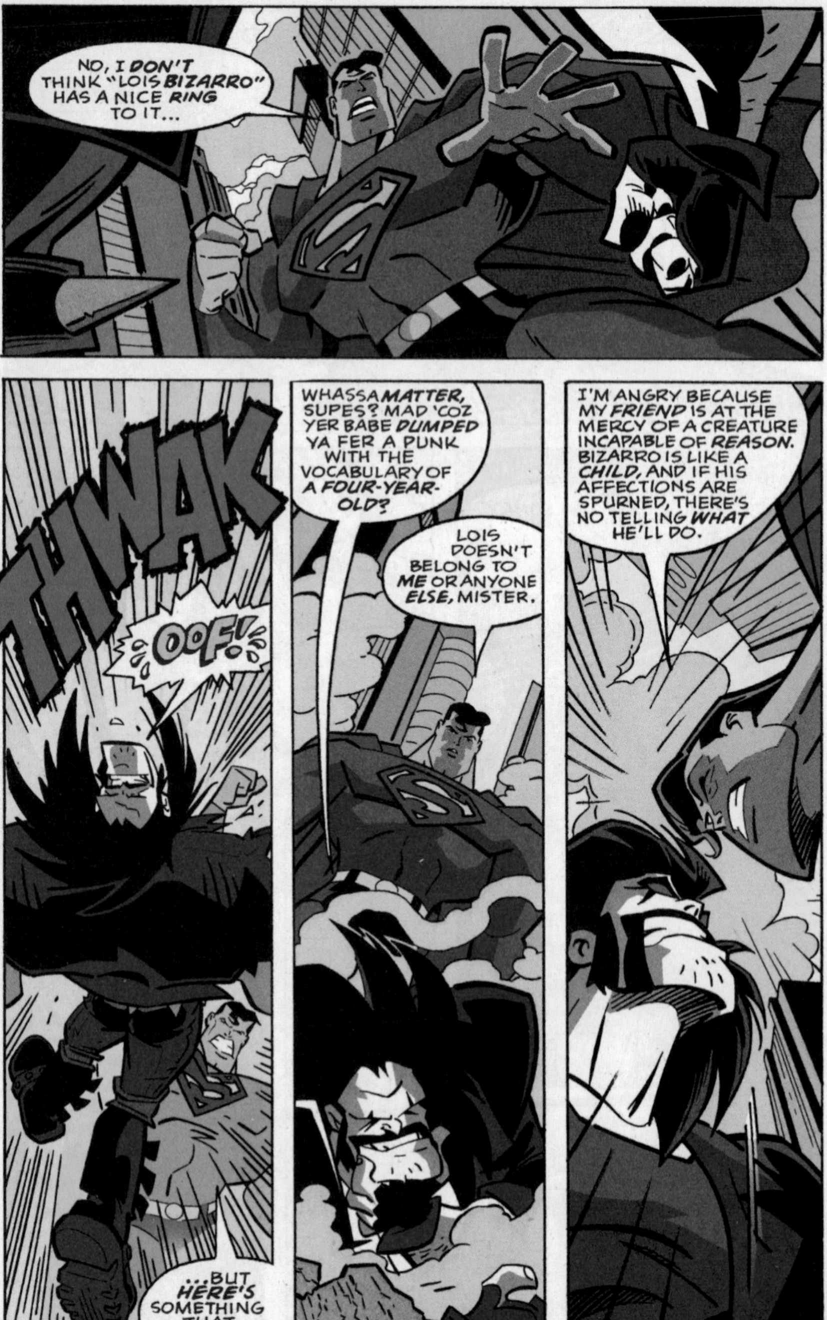
NO, I DON'T THINK "LOIS BIZARRO" HAS A NICE RING TO IT...
THWAK
OOF!
...BUT HERE'S SOMETHING THAT DOES!
WHASSA MATTER, SUPES? MAD 'COZ YER BABE DUMPED YA FER A PUNK WITH THE VOCABULARY OF A FOUR-YEAR-OLD?
LOIS DOESN'T BELONG TO ME OR ANYONE ELSE, MISTER.
I'M ANGRY BECAUSE MY FRIEND IS AT THE MERCY OF A CREATURE INCAPABLE OF REASON. BIZARRO IS LIKE A CHILD, AND IF HIS AFFECTIONS ARE SPURNED, THERE'S NO TELLING WHAT HE'LL DO.

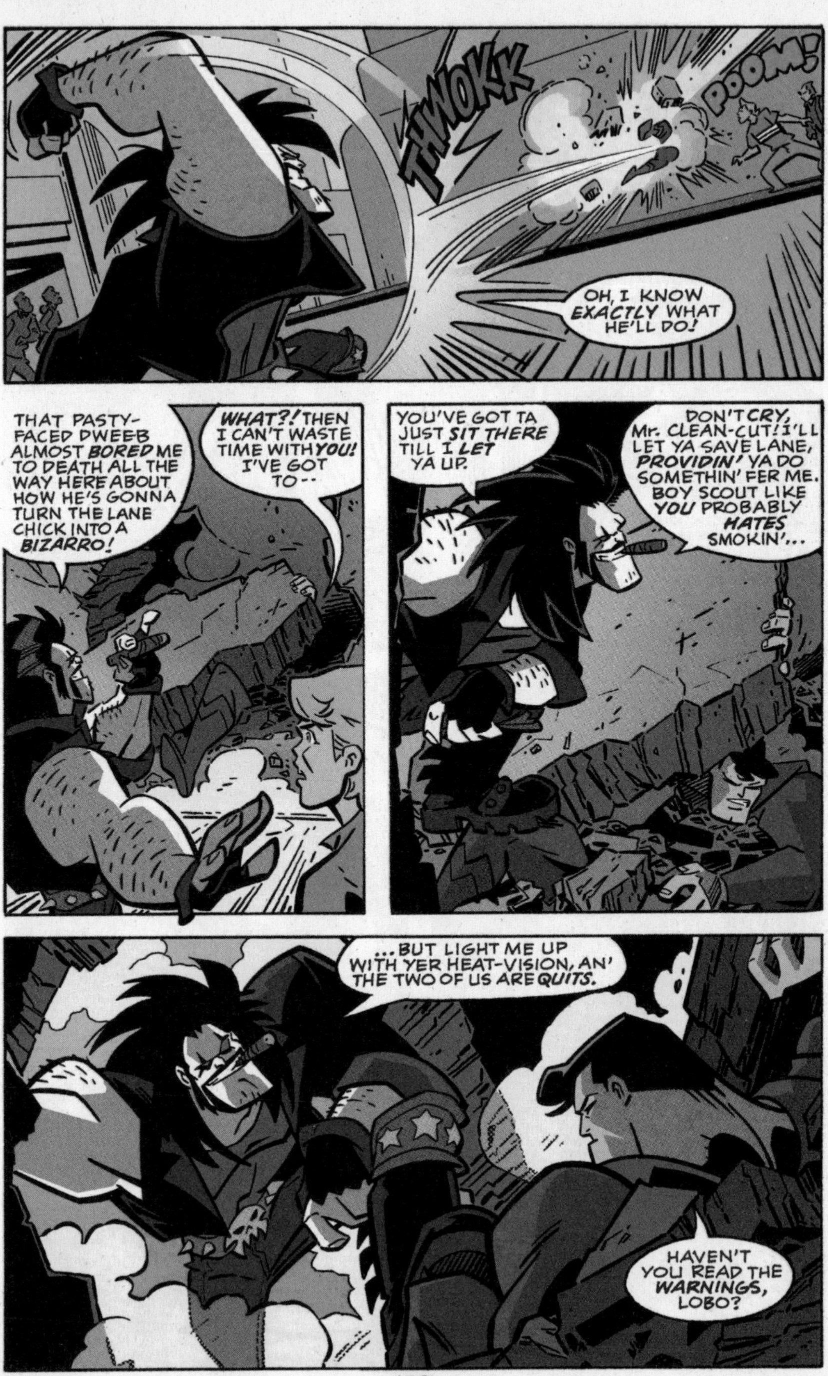
THWOKK
POOM!
OH, I KNOW EXACTLY WHAT HE'LL DO!
THAT PASTY-FACED DWEEB ALMOST BORED ME TO DEATH ALL THE WAY HERE ABOUT HOW HE'S GONNA TURN THE LANE CHICK INTO A BIZARRO!
WHAT?! THEN I CAN'T WASTE TIME WITH YOU! I'VE GOT TO--
YOU'VE GOT TA JUST SIT THERE TILL I LET YA UP.
DON'T CRY, Mr. CLEAN-CUT! I'LL LET YA SAVE LANE, PROVIDIN' YA DO SOMETHIN' FER ME. BOY SCOUT LIKE YOU PROBABLY HATES SMOKIN'...
...BUT LIGHT ME UP WITH YER HEAT-VISION, AN' THE TWO OF US ARE QUITS.
HAVEN'T YOU READ THE WARNINGS, LOBO?

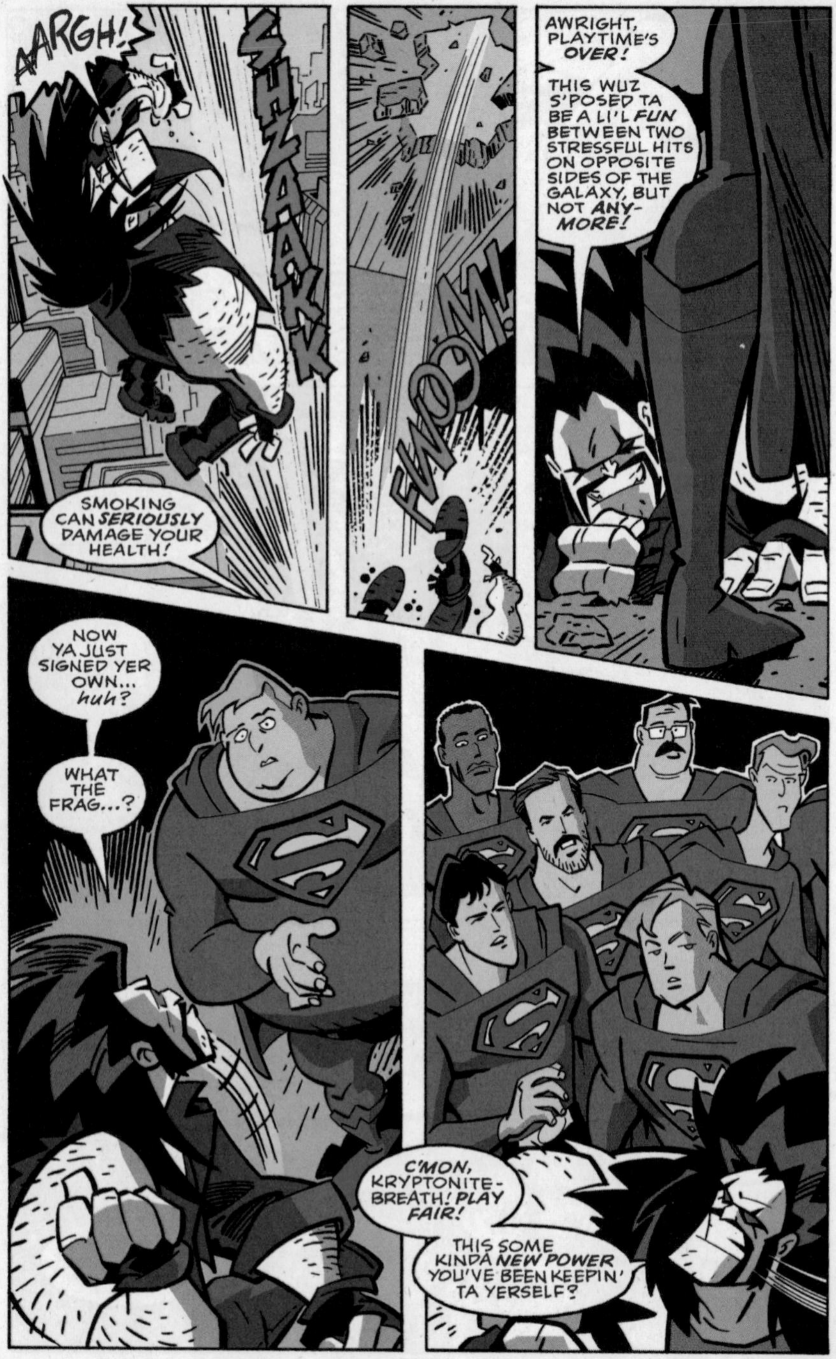
AARGH!
SHZAAKK
SMOKING CAN *SERIOUSLY* DAMAGE YOUR HEALTH!
FWOOM!
AWRIGHT, PLAYTIME'S *OVER!*
THIS WUZ S'POSED TA BE A LI'L *FUN* BETWEEN TWO STRESSFUL HITS ON OPPOSITE SIDES OF THE GALAXY, BUT NOT *ANY-MORE!*
NOW YA JUST SIGNED YER OWN... *huh?*
WHAT THE FRAG...?
C'MON, KRYPTONITE-BREATH! PLAY FAIR!
THIS SOME KINDA *NEW POWER* YOU'VE BEEN KEEPIN' TA YERSELF?

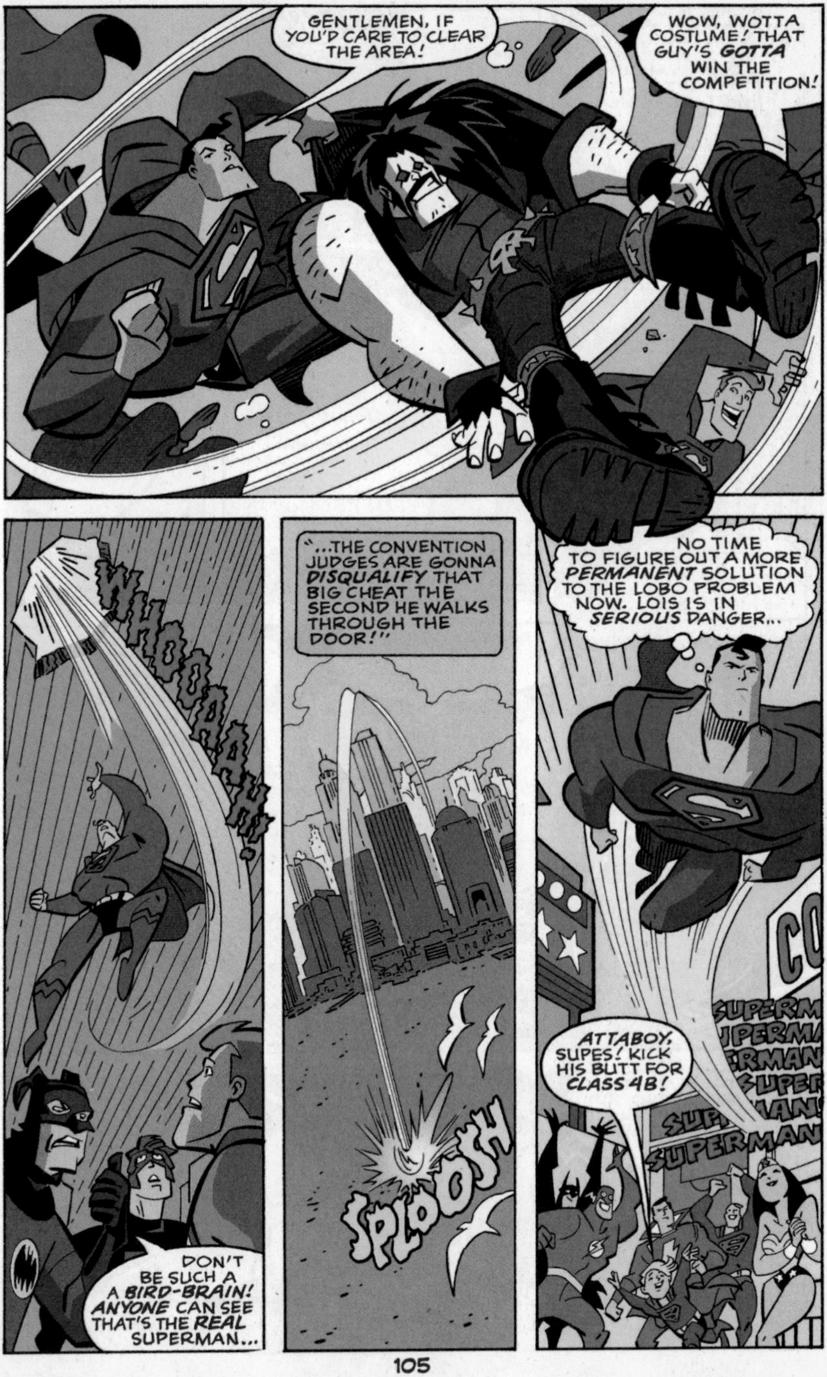
GENTLEMEN, IF YOU'D CARE TO CLEAR THE AREA!
WOW, WOTTA COSTUME! THAT GUY'S GOTTA WIN THE COMPETITION!
WHOOOAAAH!!
DON'T BE SUCH A A BIRD-BRAIN! ANYONE CAN SEE THAT'S THE REAL SUPERMAN...
"...THE CONVENTION JUDGES ARE GONNA DISQUALIFY THAT BIG CHEAT THE SECOND HE WALKS THROUGH THE DOOR!"
SPLOOSH
NO TIME TO FIGURE OUT A MORE PERMANENT SOLUTION TO THE LOBO PROBLEM NOW. LOIS IS IN SERIOUS DANGER...
ATTABOY, SUPES! KICK HIS BUTT FOR CLASS 4B!

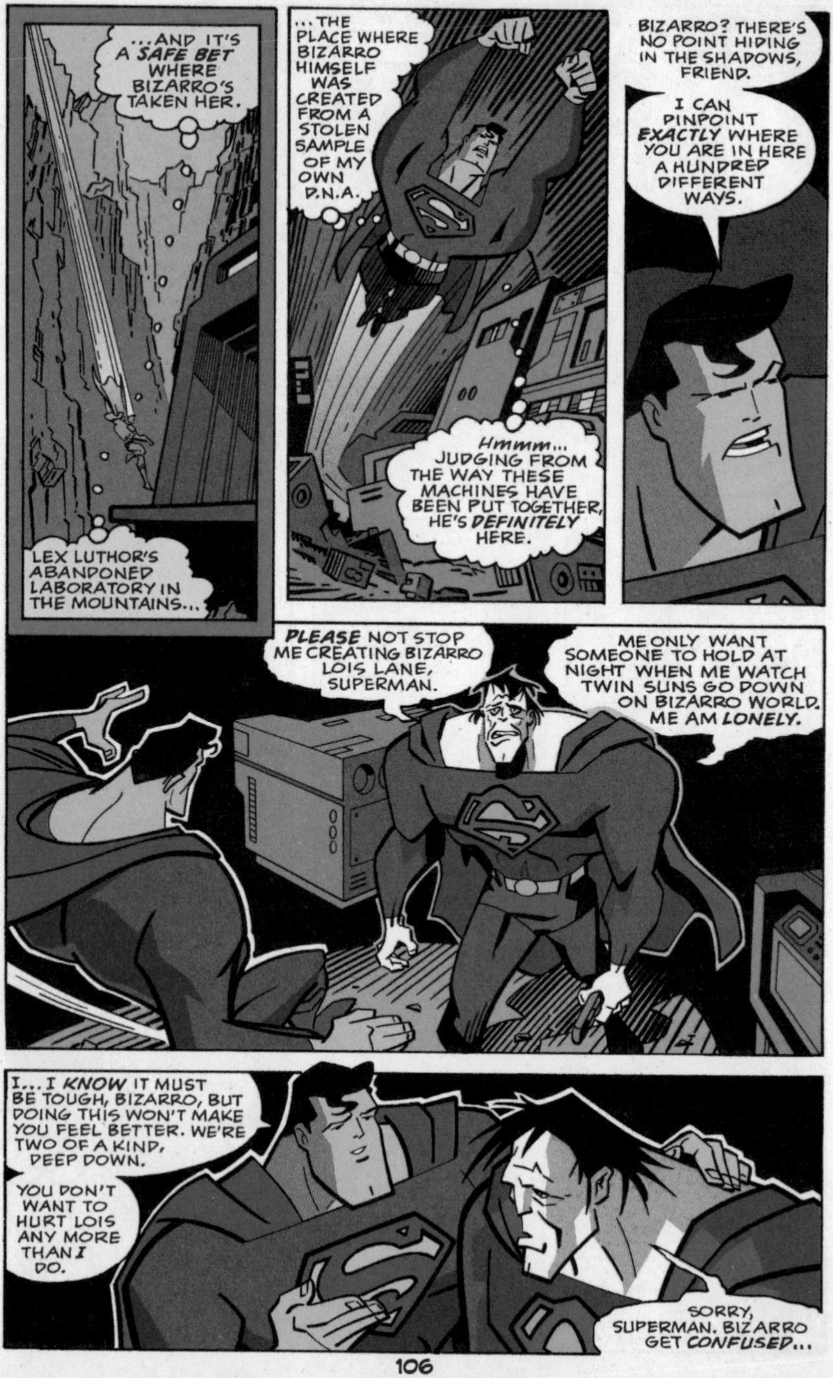
...AND IT'S A SAFE BET WHERE BIZARRO'S TAKEN HER.
LEX LUTHOR'S ABANDONED LABORATORY IN THE MOUNTAINS...
...THE PLACE WHERE BIZARRO HIMSELF WAS CREATED FROM A STOLEN SAMPLE OF MY OWN D.N.A.
Hmmm... JUDGING FROM THE WAY THESE MACHINES HAVE BEEN PUT TOGETHER, HE'S DEFINITELY HERE.
BIZARRO? THERE'S NO POINT HIDING IN THE SHADOWS, FRIEND.
I CAN PINPOINT EXACTLY WHERE YOU ARE IN HERE A HUNDRED DIFFERENT WAYS.
PLEASE NOT STOP ME CREATING BIZARRO LOIS LANE, SUPERMAN.
ME ONLY WANT SOMEONE TO HOLD AT NIGHT WHEN ME WATCH TWIN SUNS GO DOWN ON BIZARRO WORLD. ME AM LONELY.
I... I KNOW IT MUST BE TOUGH, BIZARRO, BUT DOING THIS WON'T MAKE YOU FEEL BETTER. WE'RE TWO OF A KIND, DEEP DOWN.
YOU DON'T WANT TO HURT LOIS ANY MORE THAN I DO.
SORRY, SUPERMAN. BIZARRO GET CONFUSED...

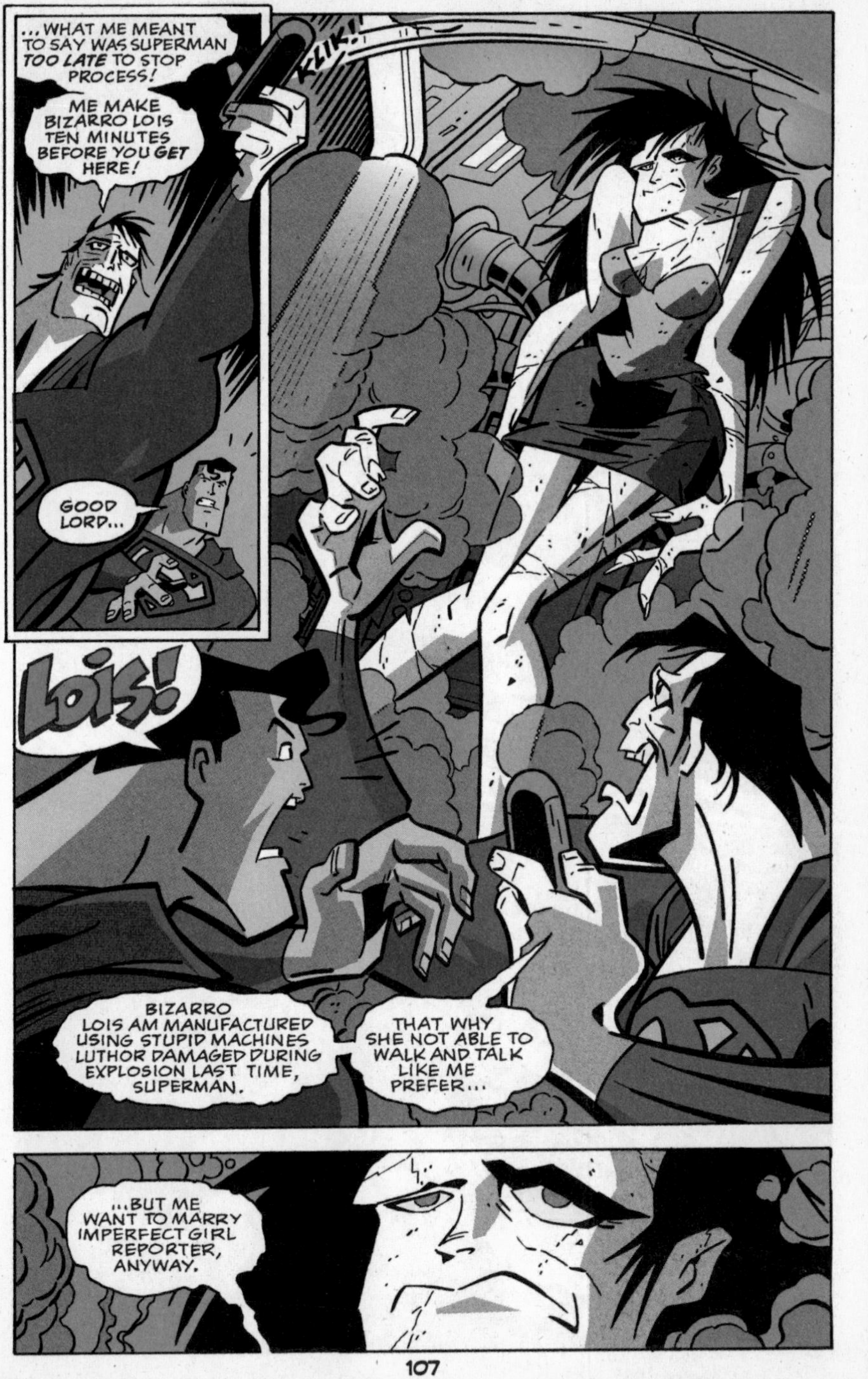
...WHAT ME MEANT TO SAY WAS SUPERMAN *TOO LATE* TO STOP PROCESS!
ME MAKE BIZARRO LOIS TEN MINUTES BEFORE YOU *GET* HERE!
KLIK!
GOOD LORD...
LOIS!
BIZARRO LOIS AM MANUFACTURED USING STUPID MACHINES LUTHOR DAMAGED DURING EXPLOSION LAST TIME, SUPERMAN.
THAT WHY SHE NOT ABLE TO WALK AND TALK LIKE ME PREFER...
...BUT ME WANT TO MARRY IMPERFECT GIRL REPORTER, ANYWAY.

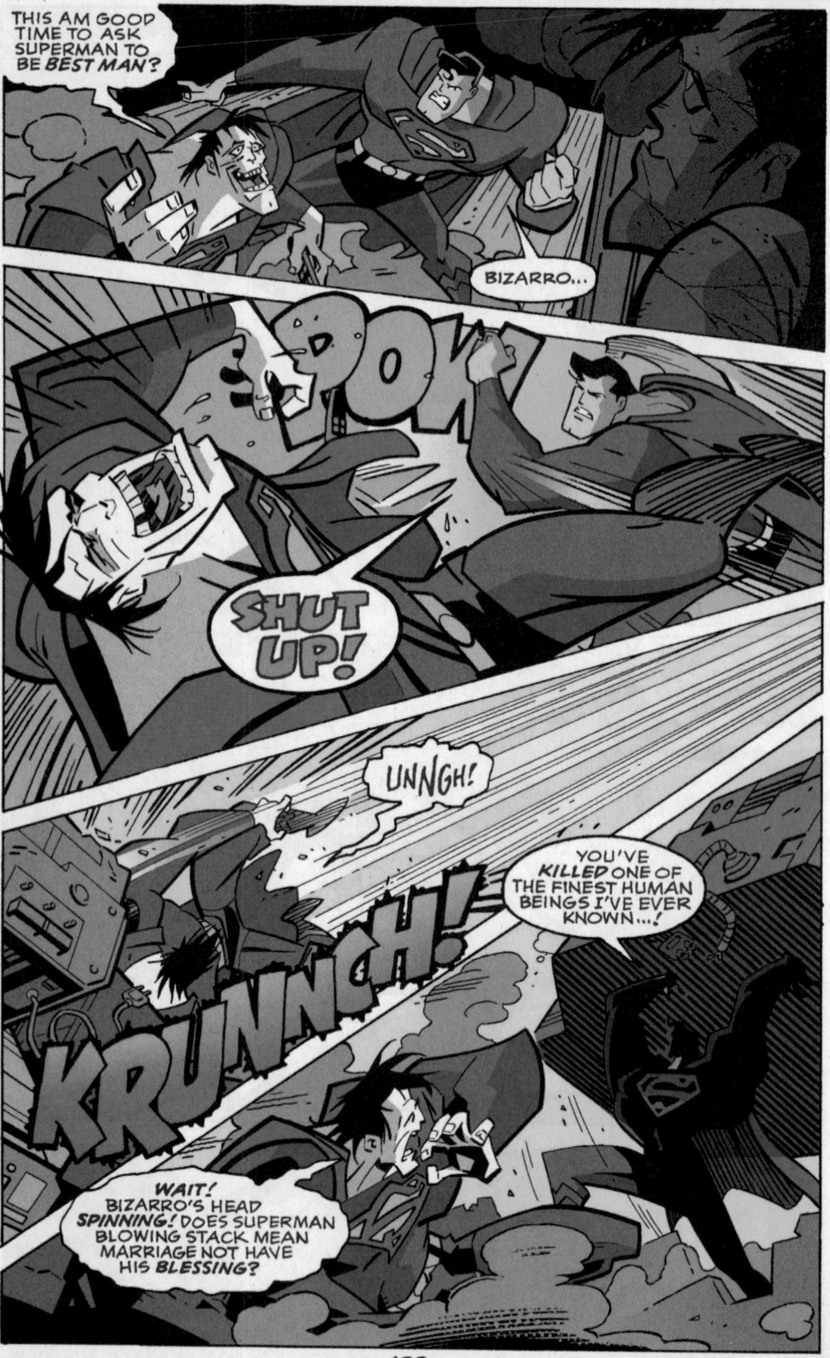
THIS AM GOOD TIME TO ASK SUPERMAN TO BE *BEST MAN*?
BIZARRO...
POW
SHUT UP!
UNNGH!
YOU'VE *KILLED* ONE OF THE FINEST HUMAN BEINGS I'VE EVER KNOWN...!
KRUNNCH!
WAIT! BIZARRO'S HEAD *SPINNING!* DOES SUPERMAN BLOWING STACK MEAN MARRIAGE NOT HAVE HIS *BLESSING?*

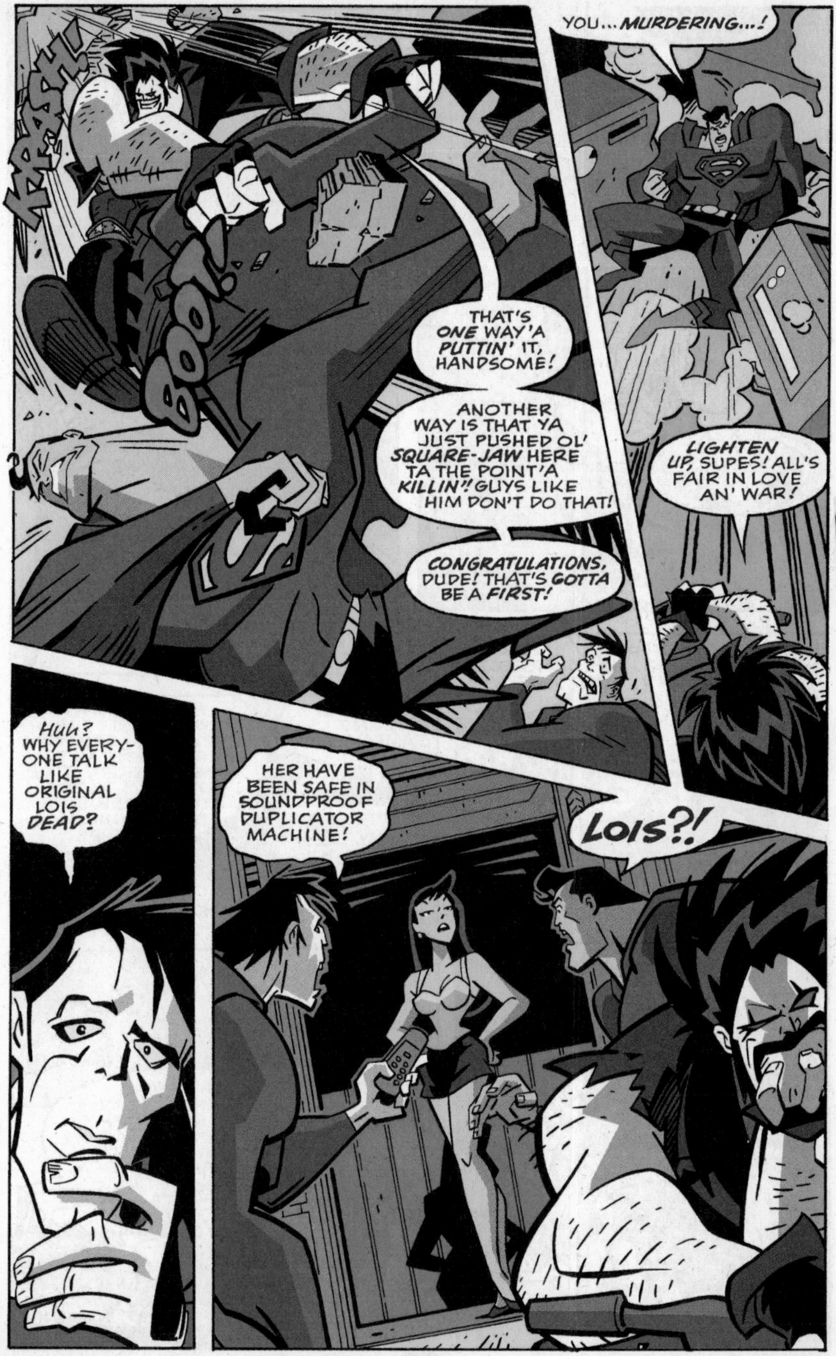
KRASH!
BOOOOM
THAT'S ONE WAY'A PUTTIN' IT, HANDSOME!
ANOTHER WAY IS THAT YA JUST PUSHED OL' SQUARE-JAW HERE TA THE POINT'A KILLIN'! GUYS LIKE HIM DON'T DO THAT!
CONGRATULATIONS, DUDE! THAT'S GOTTA BE A FIRST!
YOU... MURDERING...!
LIGHTEN UP, SUPES! ALL'S FAIR IN LOVE AN' WAR!
Huh? WHY EVERY-ONE TALK LIKE ORIGINAL LOIS DEAD?
HER HAVE BEEN SAFE IN SOUNDPROOF DUPLICATOR MACHINE!
LOIS?!

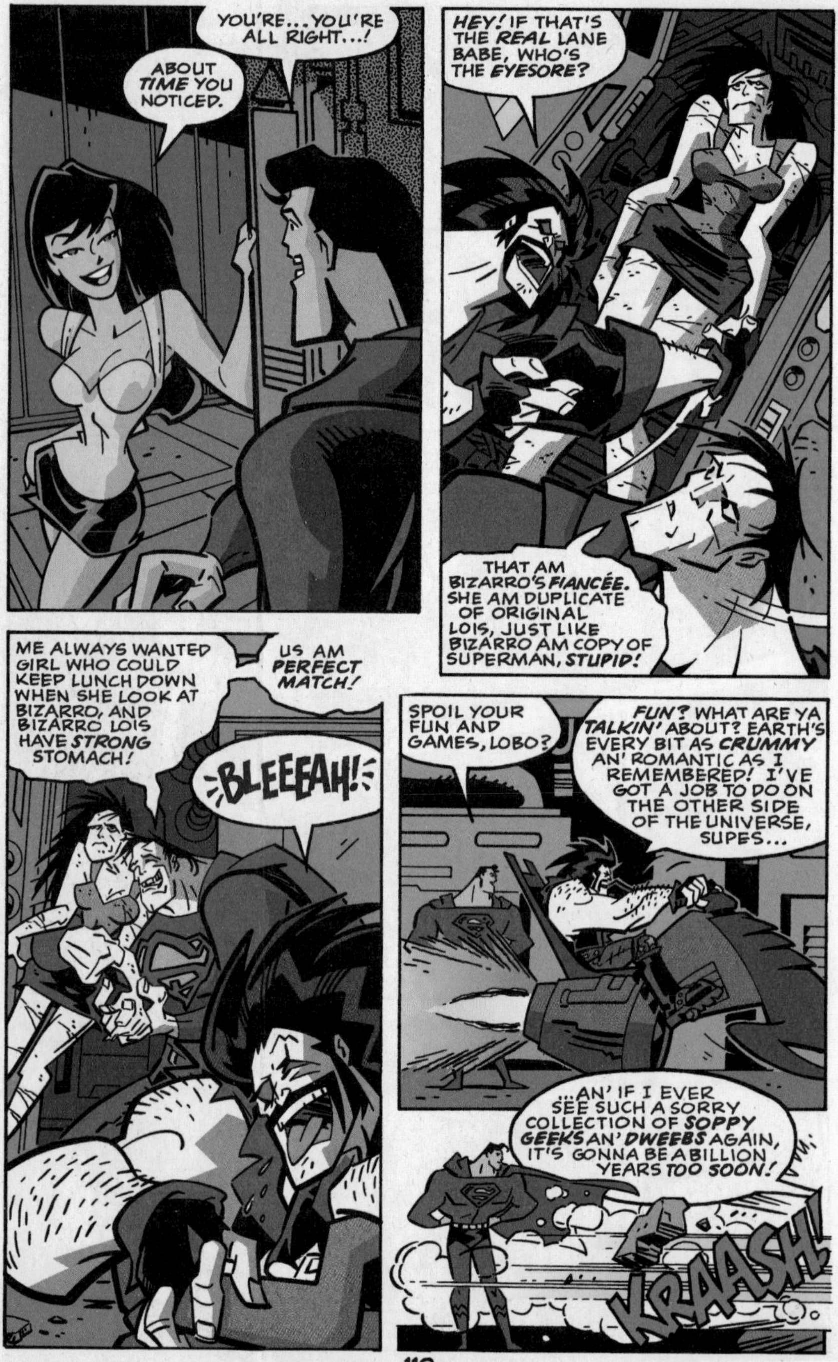
YOU'RE...YOU'RE ALL RIGHT...!
ABOUT TIME YOU NOTICED.
HEY! IF THAT'S THE REAL LANE BABE, WHO'S THE EYESORE?
THAT AM BIZARRO'S FIANCÉE. SHE AM DUPLICATE OF ORIGINAL LOIS, JUST LIKE BIZARRO AM COPY OF SUPERMAN, STUPID!
ME ALWAYS WANTED GIRL WHO COULD KEEP LUNCH DOWN WHEN SHE LOOK AT BIZARRO, AND BIZARRO LOIS HAVE STRONG STOMACH!
US AM PERFECT MATCH!
BLEEEAH!
SPOIL YOUR FUN AND GAMES, LOBO?
FUN? WHAT ARE YA TALKIN' ABOUT? EARTH'S EVERY BIT AS CRUMMY AN' ROMANTIC AS I REMEMBERED! I'VE GOT A JOB TO DO ON THE OTHER SIDE OF THE UNIVERSE, SUPES...
...AN' IF I EVER SEE SUCH A SORRY COLLECTION OF SOPPY GEEKS AN' DWEEBS AGAIN, IT'S GONNA BE A BILLION YEARS TOO SOON!
VVM
KRAASH!

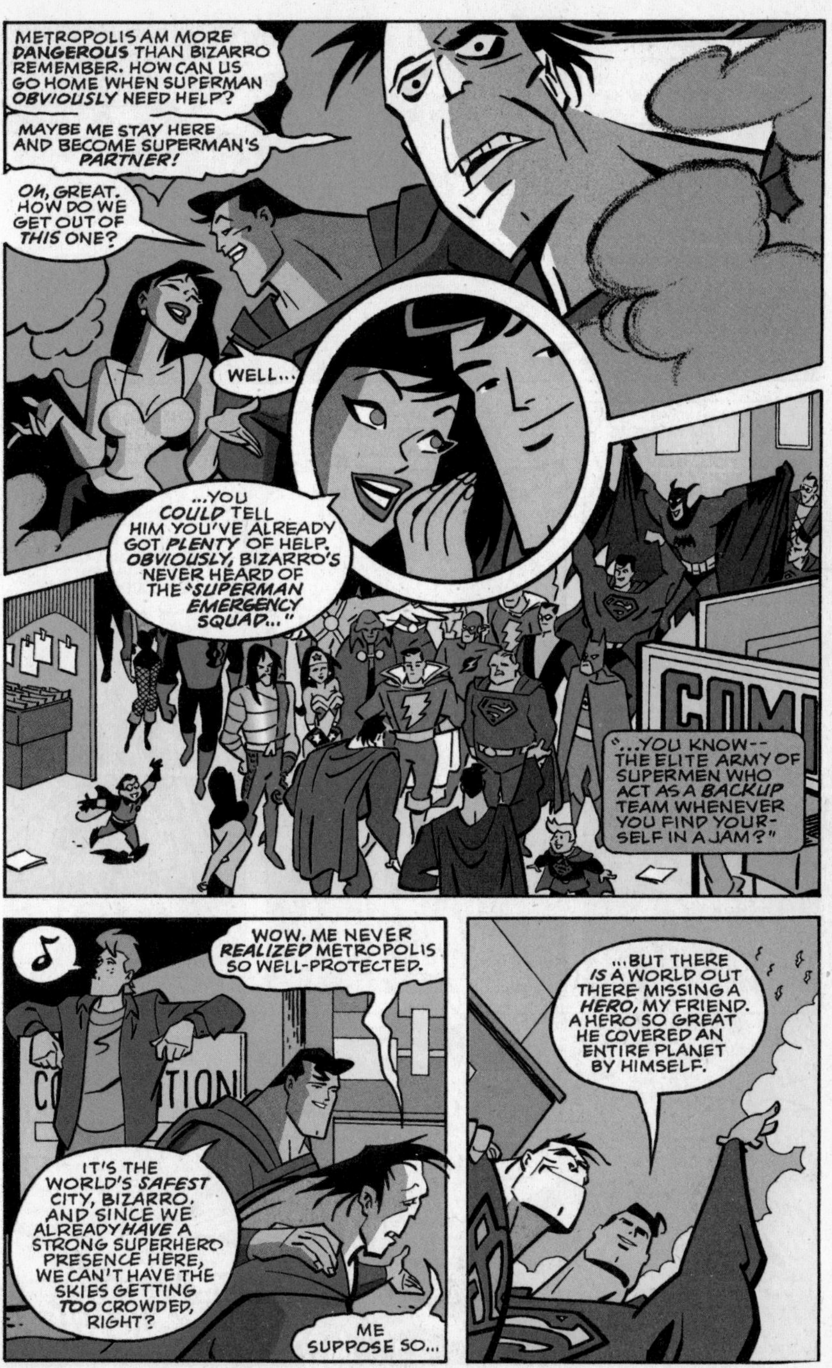

METROPOLIS AM MORE DANGEROUS THAN BIZARRO REMEMBER. HOW CAN US GO HOME WHEN SUPERMAN OBVIOUSLY NEED HELP?
MAYBE ME STAY HERE AND BECOME SUPERMAN'S PARTNER!
OH, GREAT. HOW DO WE GET OUT OF THIS ONE?
WELL...
...YOU COULD TELL HIM YOU'VE ALREADY GOT PLENTY OF HELP. OBVIOUSLY, BIZARRO'S NEVER HEARD OF THE "SUPERMAN EMERGENCY SQUAD..."
"...YOU KNOW-- THE ELITE ARMY OF SUPERMEN WHO ACT AS A BACKUP TEAM WHENEVER YOU FIND YOURSELF IN A JAM?"
COMI
WOW. ME NEVER REALIZED METROPOLIS SO WELL-PROTECTED.
IT'S THE WORLD'S SAFEST CITY, BIZARRO. AND SINCE WE ALREADY HAVE A STRONG SUPERHERO PRESENCE HERE, WE CAN'T HAVE THE SKIES GETTING TOO CROWDED, RIGHT?
ME SUPPOSE SO...
...BUT THERE IS A WORLD OUT THERE MISSING A HERO, MY FRIEND. A HERO SO GREAT HE COVERED AN ENTIRE PLANET BY HIMSELF.

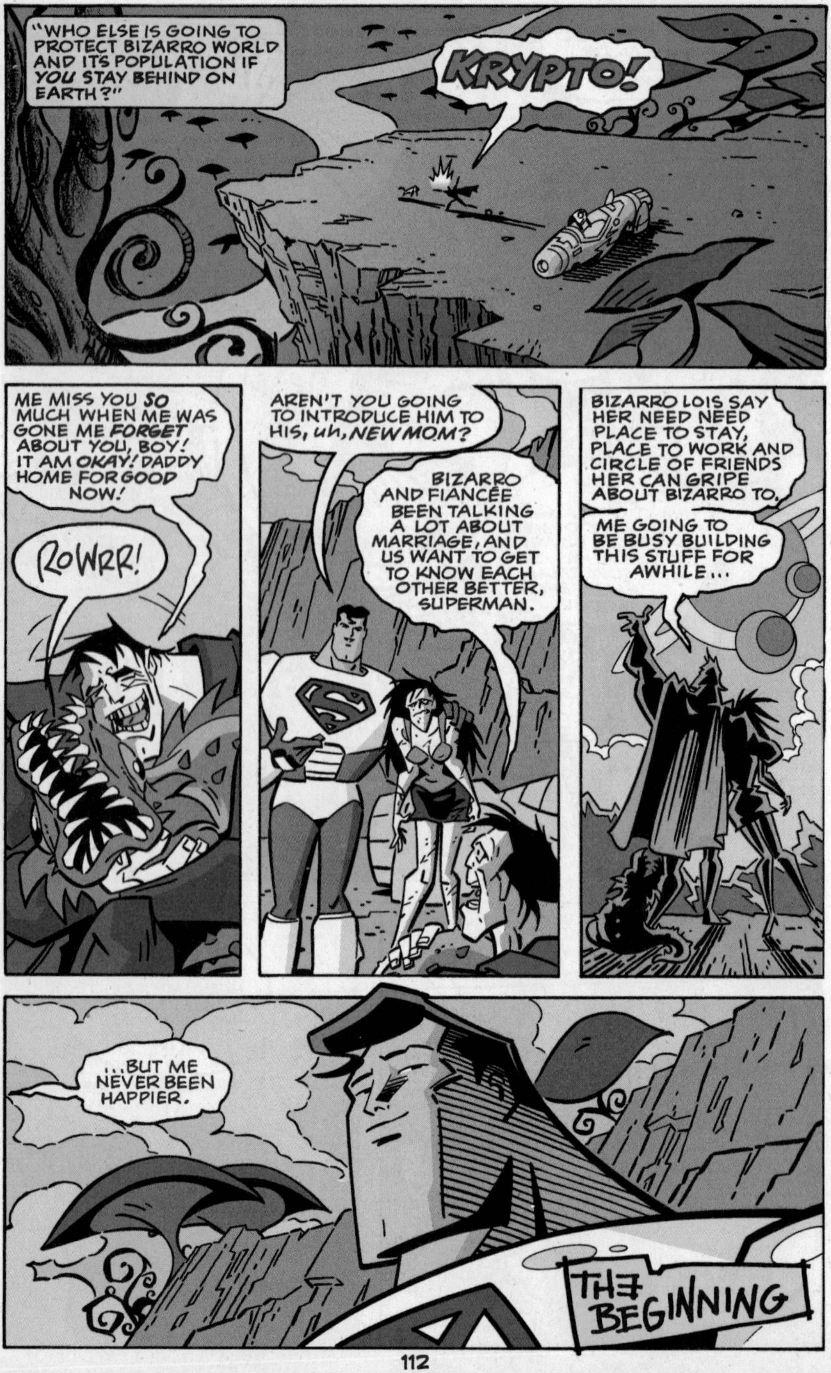
"WHO ELSE IS GOING TO PROTECT BIZARRO WORLD AND ITS POPULATION IF YOU STAY BEHIND ON EARTH?"
KRYPTO!
ME MISS YOU SO MUCH WHEN ME WAS GONE ME FORGET ABOUT YOU, BOY! IT AM OKAY! DADDY HOME FOR GOOD NOW!
ROWRR!
AREN'T YOU GOING TO INTRODUCE HIM TO HIS, uh, NEW MOM?
BIZARRO AND FIANCÉE BEEN TALKING A LOT ABOUT MARRIAGE, AND US WANT TO GET TO KNOW EACH OTHER BETTER, SUPERMAN.
BIZARRO LOIS SAY HER NEED NEED PLACE TO STAY, PLACE TO WORK AND CIRCLE OF FRIENDS HER CAN GRIPE ABOUT BIZARRO TO.
ME GOING TO BE BUSY BUILDING THIS STUFF FOR AWHILE...
...BUT ME NEVER BEEN HAPPIER.
THE BEGINNING